Meg Hutchinson

Meg Hutchinson left school at fifteen and didn't return to education until she was thirty-three, when she entered Teacher Training College and studied for her degree in the evenings. Ever since she was a child, she has loved telling stories and writing 'compositions'. She lived for sixty years in Wednesbury, where her parents and grandparents spent all their lives, but now has a quiet little cottage in Shropshire where she can indulge her passion for storytelling.

MEG HUTCHINSON

The Deverell Woman

CORONET BOOKS
Hodder & Stoughton

copyright © 2002 Meg Hutchinson

First published in Great Britain in 2002 by Hodder & Stoughton
A division of Hodder Headline
First published in paperback in 2003 by Hodder & Stoughton
A Coronet paperback

The right of Meg Hutchinson to be identified as the
Author of the Work has been asserted by her in accordance
with the Copyright, Designs and Patents Act 1988.

6 8 10 9 7

A CIP catalogue record for this title
is available from the British Library

ISBN 0 340 81820 4

Typeset in Plantin by Hewer Text Ltd, Edinburgh
Printed and bound in Great Britain by
Mackays of Chatham, Kent

Hodder & Stoughton
A division of Hodder Headline
338 Euston Road
London NW1 3BH

To the smiling friendly people of Ireland
whose welcome meets wherever you go,
I am sure they will overlook the liberties taken
regarding distances for 'sure,
'tis only a tale to be told over a glass o' porter'.

I

'Ye'll be at the church come Saturday eve, ye'll stand afore the holy altar and marry with Liam Riordan, that be my word and I'll suffer no denying of it!'

'I will not . . . I'm no daughter to you to be ordered like some servant!'

Seamus Riordan's eyes narrowed as he looked at the thin slip of a girl standing before him. Her mother had looked the same at sixteen, great wide eyes green as the forest floor, tumbling hair the colour of ripe chestnuts . . . and spirit, yes the spirit was the same too, one that stood and defied him where no man would.

'No, ye be no daughter to me,' he answered thickly, 'but ye'll do my word if it be ye wants yer mother to die in a bed!'

'But Liam—'

'Be the Riordan runt!' The interruption was cold. 'But a Riordan none the less and as such superior to all in the county.'

'Then why me?' Maura Deverell's head came up. 'If the Riordans be so superior why marry one with the daughter of a peat cutter . . . why would the *Ard Ri* want such for one of their own?'

'Kings be right,' Seamus Riordan snarled. 'The Riordans be kings in this valley, everything in it belongs to them and that has the including of ye'self. Ye will marry with my son and that be the end of it!'

★   ★   ★

There was no man to protect her, none that would stand against the Riordans. Kings? Maura thought despisingly. They were more coward than king with their sly underhand ways, waiting until the family of a man were near to starving, until every last stick had been exchanged for food, then buying the land from beneath his feet. And no man's feet stayed long on land that belonged to Seamus Riordan, they were cut before the time it took to blink an eye.

Now it was to be the turn of the Deverells unless she married with the misfit . . . but she must not call him that, not even in her thoughts! Pausing by the side of the stream that ran down from the hills Maura Deverell stared at the clear bright water. Liam Riordan was different, he didn't have the streak of cruelty and arrogance that ran through his father and brother, he was soft spoken, a smile ready on his lips whenever he might pass on the road; but it was not often Liam Riordan was seen, neither on the road nor off it.

Slipping out of her shoes she placed them in her empty basket then sat down on the springy turf, her feet in the cold water.

Why did the man keep so to the house? To be sure it was the grandest in the valley, maybe the grandest in the whole county but was that reason enough to so rarely leave its shelter?

It was not. Watching the rippling water turn red-gold in the lowering sun, Maura felt the same twinge of pity she had often felt for the younger son of Seamus Riordan. The runt, his father had called him; was that the name he used in Liam's hearing, did he know how his father thought of him? Did he have to bear that as well as everything else a cruel fate had put upon him? Once he had been more like the rest of the children of Clonmacnoise . . .

Lying back on the sweet-smelling earth she closed her eyes, her mind wandering the path of memory.

. . . He would smile and wave from the dog cart his mother

drove, and when she stopped to speak a while with the women at their doors he was always polite, always interested in all he saw.

'That one be a gentleman, sure an' it be strange to think of his coming from the loins of Seamus Riordan.'

The words her own mother had used of the lad grown to teenhood when last he and his mother had come to her door drifted in among Maura's thoughts.

Then his mother had died and he had been seen less and less until now he was hardly ever seen at all, kept closed away by a father ashamed of a crippled son, ashamed he was not strong and athletic like his brother? But where Liam had been pleasant and kindly spoken, Padraig Riordan was a complete image of his father: arrogant, overbearing and a bully ready to make money do the work should it be his fists could not.

And now they wanted her. But why, for what reason? Still she could not fathom it. Liam Riordan was a cripple, but it was a crippled body he carried and not a crippled mind! He was attractive of speech and face. There must be many a girl in Clonmacnoise, a girl of family better placed than the Deverells, who would be glad to marry with a Riordan, but the father had chosen her, selected her like so much horseflesh. She liked Liam, in many ways she pitied him, but she did not love him and she would not be traded for, like an animal in the market place!

'. . . ye'll do my word if it be ye wants yer mother to die in a bed.'

The warning was clear . . . but so was the warning of her heart: to marry into the Riordan family would be to place herself in purgatory! Never from that day would she have a voice or a will of her own.

'Did yer mother never tell ye that to lie on yer back on the ground with yer legs spread was to invite trouble?'

Her eyes flying open, Maura stared into the leering face of Padraig Riordan.

'I . . . I was thinking . . . I—'

'So was I . . . thinking that you be trespassin' on Riordan land.'

'I was not . . . I mean . . . I have to cross this place to get home.' Fear sudden and solid in her chest she inched backwards on the soft ground.

'That doesn't alter the fact you be trespassin' and that be against the law. Now what are we goin' to be doin' about that?'

There was more than the look of a bully in those narrow eyes. Maura's nerves jangled.

'You can report me to the magistrate . . . I will answer to him.'

'Why would I be doin' that when I would much prefer you answer to me!'

For the space of five seconds he watched her scramble awkwardly backwards, hands and feet digging into the spongy turf.

'This here be Riordan property and I charge a fee for the crossing of it.'

Almost as the words left his lips he moved, stamping a foot to each side of her, laughing as she gasped.

'I . . . I have no money.' She tried to scramble away, a couple of yards and she could be on her feet and away; with luck she could reach home before he could catch up to her.

'A gentleman takes no money from a lady,' he laughed again, his hot stare stroking the length of her bare legs, 'especially not from one set to become his sister-in-law.'

'Then let me go.'

'All in good time.' Bending over her he caught the neck of the dress worn thin from constant washing. 'All in good time, but first I take my fee.' Giving a tug that half lifted her by its force, he ripped the dress from neck to hem.

'No . . . o . . . o!'

The cry surged over the rippling water, echoing and re-echoing off purple-topped hills before being silenced beneath a rough hand.

'You wouldn't have yourself branded a common thief, would you?' He brought his face close. 'A girl who takes without making payment.'

'I *will* pay.' Maura twisted her head, freeing her mouth of his torrid kiss. 'I will.'

The leer of a smile spreading his mouth he snatched at the flimsy chemise, exposing pale mounds of small pink-tipped breasts.

'Of course you will.' He squeezed the tender flesh, ignoring her cry of pain. 'I'm going to make sure you do.'

She had tried to push him away . . . she had . . . she had! Stood waist-deep in the cold crystal waters of the stream, Maura made no attempt to stem the tears coursing over her cheeks.

'*What of Liam,*' she had gasped, '*if I am to marry with him?*'

It had been like crying in the wind. Scooping handfuls of water she rubbed at her breasts, trying to wash away the touch of hands and mouth.

His eyes dark with the passion driving through him, Padraig Riordan had snatched away the last of her clothes then released his own, a hungry animal stare sweeping the small figure trembling before him.

'*Don't worry about Liam,*' he had grunted, '*he won't have sense enough to realise the crust has already been cut from the loaf.*' He had pushed her roughly to the ground, his tongue flicking quickly over his thin lips, that awful abusing stare fastening on the helpless form beneath him.

'*No, Liam will never know the first slice is already gone . . . or how many more will be taken once it's brought into the house!*'

She needed no one to interpret his words, no one to explain the threat behind them. With a sob breaking in her throat she dropped to her knees, letting the sharp sting of the water rush over her chest and shoulders, wanting it to wash away the foulness of the man, to scour all trace of him from her flesh; but how would she cleanse what he had done from her mind, how could she scrub away the horror of the memory for that would be with her as long as breath filled her lungs. Padraig Riordan had raped her and threatened to do the same thing over and again once she became his brother's wife!

'No . . . o . . . o!'

Half-strangled, the heart-rent cry rushed over the water startling a covey of grey partridge using the tall rushes as cover against a harassing black raven.

She couldn't live like that . . . she couldn't. Sobs wracked the thinness of her as she plunged her head beneath the tumbling waters. But she had to live like that if her mother was to see another year!

Climbing slowly from the water she dressed in the tattered rags, holding her dress together across breasts and stomach. She would not add to the troubles that had brought her mother so near her deathbed. There had been little enough of luxury in the rough stone cottage with its turf roof, but prior to her father's death at least there had been potatoes in the storeroom and often a poached trout or rabbit to keep them company, but after the accident that had killed him, and the blight that had taken a year's crop before it could be lifted, it seemed the will to go on living had passed from Mairead Deverell and now she coughed blood with almost every breath. '*The consumption*,' Mother O'Toole from across the valley had shaken her head on pronouncing the dreaded word, '*there be no cure as be known or none the like o' which ye have the money to buy*.'

It had seemed that day as though the Passing Bell had already sounded, her mother was dying.

'. . . *ye'll do my word if it be ye wants yer mother to die in a bed*.'

Seamus Riordan's words returned; mocking, adding to the misery and pain searing her heart.

The land her father had worked belonged to Seamus Riordan, the cottage that stood on it belonged to Seamus Riordan . . . and she must belong to him also.

Blinded by tears hot in her eyes she stumbled through grass and heather damp with the dew of evening, and not until she stood among the tall sculptured crosses and tumble of ruined buildings that had once been small churches skirting the grander ruin of the Abbey of Clonmacnoise did she realise where she was.

Holding the remnants of her dress close about her, seeing her near nudity as an insult to this holy place, she walked slowly to where a tiny cell-like structure still stood. Here was the tomb of Ciaran, the gentle understanding saint who had founded the early monastery and who had been known to help the people of the valley when all else failed them.

But would the saintly Ciaran help a girl who had lain with a man out of wedlock?

'I didn't want to do it,' she whispered, 'it was not my will.'

Head bowed, shame pressing heavily on her, she fell to her knees on the hard stony ground of the tiny windowless room.

'Help me, holy Father,' she whispered again, 'help me live a life of vileness; for my mother's sake help me to enter that house, to take on a life of sin for I know no other way to stave off the hand of death, to hold her with me for as long as I can. Pray for me, gentle Saint, pray God in His compassion forgives me taking my own life the moment my mother takes her last breath.'

Trembling in the eerie shadows she listened, hoping the drift of evening air would carry an answer on its wings. But there was only silence. Rising to her feet, head still bent, she turned back into the open passing among the forest of ornately carved stone crosses and engraved tombstones, the heart inside her crippled with the pain of knowing there would be no answer from Ciaran, no plea for dispensation. Fornication and suicide, they were each a sin; despised and unforgivable by the Church, their perpetrators refused the benefit of Communion and denied a place of eternal rest in sanctified ground. Yet all of that did not frighten her as much as the silence in the chapel of Ciaran, a silence that said it was also unforgivable in the eyes of God . . . commit any such sin and hell awaited you . . . but Maura Deverell would commit them both.

Mairead Deverell staggered up from her knees to which the bout of coughing had drawn her. It could not be long now, the consumption Sinead O'Toole had spoken of took more of her strength with every passing day and soon it would take her life. Wiping blood from her lips she stared about the dark smoky room in which she had spent most of the last seventeen years. Maura, her first-born, had been birthed in the bed shoved into one corner, there also had been born the boy child that followed a year later, a babe that had not lived to see the light of his first morning. Sean was the name they had given him. Mairead's arms folded across her chest holding an unseen child, her eyes closing as she seemed to feel the nuzzle of a tiny head against her breast.

They had known he could not live, they had seen the mark of death upon him. She pressed the imagined body closer to her own, the heart inside her breaking now as it had broken so many years ago. There had been no time to fetch a priest, the nearest one had been in Clonfert and with no horse to ride Brendan could not have reached there and back before . . .

With tears squeezing beneath closed lids she swallowed against the pain of remembering.

'*The baptising has to be done.*'

Mother O'Toole, who acted as midwife to all who called for

her, had reached for the newly born child but Mairead had clung to it, her eyes beseeching a silent Brendan.

'*Mairead child!*' The old woman's voice had been gentle, full of pity. '*Ye must give the babe to yer man, let him give the blessing of holy church afore the child be laid in the ground.*'

Inside the shadowed house Mairead's inner eyes watched the drama of that bitter night unfold.

'*The child be dead,*' Sinead O'Toole had continued, 'God rest its tiny soul, now it must needs be buried.'

'*No . . . o . . . o!*'

The cry she had uttered ringing even now in her ears, Mairead stared at the bed as the answer she had given sounded again in her mind.

'*How can I bury him, how can I let him lie in the cold earth?*'

'*Child . . . child!*' The woman's arms had closed about her, the mouth already wrinkled, whispering against her brow. '*Look at your man, his also is the heart that be breaking; ye must be strong, girl, strong for the two of ye, don't be givin' him any more of the pain for 'tis my fear he won't have the standin' of it.*'

She had looked at Brendan then, at the man who had chosen to take her, and seen the agony dark in his eyes. It was his child too, he had shared in the making of it, in the wonder of its first movement in the womb, shouted in joy at its delivery and sobbed as she did at its death. She had released her hold on the precious bundle. Reaching for her husband's hand she had bitten back the sobs as the woman had taken their child.

They had huddled together; there on that very bed Brendan and herself had watched the washing of that tiny body, the wrapping of it in a clean white cloth . . . the preparing of their son for burial.

'*All be ready.*'

In the gathering dusk it seemed Sinead O'Toole held the still bundle once more towards her while the shadows whispered her words.

'*Say goodbye to your child . . . give him into the hand of the Lord.*'

'*Give him into the hand of the Lord!*' It had burst from her, ripping the heart from her body. '*Why say that when ye know there can be no salvation for him, ye knows the teaching same as me . . . there be no entry into heaven for the unbaptised.*'

Sinead O'Toole had shaken her head at that, a strange half smile touching her deeply grooved mouth.

'*This babe will not go unbaptised and no unmarked ground shall have the covering of him. Pour into a dish some of the water that be purified from boiling in that kettle and make the sign upon its brow.*'

'*No!*'

Wrapped in the silence settling over the land, Mairead lived again the moments she had lived a thousand times. Brendan had drawn away, the expression on his tired face showing the tumult in his heart.

'*'Tis forbidden!*' He had guessed the purpose in the woman's mind and rejected it. '*'Tis none but a consecrated priest can perform the rite and none but holy water placed upon the brow.*'

'*Be that the truth now!*' Eyes blackbird bright had flashed in the light of candles. '*Then p'raps with your knowledge, Brendan Deverell, ye'll be after tellin' an ignorant woman who it was consecrated John the Baptist, and who it was declared the river Jordan holy before our Saviour was baptised in its waters? I say any water that has the blessing of God asked upon it be holy and that He turns away none for whom His mercy is asked. Pour the water, Brendan Deverell, and say the words of a father for his son.*'

Mairead had risen from the bed, drawing her husband with her, and herself had poured the dish of water. Then in the dimness of the same room Brendan had taken the child into his arms.

'*Let no fear hold yer tongue.*'

The words breathed from the folding shadows had the same

gentle calmness in them now as there had been when first they
had left Sinead O'Toole's mouth, a calmness no words of a
priest had given before or since. Holding the blood-soaked rag
to her mouth, Mairead listened.

'*Words truly meant have a sweetness to the ear of the Lord.*'

'*But . . . but the child be dead.*'

The strange half smile had lingered as the bright eyes had
fastened on Brendan's face.

'*Sure an' wasn't Lazarus dead four days in his tomb afore he
was brought forth? And our own Saviour himself, lying dead in his
grave until the third day? Make your heart easy for death has no
power before God; place the sign of His son on this dead babe, name
him and give him into the love that is the salvation of all men.*'

With naught but the darkness to see, Brendan had asked a
blessing on the dish of water then with one finger had traced a
drop of it on the tiny brow.

'*Sean, Brendan, Rourke,*' she had whispered as he paused.

Repeating the names given to honour the child's father and
grandfathers he had made the sign of the cross then kissed the
already cold face and together they had laid the child to rest
among the flowers of her small garden.

There had been no more children, no more sons for
Brendan Deverell. He had loved her the same as before
and cherished his daughter, but always the pain had been
visible behind the smile, lurking deep in the eyes that never
again held that same brightness. And that small patch once set
around with blossom, that had become his own resting place.
Her glance travelled beyond the door to rest where two
wooden crosses stood side by side in the soft earth. He had
been brought there and buried by the men who had found him
dead at the foot of the hill beneath Hermit's Cave said once to
have housed a holy man. Now they lay together, her husband
and her son.

'Hold them both in your keeping, Lord.'

The prayer died on her lips as she caught sight of a thin figure stumbling towards the house.

'Maura!' It was no more than a whisper but the fear locked in it rocked the world around her. 'Maura,' she whispered again, then, the bloodstained rag dropping to the floor, she began to run.

2

———

'Do I think as how it be wise?'

Seamus Riordan looked at his elder son, feeling the same old resentment rise from the deepest part of him, resentment that this was not the child of the woman he had loved, the woman he loved still.

'I think it's after being no less wise than taking the daughter of Fergus Shea into the house, a woman who seemingly can carry no child to its full.'

'That was an accident, a trip on the stair.'

'And the second! Was it an accident that tore the second child from the womb, and it no more than seven months . . . an accident or your use of the fist?'

'I didn't—'

'Enough!' Seamus swept a hand through the air, his face a mask of anger. 'I'll hear no more. What goes between you and your wife be of no import to me.'

No one had ever been of import to his father. Padraig Riordan shifted under the gaze that carried more contempt than ever it had carried love, but then his father had never felt that emotion, not for his wife or for his sons.

'There has to be sons.' Seamus banged a closed hand on a delicate spindle-legged table, rocking it with the blow. 'And it looks to be those sons will not come from Niamh Shea, for that reason if no other then Liam must marry.'

'There will be sons—'

'Be that the truth now!' Eyes hard and cold as rock rested on

Padraig. 'And when might that be . . . this year, next? I can't wait on words. The wench be sickly, that be clear to any as looks on her. Bring her to the farrowing pen and like as not the next bed she'll sleep in will be six foot down in the earth. No, the Riordan name must go on and if not from your loins then from those of Liam.'

His own thoughts had been those of his father. Padraig's teeth clenched. Niamh might never be brought to bed of a child. But that was no fault of his, he lay with her often enough; but the Deverell girl . . . there was one would give a man what he wanted, she would stir the blood in his veins, with her he could sire a host of sons . . . and, like his father said, Niamh was sickly, giving birth or not she would not live long and then . . .

'My mind be set and there'll be no altering of it,' Seamus Riordan swept on. 'Come Saturday eve the priest will read the words over Liam and the daughter of Brendan Deverell and she will come to this house as his wife.'

'And supposing there be no child, no son, supposing Liam be no more capable in bed than out of it, what then?'

A look cold as ice-robed stone stayed on the younger man, the unconcealed contempt so deep-seated in those hard eyes striking like a blow to his face.

'Then 'twill be as it ever was, and matters taken care of for him, but take heed, Padraig, that be one matter will not be given over to you.'

'Then who, Father?' Controlling his own easily roused temper with difficulty, Padraig returned the stare. 'To carry the Riordan name a child must be born of a Riordan man and if Liam should prove incapable—'

'Then I'll do the job myself!'

'You!' Padraig half laughed. 'The father of the girl's own husband.'

'It wouldn't be the first time in the history of this world and I hold little doubt it will be the last, but this I tell you certain sure,' the older man's eyes glistened dangerously, 'wife of Liam or no the Deverell girl will not be touched by you; not one finger will be laid upon her or I'll take the heart from yer body with my own hand!'

'*I'll take the heart from yer body with my own hand.*'

Walking slowly to the part of the house given to his and his wife's use, Padraig let the words run through his mind, playing over it like the ripples of a stream.

Why? At the head of the stair he stood with his hand on the heavily carved banister. Why, for all he had done to others, had Seamus Riordan protected that girl and her mother, even now allowing them to live in that cottage?

His father was owner of this whole valley. The death of the English landowner had brought his widow to Clonfert to sit out her period of mourning, but that had been forgotten in the meeting of Seamus Riordan. What he had given the lady of Eyrecourt had obviously compensated very well for the loss of her husband, so much so she had married her Irish lover and all she had once owned was now his. But she had been far into middle age on coming to Ireland and the damp bog mists soon saw her into her grave. This Seamus had foreseen, and the wait to become valley king had not been a long one. Yet all of that did not explain why, as he had done with all other tenants, he had not turned the Deverell family from his lands.

There had to be cause. Dropping his hand to his side he walked slowly along the beautifully carpeted corridor, turning into his own room. There had to be cause, he thought again, dropping heavily into a leather-covered armchair, but what? There had never been friendship between his father and Brendan Deverell, and though Deverell's wife was polite and respectful whenever his own mother paused to pass the time of day she had never once been known to give a word to his father.

So; he stared at the peat fire burning in the grate. If there was no friendship between Mairead Deverell and his father what was the tie that bound them for there was one, of that he was certain, and what was it had given rise to the words '*I'll take the heart from yer body*'? That was one question to ponder, the other was would Padraig Riordan ever find out his warning had come too late?

Mairead Deverell looked at the girl sleeping in the small truckle bed made for her by her father when she was too grown to fit into the dresser drawer that had served for the first four years of her life. It all seemed so long ago, so long since Brendan had brought her as his bride to the clochan, this tiny stone cottage, so long since their only son had died less than an hour after his coming into the world . . . all of it so long ago. How hard those years had been, they had both worked every hour between the dawn and the dusk, him in the field he had first cleared of stones to make a tatie patch and she in the cottage looking to the thousand and one tasks that filled a woman's day. Then at night, in the bed that stood in the corner, he had held her in his arms; but though the whispering of his love for her had never ceased, the joining of his body to hers in the fulfilling of that love had become less and less until no longer did it happen at all. Had it been that desire had died in him? No, Mairead's head shook briefly at the thought, it had been the shame he thought was his, the failure to father another son.

'But it could not have been your fault!' Mairead's whispers even now were for her husband's comfort. 'The blame must have lain with me, I was not fit in the eyes of heaven to bear you more children, I gave only one daughter and now—' But she would not tell Brendan that, she would not disturb his eternal rest with the telling of the rape of his child; but neither would she let it go unpunished.

She knew what she must do. The valley kings would pay for the sin laid upon her daughter; but not with coin. Drawing her ragged shawl about her shoulders Mairead Deverell looked once more at the girl she had bathed then rocked to sleep in her arms. No, they would not pay with coin!

Going softly from the one room that was home to herself and her daughter, Mairead stood for a moment staring at the bare patch of earth within the small overgrown garden. Brendan had cleared that too then planted it with flowers for her delight, but now it was empty of all save bracken, all, that was, except for the dark narrow strip that covered him and his son. Soon it would cover her but before it did she would have justice for the wrong done her daughter.

Padraig Riordan would no doubt deny the truth of what Maura had told her and it was equally of no doubt his father would uphold him. Well, she could not blame him for that, it was natural for a parent to support their own, but for Seamus Riordan there could be no wrong in his son, she would get no justice there.

'That is why I must be doing what I do,' she whispered to the smudge of earth black in the light of a full moon. 'I know you would forbid it, Brendan, but there be no other way.'

Standing a few seconds more, a scrap of clean rag held to her mouth to stifle the cough that wracked her thin body, she listened to the quiet rhythm of her daughter's breathing. With the help of God and His holy saints . . . No – she pushed the thought away – she could not ask the help of heaven in what she was about to do.

It was as if some secret inner sense had warned of the coming of this day. Mairead touched a hand to the pocket of her patched skirt, feeling the slivers of wood wrapped in a scrap of cloth. It had been a long time in the gathering, asking passing tinkers to bring what she could not gather for herself, often waiting months for their return, but at last the tiny hole set in the wall behind her bed held all she had prayed would never be needed. But that inner sense, that soundless voice that whispered always in her heart, had not told her false and now the need was come and tonight would see her vengeance.

Stumbling slightly, tussocks of grass catching at her feet, breath rattling in her lungs, she made her way to the brook that was a silver finger of the broad river Shannon. At its edge she dropped to her knees on the dew-soaked ground, coughing into the scrap of rag and feeling the rise of blood warm in her mouth. It must be done this night, the waning of the next moon would see all chance gone for she would not live that long.

Glancing at the brilliant orb she smiled at its fullness. Deceitful so it was, the perfection of its circle denying the fact that its dying, like her own, was already well begun; that in a few short nights its glory would be eaten away and the earth would lie in darkness for three more before that brightness returned as a slim crescent. But it was this time, the time of the moon's waning, that her work must be done.

Taking the small cloth-wrapped bundle from her pocket she spread it on the grass beside her. Just inches beyond the stream's edge the moon's reflection was a great golden bowl on the gently rippling water. Stretching her hands towards it she dipped her fingers into its gleaming centre then sprinkled the tiny drops onto the slivers of wood lying in the cloth.

The powers of old would judge her asking. Crossing both hands over her breast she bowed her head, her whisper a sigh on the night.

> 'Seven twigs from seven trees,
> Thy ancient powers now give to these,
> Bathed in the moon's full light,
> Imbue them with thy force and might.'

With the last word the earth seemed suddenly to breathe, the rushes at the stream's edge riffled as the waters surged, the leaves of nearby trees rustled, whispering among themselves as a blast of wind bent their long arms towards her, while overhead the light of the moon appeared to grow, its golden phosphorescence intensifying to a silver radiance bathing her whole body in a shimmering lambent glow. Then in a breath the silence returned, the moon golden once more on the softly tumbling water.

The ancient powers had given of their answer. Mairead spread her arms, whispering thanks the night air carried over the moonlit stream. Taking up cloth and twigs she rose to her feet. She would have her revenge.

Retracing her steps she looked at the cottage Brendan had built for her when she became his bride. It had been a sign to all in Clonmacnoise, a telling that he saw no shame in the daughter of Arlen Shanley. But the shame had been there, hiding deep in her heart, though none of it had been of her doing, just as the rape of her daughter had been none of Maura's doing. Such as the father so is the son! The thought stabbing at her brain Mairead gripped her bundle tightly, her thoughts on the girl lying inside that clochan, the house so small and low it seemed as though it were sinking back into the earth from which it had been formed. She had washed the blood from her child as her own mother had washed it from her; soothed her to sleep as she had been soothed, but that would not redress the shame of rape, the pain that would fester in her daughter's heart as it had festered in hers.

A reckoning had been taken. Her steps slower now, her free hand holding the bloodstained rag against her lips, Mairead walked on towards the black shadow that was her home. Her own mother had called upon those same ancient powers, she had taken her own revenge, but it was not one so terrible as Mairead Deverell would take!

Averting her eyes from the smudge of earth black among the shadows, she gritted her teeth against the touch she could almost feel in the darkness. She would not listen to the plea she knew Brendan would have spoken, the words she could hear now in the hollow of her soul.

'Not again,' she sobbed into the stained cloth, 'I won't, Brendan, I won't let it happen again!'

Inside the house she stood a moment listening to the breathing of the girl asleep in the truckle bed, breaths broken by sobs and frightened murmurs. No, she would not let it happen again! Her footsteps soundless on the earthen floor she crossed to the hearth, holding the bundle of twigs over the glowing heart of the peat fire as she murmured.

'Thy power be their power.'

A settling of the peat sent a myriad tiny sparks bursting upwards and in the shadowed darkness Mairead's pale face smiled. Again the ancient powers had marked her asking and again they answered. She turned away, the crimson glow of the fire hindering her vision, but years spent in this room meant she had no need of lamp to light her way, and no glow of burning peat could hide what was printed in her brain. Laying cloth and twigs on the table she crossed to her solitary cupboard, reaching out the things she had put ready.

Beyond the tiny low-slung window the earth lay swathed in brilliant gold, a great banner of a moon glistening its defiant beauty before surrendering to the rise of the sun.

Taking an earthenware dish to the hearth she scooped a smattering of ash into it before returning to the table where she tore a narrow strip of the cloth, twisting it about an unused candle.

Blue, the colour of compelling, she had chosen carefully. Letting the shawl slip from her shoulders she lit the candle, holding it towards the window, mingling its light with the brilliance of the moon, drawing the power of one into the other. Turning back to the table she placed the candle at its centre.

Glancing towards the narrow bed she caught her breath, fighting back the cough rising in her throat. Maura must not wake now, she must never carry knowledge of what took place here this night; she had not been given instruction in the old ways, her daughter had not been taught as she had been taught. Tonight Mairead Deverell would call upon the ways of old but the powers of summoning would die with her. Swallowing the warm blood curdling in her mouth she touched a thumb to the ash covering the bottom of the bowl and pressed it to each twig. She could not write her name but the powers would know her signing.

Circling bowl and twigs about the bright flame she whispered softly, 'Be thou in me as I am now in thee,' then, lifting one twig at a time, she held it above the candle and recited into the velvet stillness.

> 'Elder bind Sunday, first of the week,
> Ash enthral Monday, vengeance to wreak,
> Beech in servitude Tuesday doth hold,
> Elm, Wednesday in power enfold,
> Oak govern Thursday with strength naught can break,
> With this, my asking, my nemesis take.
> Horse chestnut over Friday hold sway,
> Yew the bond to enchain Saturday.'

Over the patch that had once been a flower garden the moon silvered, seeming to halt in its path; to watch, to wait. Mairead glanced and smiled, the ancient powers were with her, guiding her hand. Quickly uncorking three small pot jars she tipped a few drops over the twigs, intoning as she went.

'With oil of Lavender,
Juniper and Sandalwood bound,
Bring thou thy powers
to my command.'

With the final word she lifted the candle and touched its flame
to the contents of the bowl, nodding to herself as twigs and oil
flared in the darkness. Tomorrow Seamus Riordan and his
sons would pay the price of their taking, tomorrow evil would
know its reward.

3

'I'll go to the priest, make confession.'

'No!' Mairead Deverell's fever-bright eyes swung to the girl rising from her knees, her morning prayer fresh on her quivering mouth. 'Ye'll speak to no priest, make no confession to a sin that was none of yer making.'

'But—'

'No, child, no buts.' Mairead's head shook briefly, the denial in it sharp as in her eyes. 'There be no fault in you, that my heart tells me. Ye have taken yer sorrow to the Lord. He will not turn His face from you.'

'But maybe mine was the making of that evil, it was thoughtless to sit as I did.'

Beneath the worn-through shawl that wrapped her shoulders Mairead Deverell's heart wrenched as she watched her daughter's lovely eyes fill with tears. Taking her in her arms she stroked the thick folds of chestnut hair, the scent of last night's rosemary wash rising to her nostrils. Brendan had always loved that delicate perfume. Swallowing the sob that thickened her throat she whispered softly.

' 'Tis a sad day for this world when a girl may not sit and rest her feet in its streams; but if you feel that by doing so ye tempted a man to wrongdoing then ask your forgiveness of God here in this house, yer words will reach to heaven as well from a clochan as from the church in Clonfert. Then when ye be finished, tidy the house and set all in its place for you and I will pass no other night beneath its roof.'

'Leave!' Maura pushed free of her mother's arms, anxiety adding to the brilliance of tears. 'But, Mother, you . . .'

Mairead's smile was gentle. 'I knows what be behind yer fears, the words of Sinead O'Toole be with me as they be with you but the evil that lies over this valley shall not touch ye again; today we will break with the past, leave its scars behind.'

'But where will we go? You are not well . . .'

'Strength will be given me.' Mairead loosened her daughter's grasp. 'Now do ye as I say, child, put the house so none can criticise, and wait ye for me here.'

'Wait!' Maura reached for her own shawl. 'The house will take no time at all, I can come with you and have that done in a trice when we return.'

Framed in the low doorway Mairead Deverell's wasted figure looked frail as a whisper in the wind but the determination in her answer was strong as the stones of the earth.

'Where I go ye will not tread. Ye will not enter Eyrecourt House, not as bride nor as one seeking redress for wrong that has been done; the taking of vengeance be given to me and that right I will claim; this day will see justice done.'

What had her mother meant? Maura watched the slight figure disappearing into the remnants of morning mist still clinging to the heath. Was she after asking the English magistrate to have Padraig Riordan arrested? But what proof would she have it was that man had abused her daughter, and without proof . . . She shivered at the thought of what would follow. Seamus Riordan was not one to forgive such a claim, he would have no pity. It would not matter to him that Mairead Deverell was a sick woman, he would have her sent to the penitentiary in Dublin . . . or, worse, demand deportation to some country beyond the sea; and herself, what would he have done with herself? He would not allow her to stay here in Clonmacnoise nor take her as bride for Liam in Clonfert. But what did it matter what Seamus Riordan did to her, it was her mother who mattered.

'Please,' she dropped to her knees, her right hand making the holy sign upon her breast, 'blessed Lord in heaven watch over my mother, keep her from the wrath of Seamus Riordan.'

'*Where will we go?*'

Maura's question rang in Mairead's mind as she pushed on towards Clonfert. The answer to that was in God's hands but wherever He had ordained her daughter must bide she prayed it would be far from this place. Only give me a little more time, she asked silently, time enough to see my child safe away from Seamus Riordan then will I gladly take my punishment for the sin I commit this day.

With a cough rising in her chest she paused, reaching for the rag already stained with blood, and as her fingers dipped into the pocket of her skirt they touched against the small jar she had pushed there before the grey wings of dawn had brushed the sky.

Holding the cloth to her mouth, her breath shallow and rasping she forced herself to go on; rest now and she knew she would never reach the fine stone house that was the home of Seamus Riordan. But she had to reach it, only that way could she save her daughter.

'*Marry her with Liam,*' Seamus had said the morning he rode his fine horse to the door of her clochan, '*marry your daughter with my son and a secure life will be hers.*'

A secure life! Mairead's colourless lips moved while in her heart she refused the offer, as she had refused it then. Secure maybe, but what happiness would her child know with a family for whom the very word was unknown, with a man who had raped her then threatened to pleasure himself again and again regardless of her being his brother's wife.

Her hand going once more to her pocket her fingers closed about the small jar, a whisper soft on the dew-wet morning. 'Forgive me, Brendan, but I know no other way.'

She had watched twigs and oil burn to ashes and as the last tiny flame had flickered into blackness she had taken the crock bowl to the door of the clochan and held it above her head, lifting it towards the brilliant orb of the moon, asking again the help of those ancient powers, on ways forbidden by the church and its teachings. She had tried. She stumbled on, the blood-stained rag pressed to her mouth. Through all the years of her marriage she had resisted using the knowledge given her by her mother, resisted taking revenge upon Seamus Riordan, but this she would not resist; a Riordan had shamed her child and that act would be avenged.

Nodding a reply to the greeting of a man pushing a peat cart, Mairead crossed the Eyrecourt bridge that spanned a narrow bend of the Shannon, then followed the road to the right that would lead her to Clonfert; but she would have no time to stand and stare at the beautiful pedimented west door or the graceful chevroned arches of the tiny cathedral of Saint Brendan the Navigator, instead she would go directly to the heavy square-built house with its regimented rows of tall rectangular windows and pillared entrance built by the English landlord whose widow had become first Seamus Riordan's whore and not much later his second wife.

Passing through the village with its low-slung turf-roofed cottages she paused, glancing at the elegant house perched on the gentle rise of ground overlooking the slow-moving river and her fingers tightened about the jar in her pocket.

Ard Ri . . . king of the valley! Seamus had certainly lived the dream, lording it over the folk from here to Clonmacnoise and further still; he had inherited the mantle of the English land-lord and he wore it well! But let him wear it. She smiled secretly to herself. Let him wear it for his lifetime . . . and after that? Nursing the smile in her breast Mairead Deverell walked on towards the house.

*   *   *

'*You and I will pass no other night 'neath its roof.*'

Maura Deverell looked around the tiny room, poor as a tinker's pocket but neat and clean as a new pin. This was her home, the only one she had ever known, if they left it where would they go? Her mother had said they must leave but it must not be so, that surely would hasten the death that lay waiting for her. No, Mairead Deverell must not leave the home her husband had built for her.

Leaving the cottage she crossed the garden to the tiny patch that was all she had time to keep free of choking weeds. Kneeling, she touched a hand to the bare earth that covered the twin graves.

'I did not lie willingly with Padraig Riordan, Father,' she whispered, 'if it be sight of me tempted him to his wickedness then I'm sorry, yet if it be he repeats it again and again then so be it, so long as Mother is not turned from her home. I will marry with Liam Riordan, I will go to the house of his father, all I ask is that you understand and if you can to forgive.'

'Be that yeself kneeling there, Maura Deverell?'

Rising quickly Maura turned to see Sinead O'Toole, her bent black-cloaked figure stood beside the open door.

'I give ye good day, daughter of Brendan Deverell and asks the hospitality of a sup o' tay.'

'The kettle is over the fire and you are always welcome in my mother's house. Come you in and take a seat while I brew the tea.' Maura's quick hand brushed tell-tale tears from her cheeks.

Taking mugs from the cupboard she added a little milk to only one of them; there was precious little left in the jug and that she would keep for her mother's return.

Sat close against the clean-swept hearth Sinead O'Toole's bird-like eyes circled the small room noting its absence of the mother, and the tears of the daughter had not been wiped before she had seen them. Her mother's house, the girl had

said. Taking the thick pottery mug Sinead stared at the
contents, but this would soon be the house of Mairead
Deverell no longer.

'Yer mother be from the house?'

Maura nodded, not wanting to speak of where it was her
mother had gone for that would lead to the telling of why. She
did not want the shame of her rape spoken of; true, Mother
O'Toole could be trusted with a secret but it was a secret she
herself could not bear even to think of.

'Gone to the grand house on the hill above Clonfert, is it?'

'You passed my mother on the way?'

First sipping the hot tea the old woman shook her head.
' 'Tis not my good fortune to have been after seeing herself this
day.'

'Then how did you know she was gone to Clonfert?'

'Many are the words I be given the hearing of though they
be not spoken by mortal tongue, and many be the pictures
carried to me on the shadows of night; pictures like the rape of
an innocent girl.'

'How—!'

The shawl slipped from the grey head, the glow from the fire
turning the bright eyes to rubies as they lifted to Maura.

'Don't be asking the how, child.' She answered the startled
gasp. 'It be beyond yer understanding, but know ye this, it has
been told no other.'

'I was thoughtless—'

'No, child.' Sinead watched the girl she had brought into the
world. 'Ye can lay no blame on yeself, ye were caught in the
beauty of nature but he that took ye, his heart was black with
lust, dark with the evil that will drive him all his days.'

Her own tea forgotten Maura hung her head. 'The . . . the
pictures, you saw the man?'

The grey head nodded, short rapid bobs like the seed head
of a dandelion swaying in the breeze.

'I saw.' Sinead sipped again.

A sob breaking from her, Maura slipped to her knees, hiding her face in the older woman's voluminous skirts. 'I'm afraid, Mother O'Toole, afraid of him and . . . and afraid of what I may be carrying inside of me.'

Putting her cup aside Sinead stroked the velvet head. 'Have no fears, there be no seed of Padraig Riordan has the growing inside of ye, ye carry no child of his.'

Not this time! Maura felt the tears well in her throat. But what of that man's threat, how long before his seed took root in her . . . how long would she suffer his abuse before she could fulfil the promise made to herself and end her own life?

Holding Maura's head between her hands, lifting it until the tear-strewn face looked into her own, Sinead O'Toole's eyes seemed suddenly to deepen, to become bottomless pools of shining darkness that drew Maura into their depths, swallowing her, enveloping her, holding her floating in a silence that stretched into eternity.

'Put that thought from ye.'

The woman's voice reached across the chasm of silence, quiet yet with a throb of intensity that beat against Maura's brain.

'It will be as Mairead Deverell has already had the telling of ye; ye'll not be forced to enter the house of Seamus Riordan as wife to his younger son nor will the elder take what ye have no wish to give.'

How did Mother O'Toole know all of this? No one had visited this house, her mother and herself had spoken to no one of what had taken place yesterday evening yet this woman seemed to have every word, it could have been she had been present in this very room. Maura's thoughts ran in circles becoming more and more confused. She knew every spoken word and those that were no more than thought; but that was not possible, nobody could read the mind of another or hear a whispered word from the other side of the valley . . . yet Mother O'Toole seemed to have done just that!

'This clochan yer father built against his marrying ye will rest in no more, sorrow it be will take ye from its shelter and in sorrow will ye leave this land; but as from a man came your defilement so from a man will come your protection.'

'My mother?' Maura asked as the quiet voice ceased and the gnarled hands dropped from holding her head.

'Ask no further word of me, child, only the voice of fate can tell you what more it is life yet holds for ye.' Drawing her worn-through shawl about her bent shoulders the woman shuffled to the door, and passing beyond into the bright clear light of a cloud-free sky she paused for a moment, staring at the two wooden crosses stood in their dirt patches, then crossing herself she murmured softly the blessing known to all in Ireland.

> 'May the road rise to meet you,
> May the wind be always at your back,
> May the sun shine warm upon your face,
> The rain fall soft upon your fields and
> Until we meet again may God hold
> You in the hollow of His hand.'

'. . . *in sorrow will ye leave this land* . . .'

The words ringing like the death bell in her mind, Maura watched the black-draped figure cross the heath towards the small plank bridge that spanned the finger of the Shannon. How could Mother O'Toole ever think such a thing? She could never leave Ireland, everything she knew or had ever loved was here. If they must leave this house and even this valley then so be it, but leave the shores of Ireland she never would.

4

The ground leading to Eyrecourt House rose gently but at the gates of the imposing building, Mairead Deverell leaned against the wall, her breath laboured. Holding the rag to her mouth she fought to control the wracking cough that seeped fresh blood into the deeply soiled cloth. Every day the cough grew worse, every day the consumption eating away her lungs left her a little weaker and at this moment had her longing for rest. But she could take no rest until her task was done and her daughter safe from the Riordan threat.

Straightening, she drew a few shallow breaths, the cool air of morning bringing no relief to the pain in her chest. The herbs left to her from Sinead O'Toole's last visit no longer made any impression on the cough that plagued, and brought no halt to the blood spilling from her mouth; but then had not the woman herself said such would be the way of it, that towards the end naught would ease the suffering. But all she had and might yet have to suffer counted for nothing when compared to that which her child would be called upon to endure unless what she had come to this house to do was accomplished. Taking another shallow breath she moved slowly along the curving tree-lined drive until she reached the house.

Now, before she was spotted by a servant! Needing the use of both hands she pushed the blood-soaked rag into a pocket before extracting the jar from another. Removing the lid she dipped a finger into the ash of the burned twigs smearing a trace of it between the stones of the house, touching the wood

of a window frame and the jamb of the heavy door. Then
moving as quickly as her wasted limbs allowed she moved to
the rear, repeating the touch to every stable and outhouse.
Taking from the same pocket the sprig of conifer she had
picked earlier she daubed ash along its length. Holding the jar
one moment longer she lifted it towards the house then, her
whisper following it, she dropped it into the well.

'What are you about there?'

The call, sharp as a knife, echoed in the space between well
and house and Mairead turned to see a stable hand watching
her from a low archway.

'A drink of yer fresh water afore I give a knock to the door.'

'Take the water with a blessing, mother, then be away with
you quickly for this house holds out no hand to beggars.'

'It's no beggar woman I be and though I thanks ye for yer
words still I'll be setting my hand upon yonder door.'

'Then if I can't be after persuading you I asks the little
people walk beside you for the master here be sharp of tongue
and rough of fist, should he see you 'twill be short shrift you'll
be after getting.'

'I thank ye for the water and I thank ye more for the
kindness of yer words, heaven smile on ye, lad.' Mairead
nodded as the young man disappeared beneath the shadowed
arch. He had spoken rightly of Seamus Riordan, the man's
hospitality was well known throughout the valley.

'The master won't have the seeing of the like of you!'

Her disdain loud as the words themselves the thin prim
woman, her mouth starched as the snowy apron that reached
to the hem of a heavy black skirt, made to slam the door shut.

'Should Seamus Riordan come to have the knowing that
Mairead Deverell were turned from his door then ye'self will
be looking for a new post but there'll be none ye'll be finding in
all of Offaly or Laois nor in all of Kildare for the man has a
long arm and a longer memory.'

With the door almost closed the woman's sour face showed a flicker of uncertainty. Beggars and gypsies rarely called at Eyrecourt, the reputation of its owner being what it was, but while this woman was poorly dressed she was spotlessly clean and her manner was certainly not that of a beggar. Posts like hers were not thick on the ground in Clonfert and less so in the rest of the valley . . . should what had been said be true, should it be that she had turned away someone Seamus Riordan might have wanted to speak with, if so then her life here would be finished.

The thought running quickly through her mind the woman opened the door just enough to stare threateningly at Mairead.

'Stay ye there,' she said sharply, 'take no step from that spot or I'll have the dogs set to hunting after ye. I'll have word of ye sent to the master but should it be the reply be one of refusing then 'twill be a bucket of water will be helping ye on yer way!'

Anxiety for her living had the woman's tongue like a black-smith's rasp. Mairead watched the door close in her face. That she could understand and forgive but one thing she would never forgive . . . the rape of her child!

'Ye'self it is, Mairead Deverell, and me set to thinking ye would never tread foot in my house; but 'tis welcome ye are and glad I am the marrying of your child with me own will see an end to old misunderstanding.'

All the hatred of years rising in her Mairead looked at the man smiling as he rose from his chair. Heavier set than he had been as a young man, with dark hair threaded with grey, eyes alert beneath beetle brows, he made a commanding figure.

'I am not come to your house for the speaking of a marriage, for that is still as I answered almost a week gone, my daughter will never be wife to yer son. Yet it is yer son that brings me here.'

'Liam?'

Mairead stared steadily into eyes that for twenty years had troubled her sleep. 'It be not that one but the other. I come to ask his father, to ask ye'self, Seamus Riordan, how will his behaviour towards my daughter be repaid?'

'Will ye sup a dish o' tay?'

Her fingers closing about the snippet of twig Mairead shook her head. It was of no consequence to this man what his son had done or who he had done it to, his action warranted no more consideration than had his father's so many years before. The lesson, if learned, had not been passed on!

' 'Tis not a dish of tea I be wanting but yer answer.'

'I take it Padraig has spoken harshly to the girl, but it will have been naught but high spirit, a lad is a lad.'

'And that be your answer?'

'What else? He be a bit big for the taking down of his trousers and setting a strap to his backside.'

'Your son needs no help in the taking down of his trousers. He did that for himself yesterday eve.'

'What's that ye be saying!'

Watching him stare at her Mairead saw the anger she had seen when a sixteen-year-old girl refused his offer of marriage, saw the hands clench and the mouth set and the same vengeance shine stark in his eyes.

'Be ye telling me my son set hand upon your child?'

'More than his hand.' Her answer was soft but with every word the man flinched as if struck by a stone. 'As with the father so with the son. He took my child against her will, forced himself upon her, then left her bleeding as you left me; you should have warned him, Seamus, warned him of the vengeance a woman can take.'

'You can't be sure . . . there be more than one man in the valley—'

'That's the truth you speak . . . but so were my child's words the truth; it was a Riordan raped her as it was a Riordan raped her mother, and as my own mother took her vengeance so will I take mine.'

'Mairead, there has to be some mistake!'

Nodding slowly Mairead felt the twig hard against her palm. 'The mistake was yours, Seamus, in not telling your sons the reward of rape. Ye heard my mother's words and can bear witness they were not empty. Never in yer life would you know true love, neither from man nor from beast, from woman nor from child, yer life would have no happiness in it and ye would give no happiness to others. Throughout the years ye have watched the truth of those words, though ye married twice there was no love and though ye sired two sons they have brought ye no pleasure. Ye thought that by bringing my child into this house as wife to Liam the strength of those words would be broken, and when you were refused then the older one reckoned on a child in her womb . . . his child . . . achieving what words could not. Now as my mother laid her curse upon ye so I lay mine.'

Reaching quickly towards him she touched the tiny piece of twig to his hand, leaving a smear of black ash from knuckle to wrist.

'See the mark of my malediction . . . Know the power of the ancient ways.'

Fever-bright, her eyes held his, seeing the leap of fear surge in them. Like many another in the country he followed the teaching of the Church but had not forgotten ways that were older by far. He knew the potency, the irrefutable force that lay in the conjuring of them, knew that once her words were uttered no tongue but hers could recall them, and that she would never do. Stifling the cough that rattled in her throat she held the twig so he could see it.

'This is the fruit of yer son's pleasure,' she said. Then as he stared at it she went on in a droning whisper as though the

words were no longer meant for him to hear but were directed
inwards to a force that was herself.

> 'Seven are the days
> Each held in thrall,
> Three are the lives
> In bond to all,
> Three the lives
> My curse enchain,
> Each pass like the days
> 'Til none remain,
> To no Riordan shall child be born
> Let house and name from this valley be torn.'

As the last word left her lips she cast the twig into the fire.
'There be yer line,' she pointed to the blazing stick, 'it will die,
burn out as that twig burns, leaving nothing behind it. This is
the curse of Mairead Deverell. Remember it, Seamus, remember it each time ye looks on yer son!'

'You have to rest, you are worn out.'

Helping the figure she had run across the heath to meet,
Maura lowered her mother to the chair beside the hearth then
set about brewing a pot of tea.

Her eyes half closed with weariness, Mairead watched the
quick movements but she knew the heaviness of heart that lay
beneath them. Her child was feared of the man who had used
her, feared he would return the same evil in his mind. And
such fear was not without base. She took the tea, holding it
between hands whose every vein showed beneath parchment
skin. Seamus Riordan had been held by the words she had
spoken but once the reality of them broke the bond they had
set he would strike back. He would come for Maura, drag the
girl with him to Clonfert, keeping her prisoner within his

house, hoping that way to force her, Mairead, to lift her curse; but the lifting would bring one equally painful for her daughter, for Seamus Riordan would never free her, she would be wed to his son.

No! She sipped the hot tea, feeling its warmth pass her throat. That must never happen, they must leave this house before the sun set.

'Mother O'Toole called this morning.'

Maura took the cup her mother drained and refilled it. She had made the drop of milk stretch by taking none herself, now she added the last of it to her mother's drink.

'Ye gave her the hospitality of the house?'

She did not need to ask a question the like of that, she had taught her daughter the value of good manners, but by asking she delayed what must be told.

'I acted as you yourself would have done.' Maura's heart contracted as she looked at the drawn face. Why had her mother insisted she go to the house at Clonfert, the deed had been done and nothing she could say would have the undoing of it.

'And what was it brought Sinead O'Toole to my door?'

'She gave no reason,' Maura answered. 'She brought nothing with her, neither did she ask anything be given except for a dish of tea but—'

'But what, child?'

'She knew!' The girl's brow furrowed, the strangeness of what had occurred striking her all over again. 'Mother O'Toole knew what had happened, that Padraig Riordan had—'

'There be no need to speak the word.' Mairead saw the horror rise dark to her daughter's eyes.

'But how could she . . . I did not speak of it.'

A faint smile touched her mother's lips. 'Nor did I, child, but things do not have to be spoken of for Sinead O'Toole to have the knowing of them. Would I be right in saying she came to comfort ye?'

'She said I could lay no blame upon myself.' With a sob wrapping every word she flung herself at her mother's knee, hiding her face in her lap. 'She said Padraig Riordan's heart was black with lust and dark with the evil that will drive him all his days; she knew my shame and she knew my fear, the dread that I might carry his child.'

Had the spell she cast come too late? Mairead felt the blood freeze in her veins. Had that man's seed quickened and even now grew in her daughter?

'Ye told her that?' Holding her breath in her lungs she waited for the reply.

'Yes, I told her.'

'And the answer, child, what did she answer?'

'That . . . that I need have no fears, I carry no child of Padraig Riordan.'

The ancient ones had not failed her. Mairead released the breath locked inside. Their powers were great as they had always been and they would keep faith with her. Seamus Riordan and his sons would know no child of their own, their house would crumble to ruin and their name be as dust . . . the valley kings would rule no longer!

'She told me I would not enter that house as Liam's wife nor would—'

'Speak that name no more.' Mairead felt the tremor that shuddered through the slight shoulders. 'Go gather up the things ye would keep, for we must be gone from here.'

Did her mother too fear Padraig Riordan would come here to this house, come looking to repeat his vile act, before carrying out his father's orders to evict them, as his orders surely would be given. Was that the reason she said they must go though the effects of today's long walk still had her breathless? But to leave now could only harm her mother, perhaps aggravate the cough that even now was wracking her thin body; but would staying here another night harm her less, would she rest knowing every moment could bring the Riordans storming to her door?

It was on account of her! Slowly drying the two cups, Maura let her thoughts run on. Seamus Riordan had turned every family from their home as fast as he bought their land, so why not the wife and child of Brendan Deverell? He had purchased their holding after the blight had devastated that tatie crop five years before. For years there had been similar failures until the only way to free his family had been for Brendan Deverell to sell the land left to him by his father. That he had done and turned to cutting peat from Blackwater bog, selling a little of it for a few pennies but mostly trading if for vegetables or for a few potatoes, but as the earth's sickness had spread and the crops of most people were failing these grew less and less, until finally the pot held naught but a fish from the river or maybe a hare from the heath; then had come the time her father had not money enough for the rent.

Holding a cup in her hands Maura stared back over the long months, seeing the pain and the shame on that face she had loved with all her heart. Her father had left the cottage, first kissing herself and her mother. He had gone to stand before the tiny cross set among the flowers he still managed to care for. Maura closed her eyes, seeing in her memory the tall figure, spare from too much hard work and too little food, set against the red-gold light of sunset, his boots half hidden by brilliant blossom, his hand outstretched to touch the cross marking the resting place of a brother she had never known, then he turned away towards the hills, their heads covered by shrouds of purple mist. That had been the last time they had seen him alive. There had been precious little at all after that yet her mother had paid the dues on the house, though it had often meant they had gone without a meal.

But now they would go, leave before the Riordans came to throw them out . . . and it was her fault! Opening her eyes she let her gaze follow her mother through the open doorway. Mairead Deverell would lose the home she loved, the place where her husband and child lay and it would be the fault of her daughter.

'I have only to marry with Liam.' Replacing the cups in the cupboard the whisper was caught in the drying cloth she pressed to her quivering mouth. That was all it would take to see her mother safe in this house. She would go to her in a moment, stand with her beside her father's grave and tell her they would not leave, that she *wanted* to marry with Liam Riordan.

But I don't . . . I don't! The cry silent in her heart she lifted the kettle from the hearth and emptied the last drops of water into the bowl in which she had washed the cups then she carried it out to the rear of the house, emptying it on the few vegetables she had managed to rear.

'It's not yourself, Liam,' she whispered, watching the water seep slowly into the boggy ground. ' 'Tis not distaste for your twisted back turns me from marrying with you, and though no love exists between us I respect and like you, but fear of your brother—'

No! Clutching the tin bowl to her chest she pushed the words away. She must not speak them, she must not think them ever again. She would accept the offer of becoming wife to Liam Riordan . . . and all that acceptance entailed!

Crossing the overgrown ground Mairead ignored the brambles clutching at her skirts and the nettles that sank sharp stings into her hands as if wanting to bar her from coming to the bare patch of dark soil. Reaching the graves she sank to her knees on the cool earth, one hand marking the holy sign on brow and breast. This would be the last time she would kneel here, the last time she would touch the soft mound that covered her loved ones.

'Sleep softly, my little son.' She leaned forward, kissing the cross that bore her child's name, smoothing the black soil with fingers that had once smoothed a baby's dark hair. 'The Holy Mother comfort ye.'

Switching her eyes to the taller cross she touched it gently. 'I thought to lie beside ye, Brendan,' she whispered into a silence it seemed the whole earth observed, 'I thought to be laid to rest here where ye'self and our child lie. It has ever been my hope my spirit would one day walk with yours upon the gentle hills of heaven but that can never be, that act I did this day for ever denies me my heart's wish, but know ye I did it for our daughter though that can bring no forgiveness. I will not be permitted the joys of being reunited with the husband and the babe I long to hold, so I ask ye, take the hand of our son in yer own and tell him of his mother's love. Take the child I was given to keep but one short hour and as ye sit with him in the sweet fields of paradise speak to him of the love he brought and which lives yet in my breast.' Touching her fingers to the cross she caressed the painted name, tears throbbing in her whisper.

'Goodbye, my love, I shall not kneel here again. Wherever I go I carry you with me in my heart. Rest in the Lord's peace, Brendan Deverell, and know always that I love you.'

5

⁓

'What have ye done? What have ye done, ye black-hearted spalpeen!'

Padraig Riordan felt his nerves quicken as he saw the anger blaze in his father's eyes; not that he wasn't used to it, Seamus Riordan had always been given to temper, but this was something more, this threatened more than a blow of the fist or a flashing of the tongue.

'I might be able to give answer if I knew what it was riled you.'

His answer was calm and even but seemed to heighten the fury dancing on the older man's face.

'If ye knew what riled me!' Seamus Riordan spat the words. 'But then how could ye have the knowing of what has been done to the daughter of Brendan Deverell?'

His father knew! Padraig's nerves jumped again. But how could he? He had not been from the house these few days and visitors to Eyrecourt were even less than few and much more than far between.

'Brendan Deverell?' He frowned, pretending to search for the name.

Watching him his father's eyes narrowed. His son had ever been a jackeen, a useless braggart striking out at those weaker than himself but always with the knowledge that the strong would not fight back for fear of his father's hand, one that could take their living with the lifting of a finger; and he, Seamus Riordan, had done nothing to curb that behaviour, he had let his elder son rampage where he would, take what he wanted where he wanted, but the abusing of Maura Deverell, that he had strictly forbidden.

'Make no pretence,' he went on, a sudden disgust thickening his tone, 'ye took the girl, forced her to lie with ye!'

Padraig thought quickly. Whoever had informed his father had no proof, there had been no one else at the bank of the stream and he had seen no one as he rode home; it was an accusing without foundation and as such he could bluff it away.

'I forced this . . . this daughter of Brendan Deverell to lie with me!' He squeezed a laugh from his throat. 'Now why would I do a thing like that when a shilling would buy any woman in Clonfert?'

'This be no woman and no whore!' Seamus's fist swept the length of an ornate sideboard, sending china crashing to the floor.

'But she is a liar.'

'What is that ye say?'

Padraig swallowed nervously. His father was nursing a high anger, but for what, a chit of a girl with nothing to her name?

'I say she is a liar,' he repeated.

Watching the pale eyes so like his own, seeing the shifting anxiety in them, Seamus knew that what he feared, that what had been told to him by Mairead Deverell was true; but he must hear it from his son's lips, the truth that would part them.

'Lying, is it?' He lowered his voice, curbing the anger flowing like crushed ice in every vein. 'Tell me, why would a woman near death from the lung fever walk the miles from Clonmacnoise to Clonfert to do no more than give a lie that could see her and her child in the House of Correction?'

She had been here to this house! Padraig lowered himself to a chair, needing the moment to absorb the fact. He had not expected this, the girls he took made no complaint neither did

their kin for fear of being sent from their homes. He should
have warned that one, told her of the retribution he could take,
that he *would* take once he had satisfied his father that he was
innocent; the girl would pay . . . by God she would pay!

'I would have thought the reason to be obvious,' he said,
adopting a careless tone, 'you say yourself the woman is sick
from the lung fever and we know there is no hope of a cure for
that and if, as I presume, they have nothing then the girl hit on
the idea of accusing me, of taking her against her will, hoping
thereby to be given money.'

It might have been true of some in this valley but not of
Mairead Deverell. Seamus thought for a moment. The woman
had passed no word with him in twenty years; she had had all
that time to take revenge yet never once had she spoken
against him, not once decried him for his treatment of her.
She had asked nothing and taken nothing even paying every
penny of rent due on that hovel she lived in though he had said
there was no need, refusing the offer of a better house in any
place she named. But Mairead Deverell still held the pride she
had shown when refusing to wed with him, a pride that
showed yet and a tongue that would accuse no man without
cause. There were lies in all of this but they were not hers, nor
did he believe they came from her child. It was *his* son was the
liar, *his* son, the bones of his body told him so yet still he must
hear it said.

'Is that the truth of it, Father, has some girl been to this
house with lies on her tongue?' Padraig had noted the silence.
His father was uncertain, that was good, it would be easy now
to convince him the girl had tried to extract money by accusing
his son of rape.

'Did the girl put a name to her attacker, did she say mine or
maybe Liam's?'

Catching the smirk that accompanied the words, Seamus
felt the disgust of minutes before thicken again in his throat,

but this time it was for himself. He was responsible for this man's attitude to the world and its creatures, his was the hand had had the guiding of him, waving away his wife's attempts at alerting him to the ever-growing deceit, the arrogance that now ruled his every action.

'Liam's name was given no mention,' he answered, a warning in his eyes.

'It wouldn't need to be, would it, Father? The misfit would not need the naming by the wench when "Hunchback" would serve her need better!' Padraig's smile of contempt was open now, spreading his lips wide. 'Was it the runt, Father? Has Liam realised at last that no woman will take him with his twisted body, that no woman will willingly—'

'Shut yer filthy mouth!' Seamus lunged forward, his hand delivering a stinging blow to the mocking face. 'We both have the knowing yer brother would not stoop to forcing the child of Brendan Deverell!'

That was it . . . that had to be the reason for his father's anger! Realisation flashed like a lightning bolt through Padraig's mind. His father had not said *any* child, he had said the child of Brendan Deverell! Could what he thought be true, had his father been lenient with that family for a reason he could only guess, that it was not the child of Brendan Deverell he protected? *'I'll take the heart from yer body with my own hand.'* Padraig smiled remembering the words. Why else would his father threaten such, why else react to the taking of a peasant wench with such passion? Unless she were not the child of Brendan Deverell but the child of Seamus Riordan! Had his father done the same as he had done, had he in the past forced that girl's mother? Lifting a hand to his cheek he touched the stinging flesh. Was his father relieving his own guilt by striking him?

'Why the concern, Father?' Like sparks struck from flint his pale eyes glittered. 'Why pay such heed when it has never bothered you before, what is so special about this girl . . . or is it your conscience that bothers you? Is it that the guilt has rested on you giving you no peace for as long as I remember? Did you in years gone do as I did yesterday eve, did you take Mairead Deverell against her will; is that why you are so considerate of the girl, not because she is the child of Brendan Deverell but the child of that man's wife and yourself?'

It could have been a blow to the stomach. Padraig watched the older man fold, his face grey as he lowered to a chair. The guess had been a good one, from this day on Seamus Riordan would raise no more hand to him.

'So that be it.' He gloated. 'That girl is your own flesh.'

Slumped in his chair Seamus seemed to speak only to himself. 'If only heaven had made it so my life would have known some happiness at least, but the Lord ruled it other-wise. Yes, I raped ye, Mairead, I took that which no man has a right to before a woman be his wife; but I offered ye marriage before and after yet ye would speak no word to me. I loved ye then and I love ye still—'

'So you raped the mother yet would condemn me for doing the same to the daughter, you get clear away—'

'No!' Seamus looked up and now the reverie was gone from his eyes and his voice was once more the chip of stone on stone. 'I did not get clear away. Her mother came to the house of my mother just as Mairead Deverell came here today. She brought with her the old magic, laying a curse that said never in my life would I know the love of woman or child nor of man or animal. Ye would do well not to laugh!' He paused, seeing the mocking smile spread again. 'Ye know for ye'self there was never any love in this house nor in the one that went before, that there is none yet. Ye be wed, tell me do ye feel love for the one ye took afore God's altar, have ye ever felt love for her or for anyone other than yeself? Ye cannot answer yes to that for even with yer lying tongue ye could not face the lie of that.

Faith in the Church be strong in this country but the old religion has never died; with some it be alive yet and with the belief comes power.'

'A curse!' Padraig laughed aloud. 'You think it was a curse keeps happiness from your house! No, Father, it is the darkness inside you, the jealousy and lust that had you at odds with our mother, with Liam and me since the day of our birth, lust for another man's wife!'

Was that the truth of it? Had it been his own jealousy and longing and not the words of her mother's curse had turned his life sour?

'So the woman came here today making her accusation, what of it? What did she hope to gain?'

The sheer arrogance of it snatched Seamus from his thoughts. There was no regret, no contrition. His son had said no word of apology, offered to make no retribution for his wrongdoing. Such is the father so is the son! Not in every respect. He ran a glance over the face that mirrored his own, the long lithe body that he had once been proud of. Not in every respect! Unlike the father the son had not one trace of remorse in the whole of him.

'Tell me,' he drew a tight breath, 'did ye force the daughter of Mairead Deverell?'

'The daughter you think might be your own?'

There was more than insult or contempt in the question, there was challenge. His words tight as the anger seething below them, his eyes on those of the man seated across from him, Seamus answered.

'My forcing of Mairead Deverell was once and once only. She was but sixteen years of age as is her daughter. I had long loved her, so much the longing for her was a fire in my veins. I had asked her many times to be my wife but always she refused until I thought desire would turn to madness. Then one summer eve it did. I was returning from the tatie field when

I saw her; dressed in white she seemed to flit like a butterfly from daisy to buttercup, a bunch of each in her hands. I caught up with her, I remember looking into her face, a face whose beauty outshone that of the flowers she held and I begged her to wed with me—' He broke off, swallowing hard against the memory. 'She refused as she had always done and as she turned from me my mind seemed to snap. I caught her by the arms, throwing her to the ground, I said she would marry me or marry no man, then . . . then I raped her, God forgive me I raped her; but as the God I call on knows, from that moment never again did I set hand upon her. It was four years later, two of which she had already been wife to Brendan Deverell, that her daughter was born. There be the truth of it, now I say again, be that truth the same of ye?'

His father could offer no threat to him, hadn't he done the same thing himself? Confident in his own security, Padraig regarded the older man with a smile of disdain.

'Yes,' he pursed his lips, disdain becoming defiance, 'yes I raped her, but if as you say she is not my half sister then where is the harm, a couple of sovereigns—'

'Where is the harm!' With rage flashing like a beacon Seamus was on his feet. 'Ye have no sense of morality and for that I must take responsibility for I never taught ye any, but for the punishment this house will suffer ye must take the blame.'

'Punishment!' Padraig looked up calmly. 'What punishment? Oh the woman can go to the resident magistrate along of Ballinasloe but her word will count for nothing when put alongside that of the son of the owner of half county Offaly.'

'The punishment I speak of will come of no magistrate, the law will have no part in it—'

Making no attempt to hide his irritation, Padraig interrupted sharply. 'Not the Deverell curse again! The rantings of an old woman is what that is, I'm surprised you take any notice.'

'A man who takes no notice of the old ways is a fool.' Again Seamus's rage seemed to fade in the face of an unseen fear. Moving to the wide fireplace he stood staring into the gleaming bowels of the peat fire. 'Mairead Deverell has the power as did her mother, and like her she has laid her curse. She brought the ancient magic to this house, touched its walls and its windows –' he looked at the hand that still bore a trace of the ash then turned, thrusting it towards his son '– she marked me!'

Glancing briefly at the hand held out to him the younger man smiled, a cold sneering smile. 'The woman touched you with her dirty paw, unpleasant I admit but a little soap and water—'

'Ye don't listen, do ye, ye jackeen!' Seamus dropped the hand. 'The curse of the grandmother worked, my house never knew happiness, held no contentment. The magic she created was severe, it blighted my life and the lives of all around me but the magic the mother works will make that seem as naught. Hers be the viciousness of a woman twice wronged.'

'Did you offer her money, that seems to override a great many wrongs.'

'The answer of a fool as always!' Seamus hissed. 'That woman would take no money, her vengeance is not to be counted in sovereigns.'

Seated in his chair Padraig Riordan felt a rush of exhilaration sweep through him. His father was afraid, the domineering, obdurate Seamus Riordan was afraid . . . and of a crazy woman and her mumbo jumbo! A half smile on his lips he said, 'Then you ride to Ballinasloe, lay complaint to the resident magistrate, tell him of the threat this woman has made, of her placing a curse upon you and have her confined to prison or to an asylum for the insane, that is where her rantings should take her!'

The mockery behind the words was not lost on Seamus. His

son knew he would never speak of Mairead's visit or of her vengeance to any outside of his family.

'Rantings,' he drew a long breath, 'rantings they may be but behind them is the power.'

'Power! Power!' The short laugh echoed across the spacious room. 'Can you hear yourself, Father? You are as mad as the woman.'

For several seconds Seamus held the breath behind his teeth but his eyes glittered as they moved over his son.

'Mad is it, I am?' he said quietly. 'Mad to believe in a power not held by the Riordans, mad to believe that never again will child be born to me or to my sons, mad to believe that all I own will be taken from me, this house come to ruin and an end to my line? Then yes I be mad but not so much I can't be telling ye that for ye that end already be come. It was many times I warned ye, many times I told ye not to take yer rampaging to that house in Clonmacnoise but ye chose not to listen so now ye'll have the reckoning of it.'

'You'll rip the heart from my body with your own hands, were those not your own words?' Pale eyes heavy with contempt stared back at Seamus's dark hair glistening as the head shook slowly. 'I don't think so, Father, we are equals now you and I, we share the same background, the same secret, the rape of a Deverell woman; add to that the fact I am a man grown and you will understand what I say, that I will take no more of your beatings.'

Clenching his hands at his sides the older man swallowed the rage ever waiting to burst like a bubble.

'Yes, I said the words and now I take them back.' He paused for a moment, the satisfaction on that younger face like the touch of a branding iron on nerves taut as a bowstring. 'I take them back so they can be exchanged. Equals it was ye said we are and that be truth, equal we be in manhood and equal we be in shame, but there it stops. This valley and all in it belongs to me while ye have naught but what I choose to give. For what ye have done, for the vengeance ye have brought down upon this house I tell ye, ye be son to me no longer. This house be closed against ye for ever. Ye will leave with no more than the woman ye married and the clothes the two of ye be wearing and ye will be gone from my land; no man whose field is mine, no tenant with the wish to remain in his clochan will give ye sustenance; as ye brought that curse upon me so I place mine upon ye. Ye be kin no longer; no stick or stone, not one penny will pass from me to ye. Sorrow be always with ye, that was the Deverell gift to ye and now I add mine, may ye ever know poverty!'

His lips blanched and tight, his hands clenched to the arms of his chair, Padraig Riordan pushed slowly to his feet.

'I thank you for the gift, Father,' he snarled, 'now I make mine to you. You may keep my wife, ride her as you intended to ride Maura Deverell, take her to your bed as you intended to take the girl you chose to be wife to Liam . . . wife to the runt and whore to the father!'

Turning on his heel he stopped short at sight of the crook-backed figure stood in the doorway. Then with a vicious laugh he pushed past, his words trailing back to the silent man.

'Ask him, Liam, ask your father how it was meant the girl would conceive should you not be able to fill her belly yourself!'

6

〜

'You and I will pass no other night 'neath its roof.'

Those were the words her mother had spoken. Maura watched the thin figure move silently about the room, her hands resting for loving moments on the rough dresser – the odd ornament on it got from some passing tinker in exchange for a meal and a glass or two of porter. This was the home of her mother's heart, the place it would ever be. Across by the grate, which for the first time held no peat fire, her mother knelt beside the chair her father had always used. Seeing the head bent low to rest upon the short wooden arm, the thin shoulders heave beneath the woollen shawl, Maura had felt her own heart breaking.

She had turned away then, gone to stand beside the patch of earth in which lay her father and brother – the depths of her calling for guidance, asking heaven to show her what to do, what she could say to get her mother to rest a few days more in this house. But heaven had not listened. Mairead Deverell was held of a fear, a fear the black heart of Padraig Riordan would send him again to her clochan, to shame her child again – the same fear she herself still held. But she had tried her best to hide that feeling, tried each way her mind could tell her to get her mother to stay – 'she would not step but a few yards from the door', 'nor go beyond the sight', 'they would go together to bring water from the stream'.

How many stones had she thrown in the path of Mairead

Deverell's decision but like chaff in the wind they had been discarded.

'What is it I should ask you, Father? What is it I should know about Maura Deverell?'

The bile of temper still full in his throat, Seamus Riordan turned his back. One son a no-good jackeen, the other a crook-back runt! The mother of Mairead Deverell had chosen her curse well.

'I asked you a question, Father.'

'There be nothing ye should know! Get ye from this room.'

The snarl held a viciousness Liam had known all his life, a cold repugnance that never failed to send him running from the presence of this man. But now the running had stopped!

'I ask again, what is it I should know about Maura Deverell?'

Liam caught the blaze of anger in the pale eyes as his father swung to face him but it was the loathing beneath that pulled at him. It was not the fault of a child he be misshapen but the child had ever suffered the brunt of blame, the child and then the man! The runt, his father called him, the misfit of the family.

'Why, ye bloody spalpeen!' Anger carrying him across the room, Seamus brought his fist hard against a face that did not flinch. 'I'll teach ye to question me!'

'That will be the first thing you will ever have taught me, won't it, Father? But at least it will be a start.'

'A jackeen!' The fist rose again. 'A bloody jackeen like yer brother!'

His head flung to one side by the second blow, Liam straightened before answering. 'Not quite like him, I am the runt, have you not said so many times?'

Arrested by the calmness of it, Seamus stared at the figure several inches shorter than himself, at the face that for the first time stared back at him without fear.

'Get out!' He turned away. 'Get your twisted body out of my sight.'

Perhaps he was meant to cry out at that, to hide in his room as he had in childhood, before he had learned to avoid that tall figure with its harsh condemning face and sharp fist. But, like the running away, there would be no more tears, they had all been shed at his mother's death, only indifference remained.

'I carry the twisted body,' he said quietly, 'but the making of it came from you.'

It was as if Seamus Riordan had stopped breathing. Not the slightest movement, no catching of breath, no snarled reply, only silence; but still his son waited.

'The name of Maura Deverell was said.' It was Liam who broke the seal of silence. 'If you will not tell me the reason then I will go to that house—'

Seamus whipped round, the usual savage gleam lighting his eyes. 'Ye'll do nothing of the kind, ye will not speak with the girl nor with her mother!'

'I am beyond the age of ordering, Father, as from this moment I am beyond your beatings . . . strike me again and I strike back, and runt though I am there is strength enough.'

'Ye heard Padraig, why ask ye again!'

'Because I wish to hear. Is it the truth he threw or just the stones of spite? Did you intend to bring that girl into this house?'

'Yes!' The cry rang against the high ceiling, a kick sending the delicate spindle-legged table crashing against the carved sideboard.

'. . . *wife to the runt and whore to the father* . . .'

The words Padraig had flung scorched in Liam's brain but no sign of their pain was reflected in his steady gaze. 'The purpose?' he asked evenly.

'He heard!' Rage no longer his support, Seamus dropped to

a chair, his head in his hands. 'But what ye heard was not all of the truth, it was no intent of mine to bring her here as my whore, nor for yer brother's pleasure, that I swear, it was wife to ye'self I asked her to be.'

He had asked her to be! Tight as his nerves were, Liam felt them tauten still further. His father had asked Maura Deverell to wed with the son he detested . . . but why? What grudge did he bear the girl to offer her marriage to his runt?

'And the answer?'

Clenching his hands at his side, he laughed silently. Why had he asked, didn't he know the answer already . . . didn't he know no girl would wed a crook back?

'I put the question first to the mother and when she refused I asked it of the girl, then when her answer was the same I told her she had the choosing, wed with you on Saturday eve or find some other place for her mother to die.'

'You sent them from their home knowing the woman was ill!'

Seamus looked up quickly and now his pale eyes were dark with something other than anger and loathing. They held the shadows of remorse and, when he answered, it was with a quietness Liam had not heard before. 'No I have not sent them from that house nor will I, they were words spoken in anger, they have no substance.'

No substance . . . but a power, a vicious power to hurt, a power his father had never recognised; though that was a lie, Seamus Riordan had ever recognised the power of cruelty, know how painful was the thorn of venom, and he had never hesitated to prick with it.

'Equals in shame.' Liam spoke quietly, each word chipped stone. 'That was what you said to Padraig, the shame of what? Rape? Is that the shame you both share, is it rape brought the vengeance you spoke of? Have you shared with Padraig in the shaming of that girl?'

This was not the son he had reared, the child that ran from him, the man that never gave answer to his insults; this man stared back with challenging eyes, asked his questions with a firmness of voice and a not-to-be-defied authority. Seamus stared at the figure framed still in the doorway, a handsome man with the fine-boned features of his mother, the same fair skin and wide brown eyes, a son a man could take pride in were it not for a shoulder that rose above the other. A cripple! A son twisted in the growing yet he had the bearing his brother would never have.

'Let God be my witness, I laid no hand upon the daughter of Mairead Deverell, it was the mother I raped, the one woman I have ever loved, the woman who will take the heart of me to her grave.'

Speaking often in a whisper, his head low on his chest, Seamus shared the truth with his son, told what had happened so many years before and of what he had learned with the visit the woman had made that morning.

Finishing softly, he said, 'I hoped the marrying of ye to that girl would break the curse her grandmother had laid upon this house, and more . . .' He hesitated. 'It be no lie to tell I hoped it would put an end to the silence her mother kept towards me, that once more she might speak . . . but when at last her words came they held no forgiveness, no absolution of the sin I committed upon her, but a refusing of ye as she had refused me and then her curse, one more terrible than that which had gone before.'

It was a just curse. Leaving his father slumped in the chair, Liam turned, going quickly to the stables. The sun had already gone from the sky and there was no moon to relieve the blackness that would wrap the land until morning but that must prove no obstacle. His was the name put to Maura Deverell, his would be the apology . . . and after that his would be the revenge. Padraig Riordan would answer for the harm he had done. He would answer to the runt.

* * *

Her mother had not listened to her plea. An arm about the thin body, Maura felt even that small weight pull at her aching muscles. How much longer could she support the stumbling form? She had begged they stay in the house until the morning, had wanted her mother to rest, sleep would help drive away the tiredness that journey to Clonfert had turned to near exhaustion. But her mother had refused to listen. She had struggled to her feet from where she knelt beside the graves of her husband and her son and waited there until Maura had joined her. Then, her hand reaching for her daughter, Mairead had turned her back on her home.

Now they were where? Maura squinted against the brilliance of a setting sun, she did not know where. Days they had walked, long tiring days with their nights spent sometimes sleeping with no more than the heather for shelter. People living in the clochans they passed were kind, giving them a share of what they had and finding them a spot to sleep that would keep the damp of dew from their bones; but each family was almost as poor as themselves, the blight had struck hard and the sickly sweet smell that lingered over the fields said the harvest of potatoes would be even less this year. How would people live? Maura's glance travelled across the wide expanse of mauve-coloured heather and the darker purple lyng. This country held a beauty that stole the heart but its people went hungry.

'I . . . I have to rest, child.' Mairead coughed, the fury of it sucking away the last of her strength.

Supporting her as she slumped, Maura drew her own tattered shawl from her shoulders. Dropping it to the ground she lowered her mother onto it then crouched beside her, holding her in her arms, trying to pass warmth into the fragile shivering body. They had to go on, to find shelter for the night. The worry of it pricked like a needle in her mind, she knew her mother must rest but the distance they travelled between each stop grew shorter while the distance between houses grew longer and longer. Held close against her, her mother coughed, catching spots of blood into a piece of cloth torn from Maura's petticoat. The bouts were getting worse, almost every step was halted by a fresh burst. With fear clutching cold at her heart, Maura stared out over the land empty of any sign of human habitation. They must not stay here very long, her mother must not sleep in the open . . . if only someone would come, help her get her mother to a barn . . . anywhere where she could rest out of the sharp touch of night. But pray as she would the world stayed empty.

Why had she agreed to leave their tiny house? Her mother would not have left without her. The Riordans would have come, Padraig or his father, and married her to Liam. Liam. She thought of that kind face, the dark smiling eyes and soft voice. He was not like the others, he had not the same arrogance or the same cruel streak; 'tis not yourself, Liam, she almost spoke the words aloud, 'tis not your crooked back keeps my heart from you . . .

'Maura!'

Her mother's tired whisper instantly brought her from her thoughts and she made to stand.

'No, child,' Mairead lifted a hand against being helped to her feet, 'I can't be going any further.'

The quiet resignation sent a stabbing chill along Maura's spine, her mother could not spend the night on the heath . . . her cough . . .

'Just a little further, there is bound to be a house just beyond the rise. Try, Mother, try to walk a little further.'

But the words seemed to make no impression and when Mairead spoke again it was with an urgency Maura had never heard before.

'Listen to me, child –' hands worn with labour clutched her

daughter's arm '– ye must leave this land of Ireland, ye must go far from the valley that saw yer birth for only then will ye be safe—'

'Leave Ireland!'

'Listen to me, daughter.' Caught by a spasm of coughing Mairead struggled to bring out her words. 'Ye must do as ye be bid. Set your back to the shores of this country for there be no peace for ye here. Seamus Riordan and his son will not see ye bide happy, 'twill be a life of misery they will make for ye.'

Her arms tightening about the frail form, Maura fought against the fear mounting inside her. Her mother had never spoken this way before no matter how bleak their lives had seemed.

'No,' she said soothingly, 'there is no need to leave this land, tomorrow we will return to Clonmacnoise and I will wed with Liam.'

Holding the rag to her mouth, Mairead pushed free of the arms circling her and in the shadowing evening her fever-ridden eyes glittered like brown stars. 'Too late,' she sputtered, 'it be too late for that, the words have been said and cannot be unsaid.'

'Words?' Maura frowned, not understanding, but her mother went on as if she had not heard.

'The powers of old have touched the Riordan house.'

The cough seized her, snatching the rest from her lips and leaving thin shallow breaths rattling in her chest. Waiting for it to subside, Maura tried again to get her mother to stand but with gentle hands she was pushed away.

'Promise me, child, promise ye will leave this land.'

Nodding, Maura shivered at the feeling that trickled along her veins, an inexplicable fear that grabbed her heart, wanting to tear it from her. Anything, she would promise her mother anything only let them move on, find shelter. Hiding her anxiety she forced her mouth to smile. 'We will go wherever you decide,' she said quietly, 'but let us leave that for the morning, tonight we must find a house.'

In the distance the sun dipped the last of its rays beneath the horizon leaving the sky robed in grey and the earth to mourn against its re-awakening; but the beauty and wonder of sunset that always held Maura breathless passed without her notice.

At the nod, Mairead had smiled then lay down, one hand touching the damp earth. Maura caught her breath. That was the way her mother always touched the earth of her father's grave, that loving gentle stroking that had her heart in every move.

'I loved no man but ye, Brendan . . .' Faint as a first breeze the words fluttered on the silence. 'I thought to lie beside ye, to rest in the sweet earth of the valley, but that will not be . . . 'tis here the Lord decrees I will lie . . . forgive me, my dear one . . . I did it for our daughter, forgive . . .'

Knelt beside her mother, Maura watched the eyelids flutter against the pallid cheeks, the fingers become still on the ground, the last sigh of breath carry the life from the thin body.

'No!' It wasn't a scream, it wasn't even a cry. Almost as soft as her mother's whisper it welled up from the depths of her as she bent to rest her head on the still chest. 'No . . . please!' she begged. 'Please, Mother, don't leave me; stay with me, I love you, I love you.' Taking the face between her hands she covered it with kisses and with each the searing, agonising realisation that her mother was dead slashed deep into her soul.

'No!' Her cry, loud now, reached into the depths of the rapidly darkening night. 'No, it's not true . . . don't leave me! Oh Mother, don't leave me!'

The scream of a vixen drew Maura back along a long tunnel of darkness. Cold bit deep into her, coldness that was the body clutched in her arms, the face pressed tight to her own. As the call of the fox rang again she lifted her head. The sky was the colour of a wood dove's wing, its vast rim edged with roseate gold. A new day . . . a day she would not hear her mother's voice or feel that gentle hand touch her own. A great sob rising in her she looked at the face that seemed lost in sleep. The purple hollows that had ringed those eyes with pain and weariness still traced their colour against the marble skin, and the unhappiness of those final moments seemed to linger about the blue-tinged lips.

'*I thought to lie beside ye . . .*'

So clear were the words that Maura's head lifted sharply, her eyes scanning the heath in search of their speaker. But the heath was empty, the words only the pain of her mother speaking inside her. Morning and evening she had knelt beside those graves whispering her love, her hand touching the covering earth no matter if it lay soaked with falling rain or deep beneath a blanket of snow. It was as if it brought her comfort, as if the knowing that one day she would rest beside her loved ones had helped her bear the anguish of losing them.

'You will be with them,' Maura whispered, laying the cold body on the ground.

She would take her mother home, back to Clonmacnoise, back to that tiny garden that once had bloomed with flowers; they would lie beside each other, her mother and father, the tiny brother she had never held. 'I will find someone to help,' she whispered again, 'I will take you home to Father.'

Covering the lifeless face with the ragged shawl she rose to her feet. Ignoring the sting of cramp that seized her muscles she began to run towards the distant hill.

7

There in the lee of the hill, where the rise flattened once more onto the heather-covered heath, a cottage! The pain of limbs cramped by her vigil forgotten, Maura ran on. There would be someone there, a cart she could borrow to take her mother home.

With almost the last of her strength she ran up to the doorway set beneath the low eaves, her hand already poised to knock before she realised the door stood open.

'Heaven smile on all in this house.'

She called the greeting taught by her mother, her light rap to the door echoing on the stillness. It died away without answer. The people might be sleeping for dawn was not yet clear spread across the sky. They would forgive her waking them, they would understand. Calling the same greeting she knocked louder and with it the door swung inward on creaking hinges.

To go unbidden into the home of another was wrong, to intrude where uninvited was foreign to her upbringing. Listening to the silence Maura hesitated. There might not be another cottage for miles, she could walk all day and meet no one. She had to wake these people, ask for their help, she could not manage alone.

Calling more loudly she stepped into the room, the dimness of it barely revealing rough stone walls and empty hearth. It was the hearth held her gaze, it was empty, no peat fire slumbered beneath a layer of ash. But fires were never left to die out, they were kept smouldering through the night, it was the only way to keep the damp air from getting to every scrap of bedding.

Accustomed now to the grey gloom her eyes swivelled to the corner that held a bed. There was no bedding! Stunned, she stared at the bare wooden boards that formed the base of the home-made bed, then more slowly circled the room. A table stood at its centre, a cupboard against the wall but no kettle hung above the dead fire and no tatie pot sat in the hearth. The cottage was empty.

'No!' Pressing both hands to her mouth, Maura stared at the emptiness then crumpled to the floor, sobs tumbling through her fingers. 'No . . . please, you can't be gone . . . my mother . . . oh help me, help me . . .'

But there would be no help. Her tears spent at last, she climbed to her feet. The cottage was deserted and its people gone. What had blighted their lives so they would leave their home, was it the failing of the potato crop or did the hand of Seamus Riordan reach even this desolate spot?

Everything that could be set upon a cart was gone. Outside the light was growing stronger, causing her to blink as she walked to the back of the house. It was unlikely a cart would have been left behind but perhaps a sled that once brought peat home from a bog, she could lay her mother on that and pull it to the last cottage they had called at, the people there would help the rest of the way to Clonmacnoise.

Undisturbed by the clucking of hens or the moo of a cow waiting to be milked the air held an eerie silence, not even a bird greeted the birth of day and no animal rustled in the overgrown vegetable patch. Unable to restrain the shiver that ran through her, Maura forced herself to walk on, she must go right around the building.

She had found no sled, no cart. Whatever might once have been here was gone. Helpless, she stared out across the heath. She could not leave her mother lying there while she went for help; even could she run every step of the way it would take hours and in that time carrion crows, foxes . . .

The thought terrifying her she started forward then screamed as something grabbed her foot, pitching her full length on the ground. Winded by the fall she lay for a moment. What had snatched at her foot, a gin trap set by the man of the house and left behind, forgotten? But being caught by a gin trap would mean pain and she felt none. Moving gingerly she eased her foot, one inch, two; nothing . . . no snap of steel jaws, no excruciating agony of metal teeth crunching into bone. Still wary she drew her foot upwards, breathing a sigh of relief when there was no sensation other than that of her own movement; whatever had caught at her had caused no injury. Sitting up she rubbed at her ankle and as she did so her fingers brushed against something cold and scaly.

With fear hard and solid in her throat she jumped to her feet, then almost cried aloud as her eye caught the rusted flaking shovel lying hidden among the weeds.

There had been nothing left behind in that tiny cottage, nothing in the area surrounding it that would be of use to her, nothing that would help get her mother home to Clonmacnoise and she could not carry that still form that far, her strength would be gone long before they reached home.

Picking up the shovel, Maura touched its broken blade. She knew what she had to do, God give her the courage to do it.

She had run all the way back to where her mother lay, every moment filled with the worry of what she might find there. But everything was as she had left it, no animal had disturbed the figure beneath the ragged shawl . . . and none must. Maura drove the shovel into the patch of ground she had cleared of rocks, feeling the shock of the hard earth jar arms and legs. She had dug the peat after her father had died but this was no soft moist bog. Heaving stone-pocked soil to one side, stopping every few minutes to free a lump of jagged granite, one of a field of such spewed across the landscape as the mountains had formed, she clamped her teeth against the searing ache that sought out every joint. She could not dig as deeply as she should, to try would see her exhausted. What little strength remained to her would be needed to move her mother.

Removing the shawl she stared at the much-loved face, its gentle mouth, its loving eyes closed in death.

'Mother . . . oh Mother!' Her tears sudden and blinding she slumped over the lifeless figure, clutching it, touching her face to the one set as cold marble. 'I promised . . . I said I would take you home, lie you to rest beside Father and Sean . . . I promised . . . I promised!'

The slight drizzle that had come with morning had slowly increased until now it fell in large spreading drops, mixing with Maura's tears as she lifted her face, sending her whisper to the heavens.

'I could not keep the promise I made, I could not take my mother back to her home to be with my father; Lord, in your mercy I pray you, bring them together in your kingdom.' Then placing one last kiss on the could brow she whispered again, 'I tried, Mother . . . forgive me.'

She had placed a shawl on the bed of the shallow grave and somehow laid that fragile body onto it but she could not let the dark soil touch that gentle face. Taking the shawl that was her own she draped it over head and hands she had brought together across the chest. Then, sobs wrenching up from her stomach, she shovelled the earth into place. But that was not enough, her mother's body must be protected from scavenging animals, that shallow grave was not sufficient. Fatigue dragging at her limbs she threw the shovel aside, then with rocks cutting the flesh of her hands she dragged them one by one until they sat in a heap across the dark patch that held her mother. Too spent to do more she sank to the ground, one hand touching the stones as her mother's had so often touched those graves set beside her home.

'Forgive me, Mother,' she murmured brokenly, 'forgive me.'

She had to leave. Clothes soaked close against her skin, hair broken free of its fastening trailing long, wet tendrils over cheeks and breasts, Maura stared down at the heap of rocks headed now with a crude cross. The shaft of the shovel, half-rotted by weather, had hit against a rock when she threw it aside and broken into two pieces. Tearing the last of her petticoat she had used the strips to tie the broken pieces together to form a cross, then wedged it in among the stones. It would bear no name. Like the grave of a pauper, her mother's resting place would know no marker. The heart inside her twisting with misery she touched a hand to the coarse broken wood, tears streaming as her fingers slowly caressed it.

'I cannot carve your name,' she murmured, 'no one will know it is Mairead Deverell sleeps beneath these stones. But it is only flesh and bone lies here; the real Mairead, tender, caring woman whose love guided and protected, shielding yet giving room to grow, that Mairead lives on in my heart, the mother I will carry with me always. We are part of one another, your love is my love intertwining on two souls. No matter where I walk, there will you be with me. I love you, Mother, nothing can ever alter that.'

Choking on the words she bent to touch her lips to the cross in a last farewell and when she straightened it was to see a figure watching her through the mist of rain. Maura felt the world shake beneath her feet. The man watching her so intently . . . it was the son of Seamus Riordan.

'It will do no good to run.'

Maura had turned away, her first step already taken when a strong hand caught her arm.

'Distance puts a space between bodies but it cannot provide refuge for the mind . . . neither does it give peace to the heart.'

The last came on just a whisper, almost like an afterthought.

Snatching her arm free, Maura looked at the man, his face streaked with rain that had soaked them both. He was different somehow, changed from the last time she had seen him. His face was handsome as it had ever been but now it was stamped with a new confidence, an authority that seemed to shout from a figure visibly taller . . . straighter; it seemed Liam Riordan stood upright for the very first time.

'I have tried running all my life,' he went on, making no further move to touch her. 'Sometimes you find a place that hides you from the world but you cannot hide from yourself, you cannot put a barrier between yourself and the pain of heartbreak. It has taken my life, Maura, don't let it take yours.'

Heartbreak! She stared at the small cairn of rough stones. Her mother's heart had been broken, broken by leaving the one place in the world she wanted to be and it was the threat of this man's family was the cause and, though she did not want to think it, everything in her said he must have known of it, how could a son not know of plans being made for his own wedding?

'It has taken mine already! There –' she pointed '– there lies my heartbreak, my mother dying on the heath like some animal; that was what your father threatened when it was I refused to wed with you. Well you can tell him now, can't you, tell him that in one thing at least he got what he wanted.'

How could a man act like that! Maura watched the compassion leap to his eyes before he turned to the grave, how could he pretend! 'Forgive us, Mairead Deverell,' she heard his quiet whisper as he made the holy sign on brow and chest, 'forgive the wrongs done to you. God rest you and give peace to your soul.'

'Is that the wish of Seamus Riordan?' Sharp and loud with

pain the cry sped away into the grey mists. 'Does he ask peace for the soul of Mairead Deverell? The woman he—'

The woman he loved. Liam could have told her the words of his father. Yes, Seamus would ask peace for the soul of Mairead Deverell, but what of her daughter's peace? Did she know what had happened all those years ago, was that a burden she would carry in her heart as well as the burden of shame his brother had laid upon her?

'Maura.' He turned towards her, an acute stab of unhappiness driving through him as she stepped quickly away. 'I cannot undo what is already done but come back—'

'Come back! You ask me that, Liam? Go back with you to Clonfert to become your wife and your brother's whore?'

The diamond brightness of raindrops glistening jewel-like among folds of chestnut hair darkened by rain were no match for the condemnation glittering in her eyes, yet Liam's own held them with an open honesty, and his voice throbbed with the hurt of her accusation.

'Do you not know more of me than to ask that? I ask you to return to take back that which should never have been taken.' He paused, at odds with the meaning that could be placed on his words. What Padraig had taken, what his father had taken before him could not be replaced. 'I . . .' he went on awkwardly, 'I ask you to return with me, to Clonmacnoise, take back your home, your father's land.'

'No.' Maura shook her head. 'I will take nothing from a Riordan! I promised my mother I will leave Ireland and that promise I will keep. I will never return to the valley.'

'Leave Ireland!' He lifted a hand, sweeping strands of wet hair back from his brow. 'To go where?'

She had not yet asked herself that question; now suddenly faced with it she realised the enormity of what she had done. She had not one penny to her name; she could walk, but Ireland was surrounded by sea and that she could not cross on foot.

'I had not thought of that as yet.' She met the questioning look with open honesty of her own.

'Then return to the cottage, stay there until you have had time to think.'

Or to give your father time to succeed, to force me into marriage with you, to keep me in a house where I would be the toy his elder son would play with? Blinking the rain from her eyes she stared at the face she thought she knew. As a child and a youth Liam Riordan had ever been polite in his speaking to her mother and there had sometimes been a quick shy smile for herself. There had been an air of gentleness about him then, now that was gone. Why had he changed . . . what had made him agree to a forced marriage, for it could be no different for him than it would have been for her? Was it really a new authority, a new confidence she saw in him or was it desperation? Was he so afraid of his father he would agree to anything, even to making her his brother's whore?

'I have given you answer, Liam, I will not change my mind. My back is turned on Clonmacnoise and that is the way it will ever be.' She tried to keep bitterness from her voice as she looked past him to where her mother's body lay covered by stones. 'You said yourself what is done cannot be undone, add to that these words; what is seen cannot be truly forgotten. I saw my mother die, saw her lie there on the wet heath, her last words being for my father, to tell him her one desire had been she be laid to rest beside him, but that desire was to be denied; can you understand what that was like, can you imagine how it feels? I don't know why your father hated my parents so much or why he should want to pass it on to his sons . . .' She looked back to him, the harshness of moments ago softened to pity in her eyes. 'Refuse the inheritance, Liam, a legacy of hate is the gift of despair, it can only destroy.'

With her gone was his life not already destroyed, what more could his father do to him? Maura Deverell was the one thing of beauty in his life, the one thing that made his existence worthwhile and now that too was being snatched away.

'Maura,' he said as she turned from him, 'I won't expect you to believe what I tell you now, but for the sake of the friendship I think you once felt for me I ask you to listen. I knew nothing of any marriage, I was not asked, given no chance to agree or to refuse, that I swear on my honour; this also I swear, my father will answer for the harm done to your mother.'

The rain had stopped and in its wake a breeze was growing, teasing the hem of wet skirts as Maura once more turned to face him. He was not pretending, this was no act put on to lure her back, to bring her to his father.

'Friendship can only be ended by harsh words and spiteful actions,' she answered quietly, 'and you have never dealt any of these, nor do I believe that is your intention now. I shall take the memory of our friendship with me and cherish it always as I shall believe you had no part in trying to force a marriage between us; as for your father, his sin will find its own punishment. Goodbye to you.'

'Maura, please!' He stepped forward, taking her hands and holding them. 'I promise you there will be no more talk of marriage, my father had no right to try forcing his cripple on you.'

Tilting her head she met eyes that could not entirely conceal their pain, nor her own their show of disbelief.

'Now 'tis my turn to ask,' she said, 'do you not know more of me than to think it is your body would keep me from marrying with you? I see no deformity when I look at you, I see only the kindness always there in your eyes; no, Liam, 'tis not you, 'tis the hate that is in your father I could not live with.'

She could have added also she did not love him but somehow the words had not come, they had been there in her mind but would not reach her tongue.

He had hoped, prayed, he would find her. He had ridden

out that night thinking she would still be at Clonmacnoise, then returned to Clonfert after finding the cottage empty, but with the first flush of each dawn since then had harnessed a carriage and driven out again. Yet his hopes of having her and her mother return with him were not to be answered, the determination in that quiet voice was all too real. A legacy of hate! He swallowed hard. A father's gift to his sons!

He had watched her go then, watched the remaining slivers of mist swirl about her slight figure as she went from him across the heath. She had refused to be driven in the carriage, said no to his offer of money, a pride shining deep in those lovely eyes. She would accept no help from him so how could he have expected her to accept his love. He had wanted to tell her what he himself seemed always to have known, that he was in love with her, that he wanted her for his wife, but the thought that her words might be only a salve to his feelings, that it was in truth his twisted back that repulsed her, held the words unspoken in his mouth; and she had turned and walked away, taking her heartbreak with her and leaving him with his.

With his arms behind his head, Liam lay in his bed, his eyes watching the play of moon shadows on the high ceiling. He had thought no grief could be as strong as that in his own heart but the cry that had come from his father as he heard the fashion of Mairead Deverell's death told him it had met its match. The colour had drained from that hard face and he had rushed from the room as though every devil in hell were at his back. Equals in shame, those had been his father's words to the older son, now he was equal also with the younger. 'Equals in pain, Father,' he whispered to the shadows, 'equals in lost love.'

8

~~~

He would not lie to her. The words Liam had spoken, they had
to be the truth . . . they must be!

The breeze that had followed the dawn had quickened,
holding her wet clothing cold against her skin as Maura forced
her tired limbs to move, but the heat of the thoughts dancing in
her mind kept all else away.

They had never been close friends, the gulf money created
had been too wide for that, but like his mother Liam Riordan
had always shown the Deverells politeness; yet it was more
than that, there had been more than good manners in that
gentle smile, and those deep brown eyes had seemed to say he
would like to stay and talk, like to be real friends; or had that
been the imagination of a growing child?

But those eyes had held that same look as he had told her he
had taken no part in his father's intention, they had been deep
and soft, brown-gold as an autumn day, and they had been
filled with truth . . . they had!

Catching her toe on a clump of heather, Maura stumbled a
few steps before regaining her balance. She had been too deeply
caught in the net of her thoughts to watch her way. But why? She
stared ahead. Why give so much concern to whether Liam
Riordan spoke true or not, why should it matter what he thought
of her or that he believe she had not enticed his brother into
committing that dreadful act? It did not matter! She walked
slowly onwards. They would never meet again so however Liam
Riordan thought of her it would give her no pain.

But it would. She caught a sob on her breath. It would!

'Good day to ye.'

As the call drifted over her thoughts Maura looked to where a man stood, one foot resting on a spade, the loose ends of a blue muffler flapping in the breeze.

'The day be filled with goodness for yourself,' she answered, the relief of seeing another person bringing a smile to her lips.

'Is it far ye've come?'

The distance between them did not hide the quick frown of curiosity nestling between the man's brows as he looked at her wet clothes.

'From Clonmacnoise.'

'Clonmacnoise, is it?' He pushed at the flat cap covering a crop of thick hair. 'That be a fair step an' ye soaked like an otter having swum the lough.'

'I was caught in the storm.' Maura heard her own unnecessary reply. The man would have to be stupid to need the explanation.

'So my eyes be showin' me.' He grinned as though having heard her thought. 'Go ye on a little ways an' ye'll be seeing my cottage, there'll be a fire to dry yer clothes and a sup o' tay to warm yer insides. My wife will be there, it's pleased she'll be to have a body to pass the time o' day with.'

Thanking him, Maura hurried on, her gratitude turning to tears of relief when she saw the tiny turf-roofed house, a wisp of grey smoke curling from its squat chimney pot.

'Clonmacnoise!' Heavy with child the young woman shook her head as she handed a blanket to Maura, taking the wet clothes and draping them over a line strung above the fireplace. 'I can't be after saying I know where that be for I've never been a stone's throw from this house except to go to Clara village to wed with my Connal at the church there. Be this Clonmacnoise a grand big town?'

Wrapping the blanket around her, Maura stared at the peat

glowing red in the grate. 'No,' she said, 'it's not big and it's not grand but it is beautiful. The Abbey church built by Saint Ciaran is ruined now but the place of its standing, on a bend of the river, has a peace I think no other place on earth could hold, and the land . . . it is so soft and green, so gentle the angels themselves might walk there.'

Yet she had left it, and in such a hurry as to get herself soaked in the leaving! Placing the wet skirt over the rope line the young woman noted the thinness of it and the lack of a petticoat that went beneath. Now why would that be? She could think but she would not ask.

'Enough with yer blabber and give the girl a sup o' tay.' Sat in a rocking chair drawn beside the fire, a shawl covering her legs, an older woman broke the silence she had kept since Maura's arrival. ' 'Tis the place of Saint Ciaran – the blessing of God rest on him – be yer home, sure an' like my daughter says 'tis a place we don't have the knowing of though ye'self makes it grand in the telling.'

Catching the glance of eyes sharp as a goshawk, Maura read the question behind it. The woman was asking why leave a place so peaceful?

'The potato crop failed three years in succession,' she answered the unspoken query. 'There was nothing to provide us with a living save the digging of peat but as times grew harder for everybody, families took to digging for themselves until eventually I could no longer bring food to the house.'

'The land has a sickness that will affect many yet; but why should it be ye'self yer family depended on?'

Maura lowered her gaze from that bright interrogation. 'There was no other child and after my father died it was left to me to provide for my mother. I . . . I did my best . . .'

'Then the Lord will look kindly on ye.'

'I couldn't keep her with me.' Maura's words were a whisper, her inner vision seeing again that thin spent figure lie down on the cold ground. 'I tried, I begged but it was of no use, she touched a hand to the heath, I saw her fingers stroke the earth then she was gone.'

It took no more asking. The woman stared at the fire. The girl's mother was dead and she herself was turning her back on the home that had held them. Giving a moment to her own remembering she looked again at the girl swathed in a blanket.

'The time of each man's passing be set down in the book of ages and no hand be given the stopping of it. We are each given a term to spend upon this earth and could it be one man could have the years of another then kings and lords would live for ever while the poor would die in their cradles. Set yer heart to ease, child, for 'tis none of your fault, it be hard to part with loved ones, none know that better than me who has seen the laying of nine children and a husband in the ground. Sore is the heart to breaking but it will mend; there will be no forgetting, for true love will not give the permitting of that, but the years bring an understanding, and in His mercy the good Lord touches the heart with solace and the pain ye be feeling now becomes bearable.'

How could her pain become bearable? Maura lowered her chin into the blanket. She had failed her mother, it was through her she lay dead out there on the heath; if only she had consented, agreed to do as Seamus Riordan had demanded . . .

' 'Tis awake yer after being.'

Blinking at the glow of the fire, Maura lifted her head, glancing in the direction of the voice and then at the window set just below the eave of the sloping roof. The light that played across the several tiny panes of glass was gold but tipped with orange. What hour was it, how long had she imposed herself on the kindness of these people?

'I ask your pardon.' She reached for her clothes neatly

folded beside her. 'I did not mean to take advantage of your kindness.'

' 'Tis like meself you'll be after being and go taking a fall if ye scrabble so.' The older woman smiled. 'Taking yer time in the dressing will not see the world at its end.'

In a curtained-off corner of the room that held a truckle bed, Maura pushed away the memories that rushed at her, memories of another such bed in another such cottage. This was clean and obviously loved as that other had been, but it was seemingly equally poor. These people had given her welcome but like so many now in Ireland they were scarce able to feed a stranger. She would thank them for their hospitality and leave. If Clara, the village the girl had mentioned, was close by she could maybe reach there before nightfall and perhaps someone would give her the shelter of a barn.

'Clara, is it?' The woman shook her head on hearing the question. 'It be several miles on from here and not to be reached afore dark. If it's to Clara ye be thinking of going then it be best ye bide 'til morning for the heath can be a treacherous place once light be gone from it. Wait ye 'til my girl returns from the field and hear the same from her.'

Thanking the woman, this time for her concern, Maura declined. Had she remained awake and performed some task in exchange for a slice of bread and a corner to pass the night in she could have accepted. But apart from fetching water from the stream she had slept almost the entire day.

The dry clothes felt warm as the blanket had been but nights spent in the open had taught a sharp lesson; cold that came before dawn bit deep to the bone and her thin dress was no barrier against it, her only hope of evading its misery was to reach the village of Clara.

Her goodbye said, she hurried from the house. Gaining a rise in the land, she paused. Several miles on from here the woman had said. But in which direction? One hand shading her eyes from the brilliance of the sun she scanned the plain laid out before her, then her free hand curled, the fingernails biting deep into the flesh of her palm.

There in the distance, small as yet but distinctly clear, the figure of a man! Liam had followed and managed to find her, had Padraig Riordan done the same?

Was the figure down there Padraig Riordan? Had he followed after her, intent on keeping his word . . . to force her to go to Clonfert . . . to rape her again and again? Maura felt her nerves crawl. Wife to Liam she might become but that would have no meaning in the eyes of his brother. Maybe she had not yet been seen! It was a slim hope, one that faded as an arm lifted, a call drifting on the emptiness between them.

The stillness that followed was heavy, binding her limbs, and in the silence Maura could hear the world breaking. She had watched her mother suffer, seen her die . . . and all for nothing! She should have known he would find her. Liam! Her hand clenched tighter, sending sting after sting biting into her flesh. Had Liam told him where she was, told his brother where to find her?

'No . . . o!' Her own cry loud as the one that had reached across that space, she clutched her skirt, lifting it clear of her feet, already half turned to run when the figure pitched forward on its face.

It is a ruse, a trick to get you to go to him! Maura's brain drummed a warning. Wanting to run, to get as far as possible from the figure still lying face-down on the ground, she willed her legs to move only to feel them refuse. Why . . . why couldn't she move? Any moment the man would be on his feet, running towards her, towards the girl he wanted only to violate.

Fear that imprisoned her limbs locked her throat as the head lifted. She had left it too late, there would be no escaping him now.

'Help . . . please.'

No other sound mingled with that cry, nothing detracted from its clearness. Why was he lying there, why not just get up and take what he had come for? Or was this some new way Padraig Riordan had found to torture her? Questions chasing each other tumbled through Maura's mind, but through them all one faint and unheard thought fought to come to the surface.

The hair – the thought kicked against the rest – the hair!

With infinite slowness the thought gained recognition and with it Maura felt the sense of movement return to her body. Padraig Riordan's hair, like that of his father, was the colour of soot and threaded with grey receding back from the temples, but the man lying on the heath . . . his hair held no grey. Recognition suddenly pouring through her she began to run back the way she had come.

It was the same man who had spoken to her that morning, the husband of the young woman who had been so kind to her. Her breath short and rapid from her dash, she bent over him as he groaned and sank once more onto his face. Then she saw the blood. It covered his hands, lay in long crimson streaks along the side of his face and neck; and the muffler, tied now about his lower leg was soaked red with blood!

'The spade,' he groaned, 'twere the spade.'

As it had only minutes before, Maura's blood chilled. A cut from a spade was the thing most feared by men working the potato fields, for inevitably it poisoned the blood and death followed soon after.

'Hold on to me, the cottage isn't far, I can help—'

'No.' A bloodstained hand pushed her away as she tried to lift him. 'Caitlin . . . back there . . . help Caitlin . . .'

'Caitlin!' Maura froze. The older woman had seemed

agitated, looking often towards the open doorway as they had talked. Her daughter had taken a can of tea to her man and was later than usual in the returning.

'What is wrong with Caitlin?' Anxiety threw the words out.

'In labour.' He clutched his leg, grimacing with pain. 'I couldn't . . . go to her, please!'

What should she do, which of the two needed her the most? She stared at the bloodstained muffler. How long had he lain in the field . . . how much blood was lost . . . was the poison already in his system? And his wife . . . Caitlin was in labour! The last could have been shouted aloud for its effect was immediate, quieting the chaos of her mind, helping her to think logically. Had Connal's accident happened soon after her passing him that morning then his blood would be strongly infected, he must get help at once . . .

'Caitlin!' Reaching a hand to her the man clutched at her skirt, gasping his words. 'She be feared . . . this be her first child . . . please go . . . go to her.'

The girl must be frightened. Maura looked down at the face twisted with pain. But this man would most likely lose his leg . . . he could lose his life.

'Ye have to go to her . . . she needs ye, the . . . the baby!'

He was right. Out there on the heath more than one life was at stake, there was the life of an unborn child, it had the right to live . . . but so had Connal.

Heaven forgive if her choosing were wrong. Dropping to her knees Maura caught at his hands. 'I will go to Caitlin, I will bring her home but first I must stop the bleeding from your wound.'

'No, Caitlin!'

Trying to push her away, to get her to leave to look for his wife aggravated his pain and he clutched again at his blood-soaked leg.

'Childbirth is natural, it has happened millions of times and it will happen millions more yet.' Maura could scarce believe the calm voice was her own as she repeated the words of Mother O'Toole.

But each of those millions of times carried its own danger. Childbirth, like poisoning of the blood, often claimed life. The thought cold in her heart she kept it hidden from her face.

'Connal,' she said quietly, 'give me the belt from your waist.' Then as he stared uncomprehendingly she repeated the words, adding, 'Please, trust me, I am trying to help.'

Fingers red from blood seeping into the muffler fumbled with the buckle of a wide leather belt. Drawing it from his waist he handed it to her.

What was it Mother O'Toole had taught her? Passing the belt around his thigh, Maura sought desperately to remember.

'Connal, Connal listen to me,' she winced at the man's gasp of pain as she pulled the belt tight, 'you have to keep the hold firm for a count of one hundred then ease it loose for a count of ten; you must do this all the time I am away, it will control the bleeding, do you understand? You must do it as I said, you can't stop.'

'One . . . one hundred and then ten.' He took the leather strip, his face blanching even paler against the bite of it.

She would bring Caitlin home then get assistance for him. Her heart thumping in her chest Maura raced across the flat heath, but she had to keep on running . . . every moment counted both for Connal and for his wife.

There . . . a dark bundle among the heather, it had to be Caitlin! Fear and pain marred the pretty face that looked up as Maura knelt beside the sobbing girl.

'Connal!' She clutched at Maura. 'He be hurt . . . his leg; it were my fault.'

Holding the girl, Maura listened as the story blurted out, using the moments to catch her breath.

'The pains, they started no more than five minutes from me

leaving the house but I didn't go back, I wanted to see Connal, it was wrong I know but I wanted—' She broke off, pressing her stomach as a fresh spasm of pain drove through her. 'I wasn't going to say the child's coming was begun,' she went on as the spasm receded, 'I meant to be home, not to give him worry but as I came up to him a stab took the sense from me and it was a cry I gave, a cry that alarmed Connal so he dropped the spade and it struck him in the leg. It was my fault, now he'll get the poison o' the blood and die, I've killed him, I've killed my Connal and I want to die . . .' Pushing free of Maura the girl sank to the ground, her fingers moving over the soft earth.

It was happening again! Maura watched the fingers that seemed to stroke the ground. Her mother had lain on the earth, had died in its cold embrace, because her daughter did not possess strength enough to carry her; nor would she have strength to carry the girl. But death would not find *her* lying on the heath. Determination the only weapon she had to fight with, she struck hard.

'Stop that!' She grabbed the girl's shoulder. 'You have killed no one but you will if you carry on with this stupidity. Feeling sorry for yourself will not help Connal or his child; the longer we sit here the greater the risk of your baby being born in the open.' She had not said the real risk lay in her own not knowing the ways of bringing a new life into the world, she had never seen a birth, only heard her mother and Sinead O'Toole discuss the bringing to bed of neighbours. Talk! She almost hauled the sobbing girl to her feet. What good would that be should the child come before they reached the cottage!

A few steps at a time, stopping more and more frequently as the pains of labour increased, Maura urged her on, keeping the note of firmness in her voice. To let leniency enter in might have her giving up trying; there would be time for apology later, a time for sympathy, but right now she could not afford it.

The cottage was at last in sight. She might have cried out with relief but it was not her cry sent birds rising into the sky, it was the strangled scream of the girl slumping against her. She had forgotten! In the worry of getting to the cottage before the child came, she had forgotten Connal might still be lying where she had left him.

'Connal,' his wife screamed again, 'my Connal, he's dead . . . he's dead!'

If she let the girl sink to the ground she might lose the chance of getting her the rest of the way home. Holding desperately to the last shreds of determination, Maura shook the trembling figure.

'He is not dead, but your screeching will bring the banshees to take him sure enough.' It was cruel but if they were to move on hard words had to be said. Letting the girl go completely to pieces would finish any chance of getting her to that cottage.

'He's dead . . . he's dead!' Her legs folding beneath her, the sobbing girl fell to the ground.

This was what she had dreaded. Maura stared at the figure hunched into itself. Dragging her the rest of the way was out of the question . . . the mother was crippled with a hip injury . . . Connal was badly hurt . . . there was no cottage she knew of in miles . . . With each avenue closing she felt a terrible desperation inside her.

'Get up . . . get up!' As anxiety threatened to become panic, she shook the girl. 'You have to go on.'

Her hand pulled at the heaving shoulder but, as with her words, the touch brought no response except for the cries of grief. She could not leave matters there, the child deserved the chance of life. Pushing down on her fears she drew a long breath. If that was what it was going to take, then so be it! Cold and hard as she could possibly make them she snapped each word.

'Get up, Caitlin . . . get up now!' Receiving no reply she leaned over the girl, cupping her chin in one hand, lifting her head to look into tear-filled eyes. Then, with one more breath, her free hand landed a sharp slap to the face.

9

Caitlin's mother needed no telling the birth was near, only her gentle eyes showing, as with all mothers, that she shared her daughter's suffering.

'Praise to heaven ye were with her.' The woman tried to get to her feet, dropping back to her seat as her injured hip refused support.

Helping the girl onto the bed, Maura straightened. Explanations could wait, Connal could not. 'A doctor,' she asked tersely, 'is there one in Clara?'

'Not there.' A shake of the head accompanied the answer. 'Nor be there such a man in Kilbeggan nor yet in Durrow, but the birthing—'

'It is not for Caitlin a doctor is needed,' Maura interrupted, 'it is for Connal, his leg has been cut with a spade.'

'The spade ye says!'

'Tullamore –' Caitlin caught her breath on fresh pain '– there must be a doctor at Tullamore.'

She could go to the place the girl had said but first she must bring Connal to the shelter of the house.

'Do you have a cart for the peat?'

'Round behind the house but—'

Already out of the door, Maura did not wait for the rest. Even now it could be too late. The small three-sided cart was stood on its end, its long handles stretching like thin arms against the rear wall of the cottage. Grabbing them she pulled it after her, running with it to where the injured man lay. I have to do it, she told herself, God give me strength to do it.

'Caitlin?' Weak from loss of blood Connal's question was a whisper.

'She is all right and you are going to be a father very soon.' She glanced at the strap set about his thigh; had he held it? There was no time to ask. Setting the cart down as close to him as possible she tried to keep her tone light-hearted, to mask the worry inside her. Forcing a smile she asked, 'Tell me, Connal, how long is it since you rode home on a peat cart?'

How had they managed? Maura's arms throbbed. Using the heel of one foot, his injured leg dragging behind him, he had pushed himself to the open end of the cart and with her help hauled himself onto the flat base, and using the same method had crawled into the house and now lay exhausted.

The older woman had stifled the cries that rose to her mouth as she had watched them enter, but stark fear shone in her face as she looked at Maura. 'He best take my bed 'til the little one be safe in the world, can ye get him to the truckle?'

Gritting her teeth, Maura heaved the near-unconscious Connal, her own legs threatening to give beneath her as finally he was laid on the narrow bed.

'How far away is Tullamore?' she asked when breath allowed.

The older woman's glance rested on the still form of her son-in-law and when her reply came it was low, kept from her daughter's hearing.

'It be too many miles for the saving of that leg. Should the good Lord be giving back the use of me own I couldn't be to Tullamore in less than a day, then there be the returning . . . Oh sweet Jesus, what can we be doing!' Two cripples and a daughter in her birthing bed!'

Too many miles . . . two cripples . . .

The words sat like lead in Maura's heart. But it would be worse than that, Connal would be dead unless something were done soon.

A few feet away Caitlin had pressed both hands to her mouth yet her cries of pain seemed somehow to cut through that of the man. Turning his head his eyes sought Maura's.

'Don't . . .' His strength flagged, the hand he tried to lift fell back limply to his side but his fever-bright gaze stayed with him. 'Don't be leaving Caitlin . . . stay . . . stay ye with her, stay pl—'

The last faded and the eyes became hidden behind closed lids. With tears stinging her own, Maura stared. Only hours ago he had been smiling, offering the hospitality of his home and now . . .

'It be no good,' the woman whispered. 'There can be no saying the doctor be to home should ye get there. I hears that there town of Tullamore has a river built by the hands o' men an' great boats sail along o' it bringing a grand manner o' things for the English gentry there, so all o' that says to me a grand town be like to have a grand number o' folk with more than one or two calling a doctor to see to them.'

'But we can't let him lie and do nothing, it will be—'

She had almost said it will be too late, but the words Maura bit back could have been said for the woman's look showed she recognised every one.

'That be in the Lord's hands,' she said quietly, 'but the birthing of a child be in yours.'

'Mine!' Maura gasped. 'But I can't . . . I don't know how!'

'Then 'tis learning ye'll be after doing. I be bound by legs that be ever ready to throw me to the ground but my mind be well enough an' I'll be after telling ye every step.'

'No . . . no . . .'

'Don't be turning yer face from me, child.' The woman's voice cracked on a sob. 'Don't let this night pluck the last of my loved ones from me.'

She was not alone in fear, it haunted the older woman too. Caitlin and her husband were all she had.

'If I fail—'

It was meant to be said only in her mind, but pushed by a tumult of nerves it tumbled out.

'It be this far ye've come and not failed,' the woman answered. 'The blessing of heaven guided yer actions this day and be sure the guiding of them it has still. Have faith, child, have faith and heaven will not forsake ye nor the ones it has given into yer care.'

Hearing the girl cry out again, indecision drained from Maura; but not the pity or concern for the injured man, he must not be ignored.

'If I place your chair close beside Connal can you see to his wound, sponge it clean and dress it?'

'To be sure.' Caitlin's mother nodded. 'There be cloths in the chest and the kettle holds water set to boil, while the bucket ye' self took to the stream is filled. Now look ye to my girl, tis meself and heaven will be with ye.'

With every nerve tingling, Maura followed each quietly spoken instruction, spreading a cloth beneath the drawn-up legs, her heart twisting as she wiped perspiration from the young face contorted with agony. Was childbirth always like this, so much pain and suffering, did it always take so many hours . . . or was there something wrong? The last jarred her nerves completely. If the child could not come of its own accord . . . Her own cry joined with that from the bed as Caitlin's head arched back on the pillow, her body writhing.

'Oh God,' Maura could not hold the words, 'let the baby come, please let the baby come!'

Across the room the older woman recognised the root of the cry. Fear! The stranger that had asked only a drink of water at her cottage was young and afraid. It was certain sure she had never witnessed the childbed before but, though it was a hard thing to call upon her to deliver the child, there was no other way. Hiding the concern that was in truth tearing her soul, the heartache every mother feels seeing her child in pain, she continued with the dressing of Connal's wound, asking quietly, 'Can ye see the child yet?'

How would she know? Would she see an arm? A foot?

'It be near now,' the woman went on quietly as before, 'fetch ye the knife from the table and pass it through the flame of the fire.'

Panic vivid in her eyes, Maura stared. A knife! Cut the child free? She couldn't, she couldn't!

Caitlin's mother knew the decisive moment had been reached, one more shred of fear and this girl would break. Fixing a smile to her lips she gave a brief shake of her head.

'Sure now, 'tis naught but the cord ye need have the cutting of. There be no sense of hurt to Caitlin or the babe, were there no truth to what I be saying then I would not be doing the asking of ye. It be the same with every child born.' She smiled again. 'Sure, 'tis the body's way o' nourishing it while it yet be in the womb but with entering the world a babe needs it no longer so 'tis separated from it.'

The cord . . . she had heard Mother O'Toole speak of such . . . and this woman, she had seen childbirth many times, she would not ask anything were it not necessary.

'Mother,' Caitlin's cry, soft and full of pain, fluttered across the room, 'help me, Mother . . . help me!'

The worn face distorted as the woman struggled to keep the tears from showing, but the glance she sent to Maura displayed the tears of her soul.

Without a word, Maura went to her. Taking both hands she drew the thin figure to its feet, almost carrying it to Caitlin's side.

'I be here, mavourneen.' The woman touched her lips to her daughter's brow, stroked the damp hair. 'Mother be close, I'll let no harm befall ye. Be strong now, strong for yer babe.'

Inching towards the foot of the bed as Maura set the knife on the cloth, she nodded. 'A minute more,' she said, 'the head be as good as out. Push, mavourneen . . . push!'

It was over. Trembling from the anxiety that had governed her every move, Maura emptied the bowl of water with which she had bathed Caitlin. It had seemed like for ever since she had first helped the girl home, but the crimson streaks of the lowering sun showed it to be just a few hours. It was the hardest thing she had ever done. With her eyes closed, she lifted her face to the sky. But no task was ever rewarded with the pleasure she had felt as Caitlin had taken her newborn son in her arms.

'*It be a great thing we have to thank ye for, I shall ever bless the day the good Lord set yer steps this way.*'

The words Caitlin's mother had said at least ten times returned to Maura as she glanced back at the house.

'*It will have my own blessing too.*' She had smiled at the girl in the bed, but as she had looked at the truckle with its unmoving form the anxiety had returned. She had lied to Caitlin, told her that Connal was recovering, but the mark of fever lay heavy on his flushed face; it could only be the poison spreading through his body. Was the joy of a new life to be swallowed in the taking of another?

Sat in her chair, the sleeping child laid in a drawer set atop the chest, the older woman had glanced at her son-in-law, her head shaking slowly. '*Sure an' the mischief o' the divil was abroad this day to take the legs of a man and none else to help in the keeping of his family; 'tis glad I am to see a grandson safe born and sad I am to know the hard life he's after coming into and him with a cripple for a father.*'

A cripple! That was how Liam Riordan had ever been spoken of. Maura turned her face again to the red-gold touching the horizon. But that morning with the rain beating down on him he had stood tall, in that moment he had seemed straight and strong as the hills that edged the rim of the valley; Slieve Bloom, her father had called them, telling her they had been formed when a sleeping giant had awakened to find himself buried beneath the earth. Annoyed at his fine new coat being soiled by the red of the stone, the giant had flung it aside and thus the mountains had been made.

Maura smiled at the memory, once more a six-year-old standing hand in hand with her father, looking out over the flat green plain that held Clonmacnoise, a father straight and tall as Liam had seemed; but as another quiet moan came from the truckle the memory faded, leaving thoughts of a baby possibly robbed of his father. Why did it have to be like this, why was there nothing to be done?

As tears thick and choking filled her throat she lowered her face into her hands.

'Tis putting the cart before the horse ye be doing.

'Mother!' So clear were the words, she called out as her hands dropped to her sides. But her mother was dead. Those words had been no more than her imagination; so much did she wish to help that young man that her mind had set words to the first sighs of evening breeze.

Think, child . . . think . . . the garden.

It was so distinct, that beloved voice, it was as if her mother stood beside her, as she often had in the tiny garden her father had created, pointing out the flowers, explaining their uses . . .

The garden! Maura's head shot round, bringing her gaze to Caitlin's tiny plot ablaze with a variety of herbs and flowers.

'Thank you,' she whispered softly, 'thank you, Mother.'

' 'Tis no objections I be holding, and 'tis certain sure I be my girl won't be after giving any.'

Clinging to any thread of hope, Caitlin's mother had listened to Maura's suggestion and now bruised a bowl of brilliant yellow hypericum with a wooden spoon before covering them with water from the kettle.

Kneeling beside the low narrow bed Maura caught her breath as she removed the cloth with which the older woman had bound the injured leg. The wound was red and angry, signs of poisoning showing around and above the deep cut.

Cleansing the surrounding skin with salt water she prayed she had remembered her mother's teaching correctly. Placing a fresh cloth in the basin held on the other woman's knees she hesitated. If she were wrong . . .

'We have the trust in ye.'

Catching the whisper she knew she could not stop now, this was their one last hope. Giving only a light squeeze to the cloth so as to leave it well soaked with the lotion she laid it over the wound.

'This must not be removed,' she explained, 'but it must be kept moist, we have to drip a little of the solution onto the dressing every few hours.'

'I'll have the doing of that.' Caitlin's mother took the cloth with which Maura dripped the solution onto the dressing.

Rising to her feet, Maura stretched her back, feeling the muscles scream their tiredness. But she could not rest them yet.

'Do you have any potheen?'

'Potheen,' the woman nodded, 'sure an' am I not told it be meself makes the best drop of it in all of Ireland. A couple o' sips will set you on your feet quicker than a smile from the little people.'

'I'm not wanting to drink it.' Maura smiled. 'I want to make a tincture that will keep for the dressing of Connal's leg, the alcohol in the potheen will safeguard the mixture, keep any impurities from it.'

'There now, if that don't be another reason for the making of potheen, though there be many a man in Ireland would be prepared to swear the forgetting of any ailment lies more in the drinking o' it than in the putting o' it onto a cloth.'

Following the direction of the woman's nod, Maura lifted a stoneware bottle from a shelf set in the wall then, having packed a jar with the bruised berries and leaves of hypericum, filled it with the colourless liquid. Returning the bottle to its shelf she set the tightly fastened jar beside it. In a few days the contents could be filtered and made into an ointment that would cleanse the poison from Connal's wound. But would it be needed? She felt her nerves tingle as the sick man moaned. Had she remembered too late, had the belt about his thigh failed to hold the poison from his system? There were long hours to go before they would know, before they could tell would Connal's leg, even his life, be saved.

Turning back she looked at the man beginning to moan and toss on the small truckle bed.

Throwing himself about will spread the evil. He needs to be helped to sleep, a deep sleep that will hold his limbs in strong bonds.

Her mother's soft voice whispered again in her mind. But what was it she must do, she'd forgotten . . . she'd forgotten!

It be there, daughter, it be there, look to the garden.

Soft and insistent the voice cut through the panic beginning to race once more along her veins and with a look at the woman sat beside her son-in-law, Maura followed the invisible pull that drew her into the garden.

Glancing at the small patch, its colours masked by the shadows of approaching night, she spoke silently in her heart. Show me which to take, Mother, don't let me harm Connal more than I have already.

It might have been that hands other than her own had gathered heart-shaped leaves of linden, grey-green leaves of nepeta and dark green sage. Maura added honey to the juice of the pounded leaves then stirred in boiled water.

Carrying it across to the bed she knelt beside it, patiently spooning the warm liquid between the man's lips.

Soon he was sleeping. Taking the remains of the medicine to the table, Maura felt the strength suddenly drain from her. Should Connal die . . . oh God, it was all her fault . . . if only she had stayed awake, if only she had taken the can of tea to the field!

Weariness, anxiety and regret fusing together she choked on tears filling her throat.

Setting her own basin on the ground at her feet, the older woman watched for a moment. This girl had shown a wisdom and a bravery beyond her years. Reaching out both hands, she called in a voice like a gentle whisper, 'Come ye here, child, come sit ye beside me.' Then as Maura settled at her knee she went on, ''Tis a wonderful compassion ye showed this day both to my Caitlin and to the son her marrying brought to my clochan. Ye have done yer best and 'tis more than grateful I be, now together we will ask the good Lord to grant the peace of mind ye cannot be giving to ye'self.' As she rested a lined hand on Maura's bent head her whispered prayer spread over the tiny room.

'God grant us the serenity to accept the things we can't be changing, give to us the courage to change the things we can, and bless us with the wisdom to be knowing the difference.'

She had refused to come home, refused to return to the valley.

Emotion burning like a red-hot brand in his chest, Liam stared at the small wooden crosses set in the patch of bare black earth.

He had pledged his word that no Riordan would touch hand to her ever again, that she would be safe here in the house she had been reared in, but to no avail. She had turned her back on all she had once known.

He would never again see her in Clonmacnoise, see her

smile shyly at him from the doorway of this tiny cottage or watch him drive by from the bank of the stream.

The bank of the stream! His fingers clenched tightly. Was that where it had happened, was it there his brother had taken his pleasure raping a young girl?

His brother! Bitterness burned like acid in his throat. Padraig had not been seen since that morning of the argument between him and their father, when he was turned from the house, cut off without a penny. But that would not be for long, Padraig was not a man to forgo the easy life, nor had he ever liked work of any kind. Yes, it was sure, Padraig Riordan would return to Clonfert, and when he did . . .

'You too? The crippled dog hoping to find himself a bitch!'

For several seconds Liam stood absolutely still then slowly turned to see his brother's mocking smile.

'You thought to find *her* here, the Deverell bitch, you came sniffing in search of more than a bone; and why not, for now she's been taken no other man will look at her, no man other than a cripple! No other *man*, but then you are not a man, are you?' The sneering laugh rang on the warm silence, the cruel eyes glittering their amusement. 'You are the misfit, the family runt!'

'Why have you come to this house?'

'Why?' The loud laugh once more an abuse of the still peace of the valley, Padraig did not see the line of white settle about his brother's lips. 'Why do you think . . . to make use of that I made use of once before . . .'

To make use! Liam's fingers tightened into fists. That was all Maura Deverell had been to him, something to be used, something to take the ache from his loins.

With his teeth clamped he stared at the face he had loved, the tall straight brother he had admired, the man he had often wished himself to be, but all of that was gone, destroyed by that last act of mindless cruelty. 'Leave, Padraig,' he said quietly, 'leave now!'

'Leave! Is that what the little trollop told you, couldn't even a slut like her take a cripple into her bed?'

'Maura Deverell is no trollop.' The words were a cold hiss.

'No!' Padraig answered, mockery hard in his gleaming eyes. 'Maybe the trull would not open her legs for a runt but they'll open for me, you can even watch, brother, see what it is you'll never have—'

There was no word, the only sound one of anger in the blow that had the mocking man staggering, then a snapped-off cry as a second fist smashed against bleeding lips.

'I won't call you a swine, that would be an insult to that animal.' His eyes blazing, Liam stared at the man rising unsteadily to his feet. 'I won't even call you contemptible for you are beneath contempt, you are not worthy—'

'Worthy, worthy of what . . . of tumbling a little slut whose living depends on our charity? Or is it that I snatched the sweetie from under your nose, I bedded the wench afore you could, is that it, brother, is that the stone in your craw? Well I'm going to make sure the stone chokes you, make sure the slut has a babe in her belly . . . Padraig Riordan's bastard—'

As before no word heralded the eruption of Liam's fury, only the sound of knuckle against flesh as his fist found its target. Taken off guard Padraig stumbled backwards into the cottage, sprawling his length across the hearth.

Eyes dark with malevolence half closed as Padraig looked up at the man standing over him. 'You surprise me, the cripple has spirit . . . But no man raises a hand to Padraig Riordan, not even his runt of a brother; that twisted back you've carried all your life will seem nothing compared to the sight you'll be once I be done with you!'

As the last word spat from his bleeding lips his hand reached for the iron poker, swinging it with all his force towards Liam's crotch, but he had sidestepped, his own quick kick catching his brother's arm to double the intended blow back against his own head.

IO

Adjusting his collar, Padraig Riordan's fingers stilled as he looked at the angry mark running diagonally across the left side of his brow and cheek. Scarred! Anger hot and livid burned like acid inside him. His face would be marked for life, and by whom? By his father's runt, the hump-shouldered lad who not once in his life had as much as said boo to a goose, the runt, the misfit, the family scapegoat. Liam had marred those handsome looks. Yet Liam was not the cause – he stared at the purple weal – the instrument, yes, but not the cause, the Deverell girl was the cause. She it was, who was the causing of all of this. Hands dropping to his sides he looked around him, eyes taking in the drabness of the cheap room; bare boards where once he had walked on carpet brought from the Orient, peeling paint instead of walls hung with hand-blocked paper, a bed of flock in place of goose feather and coverings of roughly woven twill where he had known silk . . . all of this was her fault!

Turning, he kicked furiously at the leg of the ugly wooden bedstead. None of this would have happened but for her . . . he would still be living in the luxury of his father's house instead of this poverty were it not for that Deverell bitch. Oh she had known what she was about! His fists curling into balls, he breathed hard. Lying there on the bank of that stream with legs spread and skirts up over her knees she had waited for a man, any man, waited to trap him with her pretty face and a body set to taunt and tease with its promise of pleasure, and in return a payment. Well he had paid all right but so would she, only the whore would not live with her scars! He would find Maura Deverell and when he did . . . when he did! A smile crept over his mouth, pulling at the slowly healing wound, a malicious curving of the lips that added to the disfigurement. When he did the slut would die and, after her, his brother!

' 'Twas a grand wake with its going on into the morning and the priest himself too full of ale to give the speaking of the words.'

Walking into the smoke-filled room of the ale house Padraig glanced at the group of men sat listening to one at their centre. He had not seen him here before, another itinerant passing through. Dismissing him he called for a tankard of porter, carrying it to a seat on the further side of the room. It was bad enough he must needs be in this hovel without socialising with its customers.

'Then who was it had the speaking? For a man can't be sent on his way and none said.' Long side whiskers bobbed as a listener removed his clay pipe and spat into the fire.

'And isn't that the truth now!' The man at the centre nodded. 'Well the sons of the man sat and thought – with a glass or two to help with the process – while the father sat in a chair a'waiting of his burying; and so it went on 'til it seemed the wake would see a second night. Then it was the mother of the sons asked could not another priest have the saying of the words? Well the idea was good but how to tell the first one had fallen to the potheen?'

'A problem . . . a problem and no mistake.' Several heads shook as the men looked at each other.

'A problem to be sure and every soul there knowing it must be solved if the divil in hell was not to claim that poor dead man.' The speaker paused, allowing his audience to cross themselves piously before continuing. 'But the passing of her man, though it showed as sorrow on her face, it had not the

woman quite bereft of common sense. Hands on hips she
stood on her feet, her eyes daring any dispute. "Sure an' it
can't be the fault of the Father if a sickness has overtook him,"
she declared. "Don't we all be knowing he came from his bed
to see Murphy safe in his grave but it's too ill he was to have
the doing of it?" Well it took a minute in the answering for
none wished to refute the widow in her hour of grief but then
Calum O'Flaherty, a man of some seventy years, up and
asked, "And how will ye be pulling the wool over the eyes of a
man of the cloth?" But quick as the tongue of the little people
themselves the widow answered, "By pulling cloth of a different colour over the face of this one!" With that she set her
eldest on a horse, dispatching him to Glendalough for to bring
a second priest from one of its seven churches, while with the
help of the women she packed the cheeks of the first with clean
rags then bound his jaw with a length of red flannel tied neatly
on the top of his head, ordering five men to see to the carrying
of him home and giving them to say he was suffering bad with
the mumps. Need it be said the Father kept some days to his
bed while the dead man was laid comfortable in his own.'

Idiots! Padraig drank deep of his porter. They had the brain
of animals to listen to the drivel of the man!

'I see my tale did not bring ye'self a smile.'

Padraig lowered his tankard as the stranger came to sit
beside him. 'The tongue of a charlatan affords me no amusement.'

'A charlatan, is it?' Dark eyes glinted at the insult but the
anger behind them remained controlled. 'And does the tongue
of a charlatan be lying when it says ye find ye'self filled with
anger and the cause of that anger be that mark upon yer face?'

One hand lifting to his cheek, Padraig traced the livid line.
'It would not lie,' he grated.

'And if I said it be vengeance alone will take the sting from
yer soul?'

'It still would not lie.'

'So.' The man looked into his own tankard, watching tiny bubbles break on the rich creamy surface of the dark liquid. 'Will ye be having the healing of ye'self?'

'Yes!' All the rancour, all the venom of the thoughts that dogged his mind when lying sleepless in that wretched room spilled into that one word.

'And how will ye be doing that?' A hint of disbelief bringing, as it was meant to do, a swift angry answer.

'By finding the bitch who was the cause of it, by finding Maura Deverell and killing her!'

Straightening her back, Maura grimaced against the pain biting into every muscle. Connal's leg was not yet healed and without the planting of the potato crop there would be no food for that family come next year.

'I can do it . . . I have to do it.' One whisper following the other she held back the soft moan. With the ache like a fire along every sinew, she remembered how Connal had tried to stand on his feet when the question of planting next year's crop had come up, how he had gasped and clutched at his mother-in-law's chair for support, and she recalled the look that had passed between himself and Caitlin, a look that already held the hint of desperation. The baby could not be taken to lie hours in air, which could often turn misty and damp, nor could it be left in the care of two people each of whom was liable to fall while holding it, and she had known she could not abandon them.

Pressing the dibber into the ground, a sharp sting travelled along her spine as the pointed stick hit a stone. How could this ground produce any kind of food when every foot of it was laced with rock? But that was the story in almost every part of Ireland, the fertile fields taken by English landlords while the country's own people went hungry trying to eke a living from a few inches of soil. It had been like this in Clonmacnoise after her father had died. It had been left to her to set the potatoes in the ground, to grow what vegetables she could but the valley had been mellow and its soil soft, making her tasks easier.

When the last potato dropped into its hole, Maura trod the earth over it. The sun, pale in the last of its lovely gowns, lay low in the sky already drawing clouds in over itself. There would be rain soon. Picking up the dibber and the empty potato sack she placed them in the peat cart and set off for the bog. It was near enough a mile in the opposite direction from the cottage but, like the planting, the peat had to be cut.

'*Remember now, show yer regard for the little people.*'

Smiling despite the throbbing in her every bone, she cut a tiny piece from the dark brown bed and laid it aside, the words her father had taught her a whisper on her lips.

'All honour and peace be yours, take this gift offered in respect.'

The little ritual had accompanied every aspect of daily life, a tiny beaker of milk set aside from the evening milking of their cow, the first egg taken from the hen, the first fruit or vegetable, even the first flower of spring, all laid aside for the fairy people. How many times had she fallen asleep with her nose pressed to the window, determined to see the elves, to watch the myriad coloured wings of fairies flutter in the moonlight as they danced upon the ground? But always she had awakened in her own truckle bed and always the beaker had stood in its place upon a stone, empty and washed sparkling clean, her father smiling as he told her that was the way it had been left. She had loved those stories then, stories of leprechauns and elfin kings told to her in the warm glow of the fire, held snug in her father's arms. But that was all they were, stories, and now the telling was over, finished as her parents' lives were finished. It was all gone, her childhood freedom, her happiness, her home, all snatched away by the actions of the Riordan family.

But that was unfair. Sinking the spade into the boggy sedge she cut another square of peat then lifted it into the small handcart. Not all of the Riordans had despised her family. Their mother had been pleasant in her speaking to them, and Liam . . .

The spade forgotten in her hand she stared into the gathering twilight, a strange new unhappiness stealing into her heart.

Liam had followed her, asked her to return to the cottage her father had built but she had refused, she had not trusted him to keep her safe from the despicable intentions of his brother. Despite what she had said her eyes had said something different. She had not trusted him! Now it was too late, words spoken could not be taken back. Standing there, the lemony glow of sunset turning tears to diamonds, Maura felt the sharp sting of pain drive deep into her soul. Liam Riordan would never hear her apology, he would never know the truth.

But what was the truth? She bent again to the spade as a flush of uncertainty stained her cheeks. Why did she feel so badly, why had the hurt in his eyes become a pain in her own heart? They had never been more than acquaintances exchanging the time of day as he passed the cottage, she had no feeling for him as he had none for her, so why this sense of loss, why the crushing despair of having lost something dear to her?

With the last flickers of sunlight trembling on the horizon she set the spade on the slabs of cut peat, stretching her back, eyes closed in the pleasure of easing cramped muscles; but as she opened them every part of her froze. There on the rim of the heath where land met sky, the figure of a man stood watching her.

'A blessing on all in this house.'

Maura's nerves tingled at the sound of the words called from beyond the closed door. She had grabbed the handles of the peat cart, running with it like a wild thing across the open heath, leaving it unemptied behind the house, desperate to be inside with the others, terrified that this time the figure would be that of Padraig Riordan. There had been several others passed through the valley, men who had called at the house, resting an hour before travelling on, but none had been the man that had raped her. But how long before he came, how long before a passing stranger was heard telling of a young girl staying with a family not her own, a girl whose look held fear when it rested on him, how long before Padraig Riordan got the news and put one to the other? It had to come, and with each day the coming got nearer. The voice calling from outside was not the voice of Padraig Riordan, one more time fate had spared her, but fate would not always be so kind; pray God she could leave before it turned its face away.

'The same be on ye'self.' Caitlin swung the door wide, stepping aside for the man to enter.

'Is it from Clara ye be at?' Connal asked as the visitor stepped into the light of the room's one lamp.

''Tis not Clara.' Bright eyes swept from one to the other resting momentarily on Maura. ''Twas Tullynally I last laid my head to rest.'

'Tullynally, be that right now?' Connal's interest sparked. 'Sure and the miles between here and there be many.'

'And each of them long and heavy bearing on the feet; I was getting to think no cottage was built on any one of them 'til it was I saw the daughter of the house cutting peat along of yonder bog.'

'Maura Deverell be no born daughter to my house but she be loved true as my own.'

It had been said! Her name, not her belonging! Maura caught her breath. Caitlin's mother meant well, her words were a measure of her gratitude but they might well prove to be the harbinger that would bring the evil of Padraig Riordan.

'Then 'tis twice blessed yer after being.' The stranger's glance rested again on Maura as he answered.

'And 'tis well I do be knowing it.' The older woman smiled.

Reaching the strong stick Maura had cut for a crutch, Connal set it under his arm, leaning heavily on it as he stood. 'It's welcome ye be to share our table. There be nothing grand—'

'A crust given with good heart be better than a feast given grudgingly,' the man cut in smilingly. ''Tis accepting your kindness I am and asking heaven's blessings for it.' Taking the seat indicated he listened and nodded as Connal said each name in turn but his gaze stayed with Maura as if making a mental note of her every movement.

'Aiden was the name given at my baptism but Tinker I be called by most often. Tinker, that be my trade and it's mending your pots I'll be should they have a hole in them.'

'There be none in need of the mending, praise be, but a little of the telling of Tullynally or the sights ye've been after seeing on yer journey would come pleasant to the ear for I think there must be places beautiful to see.'

Spooning the broth Maura had served the man smiled, his eyes softening. 'There be many and each vying with the other in beauty; 'tis a well-known fact the good Lord set a competition in heaven. Each of the angels had to create a garden, some with valleys and rivers, some with mountains and loughs but each so exquisite as to take the breath from a man. Well when the time of the competing was at an end the angels stood with wings folded while the Lord surveyed their handiwork. Would it be the Archangel Michael, who with one sweep of his fiery sword had cut a great valley and filled it with a river whose waters sparkled like the rivers of Paradise itself, would have the winning? Or would it be the great Gabriel, who with one breath blew the land aside, pushing it high into mountains whose peaks he set about with crowns of gold-edged cloud while covering their nakedness with vast forests of trees, the loveliness of it all causing his fellows to weep tears of joy? For a day and a night the Lord perused the result of the task He had set. Missing not one tiny flower, their colours gleaming like gems among the emerald grass, each blade and petal crafted by Seraphim, nor one fish gliding its silver elegance in the glittering waters where tiny Cherubim had set them; not one did He miss. But at the end of His inspecting He shook His head telling the hosts of heaven there was no one winner, for each of them pleased as the other, and that being so the Lord bundled the whole of their works together and placed it in the sea, setting the wee folk to live only in that land, a land that would ever be closest to His heart, a land to which He gave the name of Ireland. Sure, 'tis the jewel of the earth yer son will be growing in.'

'That is a lovely story.'

'And a true one.' The man lifted his glance answering Caitlin. 'I have visited many parts of this land and in each I have found such beauty as to rob a man of speech and when he drags his limbs from one place it has been only to be spellbound by the wonder of the next.'

'Be Tullynally such a place?' Already under the man's spell, Caitlin took up the baby, carrying it behind the curtain before giving it her breast.

Asking permission he lit a long-stemmed clay pipe, blowing out a blue-grey haze before replying. 'Sure now isn't it the way I've been telling? Such a place the angels wept at its losing, with the magnificent Lough Derravaragh and the Mount of Knockeyou to one side, and pretty Multyfarnham touching its shoulder, but like so many parts of the land it be scarred by the castle sprawled across its bosom by the British Earl of Longford; to be sure it gives the gentle face of Tullynally a look resembling the pox, for its towers and battlements rise like sores on the earth of it.'

'The English,' the older woman sighed heavily, 'sure their presence in Ireland has been long the cause of heavy hearts but with heaven's grace one day they will cross the sea to their own country and bide contented to leave this one to the folk the good Lord decreed should share it only with the little people.'

'Amen to that.' The stranger crossed himself, his glance following Maura as she collected bowls and spoons.

'And where is it ye be going next?'

'Ah now,' he answered Connal, ''tis the broth of a place I turn my face to when the morning sun rises, a spot given to that humblest of men and one of God's holy saints. 'Tis to the resting place of Ciaran I go, to ask his blessing before journeying down to Clonfert.'

'Be ye all right, child?'

The woman's concern was evident as the spoons Maura held rattled noisily to the floor.

'The water . . . it is too hot.'

How had she managed to lie? Keeping her face turned from the people watching her, Maura hid the confusion that had her face pale. Clonfert . . . the man was going to Clonfert! Would he meet with Seamus Riordan, with Padraig? They would hear of a stranger being in the village, they would seek him out, ask him.

'My thanks to the man of the house for his hospitality and the mother for her bounty.' The tinker rose. 'May heaven return it a hundredfold and peace rest on ye all.'

'And on ye'self.' Connal hauled himself to his feet. 'The night holds the promise of cold so 'tis welcome ye are to share the comfort of the fire and sorry I am to have no other bed to offer.'

'Tinkers need no bed other than the heath but grace rest on ye for the offer of yer fireside.'

'There is a place in the storeroom, it means sleeping with the taties but its walls will keep off the night air, 'tis welcome ye be to pass the night if it be suitable to ye.'

His black hair flecked with grey, his dark smiling eyes reflecting the firelight, the tinker seemed suddenly too tall for the low-roofed cottage.

'I'll do that and gladly,' he said softly and then, staring directly at Maura, added, ''tis happy I am to see there is kindness of heart still in Ireland.'

It was almost as if those last words had been meant only for her. In the dark corner hidden by the curtain that closed off the truckle bed Maura held the blanket that covered her own sleeping place on the floor beside it. His eyes had bored deep into her as he had spoken them, like fingers in her soul. Was he storing away knowledge of her, painting her likeness on his memory? Had he already been asked to look for her on his journeying? With a trickle of cold spiralling down her back, she shivered. Seamus Riordan might forget but Padraig Riordan never would, he would come for her and find her at this cottage, and in the wounds of his pride he would make the family suffer for giving her shelter.

That must not happen. She clutched the thin blanket closer against her chest. She must leave . . . tomorrow she must go.

Stepping back into the lamplight as the stranger called his goodnights she looked at the older woman. 'As Connal says the night bears the promise of being a cold one so I thought to offer the tinker man this, I can take your chair before the fire for this night.'

'The gentle heart of the Holy Mother be the match of yer own,' the woman smiled, 'take it to him now if it's wanting him to have the using of it ye be.'

His eyes had been watchful, dark and brilliant as those of a crow. With her hand on the wooden latch of the storeroom door, Maura hesitated. His look had followed her about the room even when he was speaking to one of the others, followed her as Padraig Riordan's eyes had followed her whenever they had met. Were this man's thoughts as wicked . . . his intentions . . .

'*See not evil in every man.*'

Her mother's words whispered in her memory. The man had been polite, no word had offended, she was wrong to suspect . . . to think . . .

Pushing open the door she stepped into the blackness, a cry welling into her throat as a strong hand closed over her wrist and dragged her inside.

II

◆~

'Does be nothing short of a miracle, the Blessed Virgin herself must have been after sending ye to us for without ye and the skills yer mother, may her soul rest in peace, taught to ye then there be no doubting but Connal O'Malley would be lying in his grave an' this mite with no father to see to his rearing.'

'I am only thankful our prayers were heard.' Maura smiled at the woman contentedly nursing her grandson.

'All thanks to God and his holy saints for 'tis with ye they were, but then 'twas ye'self had the carryin' out o' it all, yer own was the courage an' 'tis grateful to ye I'll be all the remainder o' my days . . . 'tis me only regret ye be choosin' not to make yer home with us.'

It was not that she had no wish to settle here, the valley that held the clochan was pretty as that which she and her mother had been forced to leave, but the tiny room, already divided by a curtain, could house no other grown girl. Yet that was not her true worry. Every day her heart feared the coming of Seamus or Padraig Riordan.

Turning, she caught the glance of the younger woman who had been slicing potatoes into a broth that held no meat. This family had little enough for themselves, the feeding of another mouth for the months of winter would see their stores gone long before the next harvest could be reaped, and that supposing the potato sickness did not spread to Connal's fields.

'Connal is near to well now,' she smiled, 'and with the fields planted there will be little for him to work at for a few months and that extra resting should see his leg good as ever it was so this is the time for my moving on.'

'Connal improves by the day,' Caitlin carried the pot to the fire, 'and as Mother says it is due to you, it was yourself planted the taties, it is yourself should stay to have the sharing of them.'

'No.' Maura shook her head. 'I . . . I promised my mother—' Sat in her chair, Caitlin's mother caught the sob that snared the rest of the words.

'A daughter's promise be sacred,' she said, 'and we'll not have the asking of ye breaking it, but know ye this, the heart and gratitude of Bridie MacGee goes with ye and wherever it be in Ireland ye finds ye'self ye'll feel my love surround ye; God grant ye the protection that will be asked of Him in my every prayer.'

'. . . *wherever it be in Ireland ye finds ye'self* . . .'

Maura hid fear behind a smile. It was no part of Ireland her mother had begged her to go.

'If it's sure you are you can't be after staying then it be as Mother says and I'll not be asking you to break the word you've given to your mother, even though Connal would build you a clochan of your own here beside this one; but I will not forget what it was you did for Connal and for me and I will tell my son often of the girl who it was saw him safe into the world.' Tears bright on her cheeks, Caitlin threw her arms about Maura. 'I will ever hope to see you return to us, God keep you safe.'

Caitlin had said the words she longed to say herself but she would never return, she must leave the shores of Ireland behind her.

'Bring what it is lies in my chest.' Her own eyes moist, Caitlin's mother pointed. Then as her daughter carried a soft amber-coloured shawl to her she glanced again at Maura. 'This was the shawl I wore to my marrying and the one my girl

wore to hers, now I give it to you. Take it –' she smiled as
Maura shook her head '– take it from a woman who thinks of
ye as her own. With God's grace ye'll have a finer shawl to
wear when the time of yer own marrying comes but ye'll be
given no gift with a greater love.'

Feeling emotions too strong to allow words, Maura dropped
to her knees beside the woman she had come to love, grasping
her hand, pressing her lips to it. Part of her own heart would
always be here in this little house. Touching a kiss to the baby's
tiny head she rose and, with eyes blinded by quick hot tears,
she stumbled out onto the heath.

Standing before the tall pedimented door of the church
dedicated to Saint Brendan the Navigator, the tinker set his
pack on the ground. He would go inside and give thanks, for
hadn't he had the luck at that tiny clochan, hadn't he got what
he had yearned for this long time! The man and his family had
treated him with kindness, had shown him the hospitality that
was bred in every Irishman, but they could not one of them
give what that girl had given.

She was beautiful. He stepped beneath chevroned arches,
paying no mind to the stone-carved animal and human heads.
Her hair had been the colour of newly ripened chestnuts her
eyes wide and emerald green as leaves in summer and her elfin
face vied in beauty with the Queen of the little people herself.
Yes, Maura Deverell had given what he desired.

Sat at the rear of the quiet nave, he watched the pale rays of
sunlight play over the altar and glisten on the tall cross at its
centre but his thoughts were in the storeroom of a tiny
clochan.

She had been afraid but he had held her fast, held her until he
had been satisfied. He could almost feel her still, the softness of
her skin, the lingering scent of camomile on her hair, the delicate
body he could have snapped with a jerk of his arm.

A black-robed figure gliding in front of the altar caught his attention, serving to remind him of his reasons for being here. Watching the priest make his devotions he knew he should do the same, yet the memory of a young girl crowded the prayers from his mind; touching a finger to brow and chest he walked quietly out into the afternoon. Today he would look for work in the village mending pots and pans, and tomorrow . . . ? Lifting his glance he stared towards a distant hill, at its summit an elegant square built mansion, its tall windows glinting in the sunlight.

'I want nothing of what is yours to give.'

Liam Riordan faced the man who for so many years had brought fear to his heart; but stood there now, with soft autumn light filling the gracious room, he knew that never again would he be afraid of his father. Their only bond had been that of fear, a bond too strong for him to break, but a young girl had broken it. What had happened to Maura Deverell had snapped the tie. Mother and daughter! He looked at the face red with anger. Father and son! Both were guilty of that worst of crimes against a woman, both had committed rape . . . and he would forgive neither.

'So you want nothing of what is mine!' The crimson face darkened. 'Then how is it ye propose to live, a runt of a man—'

'A runt, yes, Father, but a runt that has grown despite your dislike of him, a runt that can earn his own living.'

'Earn his own living, is it!' Seamus Riordan laughed scathingly. 'Doing what, answer me that, doing what? The same thing ye've been doing since it was ye came into this house? For if it be that ye be thinking on then it won't have the carrying of ye far, for 'tis bugger all ye've been doing. What have ye worn that was not bought by me, what have ye eaten that was not paid for from my purse, whose be the roof ye've slept under? Be those the skills by which ye mean to earn yer living, 'cos if so then 'tis not only deformed in the body ye be but crippled in the mind along of it!'

That was how his father had ever thought of him, a puny useless child with a twisted back, a child to be hidden from society, detested, unwanted, a child whose heart had been broken by the unkindness, the constant revulsion. But he was no longer a child! Drawing a long breath he looked at the man stood opposite, seeing the very evenness of that breath acting like fuel to a fire.

'Not every man has a heart like yours, Father.' Liam spoke quietly. 'A heart not simply oblivious to the pain of a child but one that took pleasure from it. I agree my back is not as straight as yours, also I was never the son you would have had me be, but then even my crippled mind can learn and my limbs are strong, that being so I feel certain there will be someone in this valley will not be offended by my appearance, someone who will give me work.'

' 'Tis certain ye be, is it!' Seamus drove a vicious boot into the fire, showering the hearth with a cascade of tiny glistening sparks. 'And what man will it be will be putting out his own family from their home? What man will be after taking the bread from the mouths of his children, for that is what any in Clonfert or any village within miles of it will be doing should he give employment to ye. This valley is mine, I hold every stick and stone and every clochan, and any man who goes against me will find no place in it.'

Liam's eyes had not once left the figure held tense by its own fury, now as it swung from the fireplace to face him he gave a slight bow, speaking quietly as before.

'Forgive me, I had forgotten, the valley king! Then I must leave your kingdom; like the prince in the story books, I must seek my fortune in the wide world.'

This was not the son he knew, the son afraid to speak a word

to him, one that scuttled away like a frightened rabbit each
time they crossed each other's path. Seamus Riordan felt the
first tremors of uncertainty. If it had been Padraig standing
there trading verbal blows with him he would have had no
qualms, for his elder son had ever had the quick tongue, but
this was the runt, the misfit. Yet with Padraig disowned and
banished from his life it was the misfit must carry both name
and estate. Name and estate! He crossed to a tall window that
gave a clear view over the valley. Had they not been cursed by
Mairead Deverell, had not her hand touched the stones of this
house, her malediction been pronounced on him and his sons
to the ending of his line? But they were no more than words,
the utterances of an angry woman that could not come to
anything. But the words of her own mother, had they come to
nothing?

Staring out over the soft clad beauty of land rolling away to
the village, the glistening sheen of the river in the distance,
Seamus felt his nerves quicken. Padraig was no longer son to
him and now Liam was set to leave. The Deverell curse? He
breathed deeply against the anxiety rearing within him. Was it
once more at work?

His face still to the window he masked the worry pricking at
each nerve. While things were held together there was always a
chance. 'I can't prevent the going of ye,' he said tightly, 'but
know ye this, the English landlords are finding no profit in
land sickened by the blight, they have no profit in crops that
can't be grown or from tenants with not one last farthing to
pay in rent and so they be thinking to cut their losses by the
selling of their holdings. I have money enough to buy where I
will and each buying will be of land where it is I find ye settled.
Like this valley, that land will be mine and I will drive every
man, every woman and every child from it should ye be
turning yer face from this house.'

'. . . *a legacy of hate* . . .'

The words Maura had spoken echoed in Liam's mind. It was one his father would have no qualms in bequeathing to this land of Ireland. To prevent it meant that he, Liam, must remain here in Clonfert, coming face to face daily with a man for whom he felt no respect, no affiliation; but to leave . . . He could not do it, he could not be the means whereby his father would blight the lives of so many, bring to them the suffering he had brought to his own son, vent his spite on the children of others as he had on a child born to him. Watching the back still turned to him, Liam felt the echoes of the despair that had haunted him through childhood, the despair of being unloved and rejected. His father did not want him to stay because he loved him, he wanted him to stay because that way Seamus Riordan had won again, won as he always did; but this time it would be no unconditional surrender, this time Peter would not be robbed to pay Paul!

Her back against the tumbled wall of a roofless clochan, Maura drew the soft folds of the shawl about her shivering body. This was the second week since the visit of that man, each hour of it bringing its own nightmare; the second week since the tinker had grabbed her wrist, drawing her into that storeroom, yet still the terror of it had not faded, still every night shadow brought its fears. He had held her fast. She had tried to scream but the horror of what was happening had closed her throat; then he had spoken, his voice soft as the darkness that enclosed them.

Somewhere in the bracken that was slowly swallowing the derelict house an animal shuffled, the sound of it sending tremors along her spine.

His hand had been like an iron band about her wrist. The memories returned, piling fear upon fear. The strength had drained from her, leaving her without the power to fight as he pulled her towards him. She had been almost on her knees when he had spoken again. '*I have no wish to harm you,*' he had whispered, '*I am no Riordan, neither father nor son, unlike them you stand in no danger from me. I hold you now only to tell you to get yourself from this place, leave before—*'

She had broken free then, going quickly back to the light of that living room, to the chair drawn against the fire, her brain too numb with fear to take in the quiet whispered words, to fully realise it was not rape was the thought in the tinker's mind. It was only later they had stood clear in her brain. His words had been a warning . . . a warning for her safety!

'*I am no Riordan . . . you stand in no danger from me.*'

He had known, he had known the danger she was in, the danger of being discovered by Padraig Riordan or his father. Sometimes in the deep hours of the night, she had tried telling herself they would not look for her but that had brought no comfort; Riordan pride had been insulted, that was reason enough for Seamus and his sons . . . no, not both sons, not Liam! But, like herself, Liam might be given no choice, he could not be expected to do as she had done, to turn his back on his home for the sake of a penniless girl. Perhaps even now . . .

The shrill bark of a dog fox cut through the sable night bringing a cry to Maura's lips. Lowering her face to her drawn-up knees she covered it with the shawl.

Liam had ever been kindly spoken. Beneath the covering shawl her mouth trembled. Were he the only one . . . but he wasn't and that had been her reason for leaving the family that had offered her a home; she would not have the wrath of the Riordans brought down on them.

Perhaps father or son had been to that clochan already, it could be that even now they were following her.

'. . . *no danger from me . . .*'

Had that been a lie? The answering scream of a vixen seemed to be the scream in her own soul. How could she know that what the tinker had whispered was the truth; was she simply telling herself he had wanted to warn her, when in reality what he was after doing was to flush her into the open like drawing a rabbit from its hole?

Huddled against the crumbling stones she tried to think clearly. From Tullynally he had said he came and even Connal had had no knowing of that place, word of her could not have reached so far. So where was it that man had heard of Maura Deverell? He had never visited Clonmacnoise or she would have known of it, a travelling tinker was welcomed for his news. Then was it Clonfert, was he a regular caller to that village, was it there he had heard tell? Was what Padraig Riordan had done to her and what his father had intended common talk in that place? Everyone talking of her shame! Tears, hot and stinging, forced their way beneath closed lids. 'It was none of my doing!' Taken by the night breeze the cry was folded away in the darkness.

'. . . *no danger* . . .'

The words circled, vying with the deepening cold already threatening her mind, and with each rotation followed the question: who was that tinker man?

12

Coldness like she had never known before coiled around Maura. Her limbs stiff, her crouched body unmoving, she seemed petrified as if part of the stone she leaned against.

She would not go on, she would sit here and wait for the same hand to fetch her as had fetched her mother. It would not matter her dying on the heath, there was no one to mourn her, no one would even know of her passing.

Time to get up.

Faint in the distance of her dulled mind the words floated, heard yet unheard.

Time to rise.

She did not want to rise, she was comfortable. Beneath the shawl that covered her face Maura refused to accept the words calling her, gentle as morning breeze.

The day be fresh and beautiful, 'tis waiting on ye.

It was an intrusion, a transgression of her privacy; she did not want to be spoken to. A spark of irritation flickered, a single movement in the calm dispassion of lethargy.

'Tis wasting the best of it, so ye are.

It would not go away, that voice that seemed to smile. The spark becoming a flame she lowered the shawl, squinting as the clear light of morning pricked her eyes. Who was it had spoken, who had called her back into the harshness of living?

There be sticks a plenty and dry the other side of the wall, sure and ye can be coaxing a fire from them in no time at all.

Sticks . . . a fire . . . Sluggish yet, Maura's brain began to

function. She had not thought . . . she could make a fire . . .
someone had taught . . .

Sticks. They'll not come to ye of themselves.

Silhouetted by the sunrise a figure made no move to come
towards her. Alarm breaking her freezing bonds she pushed to
her feet, the searing pain of forcing cramped muscles into life
bringing a groan to her lips, a groan that gave way to a breath
of relief when she realised the figure did not fit that of a
Riordan.

'Who are you?'

Unanswered her question hung in the air, the figure turning
away. Why had the man, for it was a man, not come closer,
why had he not shaken her awake? Keeping the questions in
her mind she picked her way stiffly over the tumbled stones,
gathering twigs fallen in their shelter. Having collected a small
bundle she laid them in criss-cross pattern, memory guiding
her fingers. She had done this very thing many times, why had
she not remembered before? Why had she spent night after
cold night when twigs of gorse and clumps of dry heather
covered the heath?

But sticks did not light themselves! At a loss for what to do
next she looked at the figure standing a distance away, and as
their glances caught she felt her hand brush against the small
box pushed deep into her pocket. Matches! She had forgotten
all about the one thing she had brought with her from her own
home!

There be trout yonder.

As a wisp of newborn smoke curled into her eyes Maura
blinked. His feet had made no sound yet he stood only yards
from the fire crackling into life. Pressing her eyelids hard
down, squeezing smoke-teased tears from them, she sought to
clear her vision but when once more she looked for his face he
was moving towards the silver glint of a river.

Trout, the man had said. Her feet needed no persuasion to

follow. Lying face down at the water's edge she smiled into its
slow-moving depths. Now she remembered. Her father had
taught her how to make a fire of sticks, taught her how to tickle
trout. Each movement slow and careful, she pushed back her
shawl, then unbuttoning her sleeve she rolled it high above her
elbow.

'*Slowly now, it be no hare ye be chasing. Let yer fingers touch
him as they'd stroke a baby in its cradle.*'

The words her father had spoken so often sounded clear in
her mind as Maura slid her hand into the water. The skin of
the fish like cool silk against her fingertips, she scarcely
breathed; slowly now, she cautioned herself, rush it and
you lose the prize! But she did not lose it and with a cry of
sheer jubilation scarring the silence she grabbed the fish she
had flipped onto the bank.

Carrying it to the fire she placed it, speared by a stick
propped on a stone, above the flames. Only then did her eyes
search for the man. Where had he gone? Why did he not stay
to share her meal? Leaving the fish to cook she returned to the
river bank. Washing herself, the cold waters clearing her mind,
she stood stock-still as realisation, soul-destroying in its truth,
struck with sudden viciousness. Climbing from the river she
returned to the fire; staring at the cooked fish she had set on a
flat stone, she could not believe what was now in her mind. 'I
could have done this for Mother,' she whispered, 'I could have
made a fire, cooked her a fish; I could have kept her warm, fed
her . . . I could have kept the life in her but instead I let her die
. . . I let my mother die!'

*The pain was too strong, it had yer brain imprisoned, 'twas no
fault of ye, my little girlie.*

Girlie! No one had called her that since . . . The sweetness
of it cutting through her misery, Maura glanced across the fire
to where the man stood speaking softly.

Yer hands could not have the holding of yer mother, it was the

time of her calling; ye have the memory of her and ye have the love,
but ye must let the pain go.

Only her father had called her girlie! Maura hardly heard words that seemed to be only in her heart. It had been his own special name for her. For a moment the smoke of the fire cleared and she saw the smiling face, the lips giving no movement to the sounds still coming to her.

Be brave my little girlie, be brave.

'Father!' As the cry burst from her, Maura reached her hands towards the smiling figure, but it was already spiralling into the grey smoke, fading with it into nothingness.

'You! But ye be dead!'

A face handsome despite its years stared coldly at the astounded Seamus. 'Dead, am I? Then 'tis the first of the resurrection ye be looking at.'

'But I heard . . . I was told . . . years ago they said yer body had been pulled from the lough.'

Dark eyes glinted black ice. 'You should not believe all it is be told to you, 'tis the evidence of your eyes you should be believing.'

'Why?' Seamus's pale glance narrowed beneath the overhang of beetle brows. 'Why have ye come here, what is it ye be wanting?'

Fingering through the high rectangle of window, the afternoon light showed no smile on the strong mouth. 'It is nothing I want from you has the bringing of me to this house, yet peace of mind dictates it be so. I come to tell ye open and fair, keep yer hand within this village, seek not to strike beyond its boundaries or ye will answer for it.'

The first shock of surprise over, Seamus laughed scathingly.

'Ye think to threaten Seamus Riordan! Ye fool, who is it ye think ye are?'

Opposite him his visitor's eyes gleamed, contempt hard

beneath a velvet cover. 'It is not who I think I am,' he said quietly, 'it is who ye *know* I am, keep that knowledge ever to the front of yer mind and with it the remembrance that it is no threat is offered to ye but a gift.'

'A gift!' Seamus's brows rose. 'What gift could ye possibly give me?'

Quiet as before the answer followed. 'The gift of time. Time to set yer house in order. The past has caught up with ye as I intend it to catch up with yer son. The dog and the pup both wagged their tails on the wrong patch, they took their pleasure where it was not wanted and now the reckoning is due. Make no mistake, this is no innocent ye be dealing with; take yer spite beyond Clonfert, ignore what I say and a harder hand than justice will strike back and the days as yet left to ye will be cut short.'

Glaring at the man his servant had shown into the room Seamus allowed a small silence to develop. What had brought him here after so long? He could do no more now than he had been able to do all those years ago. Talk? Yes he could do that but words were no weapons in Clonfert, the people of the valley knew who was their master.

'Good manners teach a gift must be thanked for.' He paused, allowing a significant gaze to wander insultingly over his visitor. 'Time was yer gift to me and time shall be my gift to ye. Three days, three days I will give ye for to be gone from these parts, show yer face after that time be up and 'tis yer own days will be cut short. Seamus Riordan counts his friends in high places, keep that to the front of *your* mind.'

'It has never been forgotten!' The answer came through tight lips. 'Accuse Seamus Riordan and the reply is long and hard, but yer English friends will be of no use to ye when next we meet.'

Reaching for the bell pull that would recall his servant, Seamus's hand stilled. He was already alone in the room. But for how long . . . from this moment on how would he know himself truly alone again? Three days he had given but three days was a long time, too long to spend looking over your shoulder. Releasing the tapestry cord he walked slowly from the house.

' ''Tis yer own days will be cut short!' As the whisper turned into a smile, he crossed the yard to the stables.

Yer hands could not have the holding . . . it was the time of her calling . . .

Maura stared at the small fire, her meal forgotten in the misery of the moment.

. . . ye must let the pain go . . .

How? The sob inside turned into a torrent that threatened to choke her. How could she ever forget? She had let her mother die in misery. It had not been pain held her brain imprisoned, it had been pride. She had refused to wed with Liam Riordan simply out of pride, her own stupid selfish pride and her mother had died because of it. What would it have mattered what his brother did to her? If her mother had to die then at least by marrying she could have ensured it happened in a warm dry bed not on the rain-soaked heath like an animal. How could the pain of that ever go, how could it ever leave her?

. . . 'twas no fault of ye, my little girlie . . .

'It was, it was!' Maura crumpled, her heart in the cries refusing the gentleness touching her pain. 'I thought only of myself . . . only of myself. I was too blind, too selfish . . .'

. . . ye have the love . . .

It was beneath and above her, on every side, within her yet not a part of her, words without a voice filling her, surrounding her, the music of it soft yet so powerful it cut through her desolation with a soothing calming quiet.

She had the love, she had always had the love of both of her parents. They had known the heartache, the gnawing grief of losing one they loved, the sorrow that rose fresh every morning and lay with them every night. But through all of that their love for her had remained strong, unchanging. Now she too must be strong.

'Thank you,' she whispered through closed fingers, 'thank you—'

'If it's praying you are then you had better make it a good one for his lordship takes badly to poachers.'

A swift gasp stopping the whispered words Maura rose quickly to her feet, a mocking laugh greeting her as she turned.

'You should have taken that somewhere else to cook it, that way I might not have found you, though I doubt that; but it's the only doubt I have for it's certain his lordship will see you sent down for poaching his trout.'

'Poaching!' Maura was puzzled. 'I have taken from no private land, I took only from the river.'

'Which is private, it belongs to Lord Portington, as does the land that stretches from Timahoe to Kildare and that means you are trespassing.'

'I'm sorry, I will leave at once. Please will you point me a way that will give no offence.'

Between them the small fire crackled, tiny pistol shots wounding the silence.

Dressed in a high-buttoned jacket of rough brown tweed cloth, plain fawn trousers caught in knee-length leather boots, a small felt hat pulled down over sand-coloured hair, a stockily built man smiled viciously.

'Oh I'll point the way right enough, it be in that direction,' he jerked his head to the right, his eyes not leaving her face. 'You are going to meet with his lordship and from there it will be goal for you, hard labour for about five years.'

'Prison!' Maura gasped. 'But it was just a fish!'

'No!' The smile widened, claiming much of the swarthy

face. 'Not just a fish, it was his lordship's fish and you, my
wench, were caught stealing it. That don't go down well with
the master, not well at all.'

Narrow eyes playing slowly over her brought a shiver to
Maura's spine. 'I have said I am sorry, perhaps if I explain—'

'Would do you no good.' The eyes returned to her face and
now they held a calculating look. 'The master of Portington
Hall is not given to listening to the lies of thieves.'

Maura's head came up sharply. 'I am no thief!'

'Then what do you call that?' A booted foot touched the
stone holding the cooked trout.

'I did not know. How can a river belong to any one person?
God gave it for the benefit of all men.'

'And the government of England gave it to one man, Henry,
Lord Portington, and he has no truck with poachers. Oh of
course, perhaps you might explain . . . others before you have
tried that trick but not once has it worked, always punishment
has been the same, goal or the colonies, it makes no difference
to his lordship.'

'The colonies?' Maura's eyes showed her lack of understanding.

'It's a way we English have of dealing with the likes of you,
thieves, vagabonds, undesirables. Ship them off to the furthest
sides of the earth and leave them there to work themselves to
death.'

Leave Ireland her mother had said. Was this the way she
would leave it, a criminal banished for ever to some far-off
land?

'You are a young woman.' Hot eyes stroked her body. 'The
years left to you are many and every hour of them will be a
torment under the burning sun of the sugar islands or Australia.'

The sugar islands . . . Australia . . . she had never heard of
either! Maura watched the vicious smile fade, the heat in the
narrow eyes burn as they swept over her breasts.

'But –' the tip of a tongue licked moistly at thick lips '– there is another way, show me how sorry you are and his lordship need never hear of your thieving.'

'I . . . I have already apologised and will do so again.'

'And nicely I've no doubt, but words are not enough.'

Words were not enough! The shiver at Maura's spine became a tremble. She had been alone that day at the side of the brook, Padraig Riordan had seemed to appear from nowhere; it had been the same then as it was now. Padraig Riordan had stared at her with fire in his eyes just as this man was doing, was the outcome to be the same, would yet another man rape her?

'Words are all I have.'

The long-barrelled gun held between his hands lifted as she stepped backwards and the awful smile returned to his mouth. 'Not all,' he licked his lips again, 'strip, everything off, let's see the rest of what you have.'

'No!' The cry held all the horror, all the revulsion that flooded like a wave along every nerve.

'Shy, are we?' He jabbed the shotgun forward, striking the steel barrel against fingers clutching the shawl across her chest. 'No need to be, there is no one but me to see.'

'No, please.' Bright tears spilled quickly onto her cheeks. 'I . . . I will speak with your master, he can send me to prison, to the colonies . . .'

'Believe me, you would not fare as well there as you will here. There are men in those colonies, men starved of a pretty face and a soft body. Prisoners and warders they all hunger and when one is satisfied the next is waiting, and every day sees more of them arriving. Think of it, not once but night after night and every night, it will not cease even when your youth is gone and your pretty face is marked by the pox.'

'Stop . . . please!' Maura covered her ears with her hands but still she heard the vile laugh.

'It rests with you –' the shotgun tapped against each hand '– pleasure me or pleasure a host. Here it will last a short while and the heath is pleasant with the smell of heather, in the colonies it will go on for years with you lying with the stink of unwashed bodies touching your flesh, rats running over you as each man takes his turn—'

'No . . .' Maura's hands dropped to her sides. 'No more, I . . . I will do as you ask.'

Her fingers stinging from the pain of his blow she fumbled with the buttons fastening her blouse and all the while those hot voracious eyes watched, every movement adding to the lust that seethed in them.

His thick lips shining with spittle he thrust the gun forward, stroking the tip of the barrel over her breasts as her chemise fell to the ground. 'Sweet,' he said thickly, 'sweet enough to keep a man happy, give him those to suck and he could forget his troubles. But they are only half of what you have on offer and half of anything was never very satisfactory to Simeon Leech, with me it has to be the whole thing, so let's have the rest off.'

Holy Mother, why . . . why is this happening to me? Help me please . . . Blind with tears of fright and shame Maura tried to pray.

'I said strip!'

The sting of the shotgun across her hands snatched the breath from her lungs as Maura loosened her skirt, leaving it to lie about her ankles.

Laying the gun on the ground he removed his jacket then unfastened the buckle of a heavy belt, letting it slide to his feet.

'And the rest –' he grinned, plump fingers wresting open the buttons on his trousers '– the bloomers, let's not forget those.'

'I think we should do precisely that.'

'What the—' With his trousers halfway down his legs he turned, the grin disappearing as he saw a mounted rider watching from a short distance.

Glancing only briefly at Maura, her arms covering her breasts, the rider went on curtly, 'You may replace your clothing, young woman, you will no longer be required to perform any service Mr Leech may have imposed upon you. My apologies for the treatment you received, it will be dealt with.'

Grabbing her clothes Maura dressed as quickly as her shaking hands would allow. With the last button in place she turned towards the man on horseback, only then seeing the woman who had ridden up beside him. In acute embarrassment she kept her head lowered as she spoke.

'I . . . I did not know the river was privately owned, in . . . in Clonmacnoise we all . . . everyone can fish the waters. I . . . I'm sorry, I did not mean to steal, I have no money with which to pay for what I have taken but I will work . . .'

'Henry,' the woman rider smiled as she looked at Maura, 'that is quite the prettiest and certainly the most genuine remorse you can have seen.'

'They are good at that, your ladyship.'

'And you, Mr Leech are good at what? Terrifying a young girl until she submits to rape?' The woman's voice was hard.

'I wasn't . . . I mean . . . it wasn't rape, she offered.'

Lifting a gloved hand the man stilled the woman's reply, saying quietly, 'You are quite sure of that? Think carefully, Leech. This young woman offered her services?'

'It was her suggestion.' Struggling into his jacket the gamekeeper stared at Maura. 'I caught her fair and square as that trout there testifies, I told her as how your lordship don't take to poachers and that it was likely a prison sentence would follow on what she had done. She became tearful at that, saying as how she couldn't face being locked up and before I could do anything to prevent it she was half naked.'

'And you?' the man asked coldly. 'You could not prevent your own clothes being removed! Perhaps in her eagerness to avoid prison the young woman snatched your clothes away as well as her own.'

'My . . . my belt, it broke . . .'

'I see. And it pulled your coat off as it fell?'

Beside him the land owner's companion, elegant in deep blue velvet riding habit trimmed with white, a black silk top hat, the base wrapped around with a white muslin veil that hung down her back touching her tiny nipped-in waist, raised a cream-calf-gloved hand to her mouth in an attempt to contain her giggle.

Retrieving the gun the thick-set man broke it before balancing it over his left arm. 'I see your lordship understands.'

'I understand a great deal more than you think.' The rider nodded. 'I understand poachers must be dealt with if we are not to be robbed completely of game.'

'I thank your lordship.' The narrow eyes gleamed triumphantly at Maura. 'With your lordship's permission I'll take the girl and lock her in—'

'A moment, Leech!' The hand rose again. 'I said I understand a lot more than you think. For instance, I recognise fear when I see it and it was stark on this young woman's face; unfortunately, I am also acquainted with men's lust, I saw it often while serving with Her Majesty's regiments and I saw it again just now. I asked you to think carefully before you answered as to whether or not an offer was made to you, now I say the answer you have given is a lie.'

'No! It's no lie, I told you true.'

The rider's glare was contemptuous. 'Do not compound your conduct by lying.'

'I was doing it to protect your lordship's interests—'

'My interests!' The first glimmerings of anger showed on the face of the landowner. 'Since when have my interests been served by rape? Collect whatever belongings you have, you are to return to England, but take care I never hear of this sort of thing again or it will be yourself is bound for the colonies.'

With his gamekeeper out of sight the rider gathered the rein of his great bay horse.

'A moment, Henry.' His companion smiled at the girl she had been watching closely. 'What is your name?'

'Maura Deverell, ma'am.'

'Mmm,' the woman mused, watching Maura drop a curtsy. 'You said you would work in exchange for that fish.'

'I did, ma'am, I am no thief.'

Impressed by the quiet dignity of the answer the woman glanced at the man already impatient to be gone.

'Well, Henry,' she raised a finely shaped eyebrow, 'what do you think, shall we make the girl work for her breakfast?'

Her glance still averted, Maura did not see the small despairing shake of the head or the resigned smile spreading across the man's face when he answered.

'I think, my darling sister, you have enough maids and that another one to dance attendance upon you will be sheer stupidity, but then I never could deny you anything; bring the wench along if you want her.'

She had thanked them both. Following at a short distance behind the walking horses Maura's relief was tinged with doubt. The woman had given her the opportunity to recompense for taking that fish, but how long was that to take?

13

'Ye know what it is I be asking?'

Sat in the tiny clochan, the air of it musty with damp and smoke from the peat fire, Seamus felt the ghosts of the past close in on him. This had been the life of his childhood. It was such a place as this he had brought Siobhan after their marrying, in a cramped house such as this his sons had been born and it was men such as the one sat opposite him now, men he had used and cheated whenever the chance was given, who had helped him climb out of it. Why had he fought so hard, lied and deceived? He stared at the dull red glow of the fire. Had it only been so Siobhan could ride in a dog cart while other women of the villages walked, was it so that his sons could wear shoes while their sons wore wooden clogs? Pressing his teeth together so hard they hurt he tried to keep out the truth, but as always it defeated him. No, it whispered in his mind. It was none of those things, he had done what he did to show Mairead what she could have had had she chosen him, done it in return for being refused, done it for revenge just as he had murdered for revenge! But this time it would not be his hand would strike the blow.

'I be knowing so I do tinkers come and tinkers go, but I'll be asking the price afore I sets my tongue to promising – this one will go for good.'

Taking the tin cup into which his host had poured a liberal amount of potheen from a stone jar, Seamus wiped the rim of it with his fingers.

'The payment is twenty pounds.'

Silence followed, silence in which Seamus wanted to fling cup and drink at the unkempt head and run from the house. But do that and the deed he was asking would need to be done by himself. He could risk asking none in Clonfert, for that reason he had ridden the miles to Clareen.

'Twenty pounds to send a man to his grave? It be a paltry sum.'

Seamus's jaw clenched even harder. 'I've known men sent to their grave with no payment at all.'

At the other side of the fireplace another tin cup was raised, the message of the words understood.

'*Sláinte.*' The toast was given quietly.

Answering in kind, Seamus swallowed the liquid, the fire of it leaving a blazing trail the length of his gullet.

'*A Laon.*' His own potheen swallowed, the wiry figure held up one finger. 'This number of days will be seeing the job done.'

Shaking his head at the offer of more of the fiery drink, Seamus rose to his feet. He wished to spend no more time here with his ghosts than he had to.

'The twenty punts!' A greasy hand touched Seamus's sleeve. 'I'll not have the doing of what it is ye wants afore ye places the money in me hand.'

Counting out four white five-pound notes Seamus held back the last of them, a threat evident in eyes and voice. 'Be sure now ye do the job afore ye takes this to any *tábhairne*, ale can cause a man to meet with many an accident . . . many a *fatal* accident.'

'My word on it.' Thin fingers grasped the final note. 'These eyes will be seeing the inside of no ale house until what it is ye've paid for be finished.'

Already stooped to pass through the low doorway Seamus straightened, an icy smile touching his mouth as he turned to look once more at the tight ferret features watching him from the hearth. 'And my word on this –' it slithered like so many serpents across the tiny room '– fail me and those eyes will be seeing nothing but the inside of a grave! *Slan.*'

Gripping the banknotes in dirt-ingrained fingers the grinning man swept a mocking bow as the door of the clochan banged shut. '*Oiche mhaith* . . . good night to ye too, Seamus Riordan.'

There were many hours yet before dawn brought light enough to see his way with any clarity. Seamus reined his horse to a standstill. The decision to come to Clareen by way of the route that climbed north beside the Delour River, even though the mountain paths were rough, had been deliberate. Clochans were further between than on the flatter plain, that meant fewer people and he had no appetite for them. Being seen meant being talked of, that was something else he had no want of. This night's errand must be known of by no other than himself and the man who had taken his money. A Judas payment . . . the coin of betrayal! A sudden flash of lightning played over the jagged peaks of the nearby Slieve Bloom, a following peal of thunder rolling through the valleys. The drums of doom! Seamus set heel to the horse. But they did not beat for him.

'Steady . . . steady, lad.' He spoke softly to the animal, its hooves slipping on loose limestone shale made more treacherous by rain now sliding in sheets from a sky split by streak after brilliant streak.

Maybe he should not try returning to Clonfert! He reined in once more. The storm seemed set for the night and that could only mean the track becoming more difficult. He could turn off for Kinnity, stay the night there, or go on to Birr. But Birr held too many people. He brushed the rain from his face. He had been there many times with the wife whose estates were now his; invited by her English friends to their elegant Georgian houses strung along Oxmantown Mall, or to Emmet Square that played host to leading celebrities and where he had seen so many artists perform. There were comfortable lodgings in Birr, Dooley's Hotel would suit well enough. Persuaded by the thought of a dry bed and the companionship of a bottle of brandy if nothing more satisfying presented itself he half settled to the idea. But at the back of his mind other thoughts nibbled. Birr might no longer be high on his visiting list but that carried no guarantee he was forgotten there. Be seen in that town and tongues would be like to wag. Better he should press on, return to Clonfert before morning aired the streets; less that was seen soonest was forgot!

The decision final he spurred the animal forward, swearing loudly as a meteoric burst of light seemed to spear the ground at its feet, sending it backing away in terror.

A Judas payment! The phrase returned as the sky split again. But the disciple of old had regretted the selling of a man and taken his own life! The horse bucking in its fear, Seamus gripped the rein. It would not be the same with him, he would not tread the suicides' path, he felt no remorse for selling a man into hell; why should he when with it lay his own safety! And, as before, there would be no proof. Seamus Riordan would suffer no penalty.

A smile of triumph curving his mouth he glanced to where he knew the track rose to snake between the ridges of high rock, catching his breath as a vivid flash outlined a black silhouette of a rider perched on a crest.

The storm had him jittery as the horse! He blinked the clouding drops from his eyes and stared into the inky blackness. It had been a trick, an after-print of the lightning flash on his vision, he had only imagined—

Before he could finish the thought a cannonade of thunder blasted along the narrow valleys, gathering its own echoes, sound swelling with resound until the ground vibrated from the powerful full-throated roar, and with it all a flash that irradiated earth and sky, binding them together in a blazing flambeau of brilliant light.

The glare was blinding. Seamus threw up a hand to shield his face but not before he saw again the solitary shape against the luminescence; outlined, it seemed to be watching like a horseman of the apocalypse.

'Who . . . ?'

Seamus's call was swallowed by thunder pealing fresh from the raging heavens while lightning illuminated the terrified horse, which kicked the air as it reared then plunged from the narrow track, carrying its rider into the blackness beneath.

His father would not be returning. Padraig Riordan rode towards the house in Clonfert. He had spotted him leaving Clonfert and following the river south. To where, Portumna? Trailing his father at a distance he had soon discounted that destination, then when Kinnity also had been bypassed he had known where it was Seamus was headed. Not all of his father's secrets had been hidden from him; he had pursued him until seeing a tumbledown clochan set back from Clareen, the pigsty where Seamus's muck was spread. And the one that raked it? He would see no more dawns.

The storm had raged on but unlike Seamus he had thought better of braving it; one man had fallen from the narrow track, he would not add to the count. He had known from previous visits of the caves that riddled these hillsides and had led his own frightened horse to the shelter of one, remaining there until the storm passed. The sky had been thick and grey forcing the labours of dawn to be hard in its struggle to give birth to light before he rode slowly to that clochan. He had heard the snores before entering, potheen was a powerful sleeping potion and the little man had swallowed his medicine well. It had been so easy. A pillow across the face and in two minutes it was over. His victim had not known what was happening. Padraig smiled at the memory. What better way for a man to die . . . someone should thank him for the kindness of his act! Or should he count those five-pound notes enough? His father hadn't gone to that cottage on a good-will visit; knowing that, he had searched the man's pockets, careful to take only paper money and leaving the coins. To take every penny would point to robbery and that in turn might cause folk to think of murder; but to leave him as he had, pillow beneath his head, coins in his pocket, it seemed he had choked to death in his sleep. Whatever it was the man had been paid to do did not matter now, nothing mattered now. Slamming open the door of the house he gave no glance to the maid's scuttling like so many mice for the shelter of their holes. Seamus was dead and Eyrecourt House had a new master; but what of Liam . . . what of the misfit? Setting the heel of his boot against the study door Padraig kicked it shut. Like he said . . . *nothing* mattered any more.

'. . . *may ye ever know poverty* . . .'

Padraig laughed softly as he opened the iron safe Seamus had kept in the corner of this room. Those had been the words his father had flung at him but now they were dead as the man himself. There would be no more poverty for Padraig Riordan, those five-pound notes were not the only wealth that was to come via his father.

'. . . *no stick or stone, not one penny will pass from me to ye* . . .'

Lifting a plain metal box from the safe to the desk his laugh echoed again as he flipped back the lid.

'Wrong again, Father,' he smiled, 'now I have it all.'

'Have you found what it is you are looking for?'

Holding a sheaf of papers in his hand, Padraig lifted a glance to the figure of his brother.

'Simply looking through what is mine.'

'Yours?' Liam frowned. 'And what will Father have to say about that?'

Returning his glance to the papers, Padraig allowed a moment to pass before answering. 'Father will say nothing, for the simple reason of his being dead.'

'Dead!' Liam's gasp was loud in the quiet room.

'As the proverbial doornail.'

Pale eyes, so like the ones he had not bothered to close after descending the valley to look at his father, glittered cold as the face of that corpse.

'You—'

'Not me, brother.' Padraig interrupted. 'I only found him. It must have been last night's storm, lightning most likely frightened his horse so that it reared, taking him with it over the ridge.'

'Where exactly?' His own eyes showing he doubted the truth of the words Liam stepped further into the room, closing the door on any listening ears.

Liam already had his suspicions. Padraig flicked through the sheaf of papers, allowing himself time to think. To tell his brother their father had been returning to Clonfert would deepen those suspicions still further.

'The road that leads to Birr,' he said as the papers settled. 'We both know Seamus had a penchant for that town, maybe the colleens there are – how would you prefer I put it? – more amenable.'

'And what was it brought yourself to following that road?' Liam's thoughts flashed to the young woman who had not left her room since this man's leaving. 'Could it have been you've forgotten Niamh, forgotten you have a wife!'

'And where is it you would have me take a sick woman, to live in some hovel where she could dig peat to get her bread? Would you have her as well as myself driven from the house?'

'I would not, Niamh is ever welcome . . .'

'But *I* am not. The misfit is telling his brother he is not welcome in this house.' Letting the papers fall to the desk Padraig's glance met with Liam's. 'Have you not grasped what it is I'm telling you? Seamus Riordan is dead, and being as I am his elder son and therefore his heir it is you, my runt of a brother, you who may be unwelcome here. But this is not a time for quarrelling, while death is a quest in the house disagreement needs be put aside. I have already arranged for the bringing of the body home but there is the matter of the wake yet to be decided.'

The fact Padraig had not answered his question was not lost on Liam but custom and respect must be honoured. Seamus would be laid to his rest with no harsh words passing between his sons. But he could not remain under the same roof as the man who had raped Maura Deverell.

' 'Tis a kindly thing ye be after doing, I know the woman of the house would thank ye.'

And the daughter of the house, would she thank him or see his tidying of these pathetic little graves as an intrusion? Rising to his feet, dusting dark earth from his hands, Liam turned to face the woman who spoke.

'God smile on the mornin' of yer day.' The woman's eyes were bird bright beneath her shawl.

'And on the rest of your own.' Liam smiled. 'Do you think the woman of the house would be taking exception should we go inside and set ourselves upon a seat?'

'Mairead Deverell would be taking no exception, indeed it is a sup o' tay herself would be offering was she here to welcome a body, but then there's been no morsel of such in this clochan these weeks past.'

'Then 'tis fortune indeed saw the bringing of my own.'

'Ye ever were a kindly lad, sure and a sup o' tay will bring warmth to these old bones.'

What was this man about, why was he here? Sinead O'Toole's watchful eyes followed the movements of a figure grown straighter since she last had the seeing of him; true, heaven had not fully straightened that crooked shoulder, but it was no longer hunched into the neck.

Taking the tin cup Liam had rinsed with clean water before filling it with fresh brewed tea, Sinead regaded him as he sat with his own cup in hand.

'I hear Seamus Riordan – mercy be given his soul – lies dead in his grand house.'

Mercy be given his soul! Liam watched the gnarled fingers make the holy sign. He had not asked heaven's blessing, he had offered no prayer for his father nor stood beside the coffin to pay his respects. But how could he? It would be the act of a hypocrite to pretend respect where there was none. As with love, that had been beaten out of him long years past.

'There be a doubt inside of ye as to the manner of yer father's passing,' Sinead spoke again, 'but there be need for none for 'twas an accident. Don't be after asking how it be I know the truth of what I say nor how it is I be knowing that bitterness be lodged in yer heart; take a firm hold to it be my counsel to ye, refuse to let it grip ye so tight ye cannot breathe, for bitterness be a canker that destroys the soul of men. It ate away that of Seamus Riordan and it will do so again to that of his first-born, but ye . . . ye have yer mother's heart and yer mother's soul, in ye be love and if ye give it the chance to live there also be forgiveness.'

Forgiveness! Liam stared into the depths of his cup. For his father maybe; he could forgive him for though rape was detestable it had been brought about by love, a love refused but one that not one single day of his living had seen forgotten. Seamus Riordan had loved Mairead Deverell with an abiding depth, loved her till his dying. But the same could not be said of Padraig. He had raped a girl his heart felt no love for, raped her to satisfy his own lust, and that could not be forgiven!

'I thank you for your asking mercy for my father and for the counsel you offer—'

'It is a hard path ye've trod all of yer life,' Sinead interrupted gently, 'and there be miles of the same lies ahead. Yer heart be breaking for love of the daughter of this house, one ye would have taken for yer own and blessed heaven for the flower it gave, even though the bud of it had been picked by your own brother. But Maura Deverell too has a path to tread, one destiny marks for her to follow.'

With surprise in his eyes Liam stared at the woman, every line on her face trailing wisdom. 'How . . . how did you know about . . .'

A smile touching her mouth Sinead gave a slow shake of her head. 'The rape of Maura Deverell? How would I not know . . . wasn't it myself brought her into this world, is it not myself had the watching of her grow, does not my heart as that of ye'self have the loving of her? There is not a fibre of that girl I don't have the knowing of and this I tell you, like her mother she holds no ill will towards ye'self, she places no blame at yer door for the actions of others. Ye have a place in the heart of Maura Deverell, one that no man will rob ye of.'

And she has a place in mine, one that will never be given to anybody but her.

It seemed the old woman had almost read his mind. Liam felt those bird-bright eyes probe deep as he took the cup held out to him and refilled it with hot strong tea.

'Maura Deverell is gone from Clonmacnoise, I fear she may go from Ireland itself. I wish she would have accepted my help but her pride was master of her needs; yet my heart she cannot refuse for it has been hers from childhood, although she does not know it she will carry it with her always.'

He had avoided her eyes but he could not hide the pain that

lay behind his words. Sinead O'Toole took the cup, nursing it between her hands, feeling the warmth seep from its metal body. Maura Deverell was not the only child whose growing she had watched. His childhood too she had observed, seeing in his young face all of one man's spite and rejection, and as the first years of manhood had overtaken him she watched bewilderment and unhappiness overtaken by acceptance that a father's pride could never be his nor would a father's love; and though with their moving to the home of Seamus's new bride she had not seen him often, that same hurt was still there and with it a new and equally obvious pain. Again Liam Riordan felt his love unaccepted; could it be that as in childhood he had been afraid to speak of it? Did his coming to this tiny house in some way relieve that pain, bring him to where he could be with her if only in dreaming?

Draining the cup of its contents she placed it on a table, noting its freedom from any speck of dust as was the whole room. His doing? It could be none other. Stood in the watery light of late autumn she drew her shawl about her head, her glance lifting to the distant mountains. They had their heads in the glory of heaven while folk such as she must bear theirs in the miseries of a cruel earth.

'Maura Deverell be gone from Clonmacnoise.'

Liam watched the face that turned to him. It seemed age was suddenly gone from it, the eyes brilliant with a glow that was no reflection of the pallid sun, and the voice, it was no longer cracked by the years but was strong, strong with a strange unmistakable power. His pulse throbbing he listened to words that, though issuing from the mouth of Sinead O'Toole, seemed to come from outside of her.

'She will go from these shores to a different one, but Ireland be a special land. The beauty of it be engraved deep at birth, it stamps itself upon the heart and the seal of it never fades; its voice calls to the soul with the softness of its valleys and the songs of its streams, drawing its own back to its gentle heart. Maura Deverell will feel that sweet pain.'

The words of the woman had ended there. Liam now watched the black-robed figure walking towards the narrow wooden bridge that crossed a finger of the Shannon. He had urged her to say more but she had simply looked at him with those bird-bright eyes and, wishing him peace of the day, had turned and left.

'. . . *she will go from these shores* . . .'

The words swam in his brain. The land of Ireland was indeed a special land, a land that heaven might have kept for itself except for the blight that took the food from the mouth and the landlords that drained money from the pocket of its poor. Maura Deverell might well feel that sweet pain but Ireland's siren song would not be so seductive that it would lure her back to Clonmacnoise.

14

The terrible storm of a few nights ago seemed to have washed the sky clear of clouds. Maura glanced at the gleaming vault that stretched into forever then at the sweep of land rolling green and gentle beneath it. She had thought how beautiful it was that day she had followed behind those horses. Wide velvet parkland cushioning the river had grazed deer that stared with large brown eyes, trees had stood with branches spread like the skirts of girls dancing at a ceilidh; it had all been so gentle and perfect but none of it had prepared her for the grace and symmetry of the handsome building set at its heart.

The woman had heard the loud gasp that had escaped her lips as they had crested a low hill which shielded the house from view until you stood above it.

'Welcome to Portington Hall.'

Maura remembered the smiles that had accompanied the words, the man and woman could have been welcoming royalty. But that had been almost her last glimpse of that laughing pair for she had been left at the stables, instructions given to a groom to take her to the kitchens. The woman's smile had been the last she had seen. The groom had handed her over to an undergroom who, seeing it as beneath his high station to deal with a ragged peasant girl, promptly passed her to a stable lad; and so it had gone on with herself given over from one to another.

The land was beautiful even in the months of winter, what she had seen of this house was grand and the people who had pushed her on to others were fed and wore clean clothes that bore no patches, so why did few of them smile?

She had tried to be friendly but her efforts to speak were cut short. 'We all have our work to do and it leaves a body no time to stand in idle chatter!' Dressed in cap and all-covering apron so white it stung the eyes to look at it, a dark-haired woman had stared down a nose thin and sharp as a knife blade, her tone brooking no argument. Not that she would have dared offer any. The nervousness that had gripped her as the head cook had gone on to bemoan the fact of 'every waif and stray in the county being landed in my kitchen' had stayed with her the rest of that day and for weeks following with her rushing to do every task set her, but listening now to that harsh voice berating a sobbing kitchen maid, Maura felt her nervousness turn to anger. There was no call to treat those stationed beneath her worse than any decent man would treat cattle!

'And you, filthy child of the bog –' the woman's anger switched as Maura turned from the low sink '– stand there with your ears flapping and I'll lay the rod to your back!'

Her reply quietly spoken, its gentle lilt contrasting with the harder English tone, Maura shook her head briefly.

'No, ma'am, you will take no rod to my back. A child of the bog I may be but I do not speak to others with a tongue the like of sour milk, nor do I have to prove my own worth by beating girls less fortunately placed.'

Her mouth open with the shock of being answered back, the cook stared at the girl whose head was held proud as that of any fine visitor to this house.

'I counted myself fortunate when brought here by your mistress but I have since realised I was mistaken.'

'You . . . you were mistaken!' the woman spluttered. 'Who do you think yourself to be!'

Her own eyes hard as brown stone, Maura held the woman's vicious stare. 'Why . . . have you not said it yourself? I am a child of the bog. But an Irish bog can be preferable to the kitchen of an English mansion for it speaks no bitter word nor raises any hand to strike. There are no chairs beside it and no table laden with food but its heart is warm and the heather that bounds it provides a soft bed. I would ask my thanks be given to the master of this house and again to his sister for the kindness they themselves showed to me, but I doubt they would be given them. As for yourself, I feel I have nothing for which to express anything but regret.'

Taking the shawl from a peg set alongside the scullery door, Maura swung it about her shoulders and, head still high, walked from the house.

'You took quite a bit of catching up with, was my brother's house so distasteful to you that you had to run away so quickly?'

The smile behind the question was free of rancour and found its own answer in the one curving Maura's lips.

'The house was not distasteful, it is a very beautiful home—' She broke off not wishing to discredit the acid-tongued cook.

'Oh dear, you too.' Eugenie Stratford, sister of Henry, Lord Portington, pulled a wry mouth. 'I have to admit I feared the same thing had happened again when I learned you had left. I have asked Henry to dismiss the woman time and again but he will not hear of it; she was the wife of a man who saved Henry's life in a place called the Khyber Pass. It is in India somewhere or other. Apparently the man fought off one of the raiding tribesmen who was about to cut my brother's throat, and got himself killed instead. It was very heroic and I will be eternally grateful, though why we must suffer that woman . . . a pension and a little house in England would be more than enough, but Henry says he has a duty towards her so she must stay . . .' The delicate shoulders in their pale blue tulle lifted despairingly. 'And as a consequence we suffer her sharp tongue; but how long I will go on suffering it . . .' She paused again then smiled. 'However I did not ask you to return so I could burden you with my displeasure but to try to make reparation for the rudeness of our cook. If I promise she will never again be allowed to treat you as I have been informed she did will you stay here at Portington?'

Would she stay? Maura thought of the beautiful corridors she had walked through in coming to this private sitting room, the carpet thick as autumn heather, the spacious landing larger than any clochan she had ever been in, paintings hanging by golden chains on every wall and the breathtaking silver of bowls and vases glittering almost everywhere; surely this must be the way queens lived.

But she was no queen and Ireland could no longer be her home. Her hands straight down at her sides she stood stiffly, afraid to move in case she brushed against some beautiful object that would break, that her boots would leave their mark on a carpet the colour of fresh cream. 'You were very kind that morning.' She swallowed awkwardly. How could she say what she must without sounding ungrateful? 'You believed me when I said I did not know that by taking a trout from the river I was stealing—'

'Is that what it was, a trout? How clever of you to know, how on earth did you catch it?'

'I tickled it.'

'You tickled it!' The other woman's delighted laugh pealed out. 'You tickled a fish! I never heard of such a thing, how absolutely marvellous, you must teach me how to do it then I can show Henry I am not the empty head he says I am.'

The woman seemed to have taken it for granted she would stay. Maura curled her fingers into her palms, searching for the words that would say she would not.

'Ma' am . . .'

Eugenie Stratford had reached for a cord, about to summon

a maid, but the apologetic tone caused her to stop. Her hands falling to her lap she looked kindly at Maura.

'Do you not wish to stay at Portington?' she asked gently. 'If it is because of that horrible man you need not be afraid, he will not bother you again. He has been returned to England. You see my brother has a genuine affection for this country, that is why he chooses to live here rather than on his estates in England. He knows of the unfairness practised upon tenants by the representatives of landowners and he will not allow that to happen here by being what is called an absentee landlord. I think you will find that those of your countrymen who live on the estate are happy to do so.'

'I'm sure they are, ma'am.' Maura's fingers folded and unfolded though her eyes were steady. 'But I cannot stay here . . . you see, I promised my mother . . .'

A frown nestled between wide blue eyes, pretty blonde ringlets trembled as the attractive woman gave a slight shake of her head. 'You promised your mother you would not stay at Portington Hall!'

She could not tell all that had happened at Clonmacnoise, of her being raped, of her fears that Padraig Riordan might yet take it into his head to find her and drag her back of Clonfert. To speak only the truth would be to say all of that and more; for the first time in her life Maura was prepared to lie.

'I have no family in Ireland, my parents and brother are dead.' That at least was the truth. She took a breath, her heart asking forgiveness for what must come next. 'Before her death I promised my mother I would go to England. She had a distant cousin who had gone there . . . a town called Birmingham . . . I promised if I could find her I would make my home with her.'

'I see, and of course you must honour the promise you have given.' The look in those blue eyes was one of understanding. 'But, if I might ask, how are you to get to England? Believe me, I intend no rudeness but passage to that country . . .'

The question though unfinished left no doubt as to its meaning. Maura's fingers touched against skirts still bearing marks of heath and mud regardless of the brushing she had given them. Her poverty was obvious. Her cheeks colouring to pink she answered quietly, 'I hoped, once I found my way to the coast, I could find work, earn enough money to pay my fare.'

Once she got to the coast! Eugenie Stratford hid her smile. The girl most likely did not know which part of the coastline to head for, which of the ports would have ships bound for England. No family, no parents and it seemed definitely no money.

'Maura – I may use your name?' Receiving a nod, Eugenie went on, 'I have a proposal. As I told you, my brother prefers to stay here in Ireland but he allows me to return home to England as often as I wish. I am making the journey next week and, if you are agreeable, I would be happy for you to travel with me.'

'That is very kind, ma'am . . .'

Her puzzled frown not quite disappearing, the woman watched the pink of Maura's cheeks deepen. 'You have reservations . . . can it be you have arranged to travel with someone else?'

'No . . . yes . . . I mean . . .'

'Exactly what is it you mean?' The smile accompanying the words showed gentle amusement at the stammer.

'It's just that I promised Bridget . . .'

'Another promise, you should be less lavish with them.'

This woman had been more than kind and her offer of travel to England was wonderful, it was madness to refuse; but even as that thought came so did the memory of a small pinched face lined with tears, a young girl begging to be taken with her anywhere, away from the vindictive hand of the cook.

'Who is Bridget?'

It was gently asked but Maura winced as if it were a lash. The groom sent to ask her to return to this house had been given orders to assure her she was under no pressure, the mistress simply wanted to speak with her and she would be free to leave the moment she wished; had word of what she was told filtered into the kitchens? It must have done, for as she crossed from the stable block to the rear of the house the scullery maid had run towards her, the mark of a fresh blow evident on her cheek. 'I know yourself will be leaving again,' she had sobbed, 'take me with ye, please, 'tis no trouble I'll be after giving . . . ye have my promise.' And she had given the girl hers. They would leave Portington Hall together . . . but how to explain that to its mistress?

With jangling nerves Maura forced her reply. 'Bridget is one of your scullery maids. Like myself, she is alone in the world. She . . . she is unhappy here and asked could she go with me.'

'Has the girl been mistreated?' Eugenie Stratford nodded at the silence following her question. 'I see the handiwork of Clara Maynard in this. I shall speak to my brother, though I fear his sense of loyalty will not see her dismissed. However, if the girl wishes, she too may travel to England with the offer of a place in one of our houses there.'

Stammering her thanks, Maura followed the prim figure of a maid come to take her back to the kitchens.

It was the answer to prayers she had not dared whisper. Travelling with the sister of so important a man as Lord Portington meant all danger was over. There were no more threats could hang over her head, she was free of the menace that was Padraig Riordan.

The wake held for the passing of their father was finally over. Accidental death had been the magistrate's finding and people for miles around had come to pay respect beside the heavy coffin stood in the morning room, tall white candles at head and foot spilling soft yellow light in the darkened room. Respect? Liam stared out of the window that for the first time in seven days had its curtains drawn back. How much of it had been genuine and how much a social obligation? The poorer folk held no love for Seamus Riordan; and his wealthy English friends? It had been clear that for them it had been a duty paid to the memory of his late wife, a duty exercised as briefly as was decently possible.

'There be a gentleman asking to see ye.'

'That was prettily done, Regan, we should see about having you put with Mrs Riordan, a *private* maid.' Padraig Riordan laughed at the girl's obvious discomfort.

'Leave that child alone!' Liam turned as the maid fled from the room.

'Leave her for you, is that what you mean, brother?'

'Shut your filthy mouth!' Liam's eyes blazed.

'Tut, tut!' Padraig rose, slow and easy, the newspaper he had been reading falling to the floor. 'The runt is not pleased. Or could it be he is worried his days of comfortable living might be at an end?'

'Comfortable living! My years of living with the father newly gone to his grave were never comfortable.'

'Ah, the twisted back, Seamus never could come to terms with that, one son a replica of his own stature and strength while the other was a deformed misfit. I wonder was my mother unfaithful, did a lover father her crook-back child?'

It was lightning quick. A first struck out and Padraig was reeling backwards. 'Say what it is you wish about me,' Liam hissed, 'but you'll speak no evil against my mother.'

Gaining his balance, Padraig's glare was pure venom. This was the fourth blow struck by that runt, there would be no fifth! Touching a hand to the sting of his chin he followed slowly from the room.

His condolences brief, the man both brothers knew as their

father's solicitor took the chair behind the heavy desk, waiting until they too were seated before opening the sheaf of papers drawn from a black leather valise.

'The last Will and Testament—'

'There be no need to go reading every last word!' Padraig's bruised temper simmered. 'My brother and myself are not fools, we know the paper in your hand holds the last words of Seamus Riordan and that those words say everything that was his is now mine, so there is no more need of your staying.'

Looking steadily over the top of horn-rimmed spectacles the solicitor answered, 'Seamus Riordan paid money to have me read his Will and I will not go taking that and not doing the job. Should it be that like a child ye cannot sit quiet to listen then I'll not take it insulting that ye leave the room; though it be advising ye I am to hear what it is be in this document.'

The rebuke adding its sting to the blow delivered by Liam, Padraig glared his annoyance.

'Then read it!' he snarled. 'And be sure of this, you'll have no more dealings with this house!'

Nothing . . . nothing was his! Padraig stared at the spot where only the day before the coffin of his father had rested.

'You did it,' he muttered, 'you did all that you threatened. "No stick or stone, not one penny will pass from me to ye". Those were the words you used to me and the ones you caused to be written in that Will, so be it. But they were not the only words you spoke that day, 'twas yourself said I be son to you no longer, but the tie of blood cannot be broken by words. I am the son of your body, the evil that tainted you taints me. Equals we were, Father, but from this day I swear the spite that drove you will find deeper life in me. Rape will not be sufficient for the girl responsible for robbing me of my true inheritance, she must pay more, much more . . . long and slow will Maura Deverell pay—'

Behind him the quiet closing of the door ended the bitter tirade but it was not banished from his mind. Swinging about he smiled mockingly at his younger brother.

'So, you are master of Eyrecourt, the misfit is the new valley king . . . we must all pay homage.'

Making no reply Liam walked to the window, looking out onto the spacious well-kept gardens. For all his faults, and they were not few, Seamus had kept house and grounds in good order; it was only the people, the tenants of his land he had shown no consideration for. But to leave all of this to him, to the son he had always thought of no consequence, of having no worth . . . Yet it was no gift of love, nor was it bequeathed from the sense of what might be best for Clonfert; it was from gall. Padraig and their father had clashed more bitterly than usual and as a consequence Seamus had written his elder son out of his Will. It was an act of malice, an obdurate cruelty that gained Seamus nothing, but it provided him, Liam, with the means of carrying out that self-made promise, the promise that Padraig would answer to him for the harm done Maura Deverell. He could see him turned from this house, from the very valley itself, taking with him the portion allotted by Seamus, that of the clothes he stood up in. But what of Niamh, what of the wife his brother had virtually ignored from the day of their wedding, could he see her denied what small comfort Eyrecourt provided?

'Father's Will has changed nothing.' He turned, seeing the mockery fade from pale eyes but the anger in them remained hard and glittering. 'This house will continue to be home to you and to Niamh for as long as you wish.'

'Charity!' Padraig laughed acidly. 'I am to live on my brother's charity!'

'Will it be so different from the life you were leading only last week, the life you have lived for years!'

Blunt as a fist the words punched through the armour of

Padraig's anger, leaving his mind whirling. This brother was new to him, this one would not turn away as he had always done before.

'Tell me, Padraig,' Liam threw every word, aiming them like missiles, 'living in another man's home, everything you touch and use provided by him, if you do not call that living on another's charity then what do you call it? We have both lived our lives on charity so why the sudden change now . . . why the aversion?'

'A father providing for his child cannot be termed charity, it is the natural order of things, I took nothing that was not rightfully mine.'

'And Maura Deverell, was her maidenhead yours to take as well? Did you see what you did to her as being in the natural order of things?'

'It bothers you, doesn't it?' Padraig's mouth resumed its sneer. 'But it shouldn't, for was she never touched by any man she would not turn to you . . . no woman would.'

No woman would! It was not the sting of those last words that hammered like nails into his heart, for no other woman mattered to him. Liam felt the truth tear at him. It was Maura Deverell, she was the only one he had ever wanted. But he would never speak to her of love.

None of the pain of that realisation showed on his face but Liam's reply held a cold condemnation.

'That might be my misfortune, but yours lies in having to buy a woman or take her in rape. Tell me, Padraig, is there or has there ever been a woman come to you in love . . . even Niamh?'

It was cruel and cutting but in his own misery Liam felt no remorse. There would be no more turning the other cheek to his brother's blows, verbal or otherwise.

'What is done is done.' He went on calmly, ignoring the gasp of rage spitting at him across the quiet room. 'To tell you

I had no idea of what our father intended will no doubt be
disbelieved, that again I cannot help; the simple fact is the
contents of that Will were as much a blow to me as they were
to you.'

'A blow from which you'll recover damn quick!'

'Let us say I'll not be dying of it.'

No. Padraig turned away, concealing the thought that had
pale eyes gleaming like ice-covered stone. Let's not say you'll
not be dying of it, for I think you will, brother. The misfit will
not be master for long.

15

‘I'm so glad herself said I could go along with you.’

Huddled in an iron-framed bed in a tiny room at the top of the large house the young girl watched Maura brushing her long hair.

‘The others said sure an’ I wouldn't be allowed and that I'd have to be running away if it was away I wanted to be, but I don't have the courage to be doing that.’

‘What others?’ Maura turned towards the girl.

‘Them in the kitchens, they said ’twas running away I'd have to be after doing.’

With the brush halfway through a thick strand of hair, Maura paused, her glance holding to the thin face. Why should the girl want to run away, wasn't this house warm and dry with a bed and a meal?

‘Bridget, why would you want to run away?’ She put the brush on the plain scrubbed washstand as the girl went on as though not hearing the question.

‘Sure an’ the house be warm an’ I be given a bed and a meal but—’

‘But?’ Maura watched the fear spring into the girl's eyes.

‘ ’Tis the little people.’

‘The little people!’

‘Shh!’ The girl shot a quick glance at the window. ‘Don't be after laughing at them for ’tis a strong dislike they have of that.’

‘I wouldn't to do anything so disrespectful, but why be afraid?’

''Cos since my mammy died I be without kin and the fairy people spirit away young folk who be alone in the world and 'tis never again do they be seen.'

The room was cold, no fire being allowed to take the chill from night air creeping in under the eaves, but that did not account for the shiver that ran through the girl's thin body; she had been thoroughly frightened, but by what?

Her hair plaited neatly for the night, Maura sat on the edge of the bed. 'Now who was it told you such tales?'

Eyes wide and almost as black as her raven hair swamped the thin face. 'It's not tales.' She shot another glance at the uncurtained window. 'It's the truth, they've seen it . . . they've seen it many times.'

'Who?' Maura asked gently. 'And what is it they've seen?'

'The servants of the house. That be why many have no smile for 'tis the awful truth they've seen, young folk taken by the little people.'

'Have you seen that happen?'

Clutching the covers she had thrown over her face the girl made no reply. Despite the cold touching her bones, Maura tried again.

'Bridget, have you seen that for yourself, have you seen anyone being taken?' Beneath the covers the girl's head shook and Maura smiled. 'Then how do you know the truth of it, how do you know it isn't a story made up to frighten you?'

'They . . . the others . . . they wouldn't be after lying.'

'No, I don't think they would,' Maura answered the muffled voice, 'but maybe they are being just a little mischievous.'

'Not Mrs Maynard, that one wouldn't have the knowing of the ways of a smile nor yet how to be mischievous.'

Not all mischief is done in fun. A vision of the hard-faced cook flashed across Maura's mental vision. And not all stories are told to bring pleasure.

'Is it Mrs Maynard told you?'

Eyes like black saucers peered over the top of the rough twill sheet.

'Herself said there had been young folk taken many times, lads and girls like me who were alone, that the fairy folk—'

'That is nonsense!' Maura drew the sheet away, smiling at the scared little face beneath it.

'No, no it's not! Sure and haven't others told me the same . . . them young folk here one day and then the next gone where no mortal eye can ever have the seeing of them, it can only be the little people.'

Climbing into the bed she had been given to share, Maura could feel the trembling of fear. The stupid lies of the cook had the girl terrified.

'Bridget,' she said softly, 'before your mother and father died did you ever know or hear of the little folk doing harm to people?' Beside her the dark head shook. 'Then why is it do you think they should spirit you away?'

'I only know it's been done. The maids and the stable boys they all know. Last time were just afore I was brought to this place. 'Twas himself, the master, had the deciding of that. I was brought before the bench for taking berries from the hedge – sure an' had I known it was stealing I was after doing then I'd never have picked them so I wouldn't – being the magistrate as well as the owner of the land, himself said I wasn't to be gaoled but brought to Portington Hall where I would be taken on as a servant. I was given the position of scullery maid, replacing a girl who only the day before had been found missing so she had, taken, said Mrs Maynard, same as the others by the little people.'

'Well you are not alone any more and soon we will be gone from here.' And free of the spiteful tongue of Mrs Maynard, Maura thought. She blew out the candle and lay open eyed in the darkness. That woman must know the young people had run away, frightened off by her sharp tongue and acid sourness, so had invented those stories to cover herself. The master of Portington and his sister would not take kindly to her behaviour so it was hidden behind those lies. But what pleasure could it give to make a young life, already hard, even harder by frightening a young girl half out of her wits?

Eyrecourt was to be his home as it had always been. Padraig spurred the horse on, feeling the carriage wheels bump over the rough path. *As it had always been!* That was the problem, the cloud blighting his life. Since his father married the English widow he, Padraig, had been the heir, the promise of one day becoming sole master, holding the temper that so often threatened to separate him from Seamus; and now Seamus was gone, the valley king was dead. And the crown prince? He was deposed.

The hand holding an ivory-handled whip rose and fell, cutting sharp across the animal's sweating flank. It was Liam had inherited Eyrecourt, Liam who was master. But not for long. His face a mask of anger, Padraig brought the whip whistling through the quiet air. By God, not for long!

He would have refused the runt's offer but that would mean having nothing but what the selling of a few items brought; true, the proceeds were good but, like his allowance, that money was too soon gone. Bitterness and frustration behind the slash of the whip had the animal cry in pain but Padraig was impervious to any feelings other than his own. Only by accepting his brother's charity had he kept home and his allowance from the estate. That had been added to, a little more of his brother's charity. Padraig swallowed hard but the action did not clear his throat of bile. Nothing Liam gave in charity would be enough, nothing short of their father's entire properties would be enough. He was meant to be master of Eyrecourt and master he would be, the valleys would not be ruled by any misfit.

Approaching the town he brought the horse to a gentle trot, allowing it time to cool off before he entered Tullamore. He wanted no inquisitive stares. Following the road that led through the busy centre to the Grand Canal, he drove to a group of buildings fronting the waterway. No one would give a second thought to a carriage being brought directly onto the wharf, goods were often collected personally by people not trusting the clumsy hands or rickety vehicles of carters; he would be thought no exception.

At the end of the quay he stopped before a low-arched warehouse then, glancing both ways, drove the carriage inside.

The tea house was full with customers. Padraig stood for a moment looking around at the tables covered with blue chequered cloths and plain white china. Lord, this was no place for a man, he would rather be in a tavern with a tankard of porter to quench his thirst.

'There be room here if you have no dislike of sharing.'

'None at all.' Padraig glanced to where a man had raised his hand. 'My thanks to you.'

'My daughter.' The man answered loudly then smiled at a dark-haired young woman sat beside him. 'It be her birthday and for a treat I brought her to the town to have the choosin' of a trinket.'

'It will need be a pretty one if it is to match its owner.' Padraig removed his hat as he smiled at the girl.

'You have brought the goods?'

Tea was brought by a plump waitress and the man glanced at Padraig as they were left alone.

Padraig answered without looking up from pouring milk into his cup, 'Yes, there are three pieces this time and each of good quality and without blemish so it's a decent price I'll be wanting.'

'Could it be you are after being dissatisfied? Maybe you should look to sell your pieces elsewhere.'

Dark hair caught the gleam of light from the window and the eyes looking straight into his were challenging.

'To be sure herself was meaning no offence.' His features dark and weather-beaten as the girl's were fresh and clear, the man smoothed the threatened rift.

'I will not say there was none taken –' the woman's hard stare remained with Padraig '– there are many like you in Ireland wanting a channel through which to sell their stolen goods, take care you do not find yourself at the end of that line.'

For a moment it felt he could not contain the rage boiling inside him. No woman had ever dared speak to Padraig Riordan this way.

'The price will be the usual one, take it or leave it!' With her skirts rustling the woman rose, now allowing her voice to be heard by those around. 'I can't be after waiting any longer, it's too excited I am; please let us be going now, Father.'

Bastard! The anger in Padraig found its vent as minutes later he followed from the tea house. The price stayed as usual though the finding of the pieces grew more difficult and the taking of them more hazardous with every time!

Making his way to a side street he entered a tavern, a tankard would help him think, but it would do nothing to ease the smarting of being upbraided by a woman!

'You'll be after accepting what be offered.' The man from the tea house spoke softly.

Crossing to a table set in a shadowed corner of the smoky room Padraig set down his tankard before answering.

'It's no longer a fair price . . . the risk has increased.'

'Sure an' when was life ever fair?' The other man placed two glasses of potheen on the table. 'For the likes of us it's a case of you takes it or you leaves it an' that one knows you not be leaving it.'

No he would not be leaving it, the money he got for what he

stole was too much to lose. Had he inherited all of Seamus's wealth then he might have whistled a different tune but as things were then this business must go on.

'. . . *may ye ever know poverty* . . .'

Words that had burned themselves into his mind flared again now. Picking up the glass the man had placed beside his tankard, Padraig swallowed a mouthful of the raw spirit, feeling the bite of it against his throat. That part of Seamus's hopes for him would never come true, not if he had to rob all of Ireland of her choicest pieces.

'You'll be wanting me to deliver what it is you brought?'

Nodding, Padraig set the glass down on the rough wood table. 'I will, and have yourself count the payment for I have no trust in that one.'

'You know that the taking of delivery has been put back some few days?'

'And the money?'

It seemed the leathery face would crack as the man smiled. 'That has the putting back along of it.'

'Damn!' Padraig spat. 'That's a nuisance could be done without!'

Having had the glasses refilled, the other man lifted his. 'Certainly it could be a bit of a one but then a ceilidh provides a man with cover for more than the tickling of a colleen.'

He was right. Padraig's brain moved quickly. A celebration with everyone within miles come to join in, and half of them returning to their homes with the brain washed from their heads by the potheen, gave the perfect opportunity for a man to take whatever he pleased. Lifting his own glass he returned the smiling '*slàinte*'. Maybe next time they met there would be more than three pieces!

'Will yourself be providing a ceilidh?'

'Clonfert will be celebrating,' Padraig answered. 'The safe bringing to bed of the English queen will be danced to there as in other parts.' That woman was regular as a milch cow, he thought swallowing his liquor. She dropped a newborn every other year while his wife . . . his wife remained childless. If Niamh had given him a son then Seamus would not have done what he did, he would never have changed his Will.

'We all must dance to the English drum but only until the day when Ireland frees herself of the drummer.' The other man set his glass hard on the table.

'The coming of it be soon.' Padraig mouthed a reply he knew was looked for though he cared neither way. Clonfert would be his by right of title deed, as for its people, what difference to them who sat in the master's seat!

'Do the goods be waiting in the usual place?'

The man was on his feet as Padraig answered. 'The carriage is in the yard of the warehouse, take what is inside, and remember –' he looked up '– the money, all of it, by this time next week.'

Watching the greasy smile as his companion turned away, he tasted the returning bitterness on his tongue. God damn you, Seamus! he thought. God damn you to hell!

'I am sorry there are such feelings of animosity between you, brothers should be united in friendship as well as in blood, but Padraig is swift to anger and his tongue often says what his heart does not mean.'

He could laugh at that. Liam looked at the woman trying so loyally to defend her husband. He could tell her that never once in his life had Padraig Riordan spoken a word he did not mean. But the hurt in those soft eyes was sore enough, he would not add to it.

'We both know that,' he lied gently, 'and we both know that the closest of brothers sometimes have their diverse opinions and that is all it is between Padraig and myself, a difference of opinion, and you, Niamh, are not to fret over such a trifle.'

A trifle! Niamh poured tea from a silver pot. That it was not. She had seen the rage on that handsome face darken to hate as her husband spoke of the new master of Eyrecourt, sensed the threat that pulsed along every line of that lithe body. Losing his inheritance to another was no trifle for Padraig Riordan, even though that other was his own kin.

'I have asked for us to move from this house, to take a place that would be our own.'

'Eyrecourt is your home.'

Across from him dusky eyes dominated a pale wan face.

'But it is not *ours*,' she said quietly, 'not in the way Padraig would have it . . . his and only his. Do you not see, Liam, there can be no peace in this house; losing Eyrecourt is a tumour in his soul that will grow and grow until it consumes us all.'

Watching the shadows of pain flicker across the pale face, Liam felt pity for her well up inside him. Niamh, too, was a misfit. She had produced no child, no heir for Padraig Riordan and for that reason, if for no other, he despised her, casting her off like some unwanted toy. She had suffered as he had, but maybe for her there was a way to end the unhappiness.

Placing the delicate porcelain cup on the heavily chased silver tray he went to sit beside her on the primrose silk sofa.

'Tumours can sometimes be cured,' he said, taking one wasted hand, 'as can unhappiness. Eyrecourt can still be Padraig's, I will give it to him.'

'Do you really think that would take the chagrin away? No,' the dark head shook slowly, 'the wound your father inflicted would fester still. What he had thought his by right of birth passed to him of his brother's charity . . . ! That would bring no healing.' Nor would it drain the poison. Niamh fell silent, letting the rest of her words exist only in her mind. Nothing would ever cleanse her husband's heart of that.

'Then *I* will leave Eyrecourt, find some small—'

'No!' Niamh's head shook more sharply. 'This house is

yours and it must remain yours. Listen to me, Liam. Clonfert, its tenants and those of the valleys suffered under your father's hand, he took the money from their pockets, but place them under Padraig and 'tis the blood from their veins he will take. His greed is not like that of Seamus, he will not buy a tenant's holding, he will wait like a vulture until starvation drives people away or sees them laid in the ground.'

And that would be soon if the potato sickness crossing the land became a blight. Liam thought of the fields he had visited, of the sickly smell coming from the land.

'You must remain master,' Niamh went on, 'you must be the guardian of Clonfert, you have to, Liam, for I fear my husband would destroy it.'

Seamus Riordan's runt, the guardian of Clonfert. It would be amusing if only it were not true. But it was! Liam remained silent. His brother's arrogance and greed would choke the life from the people . . . and Niamh, what would be done with her? One thing he was sure of was that she would not be given the love she deserved, nor the respect due a wife.

'Seamus did something more than he thought when he dispossessed his elder son,' Niamh continued to speak, 'he gave the valleys a second chance, do not fail them, Liam, do not give them back into the keeping of Padraig.'

Liam watched the gleam of desperation in the dark eyes. What she said was said out of her own unhappiness, it was not disloyalty but a genuine feeling for the tenants, the people who worked the land; their happiness as much as her own mattered to this woman. How could his brother treat her as he did, why could he not see the worth that was entrenched in her, love her for the woman she was? Still holding her hand in his, Liam smiled. 'It shall be as you wish, I will remain at Eyrecourt but I ask you too to have the courage to stay, to act as its hostess.'

'You are a very good man, Liam Riordan, I pray heaven give you long life.'

Drawing him towards her Niamh offered her cheek and as Liam kissed it the door of the room opened.

'Now if that doesn't be a sight to greet a man, his brother making love to his wife!'

Niamh had cried out at sound of that first word, now she was pressed back into the corner of the sofa, her anguished stare on her husband.

'Padraig, it wasn't—'

'Quiet, slut!'

'Don't speak to her like that!' Liam was on his feet, anger blazing in his face.

'I will speak as I wish, she is my wife. But that does not matter to you, the runt cannot find a woman to lie with him so he forces himself on his sister-in-law.'

'That's a lie!'

Seeing the fingers close into fists Padraig's pale eyes held a look not of anger but of triumph.

'Of course it is.' He smiled. 'But only we in this room know that and both of you would be expected to lie, I know I would were I in your situation when stood before a magistrate.'

'Magistrate!' Niamh gasped, dusky eyes wide with horror.

'Yes, my dear, a magistrate. A man wronged as I have been must resort to law.'

'We've done you no wrong, you know that well enough!' Liam held the pale triumphant stare. 'Threaten me if it gives you pleasure but don't frighten your wife.'

The smile curving Padraig's mouth vanished in an instant. 'It is no threat,' he grated, 'I shall bring both of you to court; *wife takes husband's brother as lover* . . . it will cause quite a scandal.'

'It is not a courtroom drama you want, is it, Padraig?' Liam's words throbbed with contempt. 'It is Eyrecourt, and this is a way you see of getting it no matter what your wife suffers in the process.'

'It was mine!' The hiss slithered across the room, spitting at Liam like a cobra. 'It was always mine and I'll see any man in hell before I lose it.'

'And any woman?'

'Yes!'

The laugh, wild and loud, brought a sob to Niamh's lips.

'Yes, and any woman! I had thought to kill you for robbing me – oh not of my wife, a barren sow is of no use to a man. No, brother, you were going to die for taking my inheritance but now I see there is another way, a much slower and infinitely more painful way than a bullet in the head, a way in which you will suffer a lifetime of deaths locked away in a prison cell. As for your lover, she will be received in no decent house, no one will speak to her or be seen anywhere near her except in a bawdy house where she belongs!'

'You swine!' One stride brought Liam to where his brother stood but Padraig made no attempt to back away from the raised fist.

'Strike!' Padraig lifted a hand to touch the fading weal on his cheek. 'Add more marks to the one you gave the night I first discovered you in my wife's bed. Leave your bruises where they can be seen by a jury, give me more evidence with which to damn you both.'

'Why?' Liam's hands dropped to his sides as he swung away. 'Why Niamh? I can understand your resentment of me, even your hatred, but why vent your spite on a helpless woman, someone who has never harmed you?'

His broad shoulders lifting in a shrug, the evil that was Padraig Riordan showed in the velvet smile gliding to his lips.

'Spite!' He raised a mocking eyebrow. 'That is your word, brother, I prefer to use "opportunity" for that is what you two have given me; the opportunity to reclaim Eyrecourt and to be rid of a wife I have no use for and for whom I certainly never had any love.' Ignoring the cry from the couch he went on. 'I took Niamh Shea for one purpose only, to breed, and that she has not done. I said a moment since that a barren sow is of no use, that is what my wife has proved to be . . . of no use . . . therefore it follows I must take another. Ordinarily the Church abhors divorce but it abhors infidelity even more.' He glanced at the woman sitting with hands covering her face. 'You remember the vow, my dear, your vow taken before the altar, "keep ye only unto him", the one I shall say I twice caught you breaking with my own brother; even the Church will not forgive that, I shall be granted a divorce, and you? There are whorehouses in Dublin, I'm sure you will find a place in one of them!'

16

'Sure an' it's going to be wonderful so it is.' Bridget's eyes gleamed with pleasure. 'I've been to no ceilidh ever in my life before, my grandmother said it was sinful for a woman to be dancing after her husband be dead and gone and my mother never would be disagreeing with her. Has yourself been to a ceilidh?'

'Some,' Maura nodded, 'but that was a long time ago, I was just a young child.'

'So why, when you were grown a wee bit, did you not go any more, was it your mother wouldn't have the agreeing to it?'

'My mother did not forbid me.' Holding the folded petticoat to her chest Maura looked back at her yesterdays, at her mother urging her to go to the celebration that would follow a marriage in Clonmacnoise and her own head shaking its refusal.

'Then why?' Bridget's question came as she whirled around the cramped bedroom, hands holding out the sides of her voluminous bloomers as though they were the wide skirts of a fabulous ball gown.

Smiling at the pirouetting girl, Maura answered, 'My mother too would attend no ceilidh after my father died and I had no wish to go without her.'

'But we'll both be going to this one, won't we, Maura? It won't be as though we be brash girls attendin' on our own, we will have each other so we will, there be nobody can raise a frown to that, not even Mrs Maynard.'

It was possibly the only thing of their doing Clara Maynard

had not given a frown to. Maura laid the petticoat on the foot of the bed. Could it be she truly had no objections to young people dancing or was it because Eugenie Stratford was all for their attending? She glanced at the dresses the sister of Lord Portington had given as gifts to mark the birth of the sixth child of the English queen. They were pretty with their colours of red and green but she would feel more comfortable in her own patched skirt, yet not to wear that to the dancing would be a slight to the woman who had shown her kindness.

'Which of them be your choice?' The smiling Bridget held a dress in each hand.

'I have no preference, you take whichever it is pleases you more.'

'Sure an' they both be beautiful so they do, I'm not after knowing which I would choose.'

That was how she had felt on the morning of her seventh birthday. Maura watched the delight and wonder in the other girl's eyes but once more her memory was showing her a different scene. A small girl tearing the wrapping from a gift handed to her by a tall smiling man, the genuine squeal of delight as she saw the jointed wooden doll, the happiness on her father's face as the child threw herself into his arms, her own clasping his neck. Then, when he set her down, another package from a chestnut-haired woman whose gentle face shone with love. There was no squeal of delight as the package was opened, only a soft gasp of wonder as two tiny doll dresses were revealed. The world held no greater treasure for the child, but the child had grown and learned, learned real treasure was the love of her parents.

'Which will I be after taking? You'll have to help me, so you will.'

Fighting the tears the memory brought, Maura managed a smile. 'They each suit you but perhaps with hair so black the red dress . . .'

'I be after thinking the same, oh Maura, you be certain sure
now it isn't your own choice I be taking?'

'I'm certain sure.' Taking both dresses from the girl, Maura
dropped the green one onto the bed. Helping Bridget into the
other she fastened tiny buttons tying the broad ribbon sash
about the thin waist, then dropped to her knees. 'This will not
be missed.' Lifting the fine cotton skirt she pulled a matching
red ribbon from the petticoat, proceeding to wind it in the
raven hair.

'There,' she stood back looking at the thin little face so
radiant in its happiness, 'there'll be no other girl as pretty at the
ceilidh.'

'Is it truly pretty I look?' The smile accepting Maura's nod
faded suddenly. 'D'you not think the queen of the little people
will be after taking that sorely?'

Perplexed, Maura watched the light that had shone bright as
carriage lamps in those wide dark eyes melt away.

'Now why would she be doing that?'

Glancing first at the window already dark with the shadows
of evening, Bridget's answer was no more than a whisper. 'It
be well known the queen of all the fairies be the loveliest of
creatures and 'tis not pleased she'll be to see a servant girl
looking pretty . . . she . . . she might have meself taken—'

'Now you stop that, Bridget O'Flaherty!' Her reply sharp as
it was meant to be, Maura caught the young girl's arms,
shaking her. 'The little people are beautiful of heart as well
as of face, they are kindly and gentle and their queen is the
kindliest of all; it would make her unhappy did she know you
could think her otherwise.'

'I didn't mean . . . I didn't want . . . Maura, will I be
punished for speaking so?'

How could anyone punish a child so pulled and torn by life
she was afraid of her every word?

'No, Bridget.' Drawing the girl to her she held her for a

moment, feeling the tremble of anxiety ripple through the spare body. 'No one will punish you, no one will punish you ever again.'

There would be no noticing a stranger at that celebration. Padraig Riordan glanced at his reflection in the mirror of the room he had taken for the night. A ceilidh was open to all who cared to come and that included men like himself who had business in Tullamore. He had not intended staying over for the night but the chances of picking up a pretty piece was not to be turned down; there was always room in the pocket for an extra coin or two, and after today each sovereign paid would be his! He pulled at the cravat, slipping it free of his neck and pushing it into the pocket of his jacket. He had shared long enough, that bitch of a woman would sneer from the other side of her face when she learned that Padraig Riordan needed no agent to sell his goods for him.

The boat would sail come first light. The Grand Canal, it was a good name for the waterway that led clear to the sea at Dublin for it was a grand quick way of getting goods to the port; overland the journey took days, each of which carried the danger of that property being discovered. But by using the canal stuff was out of the country and on its way abroad before many people were aware of its being missing.

Smoothing his hair he smiled at himself in the mirror. Tonight he would take one more piece and after that he would be in business for himself.

The night promised to be fine and clear. He glanced at the moon already riding high, turning the peaks of the distant Slieve Bloom mountains black against a silver-grey sky. A night made for pleasure with a little profit an added bonus. He followed the wide track that ran alongside the Grand Canal until it branched across Maryborough heath. After a few minutes of steady trotting, he reined the horse in. Across the velvet night the sound of drum and fiddle beckoned him on. Portington Hall lay just ahead.

Leaving the carriage in the shelter of a clump of trees, where hopefully it would not be spotted, he walked across the open ground and came to the rear of the large house. The celebration was being held in a large barn some distance from the stable block. All the better. Padraig smiled to himself. The further from the house the less was likely to be seen.

Welcomed immediately, a tankard of porter in his hand, he found himself a corner where he could watch with not too much notice taken of himself; he would wait a couple of hours, give the music and the drink a longer time to capture folks' attention and then . . .

A roll of the drum calling everyone's mind to itself he glanced about the assembled group as a self-elected speaker shouted the toast, 'A long and happy life to the new Princess Louise . . .' Lifting his tankard, his hand halted in mid air. Was it . . . was his mind deceiving him, the shadows playing tricks with his eyes? Lowering the tankard he stepped to where several bales of straw would hide him completely. It might not be her, there were many girls in Ireland with a slight figure and a beautiful face . . . but the hair, that deep burnished chestnut, that was not so usual.

It had to be her. Easing himself forward he peered around the edge of the bales. There . . . that red-brown gleam in the lantern's light, it had to be who he hoped it was, it had to be Maura Deverell!

'Oh Maura, don't you be thinking 'tis a grand night.' Her eyes challenging the gleam of lanterns strung from the beams Bridget clapped her hands in delight as the fiddles struck up again.

She had not wanted to come. Maura felt a flush of guilt. She might so easily have deprived the girl of the joy of this evening for it was a surety Bridget would not have attended without her. Well now they were here and her friend must have as much enjoyment from it as possible.

'Sure an' there can never be another so grand, not even the—'

'No, no, no!' Maura raised an admonishing finger. 'There will be no mention of fairy folk and no more thought given to them, you will enjoy your grand evening and let nothing blight it.'

The girl was altogether too superstitious. Her glance wandering over the smiling faces of people gathering around a small platform erected for the musicians, Maura's own smile faded as she caught sight of a narrow sharp-featured face, sour as the rest were happy. Clara Maynard would have preferred no ceilidh, she had no desire to see people happy. But for Bridget and herself the need to put up with that woman's acid tongue was to be short-lived, a week and they would be gone.

'Can we go nearer?' Bridget tugged at her sleeve. 'The others say Michael O'Flynn be the best clog dancer in the whole of Ireland.'

'Then I think we—' The answer lost in the acclamation of the clogger's audience, Maura allowed herself to be drawn nearer the temporary stage.

A week and she would be gone from this country for good, her word to her mother will have been kept. Maura felt the sharp stab, so like pain, strike at the birth of that thought. To leave Ireland for ever! It was like cutting out a piece of your heart. Her mother could not have known the heartache the keeping of that promise would cause or she never would have asked it. But then what was there here for her except grief? In time the hurt of parting would pass. She had heard those words as a child. Mother O'Toole had said them as she held Mairead Deverell in her arms, trying to soothe the agony of her husband's death; but it was only the years had passed, taking with them none of the torture, none of the anguish: Mairead Deverell had died with the stone of sorrow still heavy in her heart. Maura watched the skilful movements of the man's feet, heard the rhythm of their drumming on the wooden boards, but they made no impression on her senses. If only she and her mother could have left together . . . but even as they had walked away from the clochan, deep within her she had known, known her mother could never have left Ireland, left behind the love of her life. Was that what her daughter was doing? In turning her back on all she had ever known, was she leaving love? Love? A picture of a stoop-shouldered man with kind gentle eyes smiled from her soul . . . No, not love. What she had felt for Liam Riordan out there on the heath was no more than gratitude!

Outside the barn Padraig stood in the building's deep shadow. He had seen her, he had seen the bitch who had turned his life upside down, the girl he had promised himself he would kill; she was in that barn, Maura Deverell was here! He could have searched for months, travelled the length and breadth of the land before finding her, but fate in its kindness had brought him here, led him to where she was. His fingers gripping convulsively together, an almost hedonistic pleasure shot through him. He had found the way to take Eyrecourt back, to avenge himself on a runt who had robbed him of his inheritance and robbed his face of its clean handsome look, and he had found the way to rid himself of a wife who was nothing if not a burden, and now he had found the girl. Tonight he had been given more than a chance of simply taking a piece. He smiled again, a slow, lascivious, satisfied smile. Tonight the gods had smiled on Padraig Riordan.

Away to his right a sudden surge of yelling and applause spilled into the night. The barn door had opened. He pressed further into the concealing shadows. Probably some man who had come outside to relieve himself. From the building's interior the sound of fiddles striking up eased the tension that had pulled suddenly at his nerves; whoever had come out of the barn would return quickly, a ceilidh of the sort provided by a lord of the manor was such that not a moment of it was to be missed.

His breathing level once more, he settled to wait. He could let himself into that house. He ran a glance over the large façade, the stonework etched black against the lemony silver of moonlight. It would take no effort and with the noise of the celebration another sound would not disturb the dogs. But once inside in which room did he wait? With so many she could be housed anywhere; better to stay here, fortune had been with him thus far, it would not desert him now.

But she would not leave that barn alone! The thought flared like a rocket, scorching his mind with the brilliance of reality. The whole of the staff of house and estate were crammed into that barn, it stood to reason they would leave in groups. He could not be beaten now! A vicious fist slammed into the wall at his back. He could not be given this chance only to have it snatched away! But how . . . how could he get to her while others were there to see! An irritant to his mind the thoughts continued to plague, question following answer, riding in and out like waves on a shore. There had to be a way . . . The mental argument stopped as from the corner of his eye he caught a movement. He had allowed his concentration to be diverted . . . fool! He cursed himself, if he had been seen then his chances of capturing Maura Deverell were gone. With only his eyes moving he strafed the shadows. Nothing . . . no one was there. Leaning his head against the wall he freed air from his lungs in one long slow movement, eyes closed in relief. He could so easily have . . . but the thought got no further; sliced away as his eyes opened, Padraig drew back the breath as he caught sight of a slight figure walking towards the house.

It had been only a glimpse, a fleeting teasing of his mind. Moving to the rim of shadow he stared across the ground separating house and barn. Or had it . . . was what he had seen merely a projection of his own desire or was it real? Did fantasy remain so long in the eye of the brain, did it move the same as she had moved, carry its slim form as she had carried hers, was what he looked at now a delusion, a deception of his own making?

Watching the figure clear a patch of darkness cast by a setting of ornamental bushes, Padraig felt that same flush of pleasure, the halcyon gratification that followed the realisation that this was no illusion, no shadow on shadow he was watching, but flesh and blood, it was Maura Deverell!

Drawing the cravat from his pocket, his tread silent as that of a panther, he moved into the moonlight.

17

It was the truth Niamh had spoken. To give everything back to Padraig would spell the end of Eyrecourt and the valley. He would bleed every last farthing from its people without a second thought.

Why had his father done this to him? Liam stood inside the tiny chapel of Saint Ciaran, his head bowed in respect. The naming of him as owner of his estates was not done of love, Seamus would not happily give his runt the time of day; no, that Will had been drawn in a fit of temper and would have been revoked as soon as reason returned, but there had been no time, death had come to Seamus before his mind had calmed.

The people of the village and the tiny clochans scattered throughout the properties had not hidden their pleasure on finding their master was not to be Padraig but Liam, the crook-shouldered son. They had smiled and greeted him warmly at each house he had visited. Smiles in every house. He drew a deep breath, holding it in his throat. In every home except one!

Releasing the breath he made the holy sign across forehead and breast, murmuring a prayer to the saint before leaving the tiny building. Walking to a spot where the ground sloped gently he halted, his gaze following the lazily flowing Shannon.

He had been to the cottage in Clonmacnoise. There had been none there to greet him, no one to smile a welcome. The house had held a sadness, a deep emptiness that seemed to engulf him . . . a sadness matched by the emptiness of a broken heart.

His gaze caught by a great-crested grebe, the pale April sun glinting in the glorious halo of orange, red feathers contrasting sharply with the downy white softness of the long neck and curving breast, he followed the swoop bringing it to land on the river. The bird had a freedom man could never share, a freedom he knew he himself wanted; but freedom carried a heavy price and that price would be paid by Niamh and the tenants.

Niamh! He watched the bird dive in search of fish then rise into the air with consummate ease. The pain of Padraig's words to her in that room had been terrible to see and the fear of being hauled before a court and branded a whore lived with her. Yes, he could renounce that inheritance, give it all to his brother, take the freedom he yearned for. Across the river the beautifully plumed bird skimmed lightly down to the water. Watching it a moment longer he turned away. He could take his freedom . . . but he could not leave Niamh alone in her prison.

'You were supposed to be watching!'

Clara Maynard flushed under the stony gaze of her mistress but the colour that rose to her face was the mark of irritation rather than guilt.

'I did say it would be unwise to allow that ceilidh, with so many folk it's impossible to keep your eye on one.'

'Unwise!' Eugenie Stratford's eyes blazed like blue ice. 'You do not see it as unwise to allow the workers and tenants to celebrate an important event in Her Majesty's life . . . that by barring them is to make them even less tolerant of English rule? But then you would not, your low-class brain is not capable of that kind of understanding. God, why do I suffer you!'

Wincing as a pearl-back hairbrush flew past her ear, Clara stood silent. It would be her fault whatever answer she gave, so best to give none.

'Did nobody see the girl leave?' The words rang like gunshot in the quiet bedroom.

Recovering the hairbrush, Clara shook her head as she placed it on the dressing table.

'I presume you *have* asked?'

Oh how I'd like to tan the arse off you. Thoughts ran wild behind Clara's flush of colour. A bloody good hiding would do my lady the world of good, knock some of that aristocratic starch out of you!

'I asked all of the staff, ma'am,' she kept her voice even, 'it seems no one saw her leave the barn.'

'No, they wouldn't, they would be too busy watching the depth of ale in their tankard; but people do not just disappear.'

'Many of the household staff think they do.'

Eugenie looked up sharply. 'And just what do you mean by that?'

The spoiled brat of a woman knew exactly what was meant. Her hands folded across her middle, Clara's fingers tightened against the desire to slap that haughty face.

'They were encouraged to think the little people . . .'

'Little people! Not you, too, don't tell me you believe all this nonsense of leprechauns?'

'No, ma'am, I don't, but the Irish do and 'tis their doubts, their suspicions that have to be quieted; telling them those young people be spirited away by fairy folk is the best way of getting them to hold a still tongue, and a still tongue be very necessary if—'

'Never mind!' Eugenie Stratford cut in sharply. 'The fact remains the girl has run away and you are the one I hold responsible . . . You will find out why and how or you, my dear Mrs Maynard, will find yourself back in England, without a penny!'

That bitch would threaten her once too often! Returned below stairs, Clara fumed to herself. It was so easy to criticise, so easy for the wealthy of this world to find fault in everybody other than themselves; but Lady Eugenie Stratford should learn to curb that sharp tongue or could be it would be curbed for her. But just why had that wench run off? She had the promise of being taken to England only next week, of being given a new life there, that was what she had asked for, wasn't it . . . so why give it up now?

There were no such things as leprechauns, people were not just spirited away and that girl had no reason to run off. Clara's hands became still in the bowl of half-mixed pastry, a sudden thought gripping her mind tight as a vice. *She had no reason to run away* . . . Clara stared at the flour in the bowl. So had someone else done the running, and had the girl gone with whoever it was, not of her choosing but as a captive?

It had all gone perfectly. Taking his time over breakfast, Padraig congratulated himself on his previous night's work. It had taken no more than a moment to slide the cravat over the girl's mouth and jerk her backwards off her feet. He smiled, remembering the ease with which it had all been accomplished. The clump of bushes had given almost immediate cover and from there to where he had left the carriage deep shadow had continued to mask any movement. He had been forced to knock her unconscious before lifting her into the vehicle and that had been regretful, he would have preferred talking, to tell her of what it was lay in store, how the rest of her paltry life was to be spent; and she would have quite a foretaste of that before that boat reached England!

There had been no problem with its captain. A leery smile and a filthy hand clutching several coins rose in Padraig's mind. The man knew what was required of him and also how a blade would find his heart should he allow his tongue to get the better of him. White slaving was despised in Christian countries, but then slavery was a dirty word. The smile still on his lips he poured himself fresh coffee. Providing desirable goods was a much more acceptable term and the piece he had picked up last night would be acceptable in any dockside brothel.

God, what a fool he'd been! The feeling of smug gratification fell away, taking the smile with it. Lord, what a fool to have aligned himself with others when he could so easily conduct these affairs alone and that way have taken all profits into his own pocket. But last night he had come to his senses, last night had seen him take the first step along that path, the money paid for the girl he had handed aboard that boat would be his; no sharing . . . no argument . . . just his! And that was the way it would be every time from now on.

Shaking his head at the offer of a fresh pot of coffee he glanced about the dining room of the small hotel. Normally he wouldn't be seen dead in such a cheap place but there must be nothing grand on these trips, he must appear to be no different from the merchants who used the canal as a means of sending or receiving wares, even though the goods he exported were vastly different to theirs. He would, of choice, have preferred to remain in Tullamore in one of the better hotels until the returns on his investments arrived, to see the total amount for himself instead of just the sum that pair said was his due, that way the journey home to Clonfert and repeated in a week or so would be unnecessary. But then, one must not expect everything on a plate. He drank the remains of his coffee, feeling the smile return in his mind. But nor should one be satisfied with a little when there was much more to be had. Nodding to the attentive manager he settled his bill and walked out to where his carriage had been harnessed and now stood ready. There had been more than one pretty colleen dancing in that barn.

He set the horse to a trot. There promised to be good pickings between Clonfert and here and he was going to be the gatherer. Oh he wouldn't be too greedy and he would not take from Portington Hall itself a second time, but from the villages and clochans between . . . yes, he would take his choice.

Reaching a point in the road where it branched towards the wharf and warehouses lining the canal he brought the carriage to a stop. Would it not look better to return to the warehouse to be seen to be doing business there? Not many merchants stayed the night in a hotel unless they had cause to visit the warehouses next day. Last night's undertaking had been risky and he wanted to be away out of Tullamore but he should not appear over-anxious. His decision taken, he turned the horse towards the canal. An hour should be time enough to allay curiosity.

'It was you, was it not?'

Quietly spoken it nevertheless set Padraig's nerves tingling as a man and a woman stepped from the shadow of a low archway.

'Don't bother to lie,' the words snapped like icicles, 'I had my suspicions when I heard this morning that a girl had gone missing from last evening's celebrations, and here you are still in Tullamore, yet your business in this town was finished yesterday.'

'I really have no idea what you are talking about.' Over his initial surprise, Padraig's suavity of manner re-established itself and he smiled, aware of watching eyes.

'Then I will explain—'

'This is no place a lady should be expected to stand.'

He had raised his voice for the benefit of people moving about the warehouse. 'Allow me to offer you coffee in a more suitable establishment.'

Refusal on the part of the couple would draw attention.

Padraig knew they would not take that risk. Walking with them to the small tea room they had used the day before he gathered his thoughts together. They had obviously made enquiries, but had anyone seen him deliver that girl in the late hours or was this simply a bluff?

'Now,' he said, after coffee had been set before them, 'if you will tell me what it is that is troubling you . . .'

'You know very well!' The woman's eyes glinted angrily. 'A girl has gone missing.'

Stirring sugar into his drink, Padraig shrugged. 'So, a girl has gone missing, it isn't the first time.'

A gloved hand came sharply down onto the chequered table cloth. 'You fool!' the woman snapped. 'The girl was not from some far-flung village, she was a maidservant at Portington Hall!'

Padraig's eyes narrowed, his answer sliding sinuously from behind clenched teeth. 'But not the first to disappear from that house as you well know, why then should there be any fuss over this one?'

'She was supposed to travel to England with . . . with the mistress while the others . . .' She hesitated.

'The others,' the stocky man, who until now had said nothing, spoke quietly, 'they were presumed to have run away because they were dissatisfied with their lot, but the girl who went last night was known to be delighted at the prospect of going to start a new life in England, consequently someone somewhere might easily ask questions and should it be his lordship gets to hear then we could all have problems.'

'All?' His smile disdainful, Padraig counted out several coins, laying them in the centre of the table. 'I fail to see how you think I might be included, I was not present at the celebration you speak of.' If they knew that to be the lie it was they would say so now. Forcing himself to look the pair in the face he waited, and when no admonishment came he stood up.

'Wait!' The woman's eyes blazed sheer malice. 'I know you are behind this business and I warn you now. Try to cheat us, try to take the trade solely for your own and you will regret it!'

'Thank you for your delightful company, madam.' Padraig took the gloved hand in his and, as he smiled into those angry eyes, he whispered, 'Now I give *you* a warning. Get in the way of Padraig Riordan and neither of you will live long enough to regret it!'

They had guessed the girl had been abducted and they had guessed who her kidnapper was. Padraig guided the carriage away from the busy terminus of the Grand Canal with its proliferation of boats. But guessing was all that couple could do. They had no proof and they would get none here unless that captain wanted his next voyage to be in hell. Clear of the town he set the horse to a sharp canter. The girl he had carried off last night marked the beginning for Padraig Riordan, from this day he, and he alone, would supply the market with girls.

18

She had been closely questioned by Eugenie Stratford, asked again and again who had spoken to them during the evening, had someone paid them a little more attention perhaps than was usual, had they stayed close to each other all evening? And so on, question following question until she had felt she would scream; and through it all Clara Maynard had stood stone-faced and silent. But once clear of her ladyship's private salon the woman had launched her own barrage. Had there been talk of a man friend, was that the reason the girl had changed her mind about going to England, had she run away to join some man? And after the questions her slightest movement had been watched by the cook who kept her closely confined to the kitchen, allowing her outside only in order to use the privy and even then she had waited just beyond the door.

Why? Sat on the bed she had shared with Bridget, Maura's mind wrestled with every possible reason. Why had Clara Maynard refused to let her go and search for Bridget, why was she herself being treated like a prisoner?

That girl had not run away, she was much too happy at the prospect of their leaving together to do anything of the sort, on top of which she was frightened of her own shadow, she would be terrified at the thought of being out on the heath alone and in the dark. So what had happened . . . where was she?

They had stood together in that barn watching the dancers, clapping to the rhythm of the music. Then there had been the clogger, Bridget had been delighted, urging that they stand nearer the platform on which the man was to perform. That was when she had shivered a little. Excitement or a touch of night frost? Maura remembered saying she would fetch the shawls from their room and for Bridget to stay where she was, only when she had returned Bridget was gone.

If only I had not stayed to change, Maura's thoughts were condemning. She had felt uncomfortable in the pretty green dress that was the gift of Eugenie Stratford, dresses the like of that were not for a penniless girl, so she had taken a few minutes to change it for her own cotton blouse and patched skirt then removed the ribbon the other girl had insisted she weave into her hair. Her own comfort! She felt the cry rise in her throat, choking her with its censure. That had been her priority . . . her one thought when it should have been Bridget she was thinking of. She ought never to have left her not even for a moment, they should have gone to the house together . . . The last thought coming on a long day of worrying was too much. A sob breaking from her she sank to her knees, her tear-filled eyes lifting to the cheap plaster figure of a gently smiling woman set on a tiny shelf fixed to the wall opposite the bed.

'Holy Mother,' she whispered, 'what I did was selfish, I thought only of myself when it was Bridget should have been uppermost in my mind. She is little more than a child who is often afraid. Please, gentle virgin, implore your holy son to send His angels to watch over her, to keep her from harm.' Tears blinding her vision, Maura covered her face with her hands and wept.

Dusky mauve tinged at the rim with pearl, the pre-dawn sky lay over the earth like some precious veil. Soon it would give way to rose-pink streaks, the first light of morning. Staring for a moment through the meagre window of the attic bedroom, Maura knew what it was she would do, what the long hours of the sleepless night had told her she *must* do. Tying her shawl about her she lifted the latch of the bedroom door then waited, listening for any sound that said she was overheard, and when none came she ran lightly along the corridor that gave onto the servants' staircase, hardly breathing until she reached the bottom. Tiptoeing through the kitchen and scullery she let herself out of the door that opened onto the stable yard. The dogs would not bark, they were used to the scullery maids bringing ash from the kitchen range before the day was properly risen.

The bedroom had been cold, Clara Maynard maintaining that no fires be lit in rooms set at the top of the house for fear of setting the roof ablaze, but outside the air was colder still, a breath of late spring frost covering trees and ground with a veneer of white. Shivering with the bite of it, her shawl drawn close, Maura's glance ran over the brilliant expanse, past the stables, hesitating as it reached the barn where the ceilidh had been held then on to lose itself at the horizon.

'. . . *the little people* . . .'

Bridget's awe-struck voice echoing now among her own thoughts, Maura brushed it away. Wherever Bridget had disappeared to it had nothing to do with leprechauns, it was no spiriting away by fairy folk had taken her from that barn. But which way had she gone? How to know which direction to follow? Maura glanced at the ground; there were no footprints in that delicate virgin whiteness, no lead for her to follow.

Across in the stables a horse snorted, the sound among the silence jarring her taut nerves. She had no idea which way led where but every moment of indecision was a moment nearer being discovered, of being taken back into that house.

Praying the dogs would not bark she clutched her shawl tight beneath her chin and began to run.

They should both have been happy, both have been looking forward to starting life anew in England; what had happened to the dream?

So spent it was all she could do to push one foot in front of the other, Maura gazed over the wide stretch of darkening land. She had run and walked the entire day, hours and hours of searching and never seeing a soul, how could a country with so many people be so empty? No one, no one in all that time, only clochans empty and abandoned, pots and furniture left for the dust of hopelessness to cover them while always, from every field she passed, came the sickly smell of potatoes rotting where they lay, harvests ruined before they came to maturity; like the fingers of death, a sickness brushed the land, bringing famine and desolation in its wake.

Taking time to catch her breath she huddled down in the shelter of a large boulder. Those houses, she had run to each and every one of them hoping maybe to find Bridget there or somebody who might have seen or spoken to her. But each of the houses was empty.

Closing her eyes she rested her forehead on her knees, the picture of those tiny forlorn little rooms rising to her mind clear and vivid as an illustration in a book. Where had those people gone . . . had some of their loved ones died of the hunger and hardships brought by repeated failures of the potato harvests . . . was the hurt and bitterness so much it had driven them to leave their homes or, like so many others, had they been driven out by cruel landlords? Ireland was bleeding and its people suffered. Maura felt her stomach churn with the pain of it all. When would the nightmare end or would it go on until the whole land suffocated beneath the fear and hunger? So much heartbreak, so many innocents, so many like Bridget who would not know which way to turn . . . Bridget! Raising her head she looked out again over the land succumbing to the shadows of evening. She had been sure that girl would not have left Portington Hall alone, now seeing the night swallow the earth she was certain of it. Somehow Bridget had been lured away . . .

The thought stopped there, Maura's heartbeat suddenly sounding like gunfire in her ears.

Tempted away? She pressed her lips hard together, holding back a cry as the other half of that thought battered its way into her mind . . . or had Bridget been abducted?

But why would anyone want to carry Bridget off? Closing her mind to the thoughts that brought only panic, Maura tried to look at things logically. The girl was no daughter of wealthy parents, she would bring no ransom; nor was there any man so sick with love he would risk the gallows to have her beside him, and had there been a Seamus Riordan in the background ready to throw her into a marriage for whatever reason to suit himself then Bridget would surely have told of him. Her questions exhausted, Maura trembled as the reality of the only possible answer returned like a dark spectre. Bridget had to have been abducted!

Pushing slowly to her feet, the ache of tired muscles lost amid the pain of what she could only see as truth, she stared into the advancing gloom. A whole day had brought no word of Bridget, a week, a month and still it could prove the same; perhaps the girl was already returned to Portington Hall safe and sound, perhaps she herself should return there tomorrow, explain to Lady Stratford that it had been friendship had driven her to slip away from the house. Friendship! Self-reproach rising hot and fast inside her brought a touch of shame. Where was the friendship that had her giving up so soon? No, she would not return to Portington; no matter how long the search, she would carry it on until she found Bridget.

A flurry of breeze whispered against her face, stroking with the first touch of promised night frost. Shivering, Maura pulled the shawl about her, the soft warmth bringing with it a memory of a small clochan set in the lee of a hill, of a half-crippled woman and a young couple smiling proudly at their first-born child.

'. . . *ye'll be given no gift with a greater love* . . .'

Soft as the darkness out of which they came the words spoken by Bridie MacGee kissed the edge of her memory. The woman had given more than the gift of a shawl, she had given of her heart's love; could Maura Deverell do any less for that frightened girl who had looked to her for friendship?

The night would be long and not free of fear but she had spent nights alone on the heath before. With the protection of the Blessed Virgin she would do so again and with morning would continue the search.

Her prayer finished, Maura opened her eyes. Was it an illusion? She blinked against the lowering dusk, her frown becoming a smile of joy as across the distance a yellow glow winked at her.

If it was a carriage it would be gone long before she could reach it. The first flood of euphoria trailing away, Maura stared at the light; please, let it not be a carriage!

Watching for several more seconds, seeing it made no movement, she almost cried her thanks. It was no carriage.

Her aching legs forgotten she flew towards the steady gleam, her whole being throbbing with relief as she saw the shape of walls and a low roof etch themselves against the pewter sky.

It was a cottage, and this one wasn't empty!

'God bless all in this house.' She half sobbed the greeting as the door opened to her knock and she was invited in. 'Please, I am looking for—'

'We know who it is you be looking for . . . bring yourself inside, Maura Deverell, 'tis greatly pleased we are to see you.'

As the blood drained from her cheeks, her legs threatened to buckle beneath her, Maura looked into the face of Padraig Riordan.

'. . . *the days as yet left to ye will be cut short* . . .'

The words could not have been more prophetic had they been spoken by Moses himself. With his pack at his feet the tinker sat watching the kettle he had set to boil over a fire of sticks. That had been his warning to Seamus Riordan but his own had not been the tongue had tasted the sweet wine of vengeance, that had been the reserve of the Lord. 'Thrown from his horse,' the men of Clonfert had muttered over their tankards, 'rolled down the side of the stony foothills of the Slieve Bloom and found the next day stone dead, his eyes staring at some unknown horror. Sure an' wasn't it his own black-hearted sins rising up to claim him.'

Listening to them in the tavern set in the midst of the village he had kept his own counsel. He could have added to their count of Seamus Riordan's black sins, told of one some had guessed but forgotten long ago while others had never heard of it, nor of Aiden Shanley.

Reaching another stick from the pile he had collected he added it to the fire. His name had long died from the lips of the folk of the valleys but it had never truly died from the memory of Seamus Riordan, the fear that had leapt to the man's eyes that day in his fine house had been evidence of the truth of that and was probably the first truth he had ever owned, for he had spoken none of it the night of that murder . . . and murder it had been.

Steam from the blackened spout escaped in short opaque puffs, floating upwards before losing itself in the clear air of morning.

Twenty years or twenty lifetimes? The crimson flames gave way to a dark night and in it two men struggled while a boy watched from the cover of a rock. He had seen it every night of those years, see the arm lift, dark against a leaden sky, then the moon had peeked between the folds of grey, its silver smile playing over a knife . . . a knife that had sliced downwards burying itself in a man's chest.

He must have cried out then for the figure that wielded the knife turned towards him and before his trembling legs could move he was being held like a rabbit in a trap.

There had been no believing a ten-year-old boy so scared he could scarce string two words together. Seamus had been seen as the caring neighbour reluctant to tell how he had found the boy knelt over the fallen man, one hand still holding the knife protruding from his chest.

With a stick in his hand the tinker toyed with the embers gleaming beneath the kettle. His mother had clung to him, her cries following after the men sent by the magistrate to fetch him. That had been the last time he had felt her dear hands touch him or had her lips kiss his face. He had gone from that courtroom, sentenced to twenty years in the colonies, a sentence that would have been death on the gibbet were it not for the fact his victim was not dead. The man could not testify as to the lies of it all, a coma held him in a grip that did not loosen. Two weeks! Jabbing the stick into the fire he clenched his teeth against the bitterness of remembering. He had visited the cemetery set close to the Abbey of Clonmacnoise, read the wording on the headstone there, the stone set over the body of the man who had died two weeks after Aiden Shanley had been sent from Ireland.

For half of those twenty years of his sentence he had prayed. The thoughts went on twisting and re-twisting, weaving their own tapestry of misery. The boy he was had prayed nightly for some miracle, an act of providence that would bring him back to his family. But when the years passed and no miracle happened the man he had become vowed retribution, made himself a promise that one day . . . one day, Seamus Riordan would answer for the pain he had caused that family all those years ago.

And then he had returned. Dancing on its own steam the kettle lid rattled, the jangle of it spreading a circle of sound on the stillness. His heart was singing as he had made his way to his mother's home, that tiny cottage whose walls had threatened to burst apart from the store of love crammed into it. He had found it. Unable to bear the inward picture any more he dropped the stick to bury his face in his hands. He had at last returned to his home, to his loved ones, to all that memory had served to keep life in him for twenty years! But his home was almost a ruin, walls and ceiling tumbling, a shell that had broken, spilling out the love it had held until nothing remained; nothing! He cried out, a great strangled sob that sent birds screeching from the trees and wildlife scuttling among the heather. Nothing of that love remained, only a marker in the churchyard showed where his parents lay. They were gone, carrying away the hopes and dreams of a young innocent lad. Then the promise made unto himself had hardened, forged into unbreakable iron. As Seamus Riordan had destroyed so must he and his be destroyed. Yet the vengeance promised himself for so long was not to be his. Lifting his head the tinker stared into the distance. Fate had taken the father . . . but the father had two sons!

19

How had this happened? She had taken so much care, yet the fear of so many nights, so many dreams, had become reality, Padraig Riordan had caught up with her and this time there would be no escape.

Still trembling from shock, Maura huddled in a corner of the tight little room, only her eyes showing over the top of her shawl. It was as if it was meant to be, his waiting here, waiting while fate delivered her back to him. But why should heaven be so against her, what had she done to be so deserving of this cruelty? Was it because she had slipped from that house, gone against the wishes of Eugenie Stratford to search for Bridget? But she had only wanted to help a frightened girl, was that so dreadful a sin?

'A bonus . . . sure an' won't that be welcome as the flowers in May!'

Across the room the man who had opened the door to her laughed loudly, the look he shot across to her bringing fresh ripples of terror to her spine.

'This one is not to go by way of the usual channels.' Padraig Riordan did not bother to hide his words. 'I don't want her sent from Tullamore.'

'Not Tullamore.' The other man lowered his tankard, his small eyes peering at Padraig. 'Sure an' isn't it from Tullamore they always be sent? Isn't that where the boat be after sailing—'

'There are other boats and other ports!' Padraig's answer

was snapped. 'The little piece we got tonight will not go from Tullamore.'

In the short silence that followed the interchange, Maura tried to clear her mind. A boat . . . Tullamore . . . Were these two planning to send something abroad . . . but what was so special it was not to be seen in that town?

'So where is it ye be after wanting me to see that one on its way?'

'It must needs be some way off from here, I don't want the chance of our prize being recognised.'

Taking another hefty pull from his tankard then wiping his mouth with the back of his hand, the man nodded his head like a puppet.

'So! It mustn't be after being recognised . . . then just where now is it ye think this some way off from here be?'

His own tankard held between both hands Padraig twisted its base on the rough table. 'There be another place beside the canal, Robertstown . . .'

'Robertstown!' His companion exploded. 'That don't be some way from here it be a bloody big way . . .'

'And I be paying you a bloody big bonus!' The crash of tankard striking wood added to the crash of the answer erupting across the room. 'You will deliver that piece to Robertstown and hand it to the man whose name I will write for you . . . and if you wish to lie peaceful in your bed you will ensure it reaches its destination unbroken!'

His face dark as a thundercloud Padraig kicked away his chair, one stride bringing him to where Maura sat.

'You!' he breathed viciously. 'You held yourself too good to be wife to the runt, too grand for the likes of a Riordan . . .'

'It was not Liam I had no liking for.' Every syllable trembled on her lips but Maura forced an answer.

'Not Liam, it was not the misfit you had the dislike of, not his hands touching you, not his twisted body lying on your own that turned your stomach, but that of his brother!' Eyes full of hate glared down at her, each word slithering between clenched teeth, feeling for her like the forked tongues of so many serpents. 'Well now, isn't that the pity, for in a week or so you will be regretting the refusing of Padraig Riordan.'

'Regret refusing to be mistress to you . . . never!'

One hand flashing downwards caught the shawl she held tight about her, snatching her to her feet. As he held her a few inches from him, rage gleamed a lighted torch in his eyes.

'Oh but you will,' he snarled, 'wife to one man and mistress to another was not acceptable then think how acceptable this will be, you will be any man's whore, any man who has the shilling to pay for you and after that you will spread your legs for tuppence and then for a slice of week-old bread; that is what this had earned for you—' turning his head he thrust the scarred cheek closer to her face '– this was your fault, scarred on account of taking a bloody peasant! My inheritance taken from me on account of a bloody peasant! But you will pay . . . every day and every night you will pay until your body be rotting from the disease brought by the lovers you cannot refuse; the knowledge of what is to come is the scar you will carry, remember that when you lie beneath the stinking sore-riddled scum that frequent any quayside brothel!'

Her breath knocked from her as she was thrown to the floor, Maura could only watch as he strode from the house.

Refilling his tankard from a stone jar, the thick-set man smiled as he walked across to her. 'Now wasn't that the wrong thing to be doing at all, at all? What use to go upsetting the man that way and sending him off fit to fight the world?'

Pushing upright, her back supported by the cold stone of the house, Maura stared at the closed door. 'Padraig Riordan is not one to fight the world, the only people he chooses to fight with are tenants bound to his father's lands or women with no man to stand against him.'

'And ye'self was such a woman?' Eyes bloodshot from the drink played over Maura, lingering on her breasts. 'But if it be as ye says and ye don't be having menfolk to fight for ye how did Padraig Riordan come by the scar that marks his face, was that the doing of ye'self?'

'I know nothing of that scar,' Maura shook her head, 'he did not have it when . . .'

What a colleen did not say could sometimes be more than words in a book! The man drank again, wiping his hand first across his lips then down his trousers. '*Unbroken*,' Padraig had said, '*ensure it reaches its destination unbroken.*' Sure an' wasn't that what the man himself had done, and once the seal were broken then a letter could be read many times and no man the wiser. Drinking again he reached for the stone jar. Tonight . . . and a few nights to come he would enjoy a little light reading.

He was dead! With every nerve screaming, Maura stared at the man, his body half folded as he lay on the floor. He had taken it in turns to laugh and leer at her and all the time he had gone on drinking, the pleasure obvious on his mottled face as he repeated over and again what Padraig Riordan had told her. The brothels of some port, the soul-destroying life that was to be hers. Then the stone jar had become empty. Maura held her eyelids hard down over her eyes, desperate to shut out the scene that would not go away. His eyes had been bleary and almost closed from the porter, the stink of his breath reaching to her across the small space of the room.

'*Unbroken be what Riordan said,*' he had laughed again at that, '*but the filly already be broken but not by his hand, eh!*'

He had thought the remark hilarious, shouting it several times between that awful raucous laughter.

He had reached for her then, stubby fingers fastening on the neck of her blouse pulling her towards him, bloodshot eyes devouring her. '*Riordan took his ride,*' he had breathed into her face, the stench of it making her stomach retch, '*now I be taking the same.*'

What had happened next . . . what miracle had saved her? Her eyelids lifting Maura stared at the figure lying at her feet. The hand pulling at her had dropped to clutch at her breast, the other already groping beneath her skirt while his slobbering mouth was pressed against her throat.

Let the memory stop . . . let it go away! Half sobbing she pressed her fingers hard to her mouth but the sting of soft flesh against her teeth was not enough to halt the thoughts crowding her mind or erase the pictures that floated there.

Her breast had ached with the vicious squeezing, the skin of her stomach burning as his fingers had stroked beneath her bloomers and she had been helpless, her limbs refusing to move, her brain declining to accept what was happening, like a rabbit trapped in the gleam of a lantern she had stood absolutely still.

Her breath juddering with the memories that persisted she drew back from the figure, terrified the man would rise to his feet. But he had not moved since . . . he had not stirred a muscle or made the slightest sound . . . Standing with her back against the wall she fought against the sobs threatening to become a scream.

His mouth had trailed wetly over her throat, along her neck, its foulness reaching for her lips, and in that moment revulsion had released the grip on her limbs. She had pushed at his shoulders with both hands, one leg jerking upwards in an effort to kick him away. That was when he had cried out, his body doubling over, both hands gripping his crotch, and as he had half turned from her she had grabbed the heavy cast-iron kettle from its hook over the fire and swung it with all her strength against his head. He had made just one sound, a low almost animal-like grunt, then . . . nothing! As if watching a waking dream, Maura stared at the pictures moving across her mind.

Still bent double he had slid to the floor; in a silent almost graceful movement, like some enormous dark snowflake, he had settled at her feet.

How long had he lain there . . . how long had she stood wanting to run but unable to do so? Trembling with fear she forced herself to look at the huddled shape, blood matting in the greasy hair, the mottled cheek stained with a broader patch of red where boiling water from the kettle had spilt across it.

She had not meant to kill him. The terror of the past minutes rolled itself into a cry that echoed in the stillness. She had wanted only to stop the violation of her body, to push him from her and instead . . .

'Oh, Mother, why? Why is this happening to me?' The last of her strength ebbing away, Maura sank to her knees, burying her sobs in the soft wool of her shawl.

It had been a week since he had caught that bitch. Padraig Riordan tucked a blue silk cravat neatly beneath a single-breasted lemon-coloured waistcoat delicately picked out in gold thread and buttoned low on the chest to display the fine-lawn high-collared shirt. A week since he had sold her to the white slave trade. Satisfaction welling warm within him he reached for the frock coat laid out for him on his bed. This was the lifestyle he wanted . . . the lifestyle that was his due and it was one he would live to the hilt. Slipping into the coat he had had cut with the latest fashion of low collar and wide revers he fastened the single button before easing the close-fitting sleeves and touching the silk-covered buttons sewn to each cuff.

The fashion suited him. He smiled at the reflection in the long mirror, satisfied at the way the deep peacock-blue of the coat complimented fawn trousers, both adding their own touch to his confidence as well as complimenting his physique.

A perfect gentleman. He bowed to himself, laughing softly

at the image facing him from the looking-glass. That was something the Deverell bitch would never know, her companions would be the riff-raff drawn from the sewers of the earth, her lovers the disease-ridden scum of every ship that put into harbour. What would his brother say if he knew? Taking up gloves and silk hat he glanced again at his reflection.

'What would our dear brother say?' he asked, smiling. 'Why not find out . . . now!'

He had sold her, sold Maura Deverell into slavery! Drained of colour, Liam stumbled from the sitting room, his brain hardly registering what he was doing as he entered the bedroom that had been his father's. He had handed her over to some accomplice to be shipped to God only knew where and he had laughed as he said it. Laughed! Liam's fingers closed over the loaded pistol Seamus had ever kept in a drawer at his bedside. Padraig had laughed, but he would never laugh again!

The touch of cold steel against his fingers brought Liam to his senses. He had vowed revenge for his brother's rape of that girl yet the thought of Niamh's heartbreak had seen the vow unfulfilled. But this – he turned the pistol in his hand – the selling of an innocent girl into a life of degradation, turning her into a puppet that must dance to any act of debauchery . . . that he must avenge. What happened afterwards, the price the law would demand, was of no consequence; life had been empty for him since he had watched Maura Deverell disappear from sight across that desolate heathland, now knowing what he did it held no value at all. Tonight he would discharge the vow taken so many months before, he would repay Padraig in full, and after that . . . Walking quietly from the room Liam gave a mental shrug. It would not matter after that!

Returned to the sitting room he stared, refusing to believe

the sight that met his eyes. With blood streaming from her lips, her cheeks dark with the evidence of bruising, Niamh lay motionless across the wide hearth, and of his brother there was no sign. The pistol falling forgotten from his hand, Liam bent over the still form. It could only be his brother, who else would strike this gentle woman, who but Padraig would beat her senseless then leave her lying in her own blood?

Shouting for her maid, one of the few servants who had chosen to remain at the house, he gathered his sister-in-law into his arms. Her thin wasted body no more than a feather weight he carried her to her room and lay her on the bed, the frightened maid running beside him.

He should go after Padraig now, drag him from his horse and throttle the life from him; but what of Niamh, what if the cuts and bruises marring that pale face were not the full extent of her injuries? She must have a doctor and none in the house save himself could authorise that.

Watching the maid sponge the bruised face, carefully washing the blood from the still lips, Liam knew he could not leave. Padraig would return sooner or later and when he did he would find his brother waiting.

'I have to remove the mistress's clothing.'

Immersed in his own thoughts, Liam did not at first register the girl's words only hearing as she repeated them.

'Of course,' he nodded, 'I shall go to fetch the doctor myself, please stay with her until I return.'

He could have sent a stable hand, stayed with Niamh himself; but doctors could be temperamental beings, some refusing to turn out from a warm fireside. Liam touched a heel to the horse hurriedly saddled for him. It would be well for the doctor not to go refusing him!

It was five miles to Laurencetown. Remembering the words following after him as he left Niamh's bedroom, the maid calling that an English doctor was visiting at Belview House, he turned the horse's head in that direction. Pray God the man had not returned home.

Why would Padraig attack his wife, what could have riled him so? Questions drummed hard and fast as the animal's hooves. There was no love in his brother, not for the woman he had married or for the girl he had raped, there was only cruelty; a blackness of the heart that left no room for kindness or for decency, an evil that cried to heaven to be ended.

20

Niamh Riordan lay back on her pillows. She had glimpsed the invitation laid casually aside after Padraig had read it, seen the words written in beautiful copperplate on the gilt-edged card.

'. . . the honour of the company of Mr and Mrs Padraig Riordan . . .'

She watched the girl, a starched apron rustling as she moved about the bedroom.

'. . . to celebrate the birth of Her Royal Highness . . .'

Another child. She felt the pain of her own barrenness strike a coldness in her empty womb. Another child for the woman who already had given a husband six . . . while she, Niamh Riordan, had given her husband none!

It had been like a ray of sunlight on a dark morning, a quick feeling of happiness. A visit to Portington Hall, a ball, the chance of seeing old friends, perhaps of making new ones . . . it had all seemed so wonderful. But her husband had glared at her smile, laughed at her excitement. *She* go to Portington Hall! He had snatched up the card, placing it in the pocket of his morning coat. *She* accompany him, reducing him to a figure of pity for being saddled with such a wife? Or, worse still, a man to be laughed at as he entered that ballroom with a scrawny sallow-faced worn-out drab on his arm, a worthless barren sow . . . !

Each word had struck like a blow to her face, like the blows he had rained on her this evening, but the pain of them had been worse, much, much worse.

She had dressed carefully, having the girl that tended her now dress her in the pink lace-frilled gown she had worn to her wedding and dressing her hair with matching satin rosebuds, the diamonds that had been her mother's glittering at her throat and ears. She was not the pretty girl Padraig had married, the radiance had gone from her face and her eyes had lost their sparkle, but a beat of hope had throbbed in her breast as she had walked down the staircase to the sitting room, the hope her husband might see the love she had for him, might turn to her with a smile, reach his hand to her in welcome.

He had turned to her. Niamh threw back the bedcovers. But the smile on his face had been one of mockery, the hands that reached to her one of dismissal.

'*What do you think you are doing? Do you honestly think I will allow you to go to Portington Hall? You are a sight, a laughing stock!*'

The words he had flung at her bouncing like pebbles on the pool of her mind, Niamh got to her feet.

'Ma'am, ye shouldn't be leaving yer bed.'

The girl was beside her but Niamh pushed away the gentle hands, instructing her instead to bring a gown from the wardrobe.

'But ma' am,' wide-eyed the girl protested, 'ye can't be after thinking of going out, the master—'

Niamh's lips stung as she answered. 'The master is not here and I am mistress of this house. Do as I say, bring the gown, child, and have no fears for I shall see to it nothing of what I do will rebound upon your head.'

Dressed as before, Niamh touched a hand to her bare throat. The diamonds were gone, taken by her husband as he had taken every other piece of jewellery she had brought with her to Eyrecourt. But diamonds did not matter, after all, what good were diamonds to a barren sow?

Instructing the girl to fetch the head stable boy, Niamh sat at her small escritoire. Penning two letters she sealed them, and as her maid returned with the stable hand she gave a letter to each.

'Give that to Mr Liam when he returns.' She smiled reassuringly at the girl. 'It will be as I told you, no blame will come to you on account of my going out.'

'But ma' am, ye should wait on the doctor . . .'

'I am perfectly all right.' Niamh's whole body protested the lie but the smile remained on her swollen mouth as she glanced at the man staring self-consciously at his boots.

'You know my father's house?'

'I do that, ma' am.'

'Then I ask you to take that letter to him there, would you do that?'

The man looked up then away again quickly, clearly disturbed at being in his mistress's bedroom even though her maid was present.

'Yer father's house, to be sure I will, ma'am.'

'Mr Mahoney.' He had already turned for the door when Niamh spoke again. 'I would like it to be delivered right away so my father can make ready for me.'

Nodding, the man left the room, the letter tucked into the pocket of his jacket.

' 'Tis glad I am ye be going to stay in yer father's house, ye'll be happy there, I know.' The girl smiled.

'Yes.' Niamh's answer was quiet. 'I will be happy there.'

'It'll be after taking no more than the flick of a rabbit's tail for me to have ye a trunk packed and meself in bonnet and cloak.'

Reaching for her own cloak, Niamh shook her head. 'There be dresses a plenty that I left behind when I married and there are maids also.' Seeing the dismay on the young face she reached out a hand to touch the girl's cheek. 'What a worrier you are, Mary, and there's no need at all. I promise you no one will take your place. Now run along and have the small carriage harnessed for me.'

'But ma' am, ye can't be after thinking to go alone.'

Her body shouting its pain, her mouth throbbing afresh with the slightest movement of her lips, Niamh realised the effort of pretence was fast becoming more than she could uphold. Her hands trembled as she fastened the cloak but she looked steadily at her maid, willing the real suffering not to show in her tired eyes.

'No more argument, Mary,' she smiled again, 'I will be home before supper and you can have that time with the young gardener who makes sheep's eyes at you each time you pass him.'

Blushing furiously the girl made a business of opening the door. At the foot of the staircase Niamh halted.

'Spring air is like to be cool after dark, maybe I should have the white fur muff.'

Needing no second bidding the girl turned and ran back up the stairs.

She had not known how long she had crouched there in that room. Day and night, light and dark, it had meant nothing to her, only her fear was real, a fear that held her like an animal in a trap unable to escape, too weak to break the bonds; and beneath it all had been another more terrifying fear, that of Padraig Riordan returning.

It had taken the long howl of a vixen sounding mournfully over the wide countryside to bring her out of that waking nightmare. With the answering bark of the dog fox she had lifted her face from her shawl, catching her breath at sight of that figure still lying as it had fallen. The man had not moved. She swallowed hard, the memory of blood dried hard and black against an ivory-mottled skin churning her empty stomach. She had stood there, her conscience telling her to at least cover him with a blanket, while every nerve screamed at the thought of stepping closer to him. Then as the distant bark came again she had fled and had not stopped running until lack of breath saw her fall to the ground.

That was where they had found her. Crouched into herself, sobs shaking the whole of her body, she had screamed as a hand touched her shoulder.

It had been some time later, while a kettle simmered over a fire of sticks, that a woman had told her what had happened next.

'Sure an' wasn't it himself thinking the angels in heaven had been sent to fetch ye.' The woman's voice, soft with a brogue Maura did not recognise, echoed now in her mind. *'But I told him so I did, I told him ye were no more than fainted from weariness and, from the looks of ye, the same hunger that gnaws at many in this land, is that not the truth now?'*

There had been no need to answer, the woman had talked on as she had brewed a kettle of tea, and in her words Maura had heard a heartbreak that matched her own. Three years following each other the potatoes had rotted from the sickness that ravaged the fields and though there had been no man evict them from their clochan the land itself had done that.

'What good do a roof be when ye have naught to put in the mouths of yer children?' The woman's lips had trembled and her eyes glistened with tears as she had handed Maura the cup of hot tea, her head shaking its refusal to take back the drink.

Looking at her now, clutching the arm of the one child left to her, Maura felt the mountain of pity rise again inside her. Four children, the woman had said, four babies lost to the hunger and still no harvest, yet they had been willing to share what they had with her, to comfort her though their own hearts were as lead inside them.

They had asked her no questions, only listening and nodding as she told of her mother's death, of burying her some-where on the trackless heath, taking it for granted it was the failure of crops and the resulting hunger had driven them from their cottage; and of Padraig Riordan . . . of the man lying dead in that house, she had said nothing.

'*Ireland be rejecting her own.*' The woman had talked on as they shared the tea, using words to relieve the pain inside her. '*She will give no more of her bounty, her eyes be closed against the suffering of those that love her and her heart closed to their sorrows. There can be life here no more for the poor, they must seek it in foreign lands though the soul will ever cry out for the sweet bosom of their motherland.*'

She had touched the ground then, stroking the soft turf with her fingers, and Maura's own soul had cried out as she watched the movement her mother had made so many times before. It was tearing the heart from this kindly woman having to leave behind so much of what she loved in this world.

'*Maybe the English will help.*'

The woman had laughed at what she had said, a hopeless laugh filled with bitterness that added to the edge of accusation lacing her answer.

'*Taoiseach* John Russell! *Prime Minister he be but his thoughts be for his own country, for England, he gives no mind to the Irish.*'

'But he must,' Maura had insisted, '*once he knows—*'

'*Ye mean he isn't after knowing!*' The woman's husband had joined in then, his own disgust thick in every word. '*Ye means to tell that with half the folk of Ireland dead already from the hunger and the other half dragging themselves to the coast to be shipped away like the beasts, the man still be not knowing the plight of this land? I say that he does, an' I further says he has no care forrit, it would be like to suit the man fine, to suit all the English fine should every last child of Ireland leave these shores and his* Garda Siochana, *his grand police force, standing by to see them gone!*'

She could not blame them for their bitterness. Maura drew the amber-coloured shawl closer as a breeze whipped from the far-off mountains. But the plague that had the soil sour and the potatoes just skins full of foul-smelling water could not be laid at the door of any man; it was happening of nature and surely it would pass. Yet it had not passed in time to save the family of these people or to save her own mother.

When the kettle was empty of the warming drink the man had spread the smouldering sticks with the toe of his worn-through boot before dousing them with water from a nearby brook. They were following the river, he had said, it would bring them to the coast and there they would ask direction to the nearest port and hope to find a ship that would take them to the Americas, adding she could travel with them if it be she had the liking of it. She had accepted.

Now Maura sank thankfully to the ground as the man called a halt for the evening. Maybe Padraig Riordan would not look for her to be travelling with a family. The Americas! She watched the man and his son set off in search of a rabbit. She did not know where that might be, how far off, but she would go.

Climbing into the small carriage that had been a part of her parents' marriage gift to her, Niamh laid the muff on the seat beside her. Taking the reins she waved away the groom, setting the horses to a run even as the man protested. The way was long and it would take several hours to reach her destination, but time was of no importance. She called gently to the matched pair of sable mares, feeling them fret under a hand they were not used to. They too had been a gift to her, one more her husband had taken for his own use. As he had robbed her of everything. But none of that had any consequence. She smiled, a hidden happy smile; Padraig would not take anything else from her, hurt her no more with his words or his fists, she would be safe in her father's home.

Life had promised her so much. She flicked the reins, setting the animals to the gallop. Padraig had promised her so much. She would be mistress of Eyrecourt, the gracious house set on the rise overlooking Clonfert. She would be happy there, *they* would be happy there. Had she been too young to recognise the lies that had tripped so glibly from his tongue, had it been naivety or love had blinded her to them? Had the handsome face smiling down at her roused a passion nothing but marriage could satisfy?

So they had been married and he had brought her to Eyrecourt. And she had not found it the happy home he had professed it to be, but one filled with discontent, echoing with the abuse of father to son, brother to brother; and soon had come the abuse of her. Why did she not give him a son? Other women had borne his children, why not her? At first it had been said only in the heat of anger but that had changed as each month her cycle had begun, changed to a cruel, heartless taunting. Then had come the blows, savage vicious blows, each one a product of his dislike . . . no, his hatred of her. In them was all his frustration, the inward revolt against his father, the man who could, and eventually did, strip him of his inheritance. That too he had blamed her for; had she given him a son, an heir, the grandchild to assure his father of the continuance of the line, then he never would have been disinherited, his dues given instead to the runt. But she had remained childless, his barren sow!

The hooves of the mares echoed on the evening stillness but their sound made no impression on a mind lost to the screams of its own ulcerous thoughts.

She had lost him Eyrecourt, she had given it to his runt of a brother. Niamh winced as if feeling again the sting of the fists that had accompanied the tirade. Perhaps after all that was so, but the only one she had felt sympathy for had been Liam. The misfit they had called him, his father and his brother, and in a way they had been right for Liam Riordan was not as they were; he was gentle where they were cruel, considerate where they were not, going out of his way to be kind to her.

And she had repaid that kindness with Eyrecourt! She flicked the reins again, wanting the journey to be over. She had given him what deep inside she knew he did not want, what he had no desire to own, but what the pity of his heart would not allow him to refuse for fear of what would inevitably be the outcome. Seamus Riordan had feared for the continuance of his line, that much she had learned from listening at the dinner table, herself being discussed like some brood mare. He had feared his elder son would beget no heir and his younger would find no woman to become his wife. Seamus Riordan had carried a burden that had shown deep in those pale eyes set beneath beetle brows, a burden she had not learned of by listening but one some inner sense told her never left him, one she felt he would find no way of lifting. Was the fact of her inability to conceive the reason for that burden or was it something far deeper . . . something buried so deep in his soul he could no longer find it?

Now the man was dead, his burden buried and forgotten, but the evil bred in his son went on. Padraig would never forgive, never accept the loss of Eyrecourt. The action his father had taken would continue to fester inside him, to poison him, to drive him mad with the insult of it. There would be no day of rest in that house and no safety for Liam.

Liam! She smiled as the picture of that kind face with its dark gentle eyes rose to her mind's eye. He too carried a burden, but his was not a fear for Eyrecourt or the continuance of the Riordan name, his was a misery that went beyond that, a heartache that matched her own, the pain of a broken heart. Broken by the rejection of a father ashamed of a son, of the constant comparison of him to his brother . . . or was the twisted back the cross he carried? It could be any of them yet somehow Niamh knew it was none of those reasons.

Her glance caught by a raven flying dark against the last of the sun she let the thought slip away, followed by a silent prayer for her unhappy brother-in-law. Liam would ever be in her heart.

The bird calling loudly as it reached its roost she eased the reins, allowing the sweating horses to fall into a gentler pace. They had raced well, she would reach the house before midnight.

21

'Who was it showed ye the way of that?'

Maura looked at the lad watching her across the fire his father had lit, eight years . . . ten? He was no older despite too much hunger giving a gaunt look that aged his small face.

'My father taught me,' she answered, smiling though her heart still thumped from the fear of being caught as that gamekeeper had caught her. 'A sidewater of the Shannon lay not far from where we lived and trout were plenty there and the tickling of them was easy.'

The lad's father glanced across the fish he had threaded on a stick. 'Ye mean ye were allowed to fish the waters?'

'Yes.' Maura nodded. 'In Clonmacnoise the river was free to any it would feed.'

Placing one end of the stick in the ground, the other dangling the fish over the fire, the man stared into the dancing flames. 'Clonmacnoise? I can't be after saying I knows of the place but it has to be special if its waters be open to all.'

A special place! In a moment Maura was back beside a smooth flowing stream, a child laughing as her father flicked crystal drops of water over her bare feet then swept her up into his arms to sit on his shoulders, carrying her towards a small stone-built cottage, a dark-haired woman waving from its doorway. Yes, Clonmacnoise had been a special place.

'Was ye after having no English landlord claiming rights to every stream, to every inch of land?'

The dejection in the man's voice, the hopelessness did not

hide the wound Maura guessed was deep and raw inside him. It was the failure of the potatoes had driven them from their home so the woman had said, but had that been the all of it or was there something else embittering this man, something he attributed to foreigners?

'We had a landlord,' she answered quietly. 'He did not live in Clonmacnoise but in Clonfert.' She could have said Seamus Riordan was as avaricious of a man's land as any foreign-born landlord, that he grabbed at all he could, but that would not serve to heal the pain inside the man sat opposite; nothing would do that, wasn't the pain of leaving Ireland, the pain that throbbed in her own soul, a pain that would never really end?

' 'Twas fortunate ye were then.'

It was an almost sullen answer and one that brought a sharp glance from his wife who said tartly, 'Sure, isn't it fortunate we are to be having trout for supper?'

'Will ye teach me the doing of it, the tickling of a trout?' The boy glanced hopefully at Maura.

Glad the awkwardness of the moment had passed, Maura nodded. 'I will and gladly, but I warn you it cannot be learned in a moment, it takes time.'

'Which ye don't have, ye forward spalpeen.' The lad's mother touched the tousled head fondly. 'Ye'll be after eating your supper then it's sleep for ye so it is and –' she held up a hand to stop the words already on the boy's tongue '– and 'tis no arguments I'll be having.'

After the fish was eaten and everyone's hands and face were rinsed in the stream the woman settled her son to sleep, clearing a space on the handcart that held all they possessed in the world, then she placed the kettle on the glowing embers. The last of her precious tea was gone, shared with Maura when they had found her crouched and spent on the heath. Now she added leaves of dried rosemary to the kettle, the scent of the herb drifting in the steam issuing from the spout added a delicate fragrance to the soft touch of evening.

How many times had she smelled that scent? Her back against a clump of rock, Maura stared across the wide moorland to where, at the rim of the horizon, a pale moon lifted its haloed head. Taught the use of herbs by first her own mother and then by Sinead O'Toole, Mairead Deverell had many times brewed a tisane, a drink of herb tea used to cure many ailments; but rosemary or camomile she had used most often, saying they were a tonic that helped restore a tired body and ease a troubled mind, and she had also sometimes given it to quieten a child frightened by a nightmare. Accepting a cup of it now, Maura breathed deeply the aromatic perfume, raising the shadows of memories long hidden; but would it quieten the nightmare she was living now, relieve the horror her life had become? No. She sipped the warming liquid, wanting to halt the pictures its scent recalled, but as she lay beside the crackling fire they followed her into sleep.

'So unfortunate your wife could not be with us, you must allow my sister and me to call upon her once she is recovered of her illness.' Henry, Lord Portington, smiled at his guest, his blue eyes resting momentarily upon the scar now just a thread stretching a faint purple line over one side of Padraig's face, but as the glance ran over it Padraig knew again the rage he had felt on first seeing the mark his brother had left upon him! But now at least the cause of it was paying the price, Maura Deverell was well on her way to the whorehouse of some distant shore: it was not all the vengeance he had promised himself . . . but it was a start!

'That is most considerate of your lordship,' he replied, resisting the urge to touch the faded scar, 'I know that will please my wife greatly.'

'Then we will present our card shortly.'

Her brother excusing himself, moving to welcome other guests as they were announced, Eugenie Stratford tapped a lace fan against her fingertips, her glance wandering over an assembly dressed as if to outshine the queen they had gathered to honour.

'I hear, Mr Riordan, that you have gone into the exporting business for yourself, do you count that a prudent move?'

His own glance moving over a room ablaze with the light of great banks of tall candles and chandeliers, Padraig smiled. The question had not been unexpected for he had realised a watch would have been kept since that girl had gone from this house, but he knew the words were a guess; it would be surmised that any goods marketed by him would go by way of Tullamore, and that was not simply their mistake, it was his safeguard.

'Were it so, ma'am,' he answered quietly, 'then it would be more prudent than standing to be cheated twice.'

The fan tapped a little quicker. 'Cheated! Why, Mr Riordan, what can you mean?'

Broadening his smile as if in answer to some delightful item of conversation, Padraig looked directly into the attractive face, but the eyes so like those of her brother glared with a look of blue ice.

'What I mean is being in business with a partner who takes too great a share of any profit into his own pocket and that process being repeated by that partner's cat's paw.'

Nodding to a woman, the rubies at whose throat and ears gleamed like miniature fires, Eugenie Stratford's breath splintered with irritation.

'I do not advise—'

'That would be sensible!' Padraig's reply scythed her answer. 'It would also be sensible not to threaten. You see, my dear, to do that would be to bring about the most unfortunate repercussions; for example, should his lordship find out my accomplice, the woman I met at Tullamore, is none other than his own sister, and the man pretending to be her father is in reality the gamekeeper he dismissed a while back, then I fear your own ventures would be at an end and quite probably you would find yourself secluded in some God-forsaken hamlet somewhere!'

'How dare you threaten me!'

'Why not? A man should always do the things he enjoys.'

Shaking open her fan and lifting it to hide the set of her mouth, her answer was a hiss. 'Sometimes, Mr Riordan, a woman too manages to achieve something enjoyable to herself, like killing a pest . . . or a man!'

Raising her hand to his lips, Padraig laughed softly as he answered. 'That man will never be me, Eugenie . . . I live a charmed life. Like people say, the devil takes care of his own.'

A blaze of twinkling lights dancing in the moonlit distance, Niamh glanced at the fur muff lying on the seat beside her. She had forgotten nothing in her dressing.

Calling softly to the mares she smiled as they picked up their step. The servants at the house would be surprised to see her arriving alone but talk of it would soon make way for choicer items of below-stairs' gossip.

Thankful her father and brothers had taught her how to handle a carriage and pair she guided the vehicle around the sweeping circular driveway to bring it to the soaring four-columned portico which, together with elegantly matched colonnaded pavilions to each side, formed the beautiful façade of the elegant stone-built house.

Allowing herself to be handed from the carriage she tucked both hands inside the muff, ignoring the surprised looks of several footmen as she walked up the broad steps and into the brilliantly lit circular reception hall.

Her cloak removed, Niamh shook her head briefly as a maid

reached for the muff, then drawing a long breath she crossed the inlaid floor, pausing to speak to a footman positioned at a doorway giving onto a large room.

'I . . . I beg madam's pardon.' The servant's excellent reserve cracked as he listened to Niamh's quietly spoken words. 'I did not quite hear all madam said.'

Still quiet, yet with a firmness the manservant could no longer deny, Niamh repeated her words adding. 'You will please have me announced as I have said.'

Taking one step inside the doorway the footman whispered to an impressively liveried major domo whose smile, hidden only by a strong effort of will, vanished immediately he saw the small face pale beneath its chorus of purple bruises. Portington Hall had never received such a guest before nor had one asked to be announced in such a way. Bowing first to Niamh then facing into the glittering ballroom, he called loudly, 'Mr Padraig Riordan's barren sow!'

Eugenie Stratford's hand still to his lips, Padraig stiffened. He could not have heard those words, they were only in his mind. But the sudden hush broken only by gasps of women's indrawn breath and the quiet murmurs of scandalised men told him otherwise.

'Behold the devil!' Eugenie laughed behind the cover of her fan. 'Do you think he has come to take care of his own?'

Dropping the silk-gloved hand, Padraig turned, his own breath catching at the sight of Niamh walking towards him through a parted sea of people. What the hell did she think she was doing coming here, what would people think! With the speed of desperation driving his mind and his limbs he stepped towards her.

'My dearest, you should not be out, your accident . . .'

Inside the muff Niamh's fingers closed over the pistol. Sending Mary upstairs to fetch her muff had given her time to retrieve the weapon from where Liam had dropped it in the drawing room at Eyrecourt.

'It is too late, Padraig.' She withdrew the weapon, pointing it unsteadily at him, stopping him in his tracks. 'There will be no more lies, no more beatings. Was it not yourself said a barren sow be no good to a man, and yourself said that was all I was to you? A barren sow, Padraig –' she laughed a mild hopeless laugh, the pistol steadying in its aim '– but even a barren sow has some use, mine is to rid the world of the evil of Padraig Riordan.'

A smile playing over her cut lips she stared straight into a face twisted with surprise and fear, then with infinite slowness she squeezed the trigger.

A bevy of screams erupting around her she stared for a second at the blood spraying a crimson stream across the vividly white organza dress of a smiling Eugenie, then as Padraig fell to the floor she dropped the gun and walked from the room, none of the astounded assembly making a move to prevent her.

She had done what she had set out to do.

Oblivious of the maid running to bring her cloak, Niamh climbed into the carriage she had specifically requested wait for her close to the grand porticoed entrance to Portington Hall.

Padraig Riordan was dead! He would vent his spite on no other woman, make no other woman's life the misery he had made hers . . . and the heirs he had so yearned for? There would be none of those either!

Leaving the horses to make their own way she sat with the reins in her hands. He had not expected her to follow him to that ball or for her ever to retaliate against his vicious treatment. But she had and she was glad, glad he was dead. But she was sorry for ruining Lord Portington's celebratory ball and for spoiling his sister's dress.

Moonlight that had begun to pale before an oncoming dawn shone on the regretful smile. She must write a note of apology.

Liam heard the sound of horses' hooves and the grind of carriage wheels and was out of Eyrecourt House and running to grasp the halter of the tired mares even before the carriage reached the steps.

'Niamh!' Lifting her down from the seat he stared at the waxen pallor highlighted by the dark bruises. 'Your maid said you had gone to your father's house, how come you are here? I thought it was Padraig returning.'

Feeling the tremble rush through her he frowned. 'Where is your cloak? What was Mary thinking of letting you go out like this!'

Taking the lack of answers as a sign of fatigue he swept the slight figure into his arms; there would be time for answers later but now his sister-in-law was in need of a warm bed. Carrying her upstairs he set her gently on her feet but when he said he would call for her maid, Niamh shook her head.

'It cannot be long until dawn, let the girl sleep. I think neither you nor I have forgotten how to undress for ourselves.'

There had never been any airs and graces about this woman. Liam felt his heart contract as he looked into eyes ringed with shadows of weariness and heartache. Why could his brother not see the worth of the woman he had married, the love that had shone even beneath the bruises?

'If you are sure.'

Smiling as he hesitated, Niamh nodded. 'I am sure, and you too should get some sleep.'

Sleep! Walking slowly back down the stairs, Liam smiled grimly. There would be no bed for him, no sleep until his brother returned, no sleep until he was called to account for his treatment of Niamh. Reaching the hall he stared back up the staircase of the silent house. He had not been able to prevent Padraig's cruelty to Maura Deverell but there would be no more mistreatment of Niamh!

Moving into the kitchen he set a pan of milk to boil over the fire that burned all night in the polished iron range. Neither of them had forgotten how to undress for themselves! That was only one part of his youth he had not forgotten, making a cup of cinnamon-spiced hot milk was another. It would help Niamh sleep.

Pleading shock, Eugenie Stratford had retired, leaving her brother to manage the revival of the interrupted ball. Now lying in the comfort of her bed she watched the prettily uniformed maid gather the stained gown. She would have preferred to keep it with her, even to have it mounted on the wall of this room as a memento of the evening the blight of Padraig Riordan had been lifted from her shoulders.

A doctor had been called before she had been helped from the room, Henry insisting she not see that bloodied figure heaped on the floor of the ballroom a moment longer. It was too much for a woman to look at, Henry had said. Christ, that was all she wanted to do, look at that corpse and laugh! But that would have been unwise, the sister of Lord Portington must appear the delicate English rose!

'I'll try to clean the dress ma'am but blood be awful hard to wash away.'

She didn't want it washed away, she didn't ever want it washed away, she wanted it as her trophy. Keeping the thought locked behind the bars of her mind, Eugenie closed her eyes in a pseudo show of revulsion.

'Burn it,' she shuddered, 'have one of the men burn it on the rubbish heap. I never want to see the thing again, to be reminded . . . poor Mr Riordan.'

'Will I get ye a draught of something? Mrs Maynard swears by a little tincture of poppy juice in wine . . . says it brings on a real refreshing sleep, so her does.'

Of the kind those girls wake from to find themselves on
board ship in the middle of some ocean. Telling the maid to
leave, Eugenie's smile of triumph blossomed as the door
closed behind her. Padraig Riordan was no more and neither
was her opposition. Clara Maynard would continue to terrify
any orphan youngster that strayed this way and Leech could
watch for the same further afield; the white slave trade out of
Ireland would be solely the preserve of Eugenie Stratford and
so would the profits. True, she did not need the money, but
she excitement . . . it was food and wine in the endless desert
of a totally boring life.

Stretching a hand to the oil lamp placed beside her bed she
turned it down to a soft glimmer.

'Thank you, Niamh,' she laughed softly into the flickering
shadows, 'you see, Padraig Riordan's barren sow had her uses
after all.'

22

At the door of Niamh's bedroom Liam halted. He had not thought whilst in the kitchen how unseemly it was for him to go alone into his sister-in-law's room, no matter how kindly the intent. He glanced at the spiced milk steaming on the small tray. Given the mood of his brother these past weeks, should he find them in the bedroom together he was liable to place any definition upon it. That would be too much for Niamh, her heart was already broken and he could not open the way for a fresh tide of abuse.

A little way along the corridor a sound had Liam turn quickly. Padraig?

'Your pardon, Mr Liam sir, I was after thinking I heard someone moving about the house, I wasn't knowing 'twas yourself so it was.'

Quick relief flooded Liam like warm sunshine. He was not afraid of his brother for his own sake but for the pain his wicked accusing would cause Niamh.

'The mistress did not wish the house wakened.' He answered, thankful the old servant had appeared. This man had managed the household from Seamus's first marrying the English woman, he would understand the situation.

'The mistress?' The man's grey eyebrows drew together. 'But the mistress be gone to visit with her father, young Mary said—'

'The mistress changed her mind.' Liam realised the answer must sound suspicious but what other could he give? He had returned with that doctor only to hear Niamh had left Eyre-court for her father's house.

In the dim light of the corridor Liam could see the confusion on the face of the older man. Explanations needed to be given, if only out of respect for the many years the man had been with the family.

'The mistress returned some half an hour since.' He spoke quickly, wanting Niamh to get her spiced milk before it cooled. 'I was not yet gone to bed so I fetched her into the house myself. I wanted to call her maid to help her to bed but she insisted the girl be allowed to sleep, saying she had not forgotten how to undress for herself. So rather than cause her distress by arguing, I left her to it. Coming into the hall I remembered the spiced milk my mother made my brother and me when we were overtired and fretful, and I thought perhaps a cup of it might help bring sleep.' Glancing at the servant he smiled ruefully. 'But when I got to this door I wished I hadn't made it after all.'

With his brows still drawn together, the older man shook his head. 'Now why would ye be after regretting a kindness?'

If he could speak honestly to anyone it was to this man, a man who had often seen the pain of his growing and had tried in his own way to make up for the mindless cruelty of a father. Answering now, Liam smiled. 'I was so concerned for Niamh, I gave no mind to the embarrassment I would cause in taking in the drink myself.'

The frown cleared from the servant's brow. He had watched Liam Riordan long moments before deliberately shuffling his feet; he had seen the hesitation, the questioning in the mind that had kept his hand from the door of his sister-in-law's room, and knew it was no pretence. Reaching now for the tray he spoke quietly.

'Then p'raps 'twould be better for meself to be after taking that milk to the mistress.'

At the head of the stairs Liam's hand gripped the rail of the carved banister. There was a fear in the voice that called to him, alarm that trembled on his name.

His blood an icy slush that blocked every vein he turned back towards Niamh's room.

The letter lay crumpled in his hand as Liam stared into the fire. His brother was recovering from his pistol wound, but following doctor's advice would remain for the time being at Portington Hall.

He had forgotten all about that pistol, forgotten letting it fall to the floor of the drawing room, but Niamh . . . ! She had not done as she told the servants, she had not gone to her father's house – his fingers tightened on the paper – had she found the gun . . . had she shot Padraig?

Smoothing the crumpled note he read again.

. . . *my sister and I send our best wishes for the speedy recovery of health to your brother's wife after her most unfortunate accident* . . .

Did that mean Padraig had excused his wife's absence from that ball by saying she was unwell or had Niamh followed him to Portington Hall, where the injuries had been seen by people there and her husband had claimed they were caused by some accident?

Accident! Those cuts to her mouth, the bruises on her face had not been the result of any accident but of a man's cruelty. God, how could he . . . how could any man treat a woman as gentle as Niamh with such brutality!

The pistol – his eyes resting on the creased notepaper caught the word written in elegant flowing script – the one he had taken from his father's room, it had not been found by the maids when cleaning this room or it would have been handed over to himself; and Niamh had not been in possession of it when he lifted her from the carriage. But did that necessarily imply she had not found it, taken it to Portington Hall and shot . . . No! His mind rebelling at the thought, he threw the letter into the fire. Niamh would never do a thing like that.

    . . . her most unfortunate accident . . .

The words danced behind his eyes. Niamh must have come into the drawing room moments after he had gone to get the pistol from his father's room. Had she demanded to accompany Padraig and he turned on her, raining those blows to her face? Demand! Were it not for the pain in his heart he might have smiled. Since when had that woman ever demanded anything? But had that last 'accident' finally proven too much, had she indeed taken the pistol to Portington Hall and shot Padraig? That was a question he could not ask of her.

A tap at the door claiming his attention he looked up as the old manservant entered the room.

'A visitor, sir, Mr Fergus Shea. Will I show him to the library?'

Niamh's father here at Eyrecourt! How could he have heard so quickly?

'No,' he answered quickly. 'Ask Mr Shea to join me here.'

'Where be Padraig Riordan, where be the filthy black-hearted divil?'

There had been no waiting for the servant to withdraw, the explosion had come even as Fergus Shea approached the drawing room.

'My brother is not in the house.'

'Then where is he?' With fury in every line of him the man ripped apart the explanation. 'Where is the black-hearted spalpeen that goes calling himself a man? Let him try beating Fergus Shea as he has beaten his daughter, let him lift his fists to a man instead of a woman!'

It would be little use trying to calm this man with niceties, apart from which he deserved the truth. Quietly and without rush Liam told of his brother's bullet wound then of his apprehension that Niamh might have fired the shot, adding that Padraig was still at Portington Hall.

'I've come for my daughter, I'm taking her to the home where she is loved and yourself will not have the stopping of it.'

No, he would not attempt to stop Fergus Shea. Liam accepted the other man's demand. She deserved the love of her own, a love Padraig had never shown her. Leading the way he opened the door of a dimly lit room, stepping aside for Fergus to enter. Sympathy welled inside him as he watched the man fall to his knees beside the bed and throw his arm across the girl. He closed the door, leaving the father to grieve in private for his dead daughter.

It had been the old servant's cry had him running back to that bedroom, to a sight that would haunt him to his last day. Niamh, gentle kindly Niamh, hanged by the neck from the stretcher bar that ran between the posts of her bed. He had taken her down, calling her name as he cradled her in his arms, but life had already left that thin body. He had held her close against him as her body stiffened, only releasing it when the women servants begged she be shown the respect of being bathed and dressed. Dressed for death! She was gowned in her finest white lawn nightgown, her long braids twined with white satin ribbons. They had lit candles at her head and feet before bringing him back to the room. There, alone, he had prayed for the soul of Niamh Riordan, but for Padraig he could not pray at all.

Joined again by Fergus Shea, his eyes red from weeping, Liam offered the hospitality of the house.

'I'll be after taking nothing from this house except my child.' Fergus shook his head. 'I have brought my own people to see to the bearing of her home.' He was turned to leave when suddenly he looked back. 'I know 'tis none of your doing, Liam Riordan, the bringing of this telled me so.'

Taking a letter from his pocket he thrust it at Liam. The

writing was the same as on the letter Mary had given him when
he had brought the doctor . . . Niamh's writing.

'This must be private . . .'

'I would have ye read it.' Fergus made no move to take back
the letter.

> *My dearest father,*
> *Place no blame on Liam for he was ever kind to me . . .*

A feeling of intrusion had Liam's eyes skipping rapidly over
the spidery words until he reached the end, then with a grief
rising so strong it blocked the breath in his throat he read
again.

> *. . . what I do this night will see no regret following me into my*
> *grave. I can no longer live with the cruelty of Padraig Riordan*
> *and he, the man who promised before God to love and cherish,*
> *does not deserve to live. There is no place in the Church for a*
> *murderess or for one who takes her own life, but perhaps some-*
> *where in a father's heart a daughter may find a prayer.*
> *Niamh.*

'My daughter be no murderess for ye tells me Padraig Riordan
be at Portington.' Taking back the letter Fergus folded it before
replacing it in his coat pocket. 'But he will not stay for ever
beneath that roof, someday he will return to Eyrecourt and
what a colleen did not have the doing of then her father will!'

'Ye'll come with us, Maura, to the Americas, ye will so?'

Maura looked at the smiling face alight with eagerness and
anticipation as they approached the bustling port they had
been told was Dublin.

'They don't take passengers who haven't money to pay.'
Maura saw the happiness dim but she squeezed the hand that

had tucked itself into hers. 'It will be better if you go to that country and myself to another for then we will have the pleasure of visiting . . . think of all the grand sights you will be seeing on those journeys to and fro.'

'Sure an' they will be grand, won't they, Maura, and I'll be after making them often so I will for Father tells we'll have riches a plenty in our new land.'

Riches a plenty. Maura smiled. Pray heaven it would be so but the lad was already rich did he but realise, rich with the love of a family and the wealth of a country that held his heritage. He must leave Ireland, for that was his destiny, but let him never forget the spirit and the heart of the land that had nurtured him.

'Where is it ye'll be after going?'

The question his mother asked was almost lost in the noise and bustle of the busy street.

Where could she go? With not a penny with which to bless herself where could Maura Deverell go! The anxiety of knowing she was destitute and would soon be alone once more rippled along Maura's nerves but she kept her smile as she forced an answer.

'I shall look for work in this town, that will give me time to settle in my mind where it is I will be moving on to as well as giving me time to save the money that pays for my travel.'

'Ye'll be after looking for work in this place?' The man's glance skimmed the people who hurried, it seemed, in every direction, scurrying in and out of tall buildings like so many mice. 'Then it's care ye must be taking, a pretty colleen alone in such a town be running a grave risk.'

'What does that mean, Father, why is Maura running—'

His mother's hand sharp against his head ended the boy's question.

'It be naught that should be heard by little piggy ears!' she cuffed him again. 'Now ye go after minding that tongue o' your'n or it could be ye'll be finding it wearing a coat of the bitter aloes I carries in yonder chest!'

'Here, lad,' his father called, 'ye walk along o' me to find which ship in that harbour be bound for them Americas.'

His glance lifting to Maura he smiled. It was goodbye. Maura felt the sadness weigh heavy in her breast. These people had been kind to her but kindness alone would not buy her a passage to that far-off land.

As the two women hugged each other, both whispering her hopes for the friend she had made, silent tears ran down Maura's cheeks until at last unable to bear the emotion of it any longer she broke away, hurrying blindly from the quayside. Caitlin and her family, then Bridget and now this woman and her little family, had each brought a ray of light into her dark life, a spark of warmth into the emptiness of her existence . . . but all of them were gone.

Pushed and shoved by passers-by who seemed to have no thought for anything other than getting about their business as rapidly as possible, Maura wandered along one cobbled street after another, mindless of where they might lead, blind to the sight of the great Rathfarnham Castle, the beautiful Hermitage house or the gracious old Priory, not noticing as once more her weary steps carried her to the harbour with its tall-storeyed buildings and dark arched warehouses, all pushed so close together that nothing larger than a small handcart could pass between them.

She had asked at every likely looking place she had come to, saying she would do any work they might have for the payment of a crust and a few pennies. The politest of those answering doors had laughed, others had cursed, threatening to set the dogs after her or to drench her with a pail of water.

Pausing to draw in several breaths she glanced at the rapidly darkening sky, tall masts with sails furled poking long black fingers towards the scudding clouds while a brisk wind caught at her skirts, tugging at the shawl clasped about her head and shoulders. Racing clouds and a sharp wind – they were signals of a coming storm; she must find shelter. But pausing, if only to draw breath, had been the wrong thing to do, now her legs refused to move. Too tired to will herself on she stepped into a doorway, crouching at its base. As she rested her head on her knees despair settled its icy coldness in her soul.

What else could she do, where else was there to walk? It seemed since leaving Clonmacnoise she had crossed all of Ireland, and if she hadn't then she had not the heart to cross any more of it.

Shivering as much from anxiety as from the wind whipping into the doorway she drew the shawl over her face. 'Holy Mother,' she prayed through trembling lips, 'You who made the long journey from Bethlehem into Egypt, You who must have known the loneliness of being parted from loved ones, the bitterness and sorrows, help me . . .'

She had slept! Maura started as a sharp boot caught her in the ribs. Despite the keen bite of the wind she had fallen asleep. Struggling to become fully awake she could not fend off the hand that gripped her arm, dragging her roughly to her feet.

'Now what is it we be finding here? A wharf rat I'll be bound . . .'

The voice was coarse and grating, rough as the hand that dragged at her.

'Well there be a place for wharf rats so there be, but it don't be no cosy doorway but the harbour they goes into along o' the rest o' the garbage. Dublin has beggars too many filthying its streets.'

'Stop!' Maura tried to pull away. 'I am not a beggar.'

'Then how come ye be squatting in a doorway, yer head covered as though ye be a sack o' rubbish? Aah, but now isn't it the fool I am!' The voice became a hoarse laugh. 'Shouldn't I have been after knowing 'tis a woman of the streets ye are, a prostitute taking a few minutes off from her labours of the night . . . Well now, I reckon ye can be pleasuring meself while forgetting of the pennies.'

His hands on the bare skin beneath her bloomers drove the last drug of sleep from Maura's brain. Driving both hands against his chest she sent him stumbling into the shadows of the doorway and as he crashed against the stone she turned to run, only to collide with a thick-set figure passing by.

'And how many divils is it be chasing ye?'

At the sound of the voice all the life, all the hope drained from Maura. Looking up into the heavy-jowled face she saw the man she had left for dead on the floor of that cottage.

Eugenie Stratford stood beside her brother at the foot of the porticoed steps of the elegant Portington Hall watching the tall figure of their departing visitor settle into the carriage and take the reins into a gloved hand.

The threat was not gone from her life, it remained with her still. The body she had watched slump to the floor spurting blood across her dress, the corpse she had been ushered away from had been no corpse at all. A shoulder wound, she had been told, painful but not mortal, Padraig Riordan would recover. Why! Her teeth clenched in anger. Why could that stupid woman not have aimed straighter, why had the shot not killed him! But it had not, and now he was leaving. His recuperation must not be a burden to them any longer, he had said, smiling and thanking them for their care; he must return home to his dear wife.

Dear wife! Eugenie's mood blackened. No one was dearer to Padraig Riordan than himself and most certainly not that mouse of a wife. Lord! If only she had known sooner, that same night, she could have found a way of finishing the job herself; now it was too late. He was well on the way to recovery . . . alive to threaten and cheat her of the trade she had built up.

Turning away as Padraig flicked the reins she stormed into the house, going directly to her own rooms. There must be a way ... there *had* to be a way of getting rid of Padraig Riordan.

23

A dull ache throbbing behind a cloth binding her eyes, Maura listened to the sounds around her, whimpering, sobbing sounds that said she was not alone in the fear that gripped her. How long had she slept? Where was she? Gradually the mist that fogged her brain began to clear. A man . . . a thick-set man . . . a doorway? Slowly the past returned. She had slept a while then . . . With her breath catching in her throat she tried to rise to her feet, crying out as she realised she was chained hand and foot. Who had done this to her . . . why?

As thoughts whirled like petals in a storm she called out, only to gasp as a sharp blow landed to the side of her head.

'Call out again an' it'll be the worse fer yer, next time I'll tek a club to yer 'ead.'

Her senses reeling from the savagery of it, Maura held her silence. The man she had struck with the kettle, the one she had thought dead, had grabbed her as she fled from that doorway, he had forced a bottle to her lips, making her drink, then had held a hand over her mouth while dragging her away. To where? She tried to remember, to recall any building other than tall narrow houses but the pictures danced away into a blur. But that was what had happened, her sight and hearing had blurred into nothing; the drink . . . the sweet smell and slightly bitter taste . . . it had to have been a drug, something that terrified her as it had carried her into sleep! And where had he, the man who had caught her, where had he taken her?

The sound of heavy footsteps climbing several steps then

passing overhead faded, leaving only the quiet frightened sobs
that seemed to come from both sides. Taking her courage in
her hands Maura called softly. There was someone else with
her, the whimpering said so even though her call received no
other answer; then like a bolt of lightning an answer she could
not have dreamed possible flashed into her mind.

'. . . *you will be any man's whore* . . .'

Those were the words Padraig Riordan had flung at her.

'. . . *any man who has the shilling to pay for you* . . .'

But that had been no more than words, words to frighten
her and venge his spite, they had not been truly meant.

'. . . *you will spread your legs for tuppence and then for a slice of
week-old bread* . . .'

Padraig Riordan could not have meant what he had said!
Desperate in this new fear, Maura tried to push the words
from her, but like a persistent wasp they buzzed in her
brain.

'. . . *you will pay* . . . *every day and every night* . . .'

'No!' The cry choked from her. 'Blessed Mother, not that
. . . not that.'

'Remember, not so much as a whisper or it'll be over the side
wi' yer.'

Pushed with three other girls against the rails of a sailing
ship, Maura blinked against the sudden light. Was this the
dockside she had come to with the boy and his parents? She
could not tell for she had not been there long enough to
memorise any building.

'Where is it they've brought us?'

Beside her a slight girl with hair black as a raven's feather
blinked silent tears.

Afraid of the answer yet driven to ask the question, Maura
whispered, 'Is this not Dublin?'

The girl shook her head. 'I haven't had the seeing of much of the place but still I knows this doesn't be Dublin town, for where is its fine castle and grand buildings?'

Falling silent as the stocky figure returned the girl inched closer to Maura.

'Ye'll be going ashore now!' Hands as rough as the voice caught at the girl clinging to Maura's hand, snatching her away from the rail. Glaring at Maura he herded the weeping girls together. 'And ye wait there, I has a special customer waiting on ye, one who'll pay the price Padraig Riordan asked . . . and a little bit extra for me.'

The price asked! Stunned by the reality of it all, Maura watched the girls, half pushed and half dragged, stumble down the gangplank. Padraig Riordan had sold her . . . sold her into a life of slavery!

Glancing over the ship's side she shuddered at the dark water, its surface thick with floating rubbish. It would be horrible but no more so than living Padraig Riordan's vengeance. Grabbing a rope that stretched from a furled sail to the rail she hoisted herself up.

'Oh no ye don't!'

It was a harsh laugh, a sound of mockery laced with enjoyment, as strong arms closed about her, breaking her hold on the rope.

'We don't lose no cargo from this boat and certainly none which will bring the price Riordan be asking.'

His rancid breath fanning her face as the seaman laughed again Maura cried out, but the cry was gone the moment it left her lips, absorbed, hidden among the screams of circling seagulls.

'All that will bring ye be a split mouth!' he growled, slapping a filthy hand over her face. 'Now don't be making me do that, a man don't pay as much for a wench wi' a cut face even though it'll be fine wi' the healing . . . but money or no, if ye cries out again it'll be my fist against yer teeth and no messin'!'

Seeing the look in the cold eyes that glared into her own Maura knew the threat was no idle one. Controlling the retching of her stomach, which rolled with each wave of foul breath that wafted to her nostrils, she gasped as she was released.

'Ye wait there, an' no more climbing or it'll be Davy Jones's locker ye'll be visitin'.'

'Wait . . . please.' Quiet, though her nerves were screaming, the request halted the sailor and he turned to face her. 'Where are you taking me, why have I not gone ashore with those other girls?'

'Them!' He laughed harshly. 'They'll be mostly back-door trade for the whorehouses of this town, a cheap lay for sailors and the like who don't have money to spend on the quality goods, that was what Riordan had in mind for ye but I can get more by selling ye elsewhere.'

'Selling!' Disbelief vibrant in the word, Maura stared at him. 'But you can't sell a human being—'

'No?' A strident laugh cutting off the rest the man pointed to the group of girls shuffling down the gangplank. 'Tell that to them!'

Watching the last girl step onto the quay to be immediately grabbed and hustled into a closed carriage Maura felt her world spin. How could one person sell another, and into such a sordid life? Yet it was happening there, right before her eyes and it would happen again . . . to her!

'Please,' she asked again, 'you say I am not to go with the others so . . . so where am I to be sent?'

A smile broadening his mouth displayed teeth yellowed from lack of care. 'See that ship?' He stretched an arm, pointing further along the quayside to where a tall-masted vessel was loading cargo. 'That be the *Ocean Queen*, sails the Orient route do the *Queen*, and them there Oriental pashas be willing to pay well for a white woman to add to their haireems; that be where ye be goin', to a pasha's haireem.'

'A pasha's haireem?' Never having heard the word before Maura pronounced it as he had.

'That be the way of it, me little Irish colleen,' he grinned, saliva giving a shine to thick lips, 'a pasha's haireem, and once a woman be taken into one o' they then her don't see the outside o' its walls agen not once in all o' her life! Ye'll be locked up tighter than ye would be in any prison here in England and ye bein' white skinned ye'll no doubt be used as often as any one o' they wenches that's just been carted off to Lilah's brothels.'

'Don't ye try nuthin'!' The warning was growled as Maura stared towards the quay. 'I'll see ye go to the bottom afore I lets ye blow the gaff on this sweet little enterprise, ye get that inta yer head! Now ye stand where ye be, and remember, I have others be holding their eyes on ye, and when the *Ocean Queen* sails out of Liverpool ye'll be on board.'

The Orient! Maura searched wildly in her mind for some recognition, some idea of where that place might be, but there had been no books in the cottage at Clonmacnoise except a small Bible and no world traveller had ever called at its door; for all she knew the Orient could be as far away as the land the family she had travelled to Dublin with had called the Americas. Locked for ever behind four walls, for ever at the mercy of a man who had purchased her like he would an animal! With terror rising in her throat she pressed the soft wool shawl to her lips. Padraig Riordan had got his revenge . . . more so than he would ever know.

She must have been so sure, so sure the shot had killed him. Poor Lady Eugenie Stratford, Padraig's smile was pure vindictiveness, so very disappointed! There must also be one other woman with that very same feeling of disappointment, Niamh! Trying to kill him was one thing, but to disgrace him in front of all those people was something else again, something that would cost her dear; she was going to wish herself dead once he was returned to Eyrecourt.

He had apologised over and again for her behaviour, telling Henry Portington and his sister that his wife was not fully recovered of a brain fever and that his servants would be called to account for not watching a sick woman more closely. Yet it was not the servants he would bring to book but his wife. His wife! The very thought was anathema; he not only disliked Niamh, he detested her. A barren womb, a childless marriage and a lost inheritance, that had been the dowry the daughter of Fergus Shea had brought to him, a dowry as worthless and empty as herself. How long would it go on?

. . . *Till death do us part* . . .

His eyes cold and hard Padraig stared at the path leading away across an empty moor. That was the dictate of the Church but even the Church could not say when death would come; Padraig Riordan could say when it would come for his wife, though, and that would be soon. Niamh was a burden he had suffered long enough. A barren sow, it was an apt description; and now it was time to be rid of her if he were ever to have a son . . . And when he took Eyrecourt back, as he meant to do, then there must be an heir to carry it on.

How strange there had been no message from Eyrecourt regarding his wife, Henry Portington had said several days after the shooting. Would he, Padraig, wish to have a footman sent to the house to enquire of her safe return? He had declined the offer, saying had she not returned home safely there would have been someone sent to Portington Hall to enquire after her. Then Henry had remarked upon there being no enquiry after his own health.

'*My brother is not at Eyrecourt at present.*' Padraig smiled, remembering the ease with which the lies had tripped from his tongue. '*And if, as I fear, my wife has suffered a return of the fever that affects her reasoning and behaviour then there is no servant would take it upon himself to write to Portington Hall.*' Eugenie's brother had looked quizzical on hearing the answers but had said nothing more; as for his lordship's sister she had enquired after the health of neither Niamh or himself!

But then the risk attached to doing so would have been too great. Hitching the reins with one hand Padraig glanced at the sling that held his other arm almost immobile. To ask of his welfare would have choked the Lady Eugenie Stratford. The look on that haughty face as he was leaving testified with indisputable clarity that the fact that Padraig Riordan was not dead was completely odious to her.

She had built her hopes too high, and so had Niamh, but then both were impediments easily removed. Niamh would succumb to her illness and Eugenie Stratford . . . ? She would not risk exposure as a slaver, the family name could not be sullied; that would leave the field clear and empty of competition and all profits of that lucrative game would flow into one pocket . . . his!

Deep in the pleasure of his thoughts Padraig had not noticed the carriage with its two roan horses coming towards him. Then as the drumming of hooves on hard ground penetrated the barrier he had drawn around his consciousness he glanced at the driver. It was still too much of a distance to recognise the man, his features slightly hidden by the tall wing-collars of a black coat and the high black hat set low over the brow. Whose was this carriage? Drawn almost level Padraig ran a glance over the shining bodywork as it slowed to a halt, but no distinguishing feature adorned it.

'The blessing of the day to you.' Letting the reins fall slack Padraig smiled as he gave the greeting.

'Be it an accident ye've been after having?'

The driver of the black-lacquered carriage ran a swift glance over the sling.

'Nothing of any consequence.' His answer light, Padraig

raised his short-handled driving whip but before he could set the carriage moving again the door of the other one flung open and two broad-shouldered men leapt to the ground, one seizing the bridle of Padraig's horse, the other hauling him from the driving seat.

'So yer injury be of no consequence, eh Riordan, just as yer wife were of no consequence!'

Gasping as his body thudded to the ground, Padraig looked into the face of Fergus Shea.

Clinging to the wooden rail of the ship Maura tried to recall having been brought aboard. The man with a burn mark on his face, a bottle forced between her lips, a bitter taste on her tongue and then . . . but she could not remember any more, only a short struggle followed by blackness and silence until she had woken to find herself chained hand and foot, her eyes blindfolded. Had anyone on that quayside seen what was happening? Of course not, she dismissed the hope, had anyone seen her struggling with that man surely they would have intervened, set her free! Yet no one had . . . and no one would help her now.

Liam had tried to help. The picture of a gentle smile and kind eyes rose in her memory. Liam Riordan had offered back her home in Clonmacnoise and with it the promise of his protection; but well meaning as his offer had been there could have been no guarantee against the lust and spite of his brother. It would have been there at her shoulder, the shadow of its evil darkening her every day, its threat real and terrible, violating each long hour of her nights. Genuine as Liam's offer had been he could not have been at her side every minute. There had been no choice for her. She stared at the murky water, the picture of Liam replaced by that of Padraig, a look of mockery and triumph gleaming in his pale eyes. He had done all that he had threatened, gained all his twisted mind had wanted; true, Maura Deverell would be no mistress to him but she would be to another . . . and if that foreign pasha did not want her after all? Then she would be sold to another, maybe to some foreign whorehouse . . . traded like so many goods! The thought sickening her, she flung from the rail. There had to be a way to end all of this . . .

'Feelin' seasick, are we?'

Low and mocking, an abuse in itself, a laugh echoed in her ears, the rank smell of foul breath assaulting her nostrils as the returning crewman caught her arm, twisting her to face him.

'P'raps a lie down in a cabin wi' me to soothe yer brow . . .'

'I . . . I am quite well . . . please, I just need a little air.' Maura turned her face to the breeze, the stench of the man's breath too much.

'Sea air,' he laughed, casting a quick glance at the tall-masted vessel further along the quay, a steady stream of stevedores coming and going, carrying boxes and sacks, loading the ship for her next voyage, 'sea air be good for an attack of the faintin' an' ye'll get plenty o' it aboard the *Queen*; takes a few weeks to reach the Orient so chance be ye might get plenty o' summat else besides, men get to wantin' a woman summat bad after they've bin at sea a while . . .'

The laugh scratching in his throat ceased, a shout from the fore deck cutting it short.

'That be the captin,' low and hoarse the words slid from behind the yellowed teeth, 'he be wantin' ye gone from the ship. It means I'll have to try to get ye aboard the *Ocean Queen* sooner than was thought.' His grip tightening on her arm he pushed her before him, cursing as her feet slipped on the greasy deck. Reaching the gangplank he stepped in front of her, walking the narrow board backwards, using both hands to steady her as she stepped nervously onto it.

'Don't look down,' he cautioned, waiting while she summoned the courage to walk on, 'the water 'as a strange way o' pullin' a body into itself, just ye keep yer eyes on me.'

If only he would release her hands, if he loosed her fingers for just one moment . . . death in that dark refuse-ridden water would be infinitely more preferable to the life he had described as waiting for her at the end of that ship's voyage.

'Come ye on!' Increased in urgency the demand hissed at her. 'Don't mek me 'ave to drag ye to that ship!'

Hating the touch of his hands on her own, refusing to look into the grime-lined face, Maura swayed as he jerked her forwards.

That shout from the fore deck, the man urging her down the gangplank had been alarmed by it! Maura's mind suddenly clicked into motion . . . the captain . . . and he wanted her gone from the ship! Did that mean he thought her a passenger left behind when others had gone ashore, or that he knew she was abducted and was nervous of her being seen aboard his vessel? If the latter then he was part of what was happening to herself and to those weeping girls who minutes before had been pushed into a closed carriage and driven away, but if the former were true, if he did not know his ship was trading in human cargo, then . . . She opened her mouth to scream but was a second too late. As if reading what was in her mind to do the sailor jerked her the last few paces, talking loudly as he held her close.

'There ye be, missy, safe and sound on Liverpool dock.'

Her face pressed into a foul-smelling jersey, Maura felt hard fingers bite into her neck as she tried to speak, then the whisper close to her ear.

'One scream, ye Irish whore, cry out and I'll do for ye, the sea don't mind what scum be thrown into it.' Then, releasing her, he raised his voice again, playing to any who might just be showing an interest. 'There ye go, that old gangplank be a scary to one as don't know 'er contrariness. Just ye tek a breather, a minute to get ye shore legs again an' old Jud will see ye to yer next berth.'

With his hand gripped tight to her elbow he pressed her forwards, whispering again the threat to kill her. Passing low wide archways above which tall warehouses stretched towards the evening sky, past wagons being piled high with ever more sacks and boxes carried by sweating porters, Maura searched desperately for a way of escape, but where her mind had been clear in its thinking moments before it was now a whirlpool, a vortex of ifs and buts, each of them flaring and swirling only to be sucked away into a black hole of hopelessness.

'Praise be to all the saints.' From one of the shadowed archways a voice rang loud and clear. 'Is it ye'self these eyes o' mine be after seeing? My own grand-daughter . . . and me set to thinking ye hadn't taken the boat after all.'

'What!' Stopping in his tracks the sailor looked towards the shadows, at the same time twisting Maura against him, her face pressed into his shoulder.

' 'Tis grateful to ye for seeing my little colleen ashore, so I am.' The voice came loud as before. 'May the good God tek ye into heaven a half an hour afore the divil knows yer dead!'

From the gloom of the shadowed doorway a man whose dark hair was streaked with grey took a step forward, a smile disguising a whisper. 'An' be sure now that half hour be up the second ye opens yer mouth! Let the colleen go, quiet now, or it might be I have to call on him stood not a fifty yards from ye . . . they tells me these peelers be on the watch for traffickers!'

'Traffickers!' The sailor's voice, low as the one that had spoken, was sharp in his answer. 'What be ye speakin' of, there be no traffickin' 'ere!'

'Then ye'll have no objection to that peeler being hailed.'

The figure half turned as he finished speaking, a hand already halfway to the side of his mouth when the seaman spoke again. 'We don't want no peelers!' His answer was sharp but still his arm was tight in its hold of Maura.

'Then do as I say and release the colleen.'

'So ye can sell 'er an' pocket the proceeds ye'self?' The sailor laughed low in his throat. 'D'ye take me for a fool!'

Robed in the lowering dusk the man who had hailed them from the deeply shadowed doorway pulled his worn jacket slightly to one side, disclosing a bulbous-ended wooden club. 'I pray the saints ye don't be one for 'tis a dead fool ye'll be after being unless it is ye do as I tells. Let the colleen go, take yer hand from her and go back to yer ship.'

'And tell the one who be selling her what? What do I say to 'im when he asks after the money I should be fetching back . . . d'ye expect he'll believe me when I tells 'im some fly-by-night took 'er from the dockside?'

Touching a hand to the knobkerrie peeping beneath his coat the figure smiled, teeth showing white in the rapidly fading light.

'Probably yer confederate will not believe as readily as that policeman will when I hand ye over for white slaving, they gives folk the noose for that, be ye ready to feel the touch of it about yer neck?'

The talk between the two was lost to Maura, submerged in the buzzing that filled her head as she held the air in her lungs, trying to avoid breathing the rancid body smell of the man holding her.

'It's yer own neck'll get the stretchin'.' Maura's captor tried again. 'This 'ere wench be me own sister an' it's stoppin' 'er from runnin' off wi' a seaman I be doin'.'

'Yer sister, is it? Then 'tis wrong I've been an' all. Ye have my apologies, so ye have.' The shadowed figure glanced sideways to where the uniformed man had begun a slow stroll in their direction. 'It best be we tells the peeler of my mistake; it'll be after taking no more than a minute, then ye can be on yer way with meself being sorry for having detained ye.'

'No!' The word snapped from the seaman's tight mouth. 'Be no need o' speakin' to that bobby. Tek the wench but next time ye be on Liverpool dock be sure an' keep yer peepers wide open for there be many a knife gets lost in a man's back!'

'Bilge rats . . . they come ashore with every docking.' The figure from the shadows caught Maura as she was pushed roughly aside, her assailant moving quickly along the quayside towards his ship.

Her lungs feeling like they might burst, Maura gulped the evening air, oblivious of the smells of spices mixed with cargoes of fruit half rotten from a long voyage, of bilges being emptied into a harbour already rank with the detritus of the vessels it served.

'Thank you,' she gasped, 'thank—'

The rest fell away as she looked into the shadowed face of the tinker.

24

His blood pounding in his veins, Padraig looked into the face of the man who had sat watching him since the two younger ones had bundled him into the black carriage, leaving him with their father while one drove his carriage and the other drove this one.

What was this all about, why were they treating him like some thief caught in the act? He had tried asking but Fergus Shea had said no more than he had said when they met, he just sat there with his mouth clamped shut.

They were not driving to Eyrecourt. He had watched the passing countryside. So where? Beyond the carriage window the remains of a great church lifted once-graceful arches to the sky. The Augustinian Abbey of Saint Mary! Padraig felt an unaccountable fear touch cold fingers to his throat. They were driving to Ballinasloe, Niamh's girlhood home. But for what reason . . . why come all this way when Eyrecourt had been so much nearer to where they had met and where this man's daughter would be awaiting the return of her husband?

The questions, if asked, would be answered by the same silence the others had met with. Padraig felt the hot waves of anger begin to flow. But vengeance had no need of question and he would be revenged for this treatment of him; Fergus Shea and his sons would find out they could not lay hands on a Riordan and get away lightly.

Its wheels rattling on the cobblestones of a street of firestone houses built, as Padraig knew, mostly from profits made from the buying and selling of livestock, Ballinasloe having the largest horse fair in all of Europe, the carriage halted before a three-storeyed building set behind railings whose gold-painted tips gleamed the reflection of the sun.

Paying no mind to his as yet unhealed injury, Fergus hauled him from the vehicle. Calling to his sons to stable the horses he shoved Padraig before him into the house. Barking at a manservant to see they were left alone he hustled the way across a wide hall, banging the door of a book-lined study behind them.

'Why have you brought me here?' Padraig's rage bubbled to the surface. 'If you wished to see me why not do so at Eyrecourt where you could visit with your daughter?'

His stare one of pure hate, the older man's laugh cracked like ice underfoot. 'Visit with a woman of no consequence, now why d'ye suppose Fergus Shea would be after doing that?'

'What the hell is that supposed to mean?'

'It means you treated my girl as something of no worth, I think yer words to her were "a barren sow"!'

How could he know of what had been said . . . unless he had been part of that gathering at Portington Hall! But he couldn't have been there, surely they would have met . . . so how come this man knew the exact words Niamh had used when confronting him in that grand house? Eugenie Stratford! She wanted retribution for losing her control of the white slave trade. Of course, the bitch had made certain Niamh's father heard all about his daughter's visit to the Hall, it was she was the instigator of his being dragged to this house. Eugenie Stratford! Below the anger bubbling inside him a new, more deadly one simmered; there would be another choice specimen would follow in the footsteps of Maura Deverell, though the crafty Lady Eugenie would not find herself in the whore-houses of England but in the stews of some foreign port where no one would care who or what she was. Holding the thought close he looked evenly at his wife's father.

'I think you have been the victim of some foolish and spiteful gossip, you should not believe all you hear.'

'Gossip, is it?' Fergus's eyes blazed their hatred. 'Foolish ye say it is to believe what yer ears be hearing . . . so what of the things a man's eyes see, should he be after disbelieving that also?'

Padraig knew he must play this carefully, Fergus Shea was no man to be riling, and though the reason for his anger could be overcome with a few carefully worded lies, the action of it might not be so easily avoided; Fergus Shea was noted for striking first and not bothering to ask why later.

'Perhaps if I knew what it was your eyes imagine they have seen—' He broke off as Niamh's brothers entered the room.

'So I should not be believing me own ears an' now it be me eyes as well be deceiving me. 'Tis lies they've been after showing me, is what ye be telling. I should not take as truth the marks I've seen on me own daughter's face; the blackened eyes, the bruised cheeks and cut mouth, they be all fantasy, be that it? So then I should be seeing this as fantasy!'

Snatching a paper from his pocket and thrusting it at Padraig, Fergus went on, 'Read it, ye dubh-hearted spalpeen, let the black soul of ye know the cry of her whose life ye turned to torment.'

Opening the sheet of paper, recognising his wife's handwriting, the anger that seconds before had simmered to a boil gave way to apprehension. Had Niamh written her father of the treatment she had received since coming to Eyrecourt, told him of the blows?

'Am I supposed to recognise this?' He waved the paper airily though his pulse throbbed.

Fergus Shea's eyes narrowed, his thin lips showing the ghost of a dead smile. 'Makes no difference whether ye recognise it or ye don't, for ye see *I* recognises it, I knows the hand of me own daughter. Read it, ye spawn of the divil, read it and then ye'll know the reason of me waiting of ye on that road . . . *read it –*' reaching a hand to the paper he shoved it hard against Padraig's face '– read it, ye bloody jackeen or by the saints I'll drag out yer eyeballs and run them over every word!'

Dropping his glance to the paper in his hand, the apprehension pulsing in Padraig's veins slowly solidified into fear. With the words dancing before his eyes he read it twice, wanting his brain to provide a way of denying what he saw.

'That's right, ye black-hearted swine,' Fergus's voice was ice-cold rage, 'read it with care for then ye'll know the reason I have for doing what I intends. The tongue of ye broke the heart of my sweet colleen, yer fists broke and bruised her flesh until she could stand no more . . . yer cruelty drove her to take her life, now her father will take yer own!'

Fear deepened to near panic, closing Padraig's throat. This was an entirely new situation for him, no man had dared threaten him since Seamus had become master of Clonfert; for most of his life the boot had been on the other foot, *he* had always been the one to threaten and strike. Strike! The thought had his hands trembling, would Fergus Shea do as he threatened?

Wincing as the older man snatched the paper away he forced himself to speak. 'That is not the truth –' he watched the letter being returned to Fergus's pocket '– Niamh has not taken her own life, why should she? I don't know why this charade, I only know my wife is at Eyrecourt.'

His face almost as grey as the whiskers that lined his cheeks, Fergus Shea glanced at his sons standing silently just inside the study door, nodding for them to open it.

'Eyrecourt, is it, ye say yer wife be, then it seems I be wrong in my thinking, so we'll step into my front parlour, p'raps it is ye can be after telling who it is I have there!'

Flanked by the two younger men, Padraig had no way of leaving. His blood jerked through his veins as he followed Fergus into the parlour where he had courted Niamh. Courted! The thought burned like acid. If only he could have known, had there been some way of telling Niamh Shea was barren, that to wed with her would see him childless and stripped of all that rightfully should be his . . . God, if only the barren sow were dead!

Opening the door to the room where he had led, Fergus touched his fingers to brow and chest making the sign of the cross before, head bowed, he stepped into a room in darkness except for four lighted candles.

'Step ye forward.' Fergus's voice was hushed, the rage seemingly drained from it. 'Look ye into the coffin at the face of the one lying inside it, tell me ye still believe my girl be at Eyrecourt.'

The light of tall candles stood at the head and foot of a long rectangular table had not at first been enough to disclose the coffin rested upon it but as Padraig's eyes attuned to the gloom he caught his breath. It was Niamh . . . Niamh was the woman lying dead in the coffin!

'So!' Beside the candelit bier Fergus Shea faced the son-in-law he had come to detest. 'Be it ye still say my daughter don't be dead, that me own eyes be deceiving me and that there are no marks upon her face! Then I says ye be a liar, Padraig Riordan, that it were yer fists that cut and bruised, yer black tongue that had her set the noose about her own neck . . .'

Staring at the cold marble-like face, dark patches around the eyes and along the cheeks, a still-swollen mouth their own evidence, Padraig clung tight to his self-control. To show any sign of guilt, even though all he felt was relief that at last he was free of the burden of a childless woman, would be to have Shea and his sons tear him apart. Shock was his best avenue, shock and anguish.

'Niamh!' He threw himself across the coffin. 'Niamh . . . oh Niamh, my love . . .'

'Don't ye dare touch her, don't dare speak her name!' Catching the collar of Padraig's coat, Fergus yanked him upright. 'Ye sullied my girl's name while her lived, ye'll not do it in death!' A glance to his sons bringing them to his side, the older man touched his lips to the dead brow. Whispering her name once he followed sons and son-in-law from the room.

That letter, the one Shea had given him to read, it was written in Niamh's hand, it had said she was taking her own life. That he understood, but why was she here and not at Eyrecourt, had she come home in order to commit suicide; and, one more question, why in hell had he not been told of any of this, why had word not been sent to him at Portington Hall?

Following to the stables set a little distance from the rear of the house, Padraig felt a welcome sense of relief. Fergus Shea was escorting him to his carriage; in an hour he would be home and if it were that runt of a brother had known of this business and not informed him of it then it would be many a week before sense enough to know anything returned to Liam Riordan.

Reaching the carriage he set a hand to the rail of the driving seat before glancing at the others. 'I will send for the . . . for Niamh and after the funeral I shall find out the cause of her death.'

Fergus Shea's grey head shook once. 'Ye'll not be taking my girl, she be here to stay; as for the cause of her dying that be known to me already, yer taunts and yer fists had the doing o' that.'

'I would never raise my hand to Niamh nor to any woman . . .'

'Then who did that to her, who set those bruises upon her

sweet face? Not yer brother for herself denied that, so who else at that home o' your'n would strike a woman? I says ye be lying, that it was ye'self and no other beat my daughter until the only way she could see to stop ye was the taking of her own life, and for that yer own be forfeit.'

'I understand your grief—'

'Ye understand nothing save yer own greed!'

A fist lashing out with the cry caught Padraig on the side of the head sending him sprawling to the ground.

'Did yer father know that also, did Seamus Riordan know his son for the black-hearted villain and coward he is, one who could take his spleen out on a woman but tremble as ye trembles now when faced by a man . . . be that why he wrote ye from his Will, leaving all he had to yer brother? If so then I raise me hat to his memory for 'twas the clear sight he had.'

Pulling himself up by the wheel of his own carriage, Padraig saw the glint of near madness stare back at him. Only calmness on his own part would save him from this man's wrath. Drawing a breath that did nothing to ease the fear pulling at his veins he made to climb into the driving seat, but was instantly hauled away.

'Ye be driving nowhere!' Fergus signed to his sons who came to stand one each side of Padraig. 'My daughter was brought to the house of her father cold and dead, that is the way ye will be carried back to the house of yer brother; as yer wife died so will ye but where it was her own hand took the life from her body it will be my hand will take the life from yours.'

'This be madness—'

'Aye it be that, the madness of a father given back his only daughter in her coffin.'

Turning to where a rope was hung over a hook driven into a wooden roof support, Fergus lifted it down. Securing one end in a loop he held it out to Padraig. 'Niamh set the noose about her own neck, ye shall have the doing of the same.'

The last of his pretended calm leaving him, Padraig slapped the rope away. 'I'll see ye sent down for this,' he choked, 'I'll see you all sent down!'

Fergus's face suddenly relaxed, all the anger and tension leaving it. 'Maybe ye will,' he said quietly, 'but not 'til I see ye'self in hell!' Glancing again at his sons he went on. 'Sure now it seems the husband of yer sister be needing a little help so why not the two of ye be giving it to him.'

Silent as before the two men moved, pressing Padraig against the carriage, pinning his arms while their father secured his spread legs to the wheel.

'It was no true man ye were to take yer fists to a helpless woman. So 'tis no true man ye deserve to be when they lays ye in yer box.'

Rising from his haunches, Fergus reached a short-bladed knife from the same post that had held the rope and with one stroke severed the braces holding Padraig's trousers.

'My girl was a woman of no consequence to ye.' He slashed again, the stroke cutting into the soft flesh of Padraig's stomach as it cut away the underwear. 'She was a barren sow.' He murmured on as one son clamped a hand to his brother-in-law's mouth, stifling the terrified scream. 'An empty womb has no need of that which swings atwixt yer legs and as Padraig Riordan was no true man in life ye'll not be one when ye enters into hell!'

With the last word the knife rose in the air and as Padraig struggled desperately to free himself it gleamed once in the light from the stable doorway then flashed downwards, slicing away his genitals. Then, in absolute silence, Fergus Shea slipped the noose over his head and hanged him from a beam of the roof.

Catching Maura to him the tinker held her face against the rough cloth of his worn jacket. The peeler coming towards

them along the dock was after showing a mite too much
interest.

Stroking a hand over her hair he crooned in a voice loud
with sympathy.

'Ar now there, me sweet child, was ye set to thinkin' yer old
grandfather wouldn't be meeting ye? Come, 'tis tired ye are
from the voyage but there be a warm fireside and yer grandmother's arms awaiting to comfort ye.'

As the policeman paused to watch several porters carry
sacks from a berthed ship, the tinker touched his mouth to
Maura's ear, his whisper soft.

' 'Tis safe ye be now, safe as when I spoke to ye in that
storeroom of the cottage of Connal O'Malley; I told ye then ye
need hold no fear of me and I tell it to ye again. No hair of yer
head will be touched while ye be with me.'

The sobs too thick in her throat to answer, Maura allowed
herself to be led away and not until they were at a distance
from the dock did the tinker speak again.

'What were ye thinking, child, choosing to get ye'self into
the company of riff-raff like that seaman, have ye not sense
enough to know he would dispense wi' ye the minute he tired
of ye?'

The fears of those last hours had somehow faded. The
realisation something of a shock in itself, Maura's answer was
crisp.

'I did not choose his company!'

'And the *Seagull*, why that ship to travel to England?'

There was a hint of anger in the question, an accusation, as
if she had committed some folly by sailing on it. Tears and fear
having drained what little energy was left to her after the ordeal
of travelling on foot and half starved for miles to reach Dublin
only to be assaulted and kidnapped once she arrived, the
man's questions irritated. What right had he to ask, what right
to delve into her affairs?

Drawing the shawl tight about her she felt the warmth of its soft wool against the cool spring night, but not the assurance as when she was being held by those strong arms. Why had she felt like that, comforted . . . safe? There had not been that feeling when he had grasped her wrist in that storeroom. Watching him now in the fast-gathering shadows, the strong features, the powerful body, there was no wish in her to turn and run. But why? She did not know this man, he could easily be another such as Padraig Riordan or the sailor that was about to sell her into some dreadful life in the Orient. But catching the look in his eyes, the concern that rested there, she somehow knew he was not. Indignation ebbing from her, she answered quietly.

'That too was not of my own choosing, I was—'

'Wait.' Cutting short her explanation he pointed to an ale house at the end of the street. 'If ye have no objection ye can tell me whatever ye feels ye needs to in the Napier, it be warm and the landlord serves a meal that though it be plain is good. Ye need have no worry,' he smiled, seeing a look of uncertainty cross her face, 'there'll be none will bother ye, the landlord also runs a clean house . . . what I means is the Napier is no brothel.'

Feeling the colour leap to her cheeks, Maura dropped her eyes. She had no money for a meal but even a few minutes in the warmth of a fire and with people not bent on selling her . . . the prospect too inviting to refuse she nodded. Ordering the pot pie and potatoes she had said she was not hungry enough to eat the tinker smiled as she followed his lead and tucked into the hot food. It was possibly the one decent meal she had eaten since leaving Dublin, and possibly for days before that.

Their meal finished he took a drink from a pewter tankard, waiting for Maura's nod of consent before lighting a long-stemmed clay pipe. Blowing a stream of smoke towards the large brick fireplace he glanced at Maura.

'Ye were set to tell why the *Seagull* had not been a ship of yer choosing but if it pleases ye better to keep yer counsel then I'll not be pressing ye to do so, yer business be yer own and Aiden Shanley don't be a man to pry.'

Aiden. She remembered that was how he had named himself in Connal's house, but Shanley? No, he had not used that.

'Shanley,' she said the name softly, 'that was the name of my mother's family, could it be—'

'Ireland has many acres,' he interrupted, staring at the fire, 'and there be many folk bearing the name of Shanley but not all of them be of one family.'

Disappointment, a sharp stinging disappointment momentarily touching her heart, Maura managed to smile. It was stupid of her to have thought, to have hoped this man might be of her blood; but neither her grandparents nor her parents had ever talked of an Aiden Shanley.

'There is no reason for my not telling you why the *Seagull* was not a ship I had chosen to sail on . . .' Dismissing the regret that still touched her, Maura told her story, starting with herself and her mother leaving Clonmacnoise to the moment this man had rescued her from that seaman.

Padraig Riordan! The tinker blew a long stream of tobacco smoke, following it with eyes hard and cold as black ice. Like father like son, where one had trod so had the other; now Seamus Riordan was in his grave and before many moons passed his sons would be there also.

25

'Mr Fergus Shea?' Liam's look was slightly perplexed as he answered the manservant. 'You say he has refused to come into the house?'

'He has that, sir, asks would ye join him at the bottom o' the rise.'

The bottom of the hill! Liam was even more perplexed. Not wanting to enter Eyrecourt was one thing, but refusing to ride further than the bottom of the hill was another. Had he come regarding the burying of Niamh? Padraig of course would have to be informed . . . but why so far from the house? The man was obviously too upset to be thinking as normal, but then what father wouldn't be half out of his mind finding his only daughter as Fergus Shea had found his? Rising to his feet Liam followed the old man from the drawing room. Allowances must be made in the face of such grief.

His horse had been saddled earlier, his intention being to ride to that tiny cottage in Clonmacnoise. Mounting, he had difficulty controlling the desire to go there now, to leave the business of Padraig and his wife to those it concerned.

But it concerns you also. It was as if the sweet voice of his mother whispered in his mind. How could he for one moment have thought otherwise? Niamh, that gentle timid girl had been more than a sister-in-law, she had been a friend; she had never criticised or called him runt, to her Liam Riordan had never been the misfit.

Setting the horse to a trot he let his thoughts ride his mind.

Niamh had brought a smile to Eyrecourt and in that smile he had seen hope for the future . . . a kinder brother, a more caring father. What had happened to those hopes, to the dreams they had given birth to? As the months of his marriage had passed Padraig had become even more edgy, even more volatile, then had come the times Niamh had kept to her room, pleading feeling unwell, that had been when the blows had started . . . and Seamus, he had done nothing to prevent it, 'the business atwixt man and wife be sacred,' was all he ever answered when his younger son had spoken of a brother's cruelty. But then what had *he* done! His stomach twisting with the guilt of the thought he drew his horse to a halt.

'I'll say good day to ye, Liam Riordan.'

Fergus Shea nodded as Liam dismounted but did not move aside from the carriage he had driven. Glancing at the vehicle Liam felt his confusion return. This was a Riordan carriage! How come it was being driven by Fergus Shea?

'I have returned yer brother to ye–' opening the carriage door Fergus stood to one side '– he comes to ye as my daughter came to me. It was his tongue he used to torture her, naming her a barren sow, his fists that bruised her sweet flesh and his whoring with women broke her heart. All of that I took into my reckoning with him, now he reckons with a higher power by whose justice his soul will roast in purgatory. It was Padraig Riordan delivered my girl to death and it is to death Fergus Shea has delivered him.'

'Padraig!' Liam gasped, snatching back the rug which covered the figure slumped into a corner of the carriage.

'He be dead.' Fergus said as the younger man's eyes returned to his face. ' 'Twas on that very moor I took him, returning from the house of his English friends . . . but 'twere no friend he found waiting. Mine was the child he chastised, mine the daughter he tormented and sent to her grave in sorrow, therefore mine was the right for vengeance. That right

I claimed. 'Tis my hand and mine alone stilled his cruel tongue, mine filled his mouth with the object of his torment-ing, my hand sends him less than a man to his grave, my hand that hanged him. I gave him no choosing as to the way he should die, for a coward and a bully has not backbone enough to set his hand to suicide . . . now I say to ye, Liam Riordan, the carcass of a diseased pig be burned and the carcass I bring to ye be no better than that. Burn it . . . for to lay it in the sweet bosom of Ireland be a defilement o' the land!'

Shock keeping any answer from his tongue Liam stood by as the older man unhitched and mounted a horse tied to the rear of the carriage. Fergus sat the bay stallion with ease.

'Take the body of yer brother, do with it as be fitting to ye then if ye seeks retribution for the work of my hand ye knows where it is Fergus Shea can be found. But this I say to ye, think well on the suffering of one who was sent to the house of yer father in trust, weigh the manner of her living against that of yer brother afore ye comes seeking vengeance, for when ye do it will make the troubles with the English seem like nursery games, it will be such a war as none shall remain to speak of it on either side!'

Why had that tinker rescued her, what was he doing in an English seaport and – what was more puzzling – why had he paid for a night's lodging for a girl he hardly knew?

Having washed in the basin of warm water fetched to her room by a middle-aged woman with flaming red hair, Maura pulled her dark patched skirt up over cotton bloomers, memory showing her the thin figure lying with her white petticoat over face and chest. Her mother lay buried somewhere on the moor, she would never lie in that little patch of black earth beside the cottage that had been her home, the little house within the sound of a finger of the sweet Shannon river; and her daughter would never return to the house of her childhood!

The thought lying like a stone in her heart, Maura made her way down a narrow flight of stairs as the flame-haired woman came from the kitchen.

'There you be, dearie, breakfast be all ready . . . I 'opes you've no objection to eatin' in the kitchen, this be just a small 'ouse, not like them posh 'otels they be building along of the railway.'

'Thank you, but I shall not be taking breakfast.'

'What!' The woman's comfortable jowls wobbled as she shook her head. 'You'll go leaving a meal that's been paid for? Now I calls that a daft thing to do.'

'Paid for?' Maura's brows drew together.

Her jowls wobbling again, but this time from a vigorous nod, the woman smiled. 'That's what I said. Paid for last night afore Aiden Shanley left his 'ouse. You need 'ave no fears as to that one.' The woman ushered Maura before her, pressing her onto a chair set beside a table scrubbled almost white. 'I've knowed Aiden Shanley these five years and ain't a man in England I'd trust more. He told me last night . . . poor wench, you've 'ad more'n your fair share of sufferin' what with losing your mother the way you did, God rest 'er . . . asked me to watch out for you.'

'But why do all that for me? I could not rightly call Mr Shanley a friend. I have only met him twice.'

Placing a plate of bacon and eggs before her guest the woman looked keenly at Maura. 'Twice or twenty it meks no difference to Shanley, he knows a good wench when he sees one and his judgement be good enough for me. I said to him I says, "If that wench be agreeable then her can stop wi' me, we'll find her work of some sort."'

It was a kindness on the part of this woman and on that of Aiden Shanley to think of her. Maura looked at the food he must have paid for, and again the questions rose in her mind. Why was this man doing all of this, why go out of his way for a girl he hardly knew?

'Eat up now afore that food gets cold.' Smiling broadly the woman turned away into the scullery.

This woman had asked no question of her and apart from how she came to be with that ship Aiden Shanley had asked none, only listened as she told of being given help by Lady Eugenie Stratford, of her leaving Portington Hall only to be caught by Padraig Riordan. The tinker's mouth had tightened then, his eyes glinting like dark diamonds as they looked beyond her, seeming to see far into the past. Maura picked up the knife and fork. At that moment she had seen something like hatred flick across his face.

'. . . *'Tis to the resting place of Ciaran I go, to ask his blessing before journeying down to Clonfert . . .*'

Those had been the man's own words. Had he been going to that place to meet with the Riordans? That look, fleeting as it had been, had spoken only of hate when she had said the name. Was there something between that family and the tinker, did they perhaps have some hold over him . . . did he know of her own experience at the hands of the elder son? Thoughts choking her she set aside the cutlery, leaving the food untouched. Why should he not know! Padraig would boast of his doing, probably the whole of Clonfert and Clonmacnoise knew of it . . . Liam knew of it.

With colour burning in her face she pushed from the table and ran from the house, thin-soled boots rapping against the cobbles as she raced along the street, running from the disgrace of it . . . running from the disgust and contempt that must lie heavy on Liam's face.

Just days ago this room had held a different coffin, a different corpse, that of a gentle young woman dead of her own hand.

Stood alone, with only the candles set at the head and foot of the bier for light, Liam stared at the face of his dead brother.

'. . . *'Tis my hand and mine alone . . . sends him less than a man to his grave . . .*'

The words spoken by Fergus Shea seemed to whisper in the velvet silence of a house in mourning, seemed to echo among the flickering shadows of the darkened room.

He had not disturbed that slumped figure, only covering it with a travelling rug before driving the carriage back to the house. There he had followed as, still covered, it was carried to Padraig's own room. He had dismissed the menservants who had laid the wrapped figure on the wide bed, ordering he be left alone with his brother. That was when the full horror had been revealed.

Gently, his hand shaking slightly, he had drawn the rug downwards, revealing the face, the eyes wide and staring, the features twisted with terror.

'. . . *less than a man . . . filled his mouth with the object of his tormenting . . .*'

The real meaning of those words, the true vengeance of a father driven by grief beyond the bounds of reason, had sent him reeling as he had looked at the open mouth from which Padraig's genitals protruded.

How long had he leaned over the chair he had flung himself against . . . how long before he had steeled himself to look again at that mutilation, to look into eyes that had realised the revenge about to be taken?

But at last he had. He had closed those terrified eyes, removed the blood-soaked organs from the mouth, gently closing the jaw. Then he had stripped the body, washing it himself, replacing those private parts before clothing it in fresh linen. Then, and only then, had he allowed his brother to be placed in a coffin and carried to this downstairs room.

Here he had stayed. The servants had seen his solitary preparation of the body as they saw his remaining here beside the coffin, as a last act of respect between brother and brother.

But here in the silence and semi-darkness of this room he was keeping more than a vigil, he was wrestling with a problem that could pale Padraig's death into insignificance.

'. . . *think well . . .*'

Again the words seemed to swell on the darkness, to whisper from the silence.

'. . . *weigh the manner of her living against that of yer brother . . .*'

Padraig had deserved punishment . . . had he himself not thought to shoot him! But vengeance in the manner dealt by Fergus Shea . . . ! How could such be condoned, how could a brother not seek retribution?

'. . . *ye knows where it is Fergus Shea can be found . . . it will be such a war as none shall remain to speak of it on either side . . .*'

That was what retaliation would bring; reprisal for Padraig's death would set valley against valley, kin against kin. Was that what he wanted? Liam's fingers clenched with the asking. Would more bloodshed serve any purpose other than to bring pain to the hearts of women and suffering to their children?

'. . . *such a war as none shall remain . . .*'

Looking down on the dead face, Liam touched a finger to the faded scar. The fruit of contention! He withdrew his hand. How many more scars would result from hostility with Fergus Shea, how many deaths before each was pacified?

The price of vengeance! Turning away, Liam walked from the room. It was too high.

She had run from that house without leaving a word of thanks for the help that tinker had given her. Pushed and shoved by folk hurrying about their business Maura pressed herself against the wall of a low building, its small-paned window displaying pies and cooked meats, their appetising aroma drifting from an open door and making her painfully aware of her empty stomach.

She had fled without eating any of the food that man may have paid his last pennies for; but it had not been ingratitude had seen her run . . . then what? She could not say truly it was fear of that tinker man, because despite all her thoughts and doubts as to the reasons for his helping her she could no longer say in complete honesty she still held a fear of him; after all, would he have gone from the house of the red-haired woman leaving herself unguarded if he had been set to return her to Ireland, to hand her back to Padraig Riordan . . . No, she had fled from the contempt her attacker's brother must have felt when learning of what had happened on the banks of that stream, she had fled from Liam's disgust. Did he really believe it had been rape or did he think she had encouraged his brother, lain willingly with him?

'Get you from my doorway, I wants no beggars cluttering up the place.'

An irate voice cutting sharply across her thoughts startled Maura.

'I . . . I am no beggar, I was just resting.'

His razor-sharp features topping a long flour-covered apron the baker glared disparagingly. 'No beggar, eh! Then p'raps you was thinkin' to make away wi' a pie when my back be turned, bloody Irish thief! There be too many of your sort comes in off the boats wi' every tide, washes in to Liverpool like flotsam and jetsam! But you'll steal nothing from my shop . . .'

'My granddaughter be after stealing nothing from yer shop . . . this be simply the place I was after telling her to wait for me.'

It seemed he stepped from nowhere. Maura looked gratefully at the figure stood between her and the shopkeeper. Just as on the quayside, Aiden Shanley had come to her assistance. Catching her now by the arm he led her away.

'I was not going to steal . . .'

'I'm knowing that well enough, what I don't be knowing is just what *were* ye thinking to do! Have ye not learned anything since leaving Clonmacnoise . . . have ye not learned a quay-side be no place for a girl to be wandering around alone, and the streets of a strange city likewise? Why did ye leave the house I put ye in . . . was it not a room and work ye were offered?'

She could not tell him her reasons, could not name the emotions Liam's disapproval of her had roused . . . feelings that even now were difficult to hide.

'I could not stay there . . . Oh it's grateful I am for the kindness you showed me . . . but this town, the quayside, it is too much like that other, I could find no peace with the constant reminder.'

Seeing the crystal glitter of tears touch her lashes Aiden cursed himself for being a fool. Had he not experienced that same fear, found how difficult it was to live with memories, had he not felt the urge to run from them? It had been hard for him, a grown man; how much harder for a girl short yet of her eighteenth year.

'Dublin or Liverpool, they be the same to a colleen not knowing either.' He smiled. 'But while 'tis true ye can't be staying here 'tis also true ye can't go journeying far if it's a ship we have to find to be taking ye home to Ireland.'

All the earlier doubts winged along her nerves and Maura jerked her arm free. 'I'll not return to Ireland!' She choked. 'I won't go back to Padraig Riordan . . . you would have to kill me!'

Padraig Riordan! Aiden watched the hands lift to hide the tears, watched the thin shoulders heave. That name again . . . what did he have to do with Maura Deverell?

26

Nothing had changed yet everything was changed! With each tiny stone biting through the worn-out soles of her boots Maura walked beside the tinker. This was England and though the season was turning towards summer the night air bit sharply beneath her wool shawl. England . . . ! But where was the difference? Still there was little food to be spared from the houses they had called at, the people of the villages seemed almost as poor as those in Ireland, but the change lay in their attitude. It seemed the moment they heard the tongue of Ireland some became suspicious, hostile . . . calling herself and the tinker 'dirty Irish gypsies'. Could it have been worse had she stayed in Clonmacnoise? Even as the question shaped in her mind the answer shaped also. She could not have lived in the same house as Padraig Riordan, nor any place the fear of him might reach.

But Liam would have been there. A flush of shame rushing to her face she halted, pretending a stone was caught in her boot. Yes, Liam would have been there but could he truly have prevented his brother in his intention, or would he have been as helpless as herself, a witness to her degradation?

She straightened, holding the shawl close about her face to shield the blush of colour from the light of a newly rising moon, continuing to walk in silence. But her mind would not yield to silence, the thoughts crowding it shouted for recognition.

Liam would never have stood by while his brother shamed

her and that, if no other reason, had been cause enough for her to turn her back on Clonmacnoise. Brother against brother! She could not be the cause of that.

' 'Tis tired ye are, a few minutes more and ye can rest. There be a place across yonder pasture, its owner be well known to me and for the mending of a shovel or the fixing of a scythe he provides a warm meal and a place to sleep among the hay of his barn.'

A place to sleep, the soft warmth of hay . . . but that was payment for the work of the tinker, she could not expect the same and she would not take food from this man's mouth. He had already done much more than she could ever repay.

'Ye have the choice,' he had said as he had taken her from the accusation of that baker. 'Ye can make yer own way 'til ye finds where it is ye wants to be or ye can go along of me 'til it be ye finds the place ye have a mind to bide.'

'. . . *a mind to bide* . . .'

Maura felt her heart sink. The place she loved was closed to her for ever, barred by a man's cruelty and a promise made to a dying woman. Leave Ireland had been her mother's plea . . . how could she ever go back!

'Remember now, ye be my granddaughter, we be of the same family!'

Aiden Shanley's quiet caution reached among the shadows cast by a low-built house.

If only those words were true. Surprised by the vehemence of the thought she could only nod.

Had she really thought that? Snuggled deep in sweet-smelling hay, Maura pretended sleep. Had she truly wished with all her heart this tinkerman was kin to her or had that emotion been simply gratitude? Was she mistaking her own feeling of thankfulness for something other . . . for a feeling nearer affection?

'I be knowing ye don't be sleeping, Maura Deverell, and neither will I 'til ye take a share o' this broth.'

With the light of the lantern shedding on her face Maura blinked. ' 'Tis no use ye thinking ye can fool Aiden Shanley, so ye best sit up and take yer meal.'

'I'm not hungry—'

'Now that's after being a lie such as Saint Ciaran himself might find hard to forgive!'

The interruption was censorious but behind its reproof the gentleness of understanding was clear as he went on.

'I know what it is be in that head of yours and what it is be in yer heart . . . ye will not eat what the hands have not earned . . . 'tis an honourable way ye have, one which can only have been taught by honourable parents but I asks ye to remember the teaching of the holy saint himself who preached, "Turn not yer face from others, for in the taking of charity lies the giving of charity." They were wise words for the blessing of God rests upon the giver, now would ye'self be denying that farmer's wife a blessing?'

Opening her eyes Maura caught the look the shadows could not hide, a teasing smile which only partly masked tenderness behind it. Who was he, this Aiden Shanley, why had he come to this country . . . and, more than that, why did she feel so safe with him?

'I have the bowl of a shovel to be mending come the morning and a pot the woman of the house says has a hole in it. That will cover this night's meal and lodging.'

Taking his own bowl and spoon the tinker moved to the far side of the barn, leaving the lantern he had lit close to Maura. It had been a lie when she had said she was not hungry. She breathed the aroma of lamb and vegetables. She had said it from a feeling of guilt, it was not right that this man should labour to feed her.

'If only there were some way I could help but I'm no good at mending pots or straightening shovels.'

For a moment only silence answered her words. Did he think that was merely talk on her part, was that why he made no reply? A tinge of sadness came with the thought. She would not wish this man to think ill of her.

'There be many ways of giving help, tenderness of the heart be consoling to one who fears the coming of day.'

It seemed, sitting there enclosed in darkness, that his answer came from deep inside, from a man who knew the very essence of fear. Her own heart twisting with the thought, Maura stared to where he was lost in the gloom. She could not ask the meaning of those words, to pry was impolite but to make no response seemed to her to be insensitive. Torn between her feelings and the teachings of her childhood she struggled to find the answer.

Sensing her difficulty the tinker went on. 'With the coming of day the woman of the house be like to have lost her only child to the fever, 'twill be the third in as many months . . .'

'What ails the child?' Maura was on her feet, the broth forgotten in the bowl.

'It be the same as has taken many through this winter, the woman hoped that with spring going out her family would be safe, that this child had escaped the scourge that took its brothers, but the hope proved vain for the cough that wracked them to their graves came back to claim the one remaining; seems there be no cure, that death will ride the morning.'

Why had she not gone up to the house when they had arrived, why had she stayed out of sight like some criminal? She could have helped . . . surely she could have helped.

Taking the tinker's empty bowl and placing it with her own she picked up the lantern. Those people may refuse her but she could not let the fear of that deter her, she had to make the offer.

Minutes later, stood in the warmth of a small kitchen, she watched the farmer struggle to hold back the tears.

'We thank you kindly for the wanting to help,' he sniffed, 'but the doctor tells there be nothing as can be done, our little wench be going to die.'

'Did he say this when he called today?'

Embarrassed by his own tears the man did not look up at the tinker's question but kept his eyes lowered as he replied.

'He d' ain't call this day nor any at all.'

'But you said he told you there was nothing to be done.'

'And it was the truth I spoke, missy. When it was we feared the cough was taking a hold I took the cart into the town but when I told the doctor of the child's illness he said it was the same as before, the same as took the other three and that it were of no use his coming all the way here when there was naught as could be done, that it was nobbut a matter of time; now I thinks you should leave for I fear the illness might strike at you both.'

'Please,' Maura held out both hands to the weeping man, 'let me help, if it is only to sit with your wife.'

''Twould be a comfort having another woman by her side but the risk—'

'Let me worry about that.' Maura slipped the shawl from her shoulders, handing it to the tinker with the request he take it with him to the hay barn.

Holding it he met her eyes, and in his own was a look that held more than respect. ''Tis right here I'll be,' he said quietly, 'waiting for you.'

In the child's room, lit only by a candle and almost filled by an iron-framed bed, the farmer's wife sat on a low-back back chair holding the hand of a fair-haired girl who lay with eyes closed.

'Please don't send me away.' Maura spoke quickly as the woman looked up. 'I want only to sit with you.'

The sound of a voice disturbing the still quiet of the room

the girl's eyes flickered, and almost immediately a cough shook her body.

' 'Tis the same as come to take my lads, now I be going to lose my babby!'

How could she answer? Maura gazed at the pale face lying against the pillow. How did you comfort a woman whose last remaining child lay dying before her eyes.

Think girl . . . think . . .

A tremor touching her spine, Maura felt the breath catch in her chest. Those same remembered words, that same remembered voice . . . it was as if she stood again in the cottage where Connal O'Malley had lain half dead of the wound to his leg.

Think . . . think as ye were taught . . .

As she was taught! In the instant she was a child again, listening to her mother's soft-spoken voice, watching her point to flowers and herbs in a tiny colour-filled garden and telling how each could be used to combat illness. The teaching of her mother . . . the garden, could it be she would find help for this girl as she had found it for Connal?

Listen well . . .

The quiet words went on but Maura's mind filled with quick panic. She had not listened . . . she had not paid enough attention!

. . . Maura girl, quiet yer heart . . . ye have to try afore ye'll know . . .

The words had only whispered in her brain but like a silent whirlwind they swept it clear of bewilderment.

Ye have to try . . . That had always been her mother's encouragement whenever she had been unsure of her abilities. *Ye have to try afore ye'll know.* Could she try now . . . would this woman allow it?

'Did the doctor prescribe a medicine?'

'None.' A sob shook the woman's answer. 'He told her father there was naught would cure the sickness.'

'Her brothers, was their illness exactly as this one?'

The woman would be within her rights to tell her to leave this room, to go away and mind her own business. Instead she shook her head, her answer threaded as before with hopeless sobs.

'Not in every way. They each had bad headaches, aching limbs and sneezing . . . sneezing for days afore the cough, seemed more like a fever than an illness of the chest, it were the fever that got worse 'til they burned like coals . . . but with her 'tis not that way, the cough be more like the whoop of an owl and though her be flushed her body be not near so hot as was theirs.'

The fever had not yet reached its full. Maura glanced again at the small figure as a fresh bout of coughing rattled wetly in her throat.

. . . ye have to try . . .

As in Caitlin's garden it seemed somehow her mother stood beside her, urging her, telling her to at least try to help the child.

'I . . . I was taught a little of the use of herbs.' She spoke tentatively, not really knowing whether she wanted the woman to accept or refuse. 'If you would allow I might make a syrup that will ease your daughter's cough.'

The woman's face lifted, her tear-filled eyes glittering in the candle's light. 'You can help . . . you can help my babby, you knows a cure for what ails her?'

'I can make a syrup supposing you have the ingredients but I cannot say it will cure, yet I am sure it will ease.'

'I can ask no more 'cept the Lord add his blessing to the skills of your hands. Tell me what it is you be needing and heaven grant my house contains it.'

Leading the way down a bare narrow staircase the woman explained quickly to her husband what they were about then dispatched him to watch over the sick child.

'Will ye be wanting I should be away to the barn?'

The tinker's question taking her by surprise Maura looked across to him and for a fleeting moment it seemed she looked into eyes she had known for a lifetime.

'Will you wait for me there?'

' 'Tis wait for ye I will.'

Slung on a bracket over the fire a kettle breathed steam, the rattle of its lid echoing the quiet closing of the door, but in Maura's mind it seemed those brown eyes still stared deep into her.

'So what be you wanting for to make your syrup?'

Recalled by the anxious tone she turned to the waiting woman. Guidance – only her heart heard the reply – my mother's guidance!

'Would your garden hold fresh thyme and your cupboard have honey . . . a dark honey?'

Where had the memory come from? For years she had not had the need of cough mixtures taught to her mother by Sinead O'Toole. But the memory had risen strong, pray God it was a true memory.

Knowing her garden as well as she knew her tiny home the woman had needed no light but that of the brilliant full moon to gather both hands full of the plant she now handed to Maura. Then she reached a jar of thick dark honey from a cupboard set alongside a dresser holding an assortment of crockery.

Saying she would need boiling water Maura broke the pleasant-smelling leaves and tiny red blossoms into a bowl, her nod guiding the older woman in the adding of water. Stirring them a few times with a wooden spoon she added the honey.

Was that the all of it? She stared at the fragmented leaves, had she remembered everything?

As if her question had been asked aloud the quiet words her

own mother had spoken so many years before formed themselves in her mind.

*. . . thyme be aided in its healing when given the added strength
of yarrow and the flower of elder . . .*

Asking for these she breathed relief as the woman said her
garden provided both. When the silver leaves of yarrow and
the white flowers of the elder had been added to the basin
Maura remembered her dislike of the sugary taste of honey,
only accepting the mixture when a jar of her mother's pre-
served blackberries had dampened the sweetness. These also
having been stirred into the mixture, she covered the whole
with a cloth. It must be given time to infuse.

Could eternity last so long? Watching the fingers of a tin
clock move with infinite slowness Maura fought her screaming
nerves. Would any of this have effect on the illness of that little
girl, or was it merely a hope, one that morning would see fade
away with the child?

From the further side of the table the sounds of the woman's
praying whispered into her mind and Maura added her own to
it. 'Sweet Mother of Jesus, look with mercy on those who call
to you, intervene for one who has known the sorrows you
yourself knew when your son was taken from you, pray Him
return the health of her child.'

Overhead a cough rattled into the quiet, followed by a faint
cry. Sparing Maura only a glance the woman ran upstairs.

Unable to bear watching the unutterably slow movement of
the clock Maura turned her face from it but she could not
escape the doubts crowding one on the other, filling her mind
and heart with hopeless despair. If she had used the wrong
herbs . . . if the mixture should only add to the suffering of that
child . . . if she should die as many in the villages . . .

Like the brush of a hand that one thought swept the rest
away, leaving only the memory of the coughing plague that
had settled one winter over Clonmacnoise and further. Chil-

dren had died then and more might have followed except for
Sinead O'Toole's skill with herbs. The woman had come to
the Deverell cottage asking for thyme and honey when her
own was used.

'. . . *it will have the saving o' many a child . . .*'

The warm stillness of the kitchen exchanged itself for
another and Maura was in Clonmacnoise, listening to the talk
between her own mother and Sinead O' Toole.

'. . . *thyme be the herb to expel phlegm from the chest and fight
against the fever while honey will heal the lungs as well as
destroying the cause o' the coughing and if they can be had then
blackberries be a restorative and a help in the cleansing o'
impurities from the body . . .*'

Thyme, honey, yarrow, elderflower and blackberry. She
had not forgotten anything!

'. . . *the saving o' many a child . . .*'

She turned back to the cooling basin. Pray God it would
save one more.

27

Once more the tinker had given her a choice. Watching the patchwork of fields slipping past, Maura felt at ease for the first time since Padraig Riordan's raping her.

'*The choosing must be of yer own, stay here along of the people whose child yer mixture cured or travel on wi' me . . .*'

He had watched her face, seeming to read the very thoughts in her mind. Had he wanted her reply to be she would stay, make her home perhaps in the village that had been close to that small farm? If so, why had he waited more than a week, waited until the child showed the wonderful signs of recovery? The fear that had crowded her during those first days of walking with him, the fear that he meant to return her to Padraig Riordan, had returned fleetingly but common sense had set it to flight. If Aiden Shanley held any such intention there had been ample time and opportunity to act upon it; instead he had paid for food and secured her a place to sleep each night and not once had he attempted to touch her, but always had taken himself somewhere else to sleep.

As he waited for her answer a flicker had crossed his lined face, while his eyes . . . it had been as if for a moment they filled with regret. That had been the same moment her heart answered for her, telling her to trust this man who had already helped her twice. So she had chosen and he had turned quickly from her, simply nodding his grey-streaked head when she had asked to travel with him.

They had gone from that farm to the long ribbon of water the tinker had said linked the town of Liverpool to that of

Birmingham. She had heard the name of that town pass
between him and the man who operated the long narrow boat
on which they had been given passage. Birmingham must be
another port, where else would a boat be sailing to? Was Aiden
Shanley thinking to leave England so soon, to travel on to yet a
more distant land . . . perhaps the Americas? She smiled,
remembering the family she had walked those miles to Dublin
with, surely they would meet again there for America could
not be such a big country. But why go there from a different
port, would it not have been simpler to have taken ship from
Liverpool as that family had done?

She had said nothing of her reasoning to Aiden Shanley. He
had consented to her travelling with him, she would not repay
that kindness by seeming to mistrust his judgement.

They had talked together for some time. She looked at the
two men now walking together, one each side of the large horse
which towed the boat. They had not glanced in her direction
during their discussion yet somehow she knew they spoke of
her. Had Aiden Shanley made that false claim yet again . . .
had he told this man also she was his granddaughter?

'*It would raise no eyebrows that way,*' he had told her as they
had made their way to the basin of the canal where several
vessels were moored, '*a young girl with none but a grandparent
to care for her was a common sight. But should it be she was
without him then there was many a rogue . . .*'

He had said no more but the cold trickle of her spine had
finished the sentence for him. Would there ever be a time
when she would be free of that unspoken threat?

They could travel with him and welcome, so the boatman
had said, and in return she would cook and Aiden could help
unload the barge once they reached Gas Street.

Gas Street! Maura mused over the name as she steered.
Was it not a strange one for a sea port!

'I'll take the tiller.'

Her eyes on the beauty of field and pasture donning early summer finery she had not seen Aiden Shanley jump lithely aboard. Now smiling at her, he asked, 'Well now, is it not almost a match for the land of Ireland . . . would ye not think the little people themselves could be living here?'

'It is beautiful,' Maura's smile answered his own. 'So many shades of green.'

'Ah, but not the emerald of our own sweet isle.'

Glancing to where the bargee walked the towpath beside his horse, Maura touched a finger to her lips, her eyes gleaming with laughter he had not seen in her before, that impish twinkle so reminiscent of . . . but he must not think of that, he must never think of that.

'Shhh,' Maura was laughing softly, 'best not let our friend hear you speak so of his country . . . I much prefer sailing to walking.'

'And how about cooking? If you prefer that to walking then it's best ye set about it now or we will both be suffering from sore feet when it is we reaches Birmingham.'

The cabin was so tiny. Climbing down the three steps that gave access to the boat's living quarters she stared about her. It was so very small that Bridget would have vowed it was lived in by none but the little people themselves. The image of that pale face with its wide fear-filled eyes rose before her inner vision. What had happened to the girl, where had she gone? Had she too been caught by some man . . . sold like a sheep or a goat? No! Maura's fingers clenched. Please, sweet Mother of God, not that!

With the prayer constant in her heart and on her lips she prepared the meal, setting pig's liver to roast in the oven beside the small black iron stove and a pan of potato and onion to boil over its fire, but as evening gathered and the meal was eaten the stone of doubt that her prayer had reached to heaven lay heavy inside.

* * *

Birmingham was not a port. When the barge had been un-
loaded they had said their goodbyes, and now, walking beside
Aiden, she stared at the maze of buildings that stretched on
each side, the warren of streets seething with people and carts
of every description. Where did they all come from? Even in
Dublin she had not seen so many folk each scurrying like their
particular errand should have been finished yesterday. Was
the rest of the town like this, a bevy of soot-grimed buildings in
place of green fields?

'Ye've said nothing since leaving the barge, could it be yer
after regretting travelling with me?'

'No,' she answered quickly. 'Please don't think that, it . . . it
is just I thought Birmingham to be a port, another Liverpool.'

'A port . . . Birmingham a port!' His laugh rang loud in the
gathering dusk. 'Now if that don't have the beating of all,
though in a way it could be called such for there be many
trades in this town and many manufacturers export their
wares along the canals that be like veins leading from the
heart of it to link with almost every town England holds and to
the ports that line her coasts; so yes, ye could be after saying
Birmingham be a port . . . an inland port for it operates the
same.'

'You have been here before?'

'I've passed through it.'

The reply was curt. Stealing a glance at the strong profile
Maura fell silent, but in her mind the questions spoke loud.
Why had he come here to this town, and why, if he knew it,
was he so reticent to speak of it?

'This is the place, ye'll be after being welcomed here.'

Ushering her before him he turned into a dark passage that
led between a block of tall houses before opening out onto a
small cobbled yard.

'*Ye'll be . . . welcomed.*' Did that mean he would not be
staying; would he just turn and go, leaving her in a strange

town, a house she had never seen before . . . with people she did not know? Waiting for the door to open to his knock, Maura felt her spirits drop. She had come to value this man's company, to trust him, but it was more than that . . . she had come to love him. It couldn't be true! The shock of it caught her breath. How could such a thing happen? The time she had known him, been with him, it had been too short! But if her feelings for this man were no more than friendship why was the thought of his leaving her suddenly tearing the bottom from her world?

'God bless all in this house and keep the divil from its doorstep.'

'Well, I go to the bottom of our stairs! If it ain't Aiden Shanley!'

A short figure, wide as it was high, flung the door wider on its hinges, reaching for the tinker and holding him in a tight embrace.

'I thought yoh was in Ireland an' not like to come back 'ere no more.'

'Sure and Ireland be where I've been, but not to come back to see Bella James . . . now bejabers it would take the King of the little people himself to keep me from doing that and a hard job he'd have of it for aren't ye the prettiest creature this side o' heaven.'

'A slice of the Blarney Stone for breakfast as usual.' The woman laughed, holding him at arm's length. 'But then I wouldn't 'ave yoh any other way; a spark o' light in a dark entry be what yoh am. But don't let's 'ave ya standin' on the doorstep, come you in against the fire.'

Releasing his own hold of the woman, Aiden Shanley hesitated. 'I'm not alone, Bella.'

'So who is it this time?' Her eyes narrowing, she peered into the gloom behind the tinker's back. 'I won't be 'arbouring no beer swillers nor card players . . .'

'And neither would I have the insulting of yer hospitality by bringing such to yer door.' Reaching behind him he caught Maura's hand, drawing her to where she could be seen in the torpid yellow beam of a lamp that served to illuminate the room at the woman's back.

'A wench!' The surprise was genuine as a pair of busy eyes swept Maura. 'Now that be one for the book, Aiden Shanley wi' a wench. Hey!' The busy eyes spun to Aiden. 'Be yoh wed? I wants to see the marriage lines if yoh be thinkin' to bed in my 'ouse, for strumpets be summat else I don't allow.'

'I'll not be one to lie to ye, Bella, there be no marriage lines, sure and I'm after only just meeting the colleen . . .'

'Then yoh can tek your sport somewheers else.' Placing her ample figure squarely in the doorway the woman glared at her visitor. 'I'll 'ave no whorin' under my roof . . . and yoh –' the angry stare swung back to the cringing Maura '– yoh should 'ave more respect for yourself than to go earnin' ya bread by lyin' on yer back in any man's bed!'

'Bella!' Aiden's voice held a note that quietened the woman. 'There be no marriage lines as I told ye. This girl is not my wife and neither is she a prostitute, I would not taint the friendship you and I have by bringing a woman of the streets to yer door.'

'But yoh said yoh'd only just met.'

'And that be the truth of it. It be naught but a couple of weeks since the colleen left the shores of Ireland and if God had not seen to the placing of me where He did then she would have been halfway to the Orient by this time.'

'White slavers?' The hard stare softened instantly to one of sympathy, and strong hands fastened on Maura's arm, drawing her into the warmth of what proved to be a small kitchen warmed by a coal fire burning in a grate that gleamed like black silver.

'Sit ya theer, wench.' The woman drew a second chair to the fire. Taking Maura's shawl and hanging it from a peg on the back of the door she shot an accusing glance at the man who moved to warm himself at the hearth. 'Fancy leadin' me on that way, 'aving me accuse the wench!'

A smile spreading across his face Aiden caught the plump figure in his arms, planting a kiss on the lined cheek.

'Sure now I couldn't be resisting the teasing of ye.'

'Teasing, was it!' Bella twisted free. 'Then try this for size, liars get no feeding in this 'ouse!'

Dropping his arms, Aiden shook his head theatrically, holding a hand out to Maura. 'Begod and begorra, child, 'tis hungry ye'll go again tonight! And me thinking Bella James would be after seeing the fun of . . .'

'Fun!' Bella glared. 'Yoh call bringin' a young wench to a woman's door and mekin' out 'er be a strumpet fun? Well it be a bloody funny kind o' fun to my way of reckonin'!'

He had not presented Maura as a woman of the night but to stress Bella's mistake would be to fuel her anger and that, Aiden knew, presented the risk of himself and Maura being tipped back into the street to spend the night where they might. Injecting a note of contrition into his voice he said, ' 'Twas coarse and foolish so it was and it's apologising I am. I should not have thought to speak so to ye, Bella James. We'll be after wishing ye goodnight. Come, Maura child.'

Rising to her feet Maura spoke for the first time. 'You have my apologies also, Mrs James, 'tis sorry I am for the vexing of you though I'm sure Mr Shanley had no intention of offending; please do not let me be the cause of harming your friendship.'

'Harming!' The woman laughed, her eyes warming. 'There ain't nothing can do that, as for that rogue Shanley, he's bin in more hot water than a boiled egg. Now yoh, sit yourself agen the fire while I brews a pot o' tea, that'll goo nicely with a bit of ham from the bone.'

'So, I reckons yoh found the wench at Liverpool docks.'

The meal of ham and bread over and the crockery washed and returned to its place on the dresser, Bella settled herself in the armchair Aiden had tactfully avoided.

Beginning from that point Aiden told the story of their travelling together from Liverpool but he had reckoned without Bella's quick mind.

'That be all well an' good,' she said as he finished, 'but wheer there be one there's bound to be others, it teks more than one man piddlin' in the 'oss road to mek a puddle; Maura wouldn't be the only wench to 'ave bin put aboard that boat, the sort that follows slavin' as a way of mekin' a living don't tek them risks for the profit one wench would bring.'

'There were others,' Maura said quietly. 'We were together on that ship, they each told a similar story to my own, they had no family in Ireland and each had spoken with a woman who had promised them a new life in England, but once aboard they had been shackled like animals. When we reached port we were herded onto the deck, then—' She broke off, a sob taking her words.

'It be all right, wench,' Bella moved to her side, touching a comforting hand to her shoulder, 'ya don't 'ave to say more. You'll spend the night wi' Bella James an' the morning will look to itself.'

'. . . *the morning will look to itself* . . .'

The words echoing in her mind, Maura slipped out of the patched skirt and worn blouse, folding them neatly before laying them across a rush-seated chair set beside the door of the room Bella had brought her to. The woman's eyes had been moist as she had left, soft with the shadows of pity. But what was that pity for? Pouring cold water from a butterfly-painted jug into a matching bowl she washed her face, holding the drying cloth for long moments over her eyes. Was Bella James's pity an emotion that followed what she had heard or for what she knew the morning would bring?

'*Just when it be a body be thinking tomorrow be dawning, sure an' it be yesterday.*'

Words spoken so often by Sinead O'Toole whispered softly in her brain. Lowering the towel, Maura stared at the flickering shapes of candle-light on the wall. Would that be how the morning would be, the same as so many of her yesterdays; days that had found her alone in a strange world, afraid of every man who came towards her? Would Aiden Shanley have left her to fend alone?

Slipping into the narrow bed she blew the candle out, becoming suddenly afraid of the darkness that leapt in on her. Closing her eyes tight she prayed silently to be given the courage every fibre of her body seemed to tell her she would need.

As he had so often since the funeral of his brother, Liam Riordan pushed aside the meal that had been served to him. Raising a weary hand he ended the protest of the manservant, only walking in silence to his bedroom.

Sat in semi-darkness he stared deep into the crimson heart of a fire lit despite the gentle warmth of the early summer night.

'. . . *'Tis my hand and mine alone . . . sends him less than a man to his grave . . .*'

The words that had haunted his every moment and kept him from sleep, rose again sharp and vivid as the accusing face that seemed to stare at him from the crimson coals.

'. . . *ye knows where it is Fergus Shea can be found . . .*'

But he had not gone to the house of Fergus Shea, he had not sought revenge for his brother's death. The price of vengeance . . . he had looked down on that dead face as he had weighed those words then found the price too high. But had that been cowardice rather than common sense, timidity in place of loyalty? Had he told himself, standing at the foot of that coffin, that seeking vengeance would give rise to nothing but more suffering simply out of fear for his own skin . . . was he too much of a coward to stand up for Padraig?

'. . . *ye be naught but a coward . . . a runt and a misfit ye were born and 'tis a runt and a misfit ye'll die!*'

Seamus had thrown those words at him when he had been no more than a six-year-old afraid to set his horse to jumping a seven-foot hedge. A coward! Liam looked deep into the flames. Was that what he was being now? Had he given the lie – that his brother had died as the result of pneumonia caught on his ride back from Portington Hall – merely to save himself, was he even now pretending it was the safety of the lives of the men of the valleys, so many useless deaths of innocent people, that stayed his hand?

He had asked the same of the Blessed Ciaran. He had gone to Clonmacnoise, knelt on the rough earth floor of the tiny ruined chapel and asked his question. But there had come no answer into his troubled mind, no whisper to quiet his tortured heart; the answer must be of his own making.

Padraig had caused so much trouble and heartbreak in his lifetime, was his death to be a reason for causing more?

'. . . *such a war as none shall remain . . .*'

In the grate the scarlet coals settled lower in their bed, sending a shower of brilliant sparks bursting against the darkness of the chimney. That was how the valleys would look, the spark of pistol shots bursting against the crimson fires of burning houses! Liam watched the cascade flare their tiny points of light, blinking for one vibrant second before dying away into nothing, before being swallowed into the vacuum of darkness, eliminated as the lives of so many men would be eliminated, ended before their time . . . and for what! Vengeance for one life, a life that had given misery to many and true happiness to none.

'. . . *it will be such a war . . . will make the troubles with the English seem like nursery games . . .*'

Could he bring that down on the heads of the people, had Clonfert not suffered enough at the hands of the Riordans? In the darkened room the coals shifted again and it seemed the image of a face stared condemningly at him while in the hushing sound of its movement was the sneering hiss of contempt.

Coward!

The flame-formed eyes of Seamus gleamed their scarlet scorn.

'Yes, Father,' Liam whispered, 'a coward and a misfit. That is how you always thought of me, and who is to say you were not right?'

Closing his eyes on the odium gleaming in that phantom face Liam felt the sorrow of his lonely heart-breaking childhood creep once more into his heart. Even from the grave his father condemned him. Avenging Padraig's murder was what Seamus would have done and given no mind to the suffering it caused. But he was not Seamus! Opening his eyes he stared at the glowing coals.

'Vengeance carries a price I will not pay,' he said quietly. 'Be it as you predicted, Seamus, I will die a coward and a misfit.'

◆━━━◆

28

'You ain't the first body Aiden Shanley 'as fetched to this 'ouse.' Bella James watched the girl standing silent beside her kitchen table. 'His 'eart be too soft for his 'ead sometimes. Just 'ow he thinks to save every one he sees to be in need is more'n I can reckon, for Brummagem has more down an' outs than the Queen has tanners in 'er coffers.'

Nor was this the first time he had brought *her* to the house of a stranger and left her there. Reaching for her shawl still hanging behind the door, Maura hid her disappointment.

'I can only apologise for the intrusion of my being here.' She passed the shawl around her shoulders, pulling the ends across her breasts. Was this the way it would always have been had he taken her with him . . . setting her down every evening to eat and sleep at the expense of unsuspecting folk? At least this time she had worked off the price of her lodging, scrubbing out the kitchen and cleaning every stick of furniture the little house boasted.

'So wheer d'yoh reckon to go wi' not a penny to weight your pocket?'

Pride holding her head high, Maura gave the answer she had conjured while scrubbing floors. 'My mother always maintained we have family in England, I shall look for them.'

' 'Er said that did 'er?' Bella's mouth showed no hint of the respect she already held for this thin slip of a girl. 'An' did 'er say exactly where this family o' your'n was to be found?'

A faint tinge of colour stained her cheeks but Maura's head stayed up.

Bella's hands, small in comparison to her body, reached for an over-decorated teapot. 'I can see for meself the answer to that one, it be as 'er d'ain't. Well, wench, this much Bella James can tell ya, half a mile be as much as you'll travel wi'out some smart fellah tekin' advantage; there'll be plenty offerin' help and plenty who'll tek it an' all, they'll help themselves to *you*. I doh know what that country of Ireland be like, though from what was said last night it be no paradise, but this I does know, a young wench on her own be no match for some of the cunning buggers we gets round 'ere and doubtless it will be the same in any other town, so I says again, if ye be willing to throw in your lot wi' me then you can bide here. Folk from all over comes to Brummagem town and if it be you 'ave folk in England then sooner or later you'll 'ave the hearing of 'em.'

The woman had offered to find her work, she could pay her keep, it would not be charity. Thoughts wrestling with her pride, Maura watched deft movements belie the smallness of the hands manipulating the teapot. It would not be the way it had been with Aiden Shanley, she would not have to rely upon his paying her food and bed, and any penny she could keep would be saved so if and when she came face to face with him again she could return his outlay.

Taking her cup to the fireside, Bella sat in the armchair. She had read the bitterness in the girl's face, the disappointment of what she saw as desertion. They were emotions she had witnessed before and might well again but with this wench it were different . . . deeper, an almost living pain; could it be love, had the wench fallen in love with Aiden Shanley? Surely not . . . he was old enough to be her father. So what did that prove! Bella sipped the hot tea. A wench in trouble didn't take note of the age of her rescuer.

'That cup o' tea be offered in friendship.' She glanced at

Maura. 'I don't carry no obligations, ye be free to mek your own decisions.'

Murmuring her thanks, Maura picked up the cup. Her decision had been made, she would stay with Bella James.

The woman had been true to her word. Maura smoothed a hand over her skirt of warm brown Melton cloth. Bella had insisted she take that and a coat from the clothes she collected from the houses of the many industrialists who lived in the town. How could people afford to give such clothes away? Maura remembered the other woman's scornful laugh as she had answered that it was a result of money . . . money made from the labours of folk half dead from many hours and little pay; the wives and children of iron masters and mine owners buying new outfits almost every week just to show their husbands and fathers could afford it. But their waste was Bella's benefit. Passed to housekeepers to dispose of, the clothes were kept against Bella's visits with the result she paid a few shillings which found the way to the purses of the housekeepers. It was a business Bella ran with competence and in the months they had been together she had taught that business to Maura. This was the work she had promised. Maura glanced at the rows of market stalls sporting a wide variety of goods. Each evening Bella would go over every item of clothing set aside for the next day's sale, adding a penny or two extra on those she had paid to have laundered. '*The folk of Brummagem 'ave enough dirt in their lives,*' Bella had said, '*I won't be sellin' 'em any more.*'

It had seemed strange at first. Maura watched the shoppers moving between the stalls searching out the best buy, uncertainty on every work-weary face as to whether their pennies should be spent elsewhere. So it had been with her own mother; she too had evaluated the spending of every single halfpenny as life had grown harder, always denying herself first . . .

Blinking back the tears memory forced upon her, Maura smiled at a small pale-faced child resting its chin on the edge of her stall.

'Yoh'm pretty.' Eyes enlarged by the thinness of the little face stared solemnly.

'Thank you.'

'My mother says yoh be I'er-rish.'

'So I am.'

The small mouth closed for a moment, the child obviously digesting the information.

'Then what yoh doin' 'ere? Why ain't yoh in yer own country?'

It was blunt, to the point, without a trace of inhibition. To the child it was simply a question.

'I was all alone. I needed a friend so I came here to Birmingham.' It was true, Maura thought, watching the serious little face. Apart from Mother O'Toole she had no friend in Ireland. And what of Liam Riordan? A quick start, a feeling almost of guilt shot through her. Was Liam not to be counted as a friend?

'I'll be you'r friend,' the shrill voice piped. 'I think yoh be pretty.'

A smile lighting her eyes, Maura touched a finger to the soot-smudged cheek. 'Sure, and it is yourself who is pretty, I swear Brian Boru himself would have thought you the most beautiful colleen in the whole of Ireland.'

'Brian Bru –' the wide eyes studied Maura's face '– who do 'e be?'

'He was once the *Ard Ri*, a High King of all Ireland—'

'An' yoh was a princess an' 'e come to rescue yoh from a dragon an'—'

'Yoh'll need rescuin' from my boot!' An irate hand clamped on the thin shoulder. 'I've told yoh time outa number not to go wanderin' off on yer own, I've a good mind to clout yer 'ead fer

ya, p'raps that might knock some sense into it! I'm sorry 'er
pestered ya, miss,' the harassed little woman looked apologetic, 'it be 'er father, forever fillin' 'er 'ead wi' fairy tales. I tries
tellin' 'im . . . fairy tales won't feed 'er when 'er be growed, 'e
far better teach 'er summat useful.'

Her glance following the pair, the woman's hand now
clamped tight about the child's wrist, Maura's memory trans-
formed them to a man and a young girl walking barefoot amid
the grass bordering a river that gleamed molten fire in the
reflection of a setting sun.

'*Was the princess beautiful?*'

Her young face beaming with excitement the child danced
along.

'*Let me be seeing now,*' the tall man ceased walking to study
the upturned face, '*sure, an' the princess took the breath from the
body of folk who looked upon her such was the beauty of her, just as
my own little princess does . . .*'

Fairy tales . . . Maura watched the mental picture fade . . .
they would not feed that little girl's body but they would
nourish her heart for long years to come; let her have her
dreams, the legacy of a father's love; life was too hard without
it.

'. . . *I'll be yoh'r friend.*'

The words echoed and re-echoed in Maura's mind as
evening turned to night. But those you thought of as friends
had a way of fading from your life as pictures faded from the
mind. Those few weeks of travelling with Aiden Shanley had
her convinced he was a friend who would not desert her, yet he
had gone, left without a word, leaving only a gift. But she did
not want trinkets! Bending to place an unsold petticoat into the
large basket at her feet she felt the small copper pendant touch
her throat beneath the high-buttoned collar of her cotton
blouse. '*He made it for you,*' Bella had said as she had handed
her the ornament. A salve to the conscience? That was unfair!

Her own conscience stinging, Maura folded a pair of boy's trousers she had made from a torn skirt. Aiden Shanley owed her no allegiance, he had no moral or bounden duty to stay with her. What he had done, the help he had given, had been done from the goodness of his heart and she could have no complaint when he chose to go on his way.

'. . . *be always grateful for a kindness . . .*'

Her father had said that often and she tried to follow his advice, but every day brought with it a little of the pain she had felt on finding the tinker gone. True, Bella had become a much-loved figure in her life . . . yet somehow she could not replace Aiden Shanley in her heart.

It had been almost a year. Wearily Maura lifted the large cane basket, almost empty now of second-hand clothes, onto her head. The action had caused her some difficulty in those first days of being with Bella but now she managed it with ease. Answering several goodnights with her own she walked between the long rows of market stalls set in the Bull Ring close to the church of Saint Martin. The rag market, Bella had called it when introducing it to her, but she soon learned it did not deal solely in cast-off clothing. '*Frocks to furniture,*' Bella had told her, laughing, '*an' a bit of everythin' in between.*'

It had taken a while for the stallholders to accept her, strangers were not easily welcomed into a patch they thought of as their own, but Bella had soon put an end to that. '*This wench be wi' me, 'er'll stand my stall –*' with her hands on her wide hips she had stared challengingly at the faces of the other stallholders '*– an' if there be any bugger of yoh lot 'as argument wi' that then let's be 'earing it now!*'

There had been none prepared to pick up the verbal gauntlet, they knew well that Bella James was no woman to bandy words with, and from that day not one of them had spoken ill, though the faces of a few still said they disliked the idea of a 'foreigner' in their midst.

Outside the market hall the air was heavy with the smell of fish coming from the fish market stood on the adjacent corner. 'Not everyone's idea of perfume, how do you stand it?' A smile covering the whisper she glanced at the statue of Admiral Lord Nelson. Lifting a hand to the basket on her head she waited for a horse-drawn tram to pass before turning along Bell Street, following it to the narrow Old Meeting Street that wormed its way between a warren of tall houses only faith seemed to hold up. She had come to know many of the families who lived in these houses and in those of the surrounding area, hard-pressed people who struggled to survive their poverty; but despite it all they carried a sense of pride that allowed them to beg from no one.

'*I only 'as two farthings . . .*'

Pity that had risen in Maura that night rose again now. Bella had opened the door to a thin, almost emaciated woman, a threadbare shawl tied about her head.

'*There be talk along of the wharves that says you makes cures for the cough . . .*'

She had refused the mixture as a gift, insisting on leaving both of her farthings. Across the twisted roofs the bells of the church of Saint Jude rang the hour of nine. Maura paused to listen, loving the clear beautiful sound. Many churches graced this town, their beauty hiding the squalor and suffering of those that toiled long hours in the many workrooms and factories. There had been poverty in Ireland, many dying of famine that followed the sickness of the soil, but they had been spared the belching stacks of iron foundries that robed the sky in darkness and the buildings in soot. But it did no good to think of that land, her life was here now.

'Better not to stand dawdlin', Maura wench, the puddlers'll be turnin' out of the ale house along of Smallbrook Street any minute an' could be they'll tek yoh for a sixpenny woman!'

A small figure swatched in wide black skirts and dark shawl, a straw bonnet perched on the crown of her tousled head, bustled up to Maura, her own basket cradled on her hip.

A sixpenny woman. That was the term the women stall-holders used when speaking politely of the prostitutes that haunted the wharves and basins of the canals which ran like veins throughout the body of the town.

'I was listening to the bells, Mrs Steppings, they sound sweet as the voices of angels in heaven.'

'Oh ar, they sounds that all right!' the woman answered as Maura walked beside her, matching her quick stride. 'An' I reckons there'll be a few more angels singin' in 'eaven if this sickness don't bate soon, took two more poor little mites today.'

Leaving Maura and disappearing among the close-packed houses that bordered both sides of Hinkely Street the woman could be heard muttering her prophecies of deaths yet to come. The sickness was not improving! Maura hurried on. There were like to be more people, those without money to spare for a doctor, knocking on Bella's door and asking for potions to help their children. Word of the mixtures Maura could make had spread quickly and almost from the first week of her being here mothers had come seeking her help. But the cough that whooped in the lungs of those that caught it was spreading faster than she could make her medicine. Most nights she did not see her bed before dawn touched the sky and after a day in the market she was too tired to eat. '*Yoh 'ave to stop one or the other,*' Bella had protested as she gathered pots and herbs for making a fresh batch of potions. '*Go on like yoh be an' you'll be the next to be carried to the churchyard.*'

But how could she give up? Her steps quickening at the thought she hurried along Saint Jude's Passage, not looking at the church etched black and sharp against the crimson that suddenly flared across the night, changing the sky to a great scarlet bowl as the iron foundries opened their furnaces. The sight had terrified her in the beginning; she had trembled, thinking this must be the sign of those last days the priests back home had talked of, the Armageddon they had frightened the people of the valleys with. Then she had become used to the sight, admiring the grandeur of it, the awesome majesty that held the breath in her throat. But tonight she had no time to stare. Clutching her basket with one hand and her skirts with the other she ran on.

The house was in darkness. Bella should not be out collecting clothes at this hour, it was too tiring. Lifting the latch Maura stepped inside the kitchen, standing a few moments for her eyes to adjust to the darkness. Tonight she would insist upon Bella having supper in bed and no argument. The sorting of her day's trophies could wait until tomorrow.

Shadows resolving themselves into dresser and table, Maura set her own basket down, her feet moving cautiously as she crossed towards a fireplace that held no spark of life. There were matches on the mantelpiece, she would first light the lamp then make a fire. Bella would be cold when she got in.

The light spreading a pale glow about the kitchen simply added to its emptiness. Staring at the dead grey cinders Maura suppressed a shiver of sudden fear, then pushed it away. Bella had simply stayed on with one of her housekeeper friends later than usual, it was silly to worry.

Removing her coat she hung it on a peg hammered into the door before reaching for an apron to cover her skirts. Sticks and coals, she needed both if she were to light a fire quickly. Knowing Bella's habit of keeping both sticks and a bucketful of coals always to hand in the scullery she lit a candle from the lamp then pulled aside the heavy chenille curtain draped across the archway that led through to the back of the house. Her foot crunching on broken crockery she paused. A cat? Maybe a cat had found its way into the scullery and sent a pot tumbling from a shelf. Lifting the candle above her head her eyes followed the pool of pale light.

If the miscreant had been a cat then what was it had been sent crashing to the floor? There was nothing kept in the scullery that if spilled would result in such a wide-spreading puddle. A slight frown creasing her brow, her boots crunching on broken shards of pottery and glass, she felt the fear of a moment before strike again with piercing coldness. The dark stain, it reflected no light . . . it was not liquid! But if not liquid, then what? Her shaking hand sending pallid beams flickering against walls of shadow, she stared down at the opaque patch. It was unmoving, no oozing of its edge spread it further across the stone floor. Whatever the blackness was it was no puddle.

Black as ebony . . . no reflection of the candle's gleam . . . completely inert . . . the facts rushed together, crashing into Maura's brain with the force of a tidal wave; a force that brought a cry screaming from her throat.

'Bella!' She was on her knees, her free hand touching the dark skirts of the unconscious woman. 'Oh Mother of God . . . Bella!'

Behind her a movement disturbed the broken crockery. Catching her breath she was half turned when she was dragged to her feet, her head snatched back on her neck, the sharp point of cold steel pricking her throat.

'It don't be Bella.' A voice like gravel rubbing against stones hissed close to her ear. 'Now yoh 'ear what it was I would 'ave told her; there be only room fer one 'erbalist in 'Ockley an' that be Alfred Worsley, an' this knife be goin' to mek sure there be no other to tek his trade!'

29

'I were in the privy, I 'eard a sound like summat breakin' then a man rushed out from yoh'r scullery like his arse were afire.'

Having helped get Bella to the armchair in the kitchen the neighbour set busily about lighting a fire in the cold grate.

'I thought Bella had taken a broom to a stray cat and knocked summat from the shelf.' The woman paused. 'Eh wench, I be right sorry I couldn't come no more faster than I did but it teks me a while to go to the ground, my bowels 'ave always bin stubborn.'

'We be glad yoh come when yoh did, Polly.'

'But why this . . . yoh ain't bin 'aving no upper an' downer wi' anybody, 'ave ya?'

Bella shook her head then winced as the movement set her temples aching. 'I've 'ad miss word wi' none, but I could find summat better'n a few words to chuck at the toerag who done this. I'd bost 'is 'ead forrim!'

As she rose to her feet the expression of Bella's neighbour was tight. 'Yoh won't 'ave no need to break the varmint's 'ead, not when word o' this get about, for every bloke in Hockley will be bayin' for 'is blood!'

'But whoever it was did not take anything.'

'That won't butter no parsnips!' The woman's glance swung to Maura. 'We might not 'ave no fancy doo-dads, no fancy ornimunts to deck our 'ouses like them of the masters but what we do 'ave be sacred; we'll stand for nobody stealin' their way in an' messin' wi' what be ourn. I tells ya, lessen that thief be 'alfway to China by now then I wouldn't give a blind ha'penny for 'is chances.'

'Well right now I'd give a damn sight more'n a ha'penny that don't 'ave no 'ead on it for a cup o' tea.'

'Don't go botherin' wi' that.' The neighbour turned towards the scullery as Maura lifted the heavy iron kettle from its hook. 'It'll be near enough mornin' if yoh waits for that to boil over a new lit fire, I'll fetch mine, it were bubblin' when I went out to the privy.'

'Are you sure you are not hurt?' Maura looked anxiously at her friend as the other woman left the house.

'No more'n a headache, and a cup o' tea will soon see that gone. But you, wench, what did that no-good do to you?'

'Nothing . . . he . . . he was gone when I came in.'

'Gone was it!' Bella watched the slim back turn as Maura reached for cups from the dresser. 'Then what is it has placed that cut alongside your throat, be it work of them there little people you sometimes talks of?'

She had placed a folded handkerchief against the sting of her skin, raising the collar of her blouse to hold it in place, hoping Bella would not see it.

'I knows what you was at and the reason of it.' Bella caught the quick movement of fingers checking the handkerchief was still in place. 'But you can't hide the touch that has left blood on your blouse.'

'It . . . it is just a scratch.'

A scratch that was meant to take your life! The thought Bella held to herself dealt a cold blow to her stomach. The intruder had intended no harm to herself, had it been otherwise he could have finished her as she lay on that floor; but he had not come for that, he had come to harm Maura, and by the look of that blood-stained collar he had meant her to die.

* * *

Aiden Shanley fingered the plain wooden box placed on the bunk of his cabin. His business in Ireland had been only partly successful, he had not accomplished the all of that for which he had travelled these many miles.

The father had two sons . . .

That was the thought that had plagued all the months since his last visit to Clonfert, giving him no peace, no respite, every day and night bringing closer the memory of the agony of twenty years served in a penal institution, of the lash of a whip and the blow or kick of fellow inmates, until he felt he would cry out as a ten-year-old boy had cried out. And so he had returned a second time to the land of his birth. Returned to pay that long-standing debt. He could not make payment to Seamus Riordan, for fate had snatched that pleasure from his hand; that he had known, but if not the father, then the sons. If taking the life of Seamus Riordan was denied him, then the balm that was needed to end the pain of injustice must be provided by his sons.

So he had returned to Ireland, walked its green meadows, breathed its sweet air; but in all the weeks of his walking, every step he had taken had been accompanied by one burning ambition, one aim that drove him on . . . the desire for revenge.

He had found Padraig Riordan. Aiden stared at the small wooden casket. He had found the elder son, but fate had laughed a second time. Padraig Riordan lay in the earth next to his father; once again Aiden Shanley was cheated of revenge.

It was in the ale house in Clonfert village he had heard the telling, heard how the heir had met his death, struck down by the pneumonia, except . . . his informant had gazed expectantly at his tankard, resuming his narrative only when Aiden had paid for its refill . . . except the elder son had not been the inheritor of his father's house and means, nor, some had it, had he died of the pneumonia but of the hand of one of the many he had wronged.

The information had left him numbed. Twice he had been robbed of his due, the one thing he had lived for since finding his own family dead and his home a tumbled ruin. First the father and then the son, both beyond his reach . . . but there remained another!

All that night he had lain on the heath beyond the village, sleep never touching his eyelids. The sins of the fathers! He had wrestled with the thought . . . should one pay the price of another, should one man suffer retribution for the wrongs he himself had not committed?

Dawn had seen the answer set firm in his mind. What Seamus and Padraig had not discharged then the second son must. The debt of vengeance would be paid . . . and paid in full.

He had waited for the middle hour of morning before coming to Eyrecourt House, he would strike no man under cover of darkness. But the young master was gone. As if to underline the truth of what he had been told the butler had shown him into first the study and then the drawing room, all the while repeating that it had been some days since the son of Seamus Riordan had been seen at the house, that he was often absent for long periods and they had no idea when he might return.

Bitterness at once more being deprived of what he saw as his right had burned deep inside, flared each of the days he had retraced the way of his coming, smouldering each night spent unsleeping. He spoke of that inner anger to none he met during his journey yet the old woman at that cottage had read it in his face. They had welcomed him as they had that first time, Connal O'Malley and Caitlin his wife, but it was Bridie MacGee had sensed the resentment stored inside him.

'Ye've travelled the length and breadth of the country . . . by the saints and isn't that grand now.' The old woman had smiled, spooning potatoes onto a plate adorned with a large helping of

rabbit pie. '*And could it be ye've been after meeting with Maura Deverell on one of those journeys, for we've sore worried in these days since her leaving us.*'

He had thought at first to deny any knowledge of Maura except his meeting her in Connal's house but the look in the eyes that watched him seemed to know beforehand that would have been a lie. So he had told them just enough to bring a smile, that Maura was safely settled in Birmingham; of the part about her abduction and near selling into white slavery he said nothing . . . that must be left to the girl herself should she ever return.

'*Then ye has the knowing of where it is Maura Deverell is to be found?*' The meal over, Bridie MacGee's bird-bright eyes had fastened to his own and when at last he nodded she had turned to her son-in-law. '*Then 'tis the showing of the box ye must do, Connal, bring it to the table.*'

Aiden remembered the uncertain look that had passed from the man to the woman.

'*Sure and are we all not knowing we have not the way of setting that box where it belongs for ourselves! And is it not a fact that you, Connal O'Malley, searched the heath for a mile or more in every direction when it was we found the owner of it gone, left in the middle of the night and sayin' a word to nobody.*'

The man had made no demur, he had simply drawn a cloth-wrapped bundle from beneath the bed set in one corner of the cramped room and laid it on the table.

Aiden stared at it now as he had then, the words of Bridie MacGee echoing in his mind.

'. . . *'Twas almost dead, so he was . . . laid in this house near a month afore his wits returned to him. A carriage overturned and a man beneath it, ribs broken, that was what Connal came across out there on the heath. The ribs Caitlin and meself bound tight and the gash that sliced across his head we mended, but the weeks of nursing did little for his mind. That was empty of memory and the*

Blessed Mother could be thanked for that for it was plain it had once been filled with sorrows great enough to see a man crazed.'

'Did you know this man's name?'

Bridie had shaken her head at the question. *'The poor man never spoke it nor did he remember from where it was he had come . . . that box ye sees were the only thing he had and of that also he had no memory.'*

'So why show it to me?'

'Look ye inside and ye'll be knowing the reason why.'

They had watched as he had drawn the box to him and lifted the lid, seen the surprise leap to his face as he lifted the contents, Bridie herself nodding at the understanding gradually taking place in his eyes.

He had brought the box away with him. He had kept it wrapped in a cloth in the pack that held the tools of his trade, but the secret it held he carried in his heart.

'Why would anyone do such a thing, why smash every pot and bottle?'

The scullery at last cleared of the debris of the intrusion of the night before, the whole house scrubbed and re-scrubbed, one washing not enough to rid them of the feeling of violation, of strange hands touching every object, Maura settled thankfully to a chair.

Sipping the tea she had brewed, Bella kept the truth of her suspicion in check. 'Seems the work of a madman or of a drunk . . . either way 'e best be far from Hockley,' she answered instead.

'You are sure it was a fall and not a blow you suffered?'

'How many times do it tek!' Bella's smile denied the breath of exasperation. '– I 'eard a noise in the scullery as I opened the door. Thinkin' it to be a cat I shouted, then as I stepped forward me foot slipped on a broken crock and I went arse over elbow, knockin' meself out.'

'But why break in at all?' Maura persisted. 'You say every-one knows the houses of the iron workers and colliers have nothing the stealing of would sell for a penny, so where was the motive?'

She was right. Bella sipped from her cup, her gaze in the heart of the glowing fire. Stealing from any of the working folk would bring no gain; but murder . . . that would carry a high price . . . but who would be set to reap the real profit? Who was it had held a knife to this wench's throat and would have drawn it across had not Polly come in time?

'He probably come for what lies beneath me skirts.' Bella forced a smile, meeting the look that flashed to the young face. 'No, wench, I don't mean as the varmint were looking to rape me . . . this was more up 'is alley.' Raising the many petticoats worn beneath the voluminous black serge, Bella displayed two fairly large canvas bags. Attached to a band about her waist they rested one on each hip. 'Where I goes they goes,' she smiled. 'Toerags like that one can break in all they will but they won't find Bella James's money in no box under the bed.'

That was the reason Bella's small figure looked to be as wide as it was high. Despite herself Maura giggled. It was the many layers of underclothing needed to disguise the wearing of those bags.

Seeing the fleeting frown that followed the laugh, the quick touch of fingertips to the strip of cloth Maura had tied about her throat, Bella felt the hot rise of anger. The wench could so easily have been killed. The thought of it had kept her awake long into the small hours, the twisting of her insides telling what that would have done to herself.

She had liked Maura Deverell from the moment Aiden Shanley had brought her to this house, liked the quiet courage and the honesty that had shown itself to be deeply inbred . . . honest and true as the man who had rescued her from that terrible future; not that the past had been kind . . . a young

wench raped by a blackguard who had respect for nobody . . .
then having to bury her mother with her own hands, and on
top of all of that to be taken by white slavers . . . many a wench
would 'ave broken long since but this one had braved it all,
mekin' no song and dance but carryin' on quiet . . . just as her
was doing now, playing down the danger her had been in,
thinking of others afore herself. Smoothing her skirts over the
pannier-type bags, she tried to keep the emotion from her eyes
and voice – the emotion of a mother for a daughter, for that
was what this slight little Irish wench had come to mean to her
. . . a daughter she loved.

'Ya be sure that there be no more'n a scratch?' Her true
feelings hidden beneath the sharply asked question, she
sniffed. 'Y'ave put summat on it?'

'I cleansed it with marigold mixed with apple cider vinegar
and then dressed it with a paste of slippery elm and goldenseal;
it will heal and like as not leave no scar.'

Mollified, Bella accepted a second cup of tea, her own cure
for all ills. 'Ya knows your herbs,' she said, 'that much I own;
the mother that taught ya and the one that had the teaching of
'er 'as my regards as they do of many in 'Ockley, yoh've bin a
boon to many—'

Breaking off she stared for several seconds into the dancing
flames, a sudden thought pushing words aside until, 'Maura,
wench, I knows I've asked ya this afore but think 'ard. When
that bugger attacked ya did 'e say anything . . . anything at
all?'

'I can't—'

'*Think*, wench . . . *think!*'

Arrested by the unexpected sharpness of Bella's tone, by the
urgency in her voice, Maura stood with the empty teapot in
her hands.

'Tek ya time,' Bella said more softly, 'just try to remember.'

She didn't want to remember! Maura felt the jolt of fear she had felt as her head had been jerked savagely back and a cold sharp something pressed against her throat . . . she wanted only to forget.

'Try, wench,' Bella urged again.

'It . . . it was a harsh voice . . . gravelly –' Maura's hands shook as she re-lived the horror '– a man's voice, I think. He . . . he said there was room only for one herbalist in Hockley and that knife—'

Going to stand beside the trembling girl, Bella took her in plump arms. 'I knows this be 'ard for ya, me wench, but I asks ya to go on, to tell the rest.'

Her nerves breaking up the answer, Maura struggled on. 'He . . . he said that knife was . . . was going to make sure there would be no other to take his trade.'

'. . . *room for only one 'erbalist in 'Ockley . . . no other to tek his trade . . .*'

Above the girl's bent head, Bella James's mouth tightened. She had had her suspicions, now they were as good as proved true.

'Was a name mentioned?' No name was needed to convince her of who it was had broken into her home, of who it was had been ready to murder the girl who trembled in her arms, but others would need the proof before they doled out justice.

'I . . . I can't . . . I didn't hear—'

'A name!' Bella recognised the fear, but sixth sense told her a name had been spoken. 'He said a name!'

'Worsley!' Maura could no longer hold back the sobs. 'He said Alfred Worsley.'

Alfred Worsley! Bella held the shaking girl. The man had a voice that grated like a glede under a door, and it were Alfred Worsley kept the only herbalist shop in Hockley. But not for ever. Bella's features set like stone. If the men of Hockley failed to repay that night's work then Aiden Shanley would not.

30

As she sorted the clothes she had collected that day, Bella's glance lifted often to the slight figure moving restlessly about the kitchen straightening covers she had straightened a dozen times before, moving objects only to replace them in their original position a few moments later. This had been Maura since the break-in, a wench nervous of her own shadow. Was it a result of that man's intrusion into their home? Bella laid aside a gown of deep rose, its neckline trimmed with a fichu of paler pink tulle. That break-in was enough to put fear into any woman, but that sitting on Maura Deverell's shoulders was more than a fear of burglary, it went far deeper than that. Could it be she had guessed . . . come to the same conclusion she herself had? Did Maura think as she did, that it was no simple robbery that failed but an attempt at murder . . . an attempt that could well be made again . . . and was the wench carrying the knowledge she was the intended victim?

Word of what had happened had spread quietly from mouth to mouth; there would be no man in Hockley would not know of it and none, Bella felt certain, who would not be keeping an eye open for Alfred Worsley. But talk had it he was gone to London to fetch a shipment of herbs, gone the night before every pot in her scullery had been smashed.

A shipment of 'erbs! Bella thought acridly. If that toerag 'ad gone anywhere to fetch 'erbs then her arse was a lemon! True, he hadn't been seen at his place for nigh on a week but that didn't mean he wasn't skulking somewhere close by . . .

waiting his chance to strike again. Bella felt a touch of ice against her spine. She had made excuses every day to walk with Maura to and from the rag market, but there were places she could not pretend she happened to be in, places where modesty ordered the wench should be alone, the privy being one of them; the yard was dark, dark enough to hide anyone who had no wish to be seen . . . a perfect place to wait.

A sharp rap to the door had a spoon drop from Maura's hand.

'Steady, wench, it be nobbut a neighbour.'

Bella kept her voice calm but the hand that slid beneath her skirts trembled as it fastened about the carving knife. It were no neighbour rapping her door then waiting for it to be opened; such was not the way of Black Country folk, theirs was a shout of 'I be a comin' in' that reached the ears no sooner than folk came into the room. The knife grasped tight in the folds of her wide skirts, Bella rose. Whoever stood beyond that door it was no neighbour.

'Wait you there!' She held up a hand as Maura made to move towards the door. 'It be someone I be expectin' . . .' Holding the knife concealed from Maura's sight, she finished the sentence in her head . . . I've bin expctin' that sly mullock, well this time I'll mark 'is card meself. '*No proof*' that bobby at the police station 'ad said when 'er 'ad made complaint, but Bella James d'ain't need no proof to know it were Worsley had made to slit a wench's throat, that bastard was so crooked 'e couldn't lie straight in bed. Well he'd lie straight enough in a coffin!

Snatching the door back on its hinges, the knife already above her head, she stepped backwards. 'I . . . I begs yoh'r pardon . . . I thought . . . I mean I 'ad'nt . . .'

'Forgive my calling at so late an hour.'

Still stood beside the dresser Maura released her pent-up breath but the fear that had risen so quickly to her throat remained stubbornly thick.

'You are Maura Deverell?'

'Who be it wantin' to know?' Bella's fingers gripped the knife she made no attempt to lower.

'My regrets for startling you.' A man's well-modulated voice displayed no alarm at the reception he had been given. 'I was told I might find Maura Deverell here.'

'An' if ya can, so what?'

'I . . . I am Maura Deverell.' Stepping to Bella's side Maura saw a middle-aged man, his face haggard beneath a silk top hat.

'Good evening.' The hat was swept away. 'My name is Samuel Radley.'

Surprise sapping her anger, Bella lowered the knife. 'Samu'l Radley . . . of Radley's Bricks? I . . . I begs yoh'r pardon . . . I weren't never expectin' . . . but come yoh in, sir.'

Inside the kitchen the man's face looked even more drawn, the light of the lamp showing the shadows beneath his eyes, the dull gleam almost like hopelessness that played in them as he looked at Maura. 'You are Maura Deverell . . . the same who makes herbal elixirs?'

'You have complaint of them?' Her throat suddenly free of constriction, Maura's head rose defiantly. Was this one more trick dreamed up by her unknown attacker . . . some malicious lie told to discredit her potions?

'No . . . no, I have no complaint.' Samuel Radley's head shook slightly. 'I . . . that is my wife . . . has heard nothing but praise of your medicines and ointments. That, Miss Deverell, is the reason for my visit. My son is ill of the cough, so ill we fear he may not recover. My wife was told of the relief your mixture has brought—'

'Forgive me,' Maura interrupted quickly, 'I am no doctor.'

'You think I should retain the services of one!' Radley's drawn mouth smiled wearily. 'Believe me, Miss Deverell, I have tried them all but with little result. My son grows weaker with every day, the cough whoops in his lungs giving no rest . . . you are our last hope.'

'But I cannot,' Maura stammered, 'I claim no cure . . . my mixtures might help but that is all.'

Across the table sad eyes held her own. 'That is all I ask. My wife would be so grateful, as would I myself. Might I purchase some of your cough remedy?'

She had none, what had been brewing in the scullery had been spilled, destroyed as the pots were smashed, and she had made no more.

' 'Tis sorry I am, but I have no mixture.'

A frown settling on his brow, Samuel Radley's fingers whitened about the brim of his black silk hat. If gossip was not all lies this woman had made her preparations available to every family in Hockley, so why was she refusing him? Money! Was that it . . . did she think by refusing to raise the price? His lips set he stared at Maura.

'You may name your own price . . . be certain it will be met.'

The coldness of the answer, the disgust suddenly flaring in those tired eyes jarring her nerves, Maura was equally icy. 'I *ask* no payment, Mr Radley, but the people leave what they can afford, as for myself what I can do to alleviate suffering is done with thanks to God for the gift He has seen fit to give to me . . .'

'Then help my son!'

'Mr Radley.' Bella intervened quietly. 'What Maura said were true, there's been no remedies brewed in this 'ouse for a week or more . . .'

Standing silently while Bella told quickly of the break-in that had resulted in the destruction of every last pot of ointment and bottle of mixture, Samuel Radley gave a curt nod of the head as the explanation finished. 'Once more I must apologise to you, Miss Deverell, my rudeness of a moment ago was unforgivable.'

'Maura don't 'ave none of 'er cough cure.' Bella spoke again as the owner of the brickworks turned to leave. 'But that ain't to say as there be none.'

'But you said—'

'I knows what it was I said,' Bella caught the accusation, 'I said as there 'ad been no brewin' of 'erbal remedies in this 'ouse for a week or more. There was no lie in that, for the bottle that be in my basket were brewed the night afore we was broke into.'

They leave what they can afford. Samuel Radley understood. The owner of the brickworks was worth plenty!

'You have a bottle of the cough syrup my wife has heard praise of? Then sell it to me.' Taking several sovereigns from his pocket he set them on the table.

Reaching the bottle from her basket Bella handed it to Maura before turning to face their visitor, a hard-set expression on her face. 'T' ain't mine to sell, it belongs to Maura Deverell and it will be 'er will 'ave the sayin' of who it be will 'ave the getting' of it.'

With the bottle in her hand, Maura glanced at the small heap of coins, the gold of them enhanced by the gleam of the oil lamp lighting the room. It was more money than she had ever seen, more than she dreamed; with that much money she could go back to Ireland, raise a stone over the place where her mother had died, have the coffins of her father and brother removed to the grounds of the Abbey at Clonmacnoise, buried close to the chapel of the holy Saint Ciaran!

Scooping up the coins she held them in her free hand, glittering splinters of their radiance darting across her face. She could do so much for the memory of her parents.

'Thank you, Mr Radley.' She smiled at the man watching her, his mouth taut as the look in his eyes. 'But as I told you, any skills I'm after having with herbs is the gift of the Almighty; that, for me, is payment enough.'

Taken by surprise Samuel Radley hesitated. He had been mistaken in this girl, she was no money grabber. The hard set of his mouth softening he put out a hand, closing Maura's fingers over the coins, saying quietly, 'God made a wise choice when bestowing His blessing.'

Re-opening her hand Maura looked steadily at the man whose eyes held a haunted look born of desperation.

'The mixture is yours to take,' she said, 'but you must take the sovereigns also.'

A slight frown nestling between heavy brows he glanced to where Bella stood with her hands folded across her wide black skirts.

'Can you not—'

Cutting the question short, Bella shook her head. 'No, Mr Radley, I can't get Maura to change 'er mind, an' truth is, even if I could I wouldn't do no such thing. Like you've been told, 'er asks no reward for what 'er does. Now, sir, if you'll tek my words as they be intended, get you back 'ome to your babby an' give 'im that mixture.'

'I will, and thank you . . . thank you both.'

'Mr Radley,' Maura called as Bella accompanied him to the street door. 'Perhaps you might explain to your wife that bathing the child with warm water to which has been added Saint John's wort and comfrey will help relieve any aching of the bones brought on by fever or that comes with the cough-ing, and barley water to drink is an excellent relief where the chest lining is inflamed.'

The man turned again and when he spoke it was almost an apology. 'My wife . . . she is so overcome with worry for our son I could not blame her if your kind advice . . . please, Miss Deverell, would you return with me, take the nursing of the child into your own hands?'

For several seconds only the tick of Bella's tin clock disturbed the silence. Return to the home of a man who had simply walked in off the street! Maura felt the finger of caution touch her nerves. True he was impeccably dressed but . . .

'Please, Miss Deverell.' He spoke again. 'I ask this not for myself or my wife but for my son.'

Her glance meeting that of Bella she recognised that same caution; she was being told to refuse.

Watching them both for a moment she strove to find courage enough to answer; then, the words refusing to come, she reached for the coat hanging on its peg.

Sorting the clothes she had collected that day, Bella breathed her satisfaction; fortune had favoured her for there were several dresses she knew would sell for a good profit . . . but not on the rag market. Lilah Simkin liked a good frock and her money was as good as anybody else's even though it were made by running a bawdy house.

'*If not me then somebody else.*'

The words of the woman returned as they often had whenever Bella felt a twinge of conscience at selling to the keeper of a brothel.

'. . . *who knows 'ow they might be treated, least them as plies their wares in my 'ouse keeps a clean body for I 'olds with no backdoor trade . . .*'

It was a profession old as the world itself and like as not one would last as long as the other. Bella laid aside the dresses. Women with no other way of putting food into their mouths worked the streets of Brummagem, as no doubt was done in other towns; Lilah was true in what 'er said, the women of 'er establishment 'ad a roof over their 'eads, clean beds to sleep in and no client raised a hand to them, not a second time anyway.

Prostitution! Bella released a sigh. It was a trade she had no liking for yet at the same time she realised that while the world

was the unequal place it was many women must indulge in it
or strave. Thank God Maura had been spared such a life!

'I be comin' in.'

'Ya be welcome, though I 'opes it be naught bad to 'ear
brings ya to my 'ouse.' Looking up, Bella nodded to the burly
figure dressed in police uniform.

'Naught I feels you 'ad 'and in.' The police officer smiled. 'I
be mekin' enquiries as duty bids.'

'Duty!' Bella grinned. 'We both knows you enjoys it, goin'
around wi' buttons bright as medals on a general's chest . . . it
be the greatest pleasure you've ever 'ad, Bert Whitehouse . . .
unless o' course you counts that day o' the church picnic . . .'

'Now then, Bella! We agreed we'd say no more o' that.'

'I be sorry, Bert . . . You be right, we'll say no more, but ya
can't run me in for thinkin' . . . So out wi' it, why be you 'ere?'

'You've 'eard of the fire . . . the one over at Union Passage?'

'All of 'Ockley 'ave 'eard of it!'

'No doubt.' The policeman nodded, twisting the helmet he
had removed on entering the kitchen. 'It were Alfred Worsley's 'erbal shop, we thinks it could be as it were set to burn
deliberate.'

'Oh!' Bella was on her feet, the grin gone from her mouth,
the smile faded from her eyes. 'And do it be that ya thinks to
find the culprit 'ere?'

'Now Bella—'

'Don't you go "now Bella" to me or I'll throw you out,
buttons or no bloody buttons!' Bella flared. 'There be none
'ere who goes settin' fires, though to speak as I feel I could 'ave
set that toerag Worsley alight and no regret for the doin' it!'

'Best not to let folk hear ya say as much, Bella, least not
afore we 'ave the one responsible.'

'Which ain't me!'

'I 'adn't thought it, Bella.'

'Then why come 'ere!' Indignation spitting every word she

glared at the obviously uncomfortable figure fiddling with his helmet.

'I told ya, Bella, it be my duty. Regardless of my own beliefs I 'ave to follow orders and them orders be to mek enquiries.'

'So mek 'em . . . an' then bugger off!' Arms folded, Bella stared. But there bravado gave way to uncertainty. The bobbies had bin told of what had been done in her scullery, the smashing of her crockery and the spoiling of those potions . . . but did they believe this fire was an act of retribution on her part?

'It's been said that Worsley took exception to that lodger of your'n sellin' 'erbal remedies . . .'

'Supposin' 'e did!' Bella snapped, her uncertainty growing. 'What be that to do with 'is shop burnin' down?'

The policeman cleared his throat, putting off the moment of answer. 'You 'as to admit it do seem summat of a coincidence him complaining and then his shop—'

Anger her mistress now, Bella interrupted sharply. 'I admits nuthin'! I ain't seen hide nor hair of that swine Worsley, not since that night 'e tried to do for Maura . . . !'

Opposite her she saw Bert Whitehouse's expression sharpen. She had let her tongue run away with her. There was nothing to do now but tell the whole story.

'. . . so there ya be,' she finished off, ''ad it not been for 'er next door comin' in as 'er did then Maura could 'ave finished up a corpse wi' 'er throat cut.'

'Did the wench see the face of the man who attacked 'er?'

''Er d' ain't have to!' Bella snorted her disgust. 'Ain't I just finished tellin' ya . . . he spoke 'is name, 'e *told* 'er who it was held a knife to 'er throat, said it plain as I've just said it to you . . . 'ow much plainer d'ya need tellin'?'

'This Maura Deverell, is her in the 'ouse?'

Bella's look narrowed. 'Her ain't 'ere, I ain't seen 'er.'

Rising from the chair he had been invited to take, Bert

Whitehouse answered quietly, 'It be no use, Bella, the wench will needs answer for 'erself, so if it be her ain't in this 'ouse then ya best say where it is her can be found.'

Refusing would do no good. Her fingers twisting the corners of her apron, Bella nodded. 'Her be gone to the 'ouse of Samuel Radley of Radley's Bricks . . . but a word of advice afore ya goes along of there, speak of it wi' your gaffers, 'appen they won't want to risk antagonising a brick master by carryin' questioning along of 'is 'ome.'

Closing the door behind the man she had known from childhood, Bella leaned her weight against it. Worsley's shop had gone up in flames . . . but whose hand had kindled them?

Samuel Radley had not exaggerated when he had said his son was so ill they feared he might not recover. Maura looked at the child she had nursed through the day. Pale as alabaster, eyes ringed dark purple, the seven-year-old lay with closed eyes, the cough disturbing him every few minutes. Would her medicines be any more effective than the treatment he had already received? Standing looking at the boy she prayed they would.

'I've brought Master Peter's supper, miss, though 'tis me own reckoning he'll have no more luck at keepin' it inside him than he's had with all the rest, poor little mite.' Lowering the tray she had brought to a table, the young maid looked pityingly at the boy. 'Such a little chap, ain't he, miss? I don't know how his mother'll go on without him.'

'She will not have to go on without him!' It was said more sharply than intended and Maura felt a twinge of guilt as the girl apologised quickly. Smiling briefly she went on more gently, 'Mrs Radley will not lose him, you and I will not allow it . . . will we?'

Words! Maura turned to the fire as the girl scuttled away to bring the things she asked for. It seemed words were all she had, but words would not heal a sick child.

'I've come to sit with Peter myself and I will stay with him tonight, you must take some rest.'

The wife of Samuel Radley had come into the room. A slender petite woman, she bent over the child, touching his brow with her lips before looking again at Maura.

'If you have no objection, Mrs Radley, I would stay.'

'But you have not been to bed since you came, you must rest.'

'I do,' Maura answered. 'The chair beside the fire is most comfortable, I sleep while Peter sleeps.'

Blue eyes brilliant with tears the boy's mother looked at Maura. 'He . . . he will get well?'

Only God knew that. Maura glanced at the child, his eyes open at the sound of his mother's voice, a cough rattling his lungs as he called to her. She watched the woman sit beside her son, taking his little hand in her own, and in Maura's heart was a prayer, God be merciful.

'Will I take this away, miss?' Having brought the ingredients Maura had asked for the maid glanced at the food the boy had refused, bobbing a curtsy as her mistress looked round, then as Maura nodded she picked up the tray and bobbed a second short curtsy before leaving.

'What are you making?' Still holding her boy's hand Laura Radley watched Maura's deft movements.

'A poultice.'

'A poultice!' The woman's brows drew together. 'But Peter has no wound.'

Adding tepid water to the mustard and flour already in a bowl, Maura stirred it to a thick paste. 'This poultice is not for curing a wound, it is to relieve congestion . . . my mother used it to effect many times.'

'The game,' the boy looked up as Maura moved to the bedside, 'can we play the game?'

'I'll begin.' Stirring the bowl again Maura cackled over it, 'Hubble bubble, trouble and toil . . .'

'I know, I know, first a coat of olive oil! It protects delicate skin,' he added, smiling at his mother.

Having smoothed the oil over his chest, Maura spread the mustard mixture onto a clean white cloth and folded it in half. Holding it over him she cackled again, 'Water, flour and mustard seed the mixture that I make . . .'

'Placed in cloth upon my chest the sickness it will take.'

'Hmm!' Maura pretended a sniff as the pale face broke into a smile. 'It's too clever you are, Peter Radley.'

'I remembered, didn't I, Mother . . .' The boy coughed, fighting to get his words out. '. . . I remembered, didn't I?'

'Yes, my little sweetheart, you remembered.' Taking his hand again Laura Radley held it against her cheek, her brilliant eyes spilling tears they had held until now. 'Thank you,' she murmured to Maura, 'thank you!'

31

'I don't want it!' Petulant with fever the boy turned his head away. Cough medicine and poultice she could make, but she could not force the child to eat; yet without food he could not fight the sickness that held him.

Taking the bowl of beef broth to a small table alongside the chair set beside the fire, Maura thought for a moment before returning to the bed.

'Well now, Peter Radley.' She met the tired eyes that turned to her. 'We have a way in Ireland; when a person wants another to do something, they strike a bargain, one pays the other.'

'I don't have any money.'

'Oh it isn't always money they bargain with.'

'But you said one pays the other.'

'I didn't say they did it with money.' Maura smiled. 'I want you to try eating a little of the broth and in return I'll tell you the story of Michael Flanagan and the leprechaun. Do we have a bargain?'

Shaking the hand held out to her she wrapped him in a blanket, returning with him to the armchair.

'What is a leprechaun?'

'A leprechaun is one of the little people, the fairy folk who live only in Ireland. Now the first spoonful, swallow it down and I'll begin.'

Maura fed a little of the broth to the child in her lap. 'Michael Flanagan was going across to the bog of Allan to cut peat for his fire when he heard singing coming from a nearby rock. "Now who is that is after singing on a damp evening such as this?" he asked himself, and being of an inquisitive nature he crept up to the rock to take a peek, and there lying on his back in the heather, a small silver cup in his hand, was none other than a leprechaun.'

'Would he be a goblin?'

'A cousin of the same.' Maura fed more of the broth. 'Now all folk in Ireland know that to catch a leprechaun means he must grant three wishes and Michael Flanagan was no exception. Quick as a flash he grabbed the little man who wriggled like a fish in his hand.'

'Did Michael Flanagan get three wishes?'

'Ah now, we must wait and see.' Waiting while the child swallowed a little broth, Maura smiled, hadn't she herself asked that very same question of her father.

' "To be sure I have ye caught and 'tis three wishes ye must be after granting to Michael Flanagan" . . .'

Quietly, the light of the fire painting moving shadows over her face, Maura told her story intermittently, pausing to feed a spoonful of broth to the child who hung on every word.

'. . . and when he was freed from the bog his fine boots were gone, sucked from off his feet and the leprechaun had vanished.'

'Poor Michael Flanagan, he . . .'

Holding the small body against her as the sentence floated away on sleep, Maura stared into the dancing flames. The boy had eaten almost half of the broth. Words! She smoothed the tumbled hair from his forehead. They could not heal but they soothed; only heaven could do the rest.

'I have done all I can for your son, there is no use in my staying longer in your house.'

A depth of feeling hidden behind a brief nod, Samuel Radley touched a hand to his wife's shoulder as he answered.

'We are deeply indebted to you, Miss Deverell, you have our profound gratitude.'

'Gratitude is all very well, but really, Maura, you must allow my husband to—'

'I have already received all the payment I could want in seeing your son recovered.' Maura smiled at the pretty woman. 'I require nothing more.'

'Mrs James, will you not advise Maura?'

'Ar, I'll do that.' Bella glanced at the girl she had come to bring home. 'You follow your 'eart, wench, go as it guides an' you won't go far wrong.'

'You see, my dear, it is as I told you.' Samuel Radley shook his head but his eyes were smiling as they looked at Maura. 'There is a pride in the people of this Black Country of ours and it seems it is matched by another that is equally strong . . . the pride of the Irish.'

Crossing to where Maura stood beside Bella he took her hand. 'Keep your pride, girl,' he said softly, 'let no one take it from you.'

'You be sure you wanted to come back?' Seated in the carriage the brick master insisted they return home in, Bella voiced a concern that had played in her mind during Maura's absence. She had called at that fine house every day, assuring herself the girl was well cared for, and every day she had compared the wealth and comfort of that house to her own. Maura Deverell would be a fool to refuse a place there, a fool not to take advantage of the chance life was offering her, and she, Bella James, should be prepared to smile and wish her well and give no sign of the emptiness her going to the Radleys would leave.

'Mr and Mrs Radley have been very kind, they showed me every consideration but now I am returning to where I want to be . . . with you.'

It was the one place in England she wished to be. Maura

glanced through the carriage window at tall close-packed houses, long rows of buildings with the soot and dirt of factories and coal mines clinging to every nook and cranny, filming windows like dark curtains. But her heart lay in a different world; people there were poor as here, they worked as hard with as little reward, so what called in her soul, what was in the land of Ireland that could not be found in Birmingham? Her parents, the tiny babe of a brother? No, they were with her wherever she went. Leaning her head against the cushioned upholstery of the carriage she closed her eyes, a jolt of feeling pressing the breath from her chest as the clear picture of a figure formed in her mind, a figure she saw each night as she lay down to sleep; brown hair tumbled by the breeze off the heath topped a smooth brow and fine-boned face, a gentle smile touching the full-lipped mouth of a man who smiled at her. But it was the eyes that tore the heart inside her, eyes filled with a sort of longing, a desire for something he could never have. Then the figure turned from her and as it walked away she saw the slight rise of one shoulder above the other.

'Did the bobbies come to the brick master's, did they question you?'

Bella's voice dispelling the picture, Maura opened her eyes. 'Mr Radley told me of some enquiry, but I was not called. He said the police were perfectly satisfied with his assurance I had not left his house from the evening I entered it.'

'I should think so an' all! 'Ow the hell could them bobbies think either you or meself put fire to that shop?'

'Fire!' Maura twisted in her seat.

'You mean, you d'ain't know?' Bella frowned. 'But you said them there coppers 'ad been to see the brick master.'

'He told me they were enquiring after a missing person, he said nothing of a fire. What happened . . . has anyone been hurt?'

'Not to my knowin', but Worsley ain't been seen since his

shop were burned.' Talking in a low voice, Bella quickly told how the police suspected arson.

'Then . . . then Mr Worsley might be dead!' Maura said as the explanation finished.

'Ain't been no dead body found so far as I've 'eard,' Bella sounded reassuring, 'so I thinks we can tek it that no-good Worsley be alive somewheres.'

The man's shop burned! But why? Could she in some way be the cause? Settling once more into the tiny bedroom of Bella's house, Maura could not let go of the thought. Alfred Worsley had threatened her, held a knife to her throat . . . but that was not reason enough for his shop to be destroyed.

Putting away the change of underwear she had brought home with her, Maura closed the drawer, her lips forming a silent plea. Let it have been an accident . . . please let that fire have been an accident.

But as she walked downstairs to the kitchen she had the overpowering feeling that it wasn't.

'They be too fine to sell in the rag market.'

Bella touched a hand to rich mauve-coloured moire.

'Then what will you be doing with them?'

'Well I shan't be wearin' them, miss, so you can get that smile from your eyes. I'd look like the fairy on the Christmas tree done up in a frock like that. No, these be goin' to Lilah.'

'Lilah?' Maura looked up from folding laundered items into the large wicker basket she would take to market next day.

' 'Er be an acquaintance o' mine; pay a good sum for frocks like this, will Lilah. I be tekin' them to 'er this evenin'.'

'At this time!' Maura glanced at the tin clock, its fingers showing it to be almost ten.

Folding the second of the dresses, smoothing deep lace frills edging the cross-draped bodice, Bella hesitated for a moment. 'Perhaps—'

'No!' Maura laughed. 'I have no wish to look like a fairy either . . . but to be sure none of the little people would wear such a gown.'

'It is a bit of a creation, ain't it?' Covering the dresses with a square of clean huckaback cloth, Bella grinned. 'But then Lilah likes frocks that shouts their comin' . . . says they clear the way in a crowd.'

Reaching her coat from its peg, Maura giggled. 'I wouldn't be arguing with that.'

Straightening from packing the dresses into her own basket, Bella's grin faded as she caught sight of Maura already in the coat. 'Where d'ya think you be goin'?'

'Wherever it is yourself is going, Mrs James.'

'Oh!' At Maura's glint of determination Bella nodded. 'An' I'll not be arguin' wi' that.'

The basket balanced on her head, Bella's quick steps had led them through a maze of dark streets, their tall houses rising like wraiths in the moonlight, but the press of buildings had lessened as they approached the outskirts of the town. Where exactly was Bella taking them? Even in the darkness Maura recognised this was a part of Birmingham she had not visited before.

'Up ahead, by the new-fangled Curzon Street railroad station.' Bella pointed a disparaging hand towards some distant spot. 'Opened it in 1838 and just twelve years on they already 'ave plans for another nearer to the middle o' the town, I 'ears they be goin' to name it New Street. Another railroad station, pah! I asks ya, what good be them smokin' monsters to a town . . . they does nowt to benefit life as I sees, I tells ya Brummagem be better off wi'out 'em! I be glad we don't be goin' no closer than Seymour Street . . . trains be the 'andiwork of the devil!'

Unable to see much in the darkness, Maura stayed close behind Bella as she turned between a pair of tall gates, following her up a drive that crunched beneath their feet.

'We don't tek that way, we uses the back.'

Glancing at a door atop a short flight of steps and overhung by a large lantern, Maura followed the wide skirts. Bella's acquaintance must be a servant in this house, maybe even housekeeper; but why would a housekeeper wish to buy second-hand dresses like the ones in Bella's basket . . . where would a servant wear such?

Hardly given time to wonder on the subject, Maura was whisked up a flight of bare wooden stairs, along a corridor devoid of decoration to a door at the end. But once through it, the change was remarkable. The corridor was suddenly carpeted in deep rich red and lit with a series of small chandeliers, their candles throwing a soft gleam on polished wood and delicate porcelain figures. This was a house as fine as that of the brick master; surely the housekeeper was not permitted quarters in this part of it.

'Mistress says for you to go straight in.' Bobbing no curtsy the frilly aproned maid turned her back, disappearing quickly back along the corridor.

'That one will get 'er arse kicked when Lilah 'ears of 'er manners!' The basket transferred safely to rest on her stomach, Bella threw a derisory glance after the maid. 'Some folk don't know when they 'as it easy, it takes a sharp lesson to teach 'em.'

'Bella James . . . come you in, it be good to see you, that goes for you an all, come you in, wench.'

Drawn into an elegant room, Maura stared at its solitary occupant. Hair whose colour could not possibly be real was coiled in great red swathes above a face . . . Maura's breath choked in her throat . . . a face painted with rouge! Was this Bella's acquaintance, was this woman a housekeeper?

'I see you be surprised, wench, but you ain't the first.' The woman laughed. 'Many folk 'ave wondered 'ow come Lilah can afford to live as 'er does.'

'I'm sorry,' Maura stammered, embarrassed at being caught staring. 'I . . . I was thinking how fortunate you are to be in service in such a comfortable house.'

'In service!' The painted mouth widened in a laugh. 'Be that what Bella told you?'

'No.' Maura's cheeks coloured. 'No, I . . . I just thought . . .'

'Well, no matter.' The woman waved a hand heavy with rings as she turned to Bella. 'Thoughts won't cost me though I bet what lies in that basket will. Come on, Bella, show me what you've brought this time.'

Why had this woman laughed when she had spoken of her being in service? Maura watched her as Bella lifted the dresses from the basket.

'I likes both of 'em, Bella, and I knows which of my girls they will suit. Give me a minute and I'll have your money, meantime 'ow about a cup o' tea with a drop o' Methodist cream?'

'Tea wi' a drop o' rum would be welcome, but not if you 'ave it brought by the mardy little sod that showed Maura and me upstairs . . .'

'Showed 'er colours again did 'er!' The rouged lips tightened. 'Well, the wench has 'ad 'er last warnin', there'll be no more displays of bad manners in this 'ouse!'

As the rustle of taffeta skirts followed Lilah from the room Maura whispered, 'Whose house is this, who does that woman work for?'

Her own voice held lower than usual Bella answered, 'This be Lilah's 'ouse and 'er don't work for nobody, 'er be 'er own mistress. It be a story that don't leave the time for tellin' now, be it enough for you to know at this minute that though this 'ere house be a brothel it be run by a woman wi' a heart o' gold.'

'A brothel!' Her eyes wide, Maura stared at her friend. 'A . . . a . . . house of sin!'

'Don't you go casting judgement!' Bella's reply was unusually sharp. 'That be for the Lord alone to do and when He does He will tek into account the reason for Lilah doin' what her does.'

'Miss Lilah said a drop of tea would be after being welcome.'

Her eyes lifting to the figure carrying a tray into the room, Maura felt a surge of horror rush wildly through her veins.

'. . . *which of my girls they will suit* . . .'

Her fingers pressed tight to her lips held back the cry of revulsion as she looked at Bridget.

' 'Twas after you left the barn to bring shawls, I fell to thinking of you walking alone in the darkness . . .'

Twisting her hands together in her lap Bridget faltered then went on. 'I . . . I was almost to the house when a cloth was placed over my mouth and I was dragged away. For days I was kept trussed like a pig for market, it was no idea I had of where I was nor who had carried me off. Then I was put aboard a boat . . . a boat of the sort I'd never had the seeing of in all of my life . . . and while aboard I met with Aisleen. 'Twas herself saved me, for when we were fetched onto a quayside and a bothering broke out she pushed me into a warehouse, pulling a load of empty crates over us, and there we lay until dawn . . . it must have been the holy angels watched over us for we were not discovered.'

'Slavers!' Bella spat the word. 'Lord, how I'd like to see every last one o' them vermin strung up . . . but I always believed Lilah Simkin 'ad no dealin's wi' slavers, that 'er women chose to be what they be!'

'Sure, and Miss Lilah be no slaver!' The girl Bridget had introduced as Aisleen McCullough answered hotly. 'We were weeks in the walking from that dockside, not knowing where it was we were headed and many a night spent sleeping in the hedges. Finally we finished up knocking on the door of Lilah

Simkin's house and herself gave us a meal and listened to our story, after which we had the choosing, stay or go.'

'But prostitution! Bridget, how could you?'

'Was I not after telling yourselves it was the choosing we were given!' Aisleen McCullough's nut-brown stare fastened accusingly on Maura. ''Twas no whore we became, not myself nor Bridget neither: housemaids was the job Lilah Simkin offered when it was we refused any other, for that one presses no woman to do what her heart says be wrong.'

'Neither did her stand in Bridget's way tonight when it was her said her wanted to come away with Maura, nor in the way of yourself when you chose the same,' Bella said, relieved her trust in Lilah Simkin had not been destroyed, 'and 'tis welcome you both be to bide 'ere . . . though it don't be no palace.'

It is no house of sin either! Watching the two girls who sat curled in blankets on Bella's hearth rug, Maura kept the thought to herself. They had chosen to leave a post that provided each with a living . . . but where to find another? Fortune might not be so kind a second time.

'I'll bank the fire for the night, it's already past midnight, time be for sleeping.'

'No.' Maura was on her feet as Bella spoke. 'You go to your beds, I will see to the fire.'

Taking a candle to the scullery she held it over the empty coal bucket. She had forgotten to refill it! It should be left until morning, she shivered in the damp air, but that would mean Bella coming downstairs to a cold kitchen.

It had happened to Bridget as it had happened to her. Coal bucket in hand she opened the scullery door and stepped into the shadowed yard. Could it have been the same man had kidnapped them both . . . had Padraig Riordan captured Bridget as he had captured her?

'I knowed if I waited long enough I'd get you . . .' An arm

pressed across her throat, Maura was yanked off her feet, the coal bucket rattling on the cobbles as it dropped from her hand. 'I knowed it was you, you bloody Irish bitch,' a voice like gravel grated against her ear, 'you who sent somebody to lay a torch to my shop . . . Well, now I be goin' to pay you back, I be goin' to give you what you deserves an' this time it won't be no scratch to the throat, this time I'll really do for you!'

A shaft of brilliant white light blinding her vision, a burning pain searing across her chest, Maura felt the hot breath against her cheek, heard the vicious laugh as the hold on her fell away; but she did not care . . . she was floating . . . floating downwards into a world of peace and darkness.

32

The bobbies again! Lord, how many more times must her answer their questions, they'd do better to search for the swine who'd stuck that knife into Maura than go botherin' a widow woman at this time o' night! Irritation marking her every step, Bella marched to the street door breathing her anger as she threw it wide.

'God Almighty!' She stepped back in surprise. 'Ain't I been 'oping and prayin' you would come.'

' 'Tis hearing I was, in an ale house along of Wednesbury.' Aiden Shanley stepped into the kitchen, closing the door quickly. 'Tell me now the truth of it.'

'If it's Maura you be talkin' of then it's true all right.' The vexation that had put vigour into Bella's step faded, her shoulders slumping as she reached for the teapot.

'Leave that; sure, and we be friends enough to take a cup later rather than sooner.'

Gently pushing away hands that would take the pot from her, Bella shook her head. 'It be doing the usual that keeps me sane.'

Watching the squat figure move about a kitchen silent except for the echoing tick of the cheap clock, Aiden felt a swift rush of gratitude sear every vein for the luck that had him take a drink in that tavern. He had almost turned away, for the Turk's Head he knew was over lively on market day. His ale had been near finished when a man already three-parts drunk had stumbled against him; but it hadn't been a care of the fellow falling to the ground that was the reason for helping him to that seat in the corner of the smoke-filled taproom, but the words he was mumbling.

'. . . *Irish bitch . . . Alfred Worsley done fer 'er . . .*'

The tingle that had played along his spine as he had heard those words grazed again, twitching his nerves like puppet strings. He had set a tankard at the man's hand, encouraging him to ramble on, yet in his heart he had known the 'Irish bitch' he ranted about had been Maura.

'. . . *thought to get the better o' Alfred Worsley . . . I finished 'er . . . finished 'er good . . . stuck a knife in 'er throat . . .*'

'I'd 'oped you might be near.'

Aiden looked into the worried face as Bella handed a cup to him, breaking his thoughts. Waiting for Bella to be seated he asked again to hear all she could tell him.

'. . . and that be it.' She drew a trembling breath as her narrative ended. 'Thinking it were tekin' a time to fetch coals I went to see what the delay were, it was then I found 'er, blood runnin' from 'er like a stuck pig.'

His fingers white about his cup, Aiden forced breath into his lungs. The girl he had helped, that gentle smiling colleen butchered by . . .

'It was certain that this time 'er were finished. Them two wenches carried 'er into this kitchen and laid 'er there on that 'earth rug –' her voice breaking Bella wiped tears from her cheeks '– I . . . I brought a basin o' water and set to cleaning the blood from 'er poor body . . . it was then her moaned and we knowed her was still alive.'

'And now?' His fingers left the cup to close painfully over Bella's hand.

'You can rest easy, no need to break me fingers.' Smiling through fresh tears she released her hand from his grip. 'Thanks be to the Almighty, her be living.'

Watching the emotions chase across his face, Bella sipped

her tea. Aiden Shanley felt strongly for the girl he had brought to her house and there could be no doubt the feeling was returned, but it had not been Aiden Shanley's name she had called through the long nights when delirium had her senseless, it was not this man the soul of Maura Deverell called to.

She waited unspeaking until his feelings were controlled, yet the tremor in his voice as he spoke told they were by no means mastered.

'Worsley's shop were put to the torch, you says?'

Stirring sugar into her second cup of tea, Bella frowned. 'You d' ain't know? Then it were not you set it afire? I thought—'

'Sure, an' b' Jesus my hand would have set light to it had I known . . . and to the swine of the man himself.'

'Then it *was* the men of 'Ockley.' Bella heaved a satisfied sigh. 'I'd half guessed . . . the folk round 'ere be loyal to them as helps 'em, they wouldn't let no attack on that wench go by an' no retribution took. As for Worsley, when they find 'im . . .'

'They won't have the finding of him, Bella, nor will any man; he sleeps quiet at the bottom of a coal pit with a pile of stones for cover.'

Beyond the window a high moon sent shadows sliding furtively over dark walls, grey phantoms that crept across the floor feeling blindly for her bed, shadows which to her still-frightened mind took on the shapes of figures . . . figures whose face carried a pale scar or who slid towards her with a knife held above a shadowed head.

Pressing her lids hard down over her eyes, Maura tried to shut out the terrors but they were etched too deeply into her mind, burned into her brain as if put there with a branding iron. There is nothing to fear . . . it's over. She had told herself again and again during the days it had taken for her to recover from that attack upon her, repeated them endlessly in the long nights of lying awake, yet still the shadows haunted her, bringing with them memories she found hard to banish.

But among them were memories she would not have banished. Her glance strayed to the narrow bed almost touching her own. Bridget had refused to leave her side and even now when the wound was healed she insisted upon being close at hand.

'*Twas the holy saints kept that knife from killing ye!*' Bridget had said so many times. '*Twas their blessed hands guided it from yer throat, sending its blade into yer shoulder instead . . . Oh the wicked man, sure an' I hopes the police catch him soon, so I do . . .*'

Turning her face to the opposite direction, Maura tried to push the thoughts away. With her eyes closed against the flickering shadows she prayed for the peace of mind sleep would bring, but where Bridget's worried face had stared at her another took its place. Brown eyes smiling from finely cut features, hair tousled by breezes blowing off a rippling brook, a man held out his hands to her, a man whose one shoulder rose slightly above the other.

'Liam,' she whispered, 'Liam!'

'We be managing fine wi' out you fretting.' Bella pretended an impatience she was far from feeling as she looked at Maura sat against the fire. 'That there Aisleen McCullough be a hard worker, 'er has that shop set up fine, while young Bridget . . . well, her be a treasure an' no mistek. Took to the rag market like a duck to water, nor don't let nobody talk 'er into selling for a halfpenny less than her asks . . . I tells you, Maura, I couldn't do no better meself . . . they've both been godsends.'

Aisleen McCullough! Maura thought of the young, dark-eyed woman who had left that house with Bridget. She had pieced together their story, Bridget having told it in odd snatches liberally strewn with thanks to the little people.

Staring into the glowing depths of the fire, Maura smiled. Bridget had changed in so many ways while in others she had not changed at all.

Aisleen had been snatched from a clochan, a stone-built hut where her grandmother had stored potatoes, Bridget had said. She too had been brought blindfold to that boat.

. . . Herself kept me from harm . . .

The phrase had cropped up again and again in the telling, so too had the fact that Aisleen had stayed with her after their escape from the docks, that she had protected her from the unwanted advances of men they met on their travels, and that she had got them food and sometimes shelter by toiling until her hands bled from scything corn and lifting crops of vegetables; and always she had talked of a time they would be safe and happy. Pray God that time had come. Maura breathed her silent prayer. Pray God they were all safe at last.

'You 'ave no need of worryin' about 'ow that there shop be going, that young woman knows the herbs near enough as well as you does yourself. Sensible an' all 'er is, writes down in a book everything you tells 'er . . . like them there cook books some o' the fancy 'ouses by buyin'.' Shaking out a voile blouse, Bella inspected it for wear, nodding as she laid it with her more special acquisitions. ''Twas her seen to the dressin' o' that wound to your shoulder after the doctor said as it were not as bad as it seemed, bathed and poulticed it twice every day, and now the shop . . . I says again I thanks God for 'er comin'.'

The shop! Maura's mind slipped back to the arrival of a letter signed by Samuel Radley. It had expressed the gratitude of himself and his wife for her nursing of their son and also his concern that following the regretful accident which had burned down the establishment of Alfred Worsley, Hockley no longer enjoyed the benefit of a herbalist shop. If she, Miss Deverell, would consider . . .

She had not wanted to agree. His offer of a building that

would come free was nothing short of payment for the help she had given, and that she could not accept.

'*You be a fool!*' Bella had shown her displeasure. '*The brick master be wanting naught more than to show appreciation . . . a 'erbalist shop would be a boon to the folk of 'Ockley.*'

She had tried to argue with Bella, reminding her that Alfred Worsley might very soon re-open his business. Bella had turned away at that and when Maura had spoken of the possibility a second time she had replied sharply, saying, '*The man never will for he knows what waits forrim if ever 'e shows 'is face in these parts again!*'

So she had relented, but to accept only if Samuel Radley leased the premises to her, and so he had, asking a peppercorn rent of three shillings per quarter year. It was still virtually a gift but the brick master would hear none of her arguments and so the house in the recently constructed Vyse Street had become Deverell Patent Medicines. The craftsmen in gold and silver who were rapidly moving into the area were already customers and, according to Bella's delighted reports, word of the shop was spreading fast beyond this 'gold quarter'.

The last of the day's collection of clothing sorted, Bella carried those which would be laundered into the scullery and on her return she took a small cloth from the pocket of her voluminous skirt.

'I'll be 'anding this back to you, the doctor said as it were best removed while that wound to your shoulder was open.'

Pulling aside the folds of cotton, Maura smiled. 'I thought he took . . .'

'No, it weren't stolen.' Bella answered quickly, hearing the tremble. 'I took it from you.'

Her movements still causing her to wince, Maura fastened the narrow ribbon around her neck.

'You misses 'im, don't you, wench?' Bella had not neglected to see the lingering touch of fingers caressing the tiny ornament. ''E come nigh on every day but you was too far gone to know it. But 'e will be back, Aiden Shanley ain't a man to break 'is word.'

She did miss him . . . almost as much as she missed Liam. They were both a memory of home, a link with so much that was past, a happiness she would not know again.

'If you feels well enough, I'd like you to walk wi' me, I've a bit o' business to discuss an' two brains be better'n one.'

It would be refreshing to be out of the confines of the house; they had each been so kind to her, but now she was well the urge to be about her daily routine was strong.

Fastening her coat she was only part listening to Bella's chatter until the words 'a young man Bridget seems teken with' tugged at her mind.

'Bridget!' Maura's attention returned in full.

'Hmm.' Tying the shawl across her ample bosom, the older woman smiled. 'Ar wench, that were my first thought an' all, Bridget wi' an' admirer; but bein' truthful I has to admit my only real surprise be it ain't 'appened sooner, for 'er be right pretty.'

'But Bridget has never mentioned a man.'

Her black bonnet perched on top of piled-up hair, Bella tied the ribbons beneath her chin, answering at the same time. ''Er like be too shy, it be the same wi' most young wenches when a lad shows interest . . . but Aisleen says 'e be fair mannered and appears right teken wi' Bridget; walks 'er from the rag market each night then they both calls to collect Aisleen from the shop, and after what happened to you I be right grateful to 'im for that; seems 'e be a considerate lad.'

Bridget with a young man! Walking beside Bella, Maura's thoughts drifted. It would be wonderful if her friend had found a man who would care for her, who would love her, if she had found a love such as Maura Deverell would never know.

'. . . *you cannot put a barrier between yourself and the pain of heartbreak* . . .'

Those had been the words Liam Riordan had said to her that day on a rain-swept heath. He had offered friendship, offered to give back to her all that his father had taken.

'*It has taken my life, Maura, don't let it take yours.*'

In a silent whisper the words swelled in her heart, the pain of them a torrent that poured chokingly into her throat. It is too late, Liam! She wanted to cry aloud. It has already taken my life! But how could he have known, how could he ever know what she herself had not known, that Liam Riordan was guilty as his brother! Padraig had taken her virginity, but Liam had taken her heart!

He had not left the box with Bella James. Returning tools to his pack, Aiden Shanley felt the hard shape pushed to the bottom of it. Why had he chosen to carry it with him? It did not belong to him, it had simply been entrusted to him to deliver, to give to the one for whom it was meant, yet he had not. Why? He paused in his task, his fingers resting on the pack. He had sat beside the sick girl, held her hand in his, prayed the Lord give her strength to live . . . yet he had not left that box.

' 'Twas tuppence yoh said.'

Startled by the abrupt interruption of his thoughts, Aiden looked up. The face of the woman watching him was lined, her eyes shrouded with the veil of constant worry. Hard work killed horses and it came no harder than that of a nail maker and the woman who toiled beside him.

'Sure an' the job was not what I thought.' Aiden rose from his knees. 'All it took was a minute o' time; we'll not be botherin' with payment for such as that.'

Taking the pot he handed back to her, the woman gave it to a small child come to stand beside her. A ragged dress hanging from thin shoulders, feet bare from want of shoes, the girl looked at him with eyes that filled a face drawn with perpetual hunger.

'Tek that to the bucket an' scour it clean . . . mind yoh does it proper now, then set the taters to boil over the fire.'

Giving Aiden a glance that held all the questions of the world the child turned away without asking one. He had been much the same age when they had snatched him from his family; his life had been hard as the one given to this child, but where hers knew love his had known only hardship.

'I thanks yoh kindly,' the woman was holding out a hand deeply grained with the steel she hammered, two copper coins resting in her palm, 'but a job done must be paid for, yoh must needs buy yoh'r bread same as we.'

'Bread I have and cheese for the eating.' Lifting the pack to his back, Aiden smiled away the lie. 'What need would a tinker be having of more? As for pennies . . . they puts holes in the pockets such as the little people themselves would fall through, so if it's being acceptable to you I'll leave them an' be on me way.'

'This 'ouse pays its way!'

Admiration he so often felt for the families of this Black Country welled strong in Aiden. They were honest and proud of their labour, so much they could have been forged of the metals they worked.

Easing the burden across his shoulders he nodded. 'Then 'tis here will I come when I stand in need of two pence.'

Her mouth trembling the woman blinked on her tears. 'Thank you,' she murmured, 'the Lord bless yoh'r every step.'

'And Himself forbid the divil entry to this home.'

Skirting the corn fields that stretched away between Wednesbury and Bilston, Aiden was conscious of the box hidden beneath the tools of his trade but the reason of its still being there would no longer be hidden. With every stride it forced itself into his mind, demanding recognition, clamouring to be heard until at last he removed the pack from his back, resting it on the soft sweet-smelling earth.

He had not left that box with Bella James for while he had it in his keeping it was plausible he should return to Birmingham. But why did he feel it necessary to fabricate excuses? He needed none to visit with Bella, the woman was a friend of those years since his release from prison and friends did not need reasons to visit each other. But it was not Bella he thought of each time he touched that box, it was Maura Deverell! She it was whose face floated before his eyes when they closed for sleep . . . and she it was to whom he could never tell the truth of his past!

‿

33

'It be just along of 'ere.'

Her boots tapping on the cobbled street Bella made her way between streets too narrow to allow the passage of a carter's wagon; the grey sky, darkened by smoke and the soot from iron foundries, added to the gloom of blackened buildings packed together like fish in a basket.

'Charlotte Street,' Bella announced, taking a left turn away from the church of Saint Paul. 'The lad has a place 'ere, or so Aisleen tells it.'

Asking directions of a passing woman she turned into a doorway that gave almost immediately onto a flight of steep dusty stairs. Reaching a landing flanked by small rooms, each with its door wide open, a few words with the occupant saw her climbing a second flight.

Following closely, Maura felt the walls of the old house press in upon her, the damp musty odour of ancient brick and timber filling her nostrils. How could people live and work in such conditions?

'Whew . . . w!' Pausing at the top, Bella struggled to catch her breath. 'Climbin' all them there stairs don't do a woman a bit o' good, I be sweating like a robber's 'oss!'

Concealing the smile the other woman's irate words brought to her lips, Maura followed into the small room. Light from a solitary dust-streaked window filtered onto a bench set with various tools, some so delicate it seemed at first glance impossible a man's hand could manipulate them.

'Good day . . .'

From a stool set in the cut-away half circle of the bench a man turned to face them.

'Good . . . day.' Bella's breathless reply had the man on his feet and bringing a chair, the seat wiped with a rag snatched from the pocket of his canvas apron.

'Can I be of assistance?' Bright blue eyes looked at Maura as he fetched the stool from beside the workbench, again dusting it before offering it for her to be seated.

'Be you Robert Pemberton?' Her question abrupt, Bella let her glance rove over the figure that turned towards her. The room was dusty but the tools on that bench were set neatly and each in its place, and while a light film of that same dust touched hair and skin both were clean beneath it. Hands resting in her lap, Bella was approving.

'That be my name.'

'Hmmm!' Approval turning to admiration, Bella continued to stare. This man was not bought over by potential custom. He held his head high, his eye clear and steady as he looked at a body; Aisleen was not spouting hot air when her had said he was likeable.

'Then we be in the right place, though I thought never to find it among so many streets and alleys; still we be 'ere now so I'll state me business.'

Taking a paper from her pocket, Bella handed it to the man who scrutinised it carefully before looking up.

'I've seen something like this before.' He touched a finger to one of several sketches.

'That you 'ave,' Bella nodded, 'an' there it be round Maura's neck.'

His brows knitted together over questioning eyes. 'Maura . . . ? Could you be Maura Deverell, the friend of—'

'Yes, Mr Pemberton.' Maura smiled as he broke off awkwardly. 'I am a friend of Bridget and of Aisleen, so is Mrs James.'

' 'Twas Aisleen herself said as we should come see you, though I feels somehow it was Bridget had the instigating of it but was too shy to speak.' Handshakes over, Bella turned again to the reason of her visit. 'When it was I knowed you to be a worker in the gold I asked Aisleen to show you the trinket Maura be wearing now and to ask could you be making the same in silver.'

'May I see it again?'

Waiting until Maura untied the ribbon he carried the small copper amulet across to the workbench, holding it close as he could to the window, twisting and turning it, playing the light over every surface detail.

'This were made by a man who knows his trade.' Handing back the necklace he looked keenly at Bella. 'Why is it you don't be asking the same man to make one in silver?'

' 'Cos you be a worker in precious metals while he be a tinker who works wi' tin an' copper.'

'I see.' Robert Pemberton's bright blue eyes rested on Bella. 'But that tinker has the touch of a craftsman, the marks of it are on that trinket, what he has wrought out of base metal he can craft in silver and be quite like to make as good a job as myself.'

Pleased by his open admiration of the work of Aiden Shanley, Bella smiled inwardly. The lad was honest along wi' everything else; yet her shouldn't think him a lad either in years or wisdom, this here was a man of some twenty-five years and one with common sense behind that attractive face. Young Bridget would be well cared for should he decide to wed with her.

'I 'as no doubt o' that,' she answered, 'but tinkers don't be in one place long enough for to do the sort o' work I be looking to get done. But first I needs to know 'ow much I be looking to pay for a trinket such as Maura be wearing were it made in silver 'stead o' copper.'

Keeping her silence while the two talked, Maura could not

stay the thought; was Aiden Shanley's work not pleasing enough for Bella, did she see it as shoddy?

'I knows what you be thinking.' Her bargaining complete, Bella looked again at the girl sat beside her. 'And you be wrong; Aiden Shanley be as fine a craftsman as any in Brummagem but he'll settle to no workbench.'

'But why a trinket in silver, why not copper?'

There was a loyalty behind the question that blurted from the wench's lips. Bella smiled understandingly. She saw coming to this workshop as a betrayal . . . a denial of the love that had gone into his making of that tiny bauble.

'You remembers 'ow often you come 'ome from the rag market telling 'ow that there pendant 'ad been admired by folk, 'ow many times you'd been asked where it was you'd got it from? Well, p'raps them enquirings d'ain't mean nuthin' to you but Bella James could see the possibilities behind 'em. There be a market for such as Aiden Shanley made and I means to be the one to sell 'em.'

'But I still don't see . . .'

'No, wench, you don't! 'Cos you refuses to, and for why? 'Cos you thinks I be turnin' me back on a friend; but that ain't it at all, this way I can bring Aiden's work to the notice of others . . . them with the means to buy. Copper be all well an' good in its place but that place don't be the neck or wrist of a mine owner's wife.'

'Nor does silver be the metal.'

The quiet voice halting her, Bella turned a quizzical look at the man. 'Not silver . . . you thinks as Maura do . . . that them doodads should be made from copper?'

'No, Mrs James, I don't.'

Still hot from climbing those lengthy flights of stairs Bella blew an impatient breath.

'Then what does you think?'

Waiting a moment, looking from one face to the other as if

gauging their reaction, Robert Pemberton answered quietly, 'It's my opinion the metal you use should be gold.'

'Gold!' Bella exclaimed. 'I ain't bloody med o' money!'

'How many people are to begin with!' His eyes vivid with enthusiasm, he went on. 'Birmingham is becoming more and more important in the eyes of the world, the products of a thousand trades are exported along its canals and the railroad brings businessmen from every part of the country, industrialists with money to spend, money enough to buy a trinket of the best for a wife or daughter.'

And money enough to buy 'imself a clear conscience! What was it Lilah 'ad once said, summat to the effect of such men wantin' all the comforts of 'ome when they be away from it then buyin' their wives some pretty knick-knack as a way o' spongin' the feeling of guilt from their mind? Takin' a gamble on that fancy 'ouse of her'n had made Lilah Simkin a wealthy woman . . . Bella felt a smile spread along her insides . . . maybe it was time for Bella James to gamble.

'Them other designs young Bridget drawed.' Bella flicked the paper held on her lap. ' 'Er give 'em names but I don't 'ave the rememberin' . . . you tek a look, p'raps you knows what they be.'

Taking the paper, Maura looked at the sketches and in her heart a gentle voice spoke their names while a work-worn hand drew each shape in the black soil of newly turned earth. This one be the Tara brooch, it be said that once it held the cloak of Roderick O'Connor himself . . . and who was he? Maura heard the echo of that well-loved laugh, sure and wasn't he the highest of high kings of Ireland . . . and this be a torc, a collar such as Brian Boru himself would have worn . . .

Husky with the tears of memory, Maura pointed to each of the drawings in turn, repeating their names, describing each as her father had done.

'Could they be made as Maura tells . . . could *you* make 'em?'

Glancing at the tiny copper harp hanging at Maura's throat, Robert Pemberton breathed long and slow. 'I'd give ten years of my life to try.'

He had killed the jackeen of a man. He had followed Worsley from that Wedenesbury tavern, kept him in sight as he weaved his drunken way first along High Street and then Trouse Lane and onto the bare heath which bordered the derelict Union coal mine; there he had caught him from behind and snapped his head back on his shoulders, breaking his neck with one swift move.

There would be no finding him there. Aiden Shanley took a drink from his tankard. The villain was in hell where he deserved to be, in the place of no return. And where was he? With his head sunk on his breast the thought that plagued his sleep shouted now in his mind. Was he not in a living hell . . . was he not suffering the torment of knowing he had killed another human being? He drank again more deeply, wanting the oblivion of ale. But that oblivion never came, only the shadows that pointed to him, called his name in the silent hours, called him murderer!

Had Seamus Riordan known that torment, had he heard the silent voices, shuddered at shadows in the night? He too had been guilty of murder, he had killed a man; but where Aiden Shanley had taken one life, Seamus Riordan had taken two: he had ended the life of a man and destroyed the life of a boy.

But I did not kill to protect myself! The cry in his heart was strong, but for Aiden it brought no comfort in its wake. His thoughts had been for Maura Deverell, vengeance had been taken for her . . . but that did not lessen the guilt, guilt he would carry all his life; that would be his punishment, for the law could not give any. He had been careful to ensure no other had followed that night, that there had been no witness to his action; even should the body of Worsley be found there could be no proof as to who it was had snuffed the life from him: no finger but that of shadow could point to Aiden Shanley.

Maura! He smiled bitterly against his chest. She could have given so much happiness to his life, dulled the pain of years . . . but that hope was as dead to him now as was the childhood that had been snatched from him.

The choice had been his own. Shoving the tankard from him he rose, making his way through the grey fog of tobacco smoke and out into the street. He had not acted in the hot blood of fury whose anger dictated the actions of a man. Following after Worsley he had become calm, thinking out his own every move, stalking his victim as a wild animal stalked its prey; then, cold and decisive, he had carried through his intent and he had the rest of his life to pay for it!

Beyond the pool of pale light shed by the lantern hung above the tavern entrance a bank of blackness grudgingly released its hold on dark buildings. The Black Country! Aiden eased the pack on his shoulders. Wednesbury was all of that.

'Aiden Shanley . . .'

From the horizon a brilliant glow spread like a veil over the night sky, bathing street and buildings in brilliant scarlet, their outlines streaked with violet and mauve.

'Aiden Shanley . . .'

Turning in the direction of quietly spoken words Aiden smiled at the figure stood illuminated in the gleam cast by a succession of opening furnaces.

'Sure now, and isn't that me very name . . . constable.'

'Does yourself have no heart for what it is Bella be proposing . . . be it that has ye troubled, or be it that ye have no liking for Robert Pemberton? He wouldn't be after cheating her, I know he wouldn't.'

Bridget had sat, hands twisting anxiously in her lap, while Bella had told of the visit to Charlotte Street, now she looked with desperate eyes at Maura.

'I feel sure he wouldn't.' Taking Bridget's hands in her own Maura squeezed them comfortingly. The look in the other girl's eyes told where her heart was and how easily it could be hurt. 'I liked Mr Pemberton very much, he seems an honest man,' she said.

'Then if it ain't the man 'as you troubled it 'as to be the other for you've spoke not a word all through the tellin',' Bella spoke again. 'Be it you be thinkin' what I said were foolish?'

'The sketches can't be after showing what be involved in the making of such pieces as the Tara brooch; Celtic jewellery is very involved, Aiden Shanley would tell the same were he here . . .'

'Oh!' Bella's swift glance swung to the figure who up until now had sat quietly mending a torn apron. 'He talked o' such did he?'

Her black hair glistening in the light of the lamp the young woman's head lifted and her dark eyes held a glint of pride. 'Ireland had the working of the gold long years afore the skills of it were learned in Birmingham, the father of my grandfather and his before him had the skills that were ancient when your fabled King Arthur lived, and those skills survived, they live on still in the hearts and hands of the people of Ireland; Aiden Shanley is after knowing that, 'twas himself talked of the intricacies of crafting Celtic pieces.'

Was that all he had talked of? Watching the colour settle in the woman's flushed cheeks, Bella was curious. The pair had talked between themselves on the occasions of Aiden Shanley's visits to Maura's sickbed, and, now she came to think of it, theirs had often been the suggestion behind herself and Bridget snatching an hour or two of rest while they sat with Maura. Had it been more than a wish to help with the nursing had that offer being made . . . was it more than one girl Aiden came to see?

'So you be thinking the mekin' o' jewellery such as you speaks of be beyond the capabilities o' the man I talked with today!'

Aisleen McCullough's dark eyes met with those of the older woman and in them could be seen no hint of apology. 'Some pieces, yes, Mrs James, I do.' Bridget's gasp causing her to pause only a moment, she went on, 'But from what little I have seen of Robert's work I believe that time and practice will be after giving him the skills he lacks.'

'Well that be honest enough,' Bella answered. 'Seems all three of you 'as a likin' for the man an' you 'olds he be clever with 'is craft, yet I sees by the look of two of you I be wrong to think of 'aving him mek them trinkets.'

Releasing Bridget's hands, Maura glanced first at Aisleen's flushed cheeks and then to Bella. 'I'm not after thinking that and neither is Aisleen. Truth is we both likely have the same fear . . . that gold be too costly a metal . . .' Seeing the nod of Aisleen's head she rushed on. 'There are precious few people around here can afford to buy copper so how many could have the buying of gold? And the industrialists and businessmen you and Mr Pemberton talked of, I'm thinking they wouldn't care for the back streets of Birmingham any more than they would any other city; should it be that which Aisleen and myself are feared of becomes fact then your money will have gone and 'tis nothing you'll have to show for it. It be *you*, Bella, *you* and your well-being is all that holds each of our hearts.'

'I thanks you for that.' Her answer thick with suppressed emotion Bella reached a hand to the girl come to stand beside her chair. 'I thanks all three, you be good wenches and I knows what it be you means when you speaks of 'aving the 'olding of another in your 'eart for mine 'olds each of you . . . you've filled it wi' a love I never thought to feel again and I thanks the good Lord nightly for 'Is bounty in sending you to me. Now,' she sniffed, patting the hand resting on her shoulder, 'Maura, brew a pot o' tea an' Bridget set the cups to the table while Aisleen an' meself meks a bite o' supper, an' while we 'ave the eatin' of it I'll tell you the rest o' the plan that be shaping in my 'ead.'

A house along of Vyse Street!

Maura slipped her cotton nightdress over her head. What Bella had told them had dumbfounded them all. She had realised for herself the improbability of wealthy folk looking to the maze of back streets when shopping, especially when the article they sought was of so precious a metal, and so she proposed one of the new dwellings being erected over ground that had formerly been gardens but was now rapidly disappearing beneath rows of tall terraced houses.

'*I think Robert Pemberton be right in his saying that the next few years will see Vyse Street, Spencer Street an' the others that be goin' up soon become the very 'eart of the gold in Brummagem,*' Bella had said. '*That will be where the nation an' its fellows will come for their joollery, an' Bella James means to be there when they does.*'

She had lifted her black skirts then, removing the canvas bags tied over her hips and emptying a stream of sovereigns onto the table. The results of a lifetime of hard work.

But was she throwing those results away . . . would what she proposed fail and leave her penniless . . . was her faith in Aiden Shanley's trinket ill-founded?

If only the tinker were here to advise . . . Bella would listen to him.

Slipping into bed she blew out the candle. Why had he not returned . . . why had he not kept his promise? Perhaps his heart had drawn him home to Ireland.

Her prayers said, Maura drifted slowly in that dream state

that hovered between sleep and waking and in it she walked the soft green banks of the Shannon, its sweet breeze touching her face as she turned towards a voice that called, smiled at eyes that smiled at her, ran into the arms of a man come to meet her; but those arms were not the arms of Aiden Shanley.

'Liam . . .' Beneath the covering night the name rested like a smile on her lips.

34

'Wasn't it meself should have been knowing the law has a long arm and a sharp nose?'

'But the bobbies, they d'ain't ask about . . . about you knows who?' Anxiety deepening the lines worry and want had long ago laid on her face, Bella James watched the face of the tinker across her kitchen table.

'Not one single word,' Aiden Shanley smiled, 'though I says it readily enough, when it was I saw it was the *Garda Siochana* stood in that scarlet glow I felt me own days as a free man were ended.'

'The police fair put the wind up anybody,' Bella agreed sympathetically.

'Ah now, Bella, that's not after being all of the truth, a body needs fear the law only if they have broken it . . . and Aiden Shanley has done that all right.'

Across the table Bella's protective instinct rose. 'It's work you've saved the law by killing that swine and no doubt saved Maura's life into the bargain, for it be certain as night follows day he would 'ave tried to do for 'er again; we all be better off for seein' the last of scum like Worsley and it be sure we'll 'old no funeral feast!'

'No.' Aiden nodded slowly. 'There'll be no ceilidh will send him to his rest.'

'Rest . . . pah!' Bella answered scathingly. 'If there be justice in hell he'll never be given rest . . . may the divil set 'im to stokin' the furnaces of hell for all of eternity!'

His dark eyes twinkling Aiden chuckled. 'Ah, the gentle mercy of woman . . . the holy angels protect me from it.'

'And from them bobbies . . . be you sure it were not to do with Worsley they took you from the street?'

His head shaking from side to side, Aiden looked at the woman who had long been his friend. Maybe he ought not to have come to this house but just gone away, a letter would have served just as well. But a letter would not have shown him the face of his friends or that one face he so dearly longed to look upon again . . . the face of Maura Deverell.

Letting a smile cover his thoughts he answered, 'Sure it is I am, sure as I be looking at the finest woman . . .'

'You can let the blarney lie where it belongs!' The reply was sharp but Bella's eyes held a sorrow that went deep. The penalty for murder was the scaffold and to know Aiden Shanley was sentenced to that was something her heart would not bear.

'Bella.' He spoke quietly, all trace of teasing gone from him. 'I told you when first we met of the governor of the penal settlement I was sent to, how he watched my behaviour, how he came to believe a young boy who vowed he had done no crime and as a consequence took me into his service in the residence and by some miracle after my time was done organised my coming to England with him on his return . . .'

What the 'ell 'ad all this to do with bein' arrested in Wednesbury? Impatience niggled at Bella, taking some effort to repress.

'. . . after he gave me leave to go my own way it was thinking I was never to hear more of him . . . but it was himself had me found and brought here to Birmingham.'

'But you served your time . . . and done your years . . .'

'Hear it all, Bella.' He held up a hand. 'It was not arrested I was after being, it was requested.' Smiling at her frown he went on. 'The governor is a prison governor no longer but a member of Her Majesty's government. They've heard complaints coming out of Ireland so they have, complaints of young people suddenly disappearing . . . rumours of a traffic in white slaving, rumours that must be stopped before they reach the ears of the Queen.'

'But what be this to do wi' you? Aiden Shanley be no white slaver!'

'No, but he is an Irishman.' Aiden's hand dropped to rest on the table. 'He also has the trade of a tinker and as such can travel the length and breadth of that sweet isle and not draw a second look from any. Look into your heart, Bella, look and you'll see that I couldn't be after refusing the man my help for it was himself helped me.'

'That be true,' Bella sniffed, 'but 'ow does 'e expect you to nab them traffickers . . . why don't they set the bobbies to doing it?'

'The *Garda Siochana*—'

'The *Garda*! For why would you be speakin' of them?'

Bella and Aiden looked quickly at the girl drawing back the chenille curtain that closed off the scullery.

'Aisleen, wench . . . you be early—'

'Why do you speak of the *Garda*?'

Surprised at the trembling in her words that had cut short her own, Bella saw the look in the dark eyes that were riveted to the face of Aiden Shanley, and understanding spread a chill in her stomach. The wench had feelings for him . . . but his feelings were for another.

'Aiden was simply saying that the police—'

'The police!' Behind Aisleen the other two chorused the word.

Reaching a ladle from a drawer Bella loosed a short sharp breath as the three young women entered the kitchen. 'Sour milk gives me a belly ache an' questions gives me a 'eadache! Yet it's nowt 'cept questions I'll be gettin', most o' which I'll 'ave no answer for so it's best you does the tellin' yourself, Aiden Shanley.'

Helped by the three of them, Bella ladled a meal of broth into bowls set out by Aisleen, noting as she did so how those black eyes scarcely left Aiden Shanley. Had he noticed the same? Had he seen the worry in the girl's look . . . did he realise the cause behind it . . . was that why he told them nothing of the death of Worsley?

'So they think by going home to Ireland you will be able to discover who it is be abducting young folk . . . don't they realise the danger they are after sending you into?'

'Would yourself have me refuse, Aisleen?'

The chiding was gentle but Maura heard it and herself answered, 'No, but . . . but please take care.'

'Maura won't be asking you not to go, but I asks you; the men that put me on that boat would have no second thoughts about cutting the throat of another . . . it's to your death you be after going should they find you out.'

'They won't be finding me out, Bridget, set your fears to resting.'

The timid girl that had once been caught in the net of slavers now answered hotly, 'Why should they not? Is it you be thinking yourself guarded by the saints themselves?'

'No, Bridget.' Aiden smiled, knowing the concern behind the flare. 'But it is myself will be asking their protection just the same.'

'So you are going back to Dublin pretending to be seeking to buy girls for a trader in this country . . . and that trader will be the member of Parliament you talked of?'

Meeting Maura's eyes he nodded. 'I shall be safe, girl dear, have no fears for me.'

But she did have fears for him. Collecting the empty soup bowls Maura carried them into the scullery. Bridget was not being fanciful when she said those men would kill. Trying to uncover them, to put an end to their wicked practices was to put his own life at risk and that was the fear that tore at her.

'You can journey to Dublin,' Aisleen was saying as Maura returned to the kitchen, 'but 'tis no seller you'll be finding at the docks there, but only the men who loads the victims onto the boats.'

'Then they will—'

'They'll tell nothing!' Her eyes locked on Aiden's, Aisleen cut Bella short. 'Sure, they'd sooner sup with the divil himself than tell the names of them whose filthy work they do, even supposing it's themselves knows those names.'

'Then 'tis none but the little people themselves could be after telling who they be.'

Across the table Aiden smiled. 'Should I have the good fortune to catch myself a leprechaun then you can be sure, Bridget dear, I'll be after asking him that very thing.'

''Tis no leprechaun you'll be finding in Dublin, nor no organiser of white slaving neither!'

Switching his glance to Aisleen, the carefree smile faded from Aiden's eyes as he saw the anxiety in hers. 'Now why would that be? We know there be traffickers in Ireland, you three girls be proof of that.'

'And how many of us were taken in Dublin itself . . . have you spoken to any taken there?' Hesitation her answer, Aisleen went on. 'I don't be after saying none do get captured in that city but it be likely that most are abducted from the villages and sent there to be sold off like cattle.'

'But Dublin—'

'Be the wrong place to look if it's top dogs ye be after!' Aisleen interrupted again. 'You'll find at least one of them in Tullamore and another not so many miles from there.'

'Tullamore!' Aiden's face took on a thoughtful look. 'That be where the Grand Canal runs from.'

'And boats that carry cargo other than linens and laces.'

Aisleen's voice lowered, pain evident in her face. 'Tullamore be where I was placed on such a boat but before I was put aboard I saw the face of one responsible for my taking, I saw money go from hand to hand. Oh it was wearing no fine clothes she was—'

'She!' Bella gasped. 'Be you saying it were a woman 'ad you captured?'

'I saw . . .' Aisleen half sobbed, 'I saw the face I'd had the seeing of so many times and the clothes she wore, the dress of a village woman, could not hide her from me. The woman was Eugenie Stratford.'

'Lady Stratford! Aisleen, you must be mistaken, she helped me . . . she was going to bring Bridget and myself with her to England.'

'It was herself kept you from Leech? Oh, I be knowing all about that,' Aisleen answered Maura's protest. 'Who do you guess helps milady in her evil doings? Leech! The man sent from Portington by her brother, only he didn't go far, he it was with her at Tullamore.'

'Aisleen, you—'

'No, Maura, I have made no mistake . . . do you not think I haven't had thoughts of such myself! Night after night since that moment they have been with me but nothing changes. My grandmother was laundress to Portington Hall and no sooner could I walk than I would go with her. It's knowing Eugenie Stratford I've been since both of us have been children and it was herself I saw that day. Take me with you, Mr Shanley,' she swung her glance to Aiden, 'take me with you . . . I can point to the woman who has broken so many hearts.'

It had been a long argument, with Aisleen pointing out that coming face to face with one of her victims would counter any denial, and Bridget too had demanded she be allowed to go to face Eugenie Stratford for it was from Portington Hall she herself had been snatched. But Aiden had proved adamant. Bridget had not been handed over by that woman, he had said, and though Aisleen had the evidence of her own eyes how to turn that evidence into proof was something would task the little people themselves. So he had refused both of them.

He had insisted no more be said of his returning to Ireland, turning the conversation instead to Bella's proposed venture into the selling of gold jewellery, listening intently to all she said of Robert Pemberton, agreeing that a house whose front room could become a shop was the right thing to buy. Then he and Aisleen had fallen into a discussion of Celtic pieces, he agreeing upon its intricacies and saying the very unusualness of it would prove a selling point.

Then he had said his goodbyes. Glancing at the dawn pearling the sky beyond the small pane of glass that was her bedroom window, Maura felt the same twist of her heart she had felt then. It seemed it was more than a parting from a friend, the pain went deeper than that, almost as deep as the gift he had left her with.

She had walked with him to the street, wanting to be with him to the last moment. Only the high moon had given light as he touched his hands to her shoulders, the silver of it glinting on his hair, touching his face and showing her the emotion he too was torn with.

'*Girl dear,*' he had said softly, '*this be no true parting for you be in my heart for ever; wherever I go I can look for you in my soul and there will be your sweet self smiling back at me.*'

He had held her for a moment, looking down at her in the moonlight, then had brushed the spilling tears from her cheeks. '*No tears, little one,*' he had murmured again, '*the life of Aiden Shanley has known enough tears, I want to see only your smile when I search for you in the long nights . . .*'

She had tried to cling to him, to keep him with her a little longer, wanting to confess how much he meant to her, but he had released her fingers and set her arms gently to her sides. Then he had lifted the pack from his shoulders, taking from it a box which he handed to her. '*This came into my keeping in the auld country* –' staring at the lightening sky, Maura now heard the quiet words whisper in her mind '– *it was given by those ye'll have the remembering of for it was no other than the mother o' Caitlin, Bridie MacGee herself. A sick man it was they had brought to their cottage, one they had nursed 'til one day he had walked from it and never a word to tell who he was; this box, forgotten by him, is all they had to show ever he had bided beneath their roof. Open it when it is ye are alone, girl dear.*'

He had turned from her then, swallowed into the closing darkness as though he himself was naught but shadow.

The others had glanced at the box as she had re-entered the kitchen but they had asked no question, the traces of her tears telling them it was too soon.

Slipping from the bed she padded silently across to the chest of drawers stood against the wall, taking the box from it. She had lain half the night with that box beside her, going through its contents again and again, unable to believe what it held.

The light of the new day not yet strong she lit the stub of candle, drawing it close to the bed before climbing back beneath the covers.

How long had Aiden Shanley carried that box? She stared at the small plain wood casket. How long had it lain in Bridie's cottage . . . just how sick had its owner been? Her fingers traced smooth edges while her mind churned with the chaos of thoughts the hours of the night had not answered.

They had nursed the stranger . . . mended the bones of a broken body . . .

Aiden had told her no more but was there more? Leaving without a word of himself, forgetting something that was obviously precious to him, was that not the action of a man sick at heart?

Lifting the lid she looked at the contents tied together with a ribbon of brown velvet and beneath it her name, written in a flowing elegant hand. *Maura Deverell.*

Letters! Taking them out she held them with trembling fingers. Letters written to her! Releasing the ribbon she took the first one. Tilting it towards the pale light of candle flame she read:

> *My dearest love,*
>   *Those are words I can never say to you, but my soul cries out to speak them . . . my dearest love . . . that you will ever be, my one eternal love. I have known of that for so long but how could I tell you what it was my heart held, how could a cripple and a misfit speak to you of love . . . how could I bear to watch you turn from me again?*

There was no more, no name written beneath the words that simply died away as if the pain of writing them was too great, as if it tore the very depths as it tore her in their reading.

Her eyes blurred with warm tears, she took the next. She had read each of them many times last night, every word was engraved on her heart but still she read again:

> *Maura, my dearest one,*
>   *I walk the soft earth of the valleys and you are there beside me, I breathe the sweet breezes of the Shannon and you are near. I see your smile in the beauty of morning and your eyes in the gentle fall of evening. You are with me always but when I turn to touch your hand I am alone and heaven has gone from me: for you are my heaven. My love enfold you always,*
>   *Liam.*

Sobs trembling in her throat, breath held against the waves of emotion surging in every vein, she rested the last of the letters against her chest. They had all spoken of the same thing, Liam Riordan's love, a deep soul-abiding love . . . and it was for her. Liam had the feelings for her that time had shown she held for him.

. . . how could I tell you what it was my heart held . . .

Hadn't she asked herself the same thing, known that she could not speak those words to him?

. . . how could a cripple and a misfit speak to you of love . . . how could I bear to watch you turn from me again?

Was that what Liam had thought that day on the heath; despite her telling him it was not, had he still believed it was his twisted shoulder had her turn from him?

Her heart breaking at the thought of the hurt he must have suffered, a whisper broke from her. 'No . . . please don't think that . . . you are no cripple nor any misfit in my eyes!'

But he had thought that . . . he surely must think it yet . . . had the pain of such thinking been the reason behind the illness of the man who had walked from Bridie's cottage, his heart so sick even these letters had been forgotten by him?

'Liam,' she whispered again, 'forgive me . . . please forgive me.'

35

They had each argued against it. Sat in the tea shop close to the dock of Tullamore, Maura sipped the tea a young girl had served her with. She could not go chasing back to Ireland, they had said, not alone!

Bridget had sobbed her anxiety and Aisleen had frowned her worry when Maura had flatly refused their plea to accompany her, but at last had agreed to her request that Aisleen carry on the work of the herb shop and Bridget help with the collecting and selling of clothes.

Only Bella had seen the hidden torment, only she had recognised the need lying deep beneath the decision, understood the sorrow behind troubled eyes.

'Go, wench,' she had said after the other two had left the house, Bridget in tears, as they went to their place of work. Bella had folded plump arms about her. '*Go find the 'eart that calls to you for 'til you does there'll be no peace in your own. 'Tis 'ard to part wi' you for I think on you as my own but harder it's been for me to watch that heart o' your'n crack a little wider every day. Go wi' my blessin's and remember only that there be love for you 'neath this roof and it's achin' my arms will be 'til they 'olds you again.*'

Releasing her, Bella had pressed several coins into her hand declaring should she not accept them, use them to buy the safety of passage on a credited passenger ship, then she would be tied in the cellar 'til sense returned to 'er brain! And it was Bella herself had walked with her to the canal basin in Gas

Street, arranging with a boat family well known to her to deliver Maura to Liverpool, charging them to see her safe into the keeping of a captain they knew and could trust. They had done as Bella asked and in turn the sea captain had seen her safe aboard the boat that had brought her along the Grand Canal to its junction at Tullamore.

But what should she do now, ought she to set off at once for Clonmacnoise or stay overnight in this town?

'A room, is it!' The young serving girl's quick glance ran over Maura counting coins onto the table. 'There's after being a hotel just behind the wharf.'

Adding a penny to the payment of her bill, Maura smiled her thanks.

'But should ye not be liking a hotel, should ye want something less grand there be Kate Fitzgerald, but she takes only quality . . .' Blushing at the words that had slipped out the girl scooped the coins and scuttled away.

Only quality. Drawing the shawl that had been Bridie MacGee's gift to her about her shoulders, Maura rose. The girl could not be blamed in thinking her another destitute woman come to the dock in search of free passage to Dublin. Bella had been irate when she had refused to carry the carpet bag packed for her, but she had stood firm; she would return to Ireland as she had left. She had seen the tears sparkle on that dear lined face as Bella had hugged her one last time whispering God keep her safe.

Heaven had heard that prayer . . . may it guard her footsteps safe to Clonmacnoise. Weaving between the tables with their bright blue chequered cloths she did not notice the glance following her to the door, or the heavy-set figure brush aside the attentions of the serving girl.

He had thought, as he had seen her enter the tea rooms, that this one be another likely piece, one more to add to the collection gathered for that wealthy Englishman; but what had promised to be the plum in his cake could prove to be the stone that choked him!

He had not believed at first, his thinking had been that his eyes deceived him. Leech rose, tossing a silver coin onto the table. But as the light from the window had caught her face then he had known it was no deception, no trick of sight; the face he watched across the room was that of the bitch who had got him dismissed from his post as gamekeeper at Portington Hall and ordered from Ireland . . . it *was* Maura Deverell. But he had not obeyed the orders of his high and mighty Lord Portington, he had not left this country and neither would the woman his eyes followed; she would be found a place . . . the river . . . a stretch of ground somewhere beneath a high cliff . . . a bed beneath the heather of a wild moor . . . ? What did it matter where so long as she was dead!

Leech was a fool! Lady Eugenie Stratford's impatience shone like gemstones in her cold eyes. What if the woman he professed to have seen in the tea rooms was who he thought her to be, what could she prove? Get the business of the night finished and she could be dealt with.

It had been exhilarating . . . the whole thing was exciting, a drug in her veins that always left her wanting more . . . and she would have more.

It was too many, Leech had said, telling her what that tinker had asked, six girls was too large a shipment all in one consignment, it would be bound to cause a stir should so many pieces go missing at any one time.

Pieces! Eugenie Stratford laughed to herself. It was an apt description, that was all these Irish peasants were, pieces of worthless humanity, of no account except to a whorehouse; and there would be no one would question the reason a girl should run from a dung heap of a home or the starvation of failed potato crops. So they had been gathered and in an hour or so she would take payment.

'Where do you have them?' She glanced at the man sat beside her in the small trap.

'In his lordship's warehouse.'

'Sedated?'

'Poppy juice. They sleep like the dead, but just in case I have them gagged, bound and wrapped in sacks.'

'Excellent.' Eugenie smiled at the answer. No one would dare question cargo being loaded onto her brother's boats, no matter what the hour. Maybe that was the one drawback to the game, maybe next time she should use a vessel not of the Portington line, the risk of that could heighten the excitement. But for now she must be satisfied. Drawing her cloak more firmly about her she watched her accomplice draw a watch from his pocket. Leech was getting anxious. Semi-darkness hid her smile. She liked that . . . an anxious man was the more easily dominated.

'The girl has taken a room with the widow Fitzgerald, you say?' It was deliberately asked, not out of interest in where it was the girl lodged but as a ploy to keep Leech twittering, and Eugenie saw with satisfaction how well it worked. If she herself could experience no surge of nerves at this evening's work then at least she could enjoy watching it in someone else!

'I saw her go to the house.' Leech returned the watch to his waistcoat pocket.

'And?'

Across the town a church clock boomed the hour, causing Leech to start nervously. The quicker this night was over and that wench dead the happier he would feel.

'And?' Eugenie Stratford's foot tapped irritably as she repeated her question.

'I waited. After a few minutes she came out and I followed her to the stage office, she must have been enquiring about tomorrow's coaches.'

'But you, of course, do not intend she take one.'

'I've made sure of that, in fact I made sure she never returned to the Fitzgerald house.'

It was no more than she expected. Eugenie listened to the sound of the last chime fade into the darkness. But just which way had the alarmed Leech gone about achieving that?

'I caught her in a back alley that gives onto some warehouses that are being demolished over towards the east dock.' He began to explain as though he had been asked. 'She took a wrong turn a few minutes after leaving the stage office, it be easy done among the back streets. I asked could I be of assistance then afore she could answer I caught her a blow that knocked her senseless.'

'You fool!' Eugenie slapped a hand against her knee. 'What if you were seen!'

This woman thought herself to be the only one with a brain, but this time she was wrong. Leech smiled into the collar of his jacket. 'But I wasn't,' he said smugly, 'I made sure of that.'

'And the girl, you made sure of her also?'

'Gagged and tied in one of them broken warehouses, maybe I'll feed her to the fish in the canal . . . if the rats haven't already finished her off.'

'Do what you like with her but be certain you manage it discreetly, Tullamore can do without the attentions of the police.'

Was it perhaps time to replace her collector . . . to take another to gather up those pieces? The thought warm in her mind, Lady Eugenie Stratford allowed herself to be helped from the trap.

Do what he liked with the Deverell woman! Leech smiled. He would do that all right; hadn't he already felt the touch of that soft flesh as he'd half carried her into that derelict building, hadn't he pulled open blouse and chemise, taken each of those firm breasts into his mouth, pulling on the small

nipples? Oh, he knew what he liked and it was what he would
have when this bit of business was concluded. Maybe he
should have helped himself to more then and there . . . he
could have had the same again later . . . In the darkness his
flesh hardened, throbbing against his stomach. He could keep
the wench there, take her as many times as his appetite
demanded . . . and he had a large appetite. Standing in the
rim of darkness unreached by the light of flaring torches and
braziers set along the dock, he grinned again. Maura Deverell
had not brought him financial gain but he would take his profit
in different coin; she would provide him with a wealth of
entertainment before she died!

He had played a quiet hand. Aiden Shanley eased his cramped
legs. On that ship out from Liverpool he had offered his
services to the cook, mending pots brought from the galley
and in return he had been fed, eating with the crew and taking
a pipe of tobacco later as they talked and played cards. And
one of them had supped the potheen too well, heavy drunk he
was when Aiden had said there was no truth to the tales of
white slaving.

'*No truth . . .*' the man had slurred, '*no truth, is it? And hasn't
Ben Jackson earned 'ishelf a nice little nesht egg from the doin' of it,
and more he'll 'ave to the puttin' if there be cargo o' the right shhort
waitin' along o' Dublin.*'

It had taken a little more potheen to get a name but, his
tongue loose and his brain fuddled, the man had talked freely.
The feeder boat came along the canal from Tullamore, a boat
that, being the property of a lord, was not subject to any
question concerning cargo. Now that boat was being made
ready to sail for Dublin where it would transfer its goods to
ships bound for England, and if fortune favoured Aiden
Shanley this night then it was that some cargoes would never
be carried again.

'You be sure he said tonight?'

Aiden's nod answered the quiet whisper. The man stood at his side in the shadows was from Scotland Yard. He had acted his part well. Being introduced to the collector he had pretended to be a businessman who, running a chain of select houses of pleasure in London and Birmingham, wanted only the best for his clients.

It had been little less than two days after his leaving the boat, of following the trade of tinker around Tullamore that he had been contacted, approached in a tavern by a heavy-set man whose accent marked him as English. Word had been passed to the government minister who himself was staying at Portington Hall, now it remained to be seen whether that louse of a collector would show.

'Christ, I hope nothing's been said up at that house, the Yard's been done out of a prize too many times by people talking where they shouldn't!'

Beside him the detective was getting restless. The man couldn't be after being wronged for that. But he needn't worry that a loose tongue had upset the tatie cart, the governor had been no corncrake while at that penal colony and he was not like to be given to chattering thoughtlessly now he was in government. Aiden shifted position again. They had stood here so long wasn't himself after feeling his legs were part of the ground.

Across the darkness the same clock boomed. Aiden tensed. The church of Saint Catherine was marking the half hour. Eleven-thirty had been the time arranged . . . would the arrangement be kept? One minute . . . two . . . Aiden forced himself to stand calm. Then it was there; a match struck among the deeper shadow and extinguished as quickly. Three times in succession the move was repeated and Aiden felt the man beside him release a pent-up breath. It was the signal . . . a match lit three times . . . the collector was here.

'You have what I asked?'

The detective stepped forward as a man, moving surprisingly quietly for his bulk, came into the deep arch of the warehouse.

'I have it, all six pieces . . . now let's have the money.'

'I see the goods before I part with money . . . I find it's too late for regrets once payment has been made; and as I said in the beginning I take nothing inferior, I see before I buy.'

'That don't be what I agreed!' Leech hissed.

'It is what I agreed.'

The governor had known his man! Aiden admired the calm with which the police officer answered the other man's anger.

'We can't be standin' round while you inspects them goods,' Leech was saying, 'this don't be no bloody horse sale!'

'Precisely. That is yet another reason for inspecting what it is you have to offer; any imperfection in the purchase of a horse can be recouped in breeding stock but your . . . "pieces" . . . cannot be used that way: so either I inspect them now or the deal is off.'

Lord, had not the blessed Saint Ciaran himself no more courage than this man! Tight as fiddle strings Aiden's nerves twanged. If this collector fellow turned away now . . .

'How do I know you have the money?' Leech snarled again.

In the gloom of the arch the other man reached into his pocket. 'Twenty-five a woman, one hundred and fifty pounds altogether.' He waved a bundle barely visible in the deep shadow. 'Let us go inside where you can light a lantern and count it for yourself.'

'The *Garda*—'

'Could take it into their head to patrol the dock at any moment –' the notes were waved again before being returned to a pocket '– therefore if you have any interest in disposing of your collection then I advise you do so quickly.'

What was being said between the two men fading from his

mind, Aiden concentrated on the shadow moving along the perimeter of darkness that clothed the line of buildings facing the canal. Another of Scotland Yard's constabulary . . . an agent of the English government . . . or an assassin in league with this seller of human flesh? He stared at the moving figure. It was so light and soundless on its feet it might even be one of the *Daoine Sidhe* themselves, one of the little people . . . except they wouldn't be part of the evil of this night.

'What is taking so long?'

It was a woman's voice . . . the shadow was a woman! As silently as she had moved, Aiden moved the same, positioning himself at her rear. Whoever the newcomer was she was well acquainted with the business in hand.

'He wants to see the pieces.'

The seller had not turned to look at the woman; obviously she was an integral part of his filthy operation. Aiden's hands clenched together. One woman helping to sell another into degradation? It was almost as much as he could do to keep himself from striking them both . . . but he must or the whole thing might come to nothing and this pair would be free to carry on their devil-ridden practices elsewhere, for without the actual handing over of their captives and accepting payment there was no proof of slaving.

'I want more than just the seeing of what you have on offer, I want to inspect them. I pay extraordinary prices and for that I need assurance the goods I buy are unmarked.'

'Inspect!' The answer was sharp as a whiplash slicing the darkness. 'There is no time for inspection. I tell you each piece is flawless.'

'And I tell you . . . madam . . . that your word is not quite good enough; either my requirement is met or you can go on your way.'

The hiss of breath was sibilant, the rustle of a snake. This woman was not used to the insult of dismissal. Aware that she might turn and slip away, Aiden took one step nearer. Scotland Yard might be willing to have the losing of a trafficker in women but Aiden Shanley was not.

For several moments no one spoke, then the detective turned away. He was leaving! Bracing himself for the fight that must come, Aiden was halted by the woman's voice.

'Wait!' She moved further beneath the arch before adding, 'The goods you ordered are inside. Leech, open the door.'

So the collector was the man Leech, the man both Bridget and Aisleen had spoken of. With cold anger displacing tension, Aiden waited as the man produced a key, then followed the others, keeping himself between them and the doorway.

'They be over here.' A lighted lantern in his hand Leech kicked aside a bundle of sacks covering a huddle of bound and gagged women.

'They appear unwell.' The detective frowned as Leech dragged the women to their feet.

'A little woozy is all. Poppy juice keeps 'em quiet but it also leaves 'em drowsy. It'll wear off soon enough.' Slapping one girl hard across the face, Leech laughed as she moaned. 'See what I mean!'

Taking the lantern for himself the detective moved around the group of whimpering women. The attention of Leech and the woman was on him, but Aiden's ear had been caught by the softest of movements behind him. Turning only his head he raised a finger to his lips as the government minister and a companion moved, wraith-like, to his side.

'I see that they are alive!' The detective's answer carried in the silence. 'But that is not condition enough. I wish to see their bodies . . . the amount my clients pay for an evening of pleasure demands they are given impeccable quality both in wine and in bedfellow.' Handing back the lantern he took the wad of white five-pound notes from his pocket and stood tapping them idly against his fingertips.

Her back to Aiden the woman stamped a foot, the sound echoing against the high roof.

'There . . . see for yourself!'

Beside Aiden the minister placed a restraining hand on his companion who had caught a sharp breath, making to step forward as the woman snatched at the clothing of a captive, ripping it away.

'And this one and this one!' Repeating her action until all six stood naked she glared at her unperturbed customer. 'Is that satisfactory or shall I have them lie down and you can try them out for yourself . . . make sure your purchases have not been opened!'

'That will not be necessary, please cover them while I pay the money to your director.'

'Director!' The reply spat like venom, the woman snatching the wad of notes. '*I* am the director . . . the business of slave trafficking is mine . . .'

'That is all I wanted to hear.' Like greased lightning, the detective's hand closed over the gloved wrist. 'I arrest you . . .'

'Eugenie!' The figure the minister had restrained strode forward, his face a mask of disbelief. 'Eugenie, what have you done?'

'Done?' She turned slowly, an indolent smile spreading as she moved. 'I have amused myself, Henry, found a game that gave me pleasure, something nothing else in this misbegotten corner of the world could ever do.'

'But slaving!'

Catching the nod of the minister, the detective released his grip and Eugenie Stratford brushed her wrist as though removing some obnoxious insect.

'Really, brother dear, you needn't sound so slaughtered; these women are of no consequence.'

Coming to stand beside them the minister glanced at Lord Portington's stricken face. 'Now you see why it was I asked you to accompany me tonight; had you not seen and heard for yourself you would not have believed, though in honesty I confess I was not aware of your sister's complicity in all of this.'

In the light of lanterns carried in by the grooms, brought should assistance prove necessary, Eugenie Stratford cast a haughty glance at the man stood beside her brother. 'And now you are aware, what do you hope to do about it? You can hardly arrest a member of one of England's highest and oldest aristocratic families; now Leech you can arrest—'

'Watch him!'

The detective's shout rang out as the lantern Leech held hit the ground. In the shuffle that followed, Aiden felt himself shoved by a groom and Leech was gone into the night. Cursing the one who had stepped in his way, Aiden ran onto the dock, covering its length several times before a call halted him in his tracks.

'Man in the water . . . gone under the keel!' A sailor on watch waved from his ship. 'If you be running after a man I guesses you'll find 'im soon as 'e comes up from Davy Jones's locker, for I seen 'im come from that warehouse goin' like the divil were at his 'eels; reckon the divil catched 'im an' all cos 'e went arse over 'ead into the water.'

Leech had paid his dues, but what of the woman? Aiden turned back to the warehouse. Would Lady Eugenie do the same?

36

Oh sweet Mary, look down on me with pity, sweet Mother of God, help me!

Her screams of terror swamped by the neckerchief her attacker had fastened about her mouth, Maura twisted frantically as a rat scampered across her bared breasts. It was Leech had kidnapped her, caught her from behind then struck her on the side of the head. But he had twisted her to face him before landing that blow and she had known him instantly. Leech, the man who had tried once before to assault her; and he had said he would be back . . . Oh God, he would be back! Convulsive shudders shook her like a rag doll, panic robbing her of her senses so she screamed again and again against the stifling cloth.

But he had not returned! Slowly the realisation fought the madness of panic. Had he merely said that to add to her fright, had he in reality left her here to die . . . to be devoured alive by creatures she could hear twittering all around her? The thought relighting the flames of horror she trembled violently, screaming again as a long-tailed grey creature ran across her skirts, her mind begging the Holy Virgin to take her now . . . let her die now!

'Sure now, and isn't that a beag creature, and isn't it yourself being a silly wean to be bothered by it!'

Half laughing, half rebuking, the words her father had used to her when as a child she was startled by a kestrel shrieking as it swept over the stream somehow forced their way through the blanket of fear that swamped her brain, soothing now as then. The rat *was* only a small animal and she *was* behaving like a little child letting it frighten her. Clinging onto the idea she strove to think logically.

Leech had dragged her from that alleyway but he had not forced himself upon her in the way she had expected. He had struck her, knocking the senses half out of her before tying her hands and feet and setting a gag to her mouth. Then he had quite slowly and calmly unbuttoned her clothing . . . not the action of a man in a hurry to take what he had caught . . . he had fondled her breasts, set his mouth to her nipples and then had left her . . . again not the action of a man hot for rape. What was it he had said? '*Not now . . . not all at once, we will keep the rest for later.*' That meant he must be intending to come back, to finish . . .

Swallowing hard against the fresh tide of panic rising in her throat she glanced at a grey patch beyond a broken window. The greyness of evening? But it had been growing dusk when he had dragged her into this awful place. How long had she lain unconscious following that second vicious blow . . . an hour . . . more? The numbness of her body said it had to have been many hours. The greyness of dawn then? She glanced again at the pearl-coloured patch she knew must be sky. Why so long . . . just when did Leech mean to return . . . and what dreadful things had he in mind? It was not the heat of passion that had driven him to do what he had but the coldness of vengeance . . . a cold calculated vengeance that would not let her live!

The last thought sending spasms of horror crashing into her mind she fought for self-control . . . give way to her fear now and she might never surmount it. Breathing long and deep, her nostrils sucking in draughts of mould-stenched air, she looked about her at beams of rotten wood and decaying brickwork, then again at the broken window. Maybe if she could reach that she might attract attention. But how? She could not call out . . . and neither could she sit here waiting for the worst to happen.

Resolved that some move had to be made she used her heels to push herself across the debris-strewn floor, rubble tearing at her skirt, her shawl snagging on protruding masonry. The window had seemed much closer as she lay sprawled on the other side of the room . . . was that because, fully recovered of her senses, she could now gauge its true proximity . . . and also was more fully aware of her danger?

Her spine touching against the wall she could not give herself the luxury of rest but pushed and twisted, inching her way upwards until she was at last on her feet.

Outside, the alley was forlorn, broken windows looking out on a deserted world like sockets robbed of eyeballs. Maybe no one passed here in a day; Leech must know this town well, perhaps it was knowing she would not be found had caused him to leave her here.

Behind the gag sobs choked her throat while tears blocked out sight of the alley. She could expect no help.

Think my wean . . .

A whisper in her mind, that loved voice seemed again to speak, quieting the tumult of dread threatening to overwhelm her.

. . . 'tis no panic shows the way . . .

Father! Behind the cloth that bound her mouth the cry was soundless. As tears spilled onto her cheeks she lifted her hands in an imploring gesture, her eyes falling on the binding that held her wrists. It bit into her flesh, a thin twist of string . . . thin enough to cut on the jagged glass still protruding from a rusted iron window frame?

Breathing her thanks to the parents who had ever guided her to think on a problem, she sawed the string back and forth across the splinter of glass, her heart leaping with relief when it parted. Snatching it away she freed her mouth, tossing the neckerchief from her, then quickly untied her ankles. Thank the saints! She was loose of her bonds.

The sound of a boot on cobblestones caught her in a vice of fresh terror as she quickly fastened up her clothing. She was free of her shackles but was she free of Leech?

'I trust you can have no objection to my returning to Portington Hall until my transportation to whatever place it is you will be taking me.'

The woman had shown a coolness that was little short of audacity. Aiden Shanley poked a stick into the fire he had built in the lee of a high rock. Eugenie Stratford had not so much as blinked the lid of her eye on hearing the report which said Leech might have gone to drowning in the canal, but stared at the *Garda* from Scotland Yard who himself looked for direction to the government minister. There had been a discussion as to whose carriage she would ride in but again the woman had taken her own way.

'I will drive my own trap!' There had been no request, simply a statement of fact. A breeze catching sparks disturbed by the stick spread them in a lacework of tiny spangles, sparkling against the velvet blackness of night. Watching them, Aiden smiled. Having liking for Eugenie Stratford or not, her quickness of mind demanded respect.

Her nostrils widening she had glared at the *Garda* reaching a hand to restrain her as she stalked from the warehouse, leaving the men to make their decisions on what was to follow.

Now had that not been a fierce dear mistake? One which hadn't a titter of wit? Lifting his kettle from the fire, Aiden scalded the spoonful of tea leaves in his tin mug. Sure, it made no sense at all, but more than one hour had passed before they realised the extremes of it.

Eugenie Stratford had climbed into her trap and laid the

whip to the horse, scattering stevedores who in their haste to escape hooves and wheels dropped bales and barrels, bumped into casks and stacked boxes waiting to be loaded, sending cargo careering in every direction and so cutting off the path of carriages trying to follow in her wake. It had been bedlam as the woman knew well it would be.

Sipping the hot strong liquid, Aiden continued to stare into the glowing fire. It was racing full tilt into the darkness she had been after doing and none to see the way she had taken; but the way had proved to be south. Into the Slieve Bloom it was she had dared send that horse, driving it hard along Bealach's, lost in the jet blackness which robed the mountains; and it was in the Slieve Bloom they had been after finding her: broken and dead beneath the wreckage of the trap gone over the edge of one such path.

An accident? He sipped again at his tea. Aiden Shanley would not have the believing of that. From what he had seen of Lady Eugenie Stratford she was not the woman to spend the rest of her life in a prison cell. To the divil it was she had sold her soul with sending folk to slavery, and it was herself had delivered up her dues that night. It was knowing what she was after being about so she was, and that to drive carriage and horse from the track and over the cliff.

The traffickers were finished and Henry Portington had vowed it would never rear its head in Ireland again. Every boat he owned would sail to Dublin only after being inspected by men he would employ for the task and the same process would be repeated not only in that port but at Liverpool before and after being relieved of its cargo, and the same rule would be asked by the minister in London for to be applied to every port.

There had been no more for Aiden Shanley to do; he had been thanked by the man who had once been prison governor but had refused the offer of passage back to England.

Adding fresh sticks to the fire he watched bright flames dance with the shadows.

The call of his blood had been too strong; the whisper of purple mountains, the murmur of remembered streams and the balmy softness of air sighing over heather-filled heath, all had cried out to him . . . Ireland, the land of his nurturing, had called to him and he could not turn away. Just once more he would look upon the place that had been home, once more he would kneel at the resting places of those he loved; only then could he leave.

It had been a young lad. Maura eased the breath from her tight lungs in a slow silent stream. She had frozen at the thought it was Leech returning but the steps had grown fainter and at last she had peered around the edge of the broken window to catch sight of a ragged-trousered boy turn a corner. As she waited, ensuring no other followed his way, a nightmare of thoughts had snapped and roared in her brain but she had forced herself to stay where she was.

Dipping both hands in a fountain set outside an imposing stone building she splashed water onto her face. If only she could strip away her clothes, wash her body free of that man's touch . . . but that must wait until she was far from Tulla-more. Smoothing her hair with damp hands, brushing the dust of that debris-strewn floor from her skirts she glanced about the quiet square. She could not stand long, every moment promised the horror of being found by Leech. Quenching her thirst from the trickle of water spewing from the mouth of a finely carved porpoise, she was startled by a tug on her skirt. A cry gurgling into the cold water she raised her head.

'Would ye be after having a ha'penny to give?' Her nerves screaming, Maura looked at the face of a small beggar boy.

'I was not meaning to fright ye,' he smiled, showing gapped teeth, 'it was thinking ye might give a poor beggar a ha'penny, so I was.'

Shock still holding her tongue, Maura reached for the small leather pouch that held her money, but her pocket was empty. The sovereigns . . . what was left of the money given to her by Bella . . . it was gone! Leech . . . he must have taken it after knocking her unconscious.

'I . . . I'm sorry,' she stammered, 'my money . . . I must have been robbed.'

'Is it just arriving ye are in Tullamore?' The boy lifted a quizzical look to her dismayed face, adding, as she nodded, 'Then isn't it meself can tell you it was no beggar cut yer purse for news of it would have spread fast as flame on a dry heath . . . was it passage on a boat ye were after hoping to spend coin on?'

His glance taking in her torn skirt, the snagged shawl she pulled close about shoulders still shaking, it seemed he disbelieved she could ever have had money enough to buy any such thing, yet he waited for her answer.

'It was not.' Maura glanced nervously around a square growing busier with people. She could not afford time to gossip. 'It was a seat on the coach to Clonfert.'

A sudden grin spreading so far across his face it touched the streamers of black hair tumbling over his ears the boy snatched at her hand, pulling her after him as he set off along a wide street.

'Clonfert is it . . . ?' The words floated over the ring of his boots on the cobbles. 'Well now, do I not be knowing the very way to be getting ye'self there.'

Minutes later, breath heaving in her chest, Maura watched the lad, his hands gesticulating as he talked with a white-whiskered man and a woman whose black cotton bonnet bobbed as she listened.

' 'Tis to Clonfert himself will take ye.' The boy waved and turned, racing away without a backward glance.

'Sure, and doesn't it be after earning a smile from the Almighty to be helping a body, though 'tis sorry I am we don't be going the whole of the way to Clonfert,' the woman had said after being thanked. *'' Tis fortunate ye was in arriving for in another minute it's gone we would have been; one horse pulling a caravan be no match for a coach and team but if it's not a hurry ye be in then 'tis welcome ye are to ride with us and Flynn will set you on the road to the town when it is we draw near.'*

Sat on the steps at the rear of the prettily painted caravan, Maura watched the morning give way to the golden somnolence of afternoon. The desolation she had felt on discovering her money stolen had not all been on account of those coins. Her letters, the only things she had brought with her from England, had they been stolen too? Thank God she had not trusted them to the pocket of her skirt or yet to the inside of her chemise, for in either the man Leech would have found them. But they were safe. She pressed a hand to her thigh, feeling the small flat package nestled deep in a pocket sewn into her petticoat. She could not hope to meet with Liam Riordan, to look on that gentle face. That was a blessing she had renounced when turning from him that day on the heath, but whilst she had those letters she had a little of himself to keep, to hold alongside an image in her heart, an image that would never fade.

'The house of Bridie MacGee is what ye'self talked of?' The woman came to climb the steps, settling beside Maura.

'You know Bridie?'

The black bonnet bobbed. 'Sure, and is not Flynn and meself after knowing every clochan 'twixt Tullamore and Clara down to Clonony and Banagher and back through the villages of Kilkormac and Blue Ball in a circle which brings ye again to

Tullamore. The cottage ye were after speaking of lies a few miles beyond Clara, that I knows though it's never to its door this cart has been, and Clara lies in that direction.'

Her glance following the way pointed, Maura felt her pulse leap. Liam had been nursed in Bridie's house, perhaps he might since have returned to claim the box he had left there, perhaps Bridie could tell her he was fully recovered of his illness.

'Thank you and your husband for bringing me this far,' she said, then jumped to the ground.

'But it be a ways yet to Clonfert!'

Maura's answer held a smile. 'It is to Clonfert I will go, but it is to see Bridie and her family I want first.'

'The holy angels guide yer steps and forbid the divil to cross yer path,' the woman said softly, raising a hand in farewell. 'And may it be ye finds what yer heart be seeking after.'

'. . . *what yer heart be seeking after* . . .'

The words staying with her, Maura watched the caravan lumber steadily out of sight. The wish was a kind one but it could never be fulfilled. Her heart was seeking for more than news of Liam, it sought his face, his touch, the sound of her name on his lips . . . it sought the love of his own heart. But that was a hidden love, one never to be spoken aloud, as her own must never be. That would remain locked away deep inside, its seal unbroken all the days of the life she would return to in England. And Aiden Shanley . . . would he return to that country as he had said, would he speak of that love she had seen in his eyes?

Setting off across the heath she smiled softly to herself. She had listened to Bella talk a long time that last morning in Birmingham, listened as she told of Aiden Shanley, the young man who had taken the blame for a fight that had broken out between her own husband and another prisoner, taken the five-year addition of sentence that followed so a man already dying of a tumour in his stomach could end his days in freedom; of a man wrongly accused when only a boy then given twenty years in place of a man he had seen commit murder. But that was not all of what Bella had confided. Aiden Shanley had finished the years of his sentence but his punishment had not ended with the opening of those prison gates. He had returned to Ireland only to find the home he had loved an empty shell. The parents his boy's heart had worshipped were long in their graves and the sister he had cherished gone from the home of her marriage; but there had been one star shone in the darkness, a star he had found in the cottage of Bridie MacGee, Maura Deverell . . . the child of his own sister.

37

Only the light of a lamp shining a golden speck in the vast darkness had guided Maura's steps the last of the way. It had been late afternoon when she had left that caravan, she had not thought the walk across the rough moor to take so long, but then night had ever followed quickly on the heels of evening. The words of the caravan woman had been heard in heaven, the holy angels had guided her. With a smile on her lips she had lifted a hand to the door closed against the night air, tapping as she called softly, '*God bless all in this house.*'

The wait of a few moments had told her the glances that had passed between the family, looks maybe of consternation, for visitors were few on the heath at night. But then the door opened and light had fallen across her face.

Morning breeze cool on her cheeks, Maura smiled remembering the events of the previous night, the delighted gasp of Connal as he recognised the figure stood on the doorstep.

They had made her so welcome; Bridie almost weeping with joy at seeing her safe and Caitlin repeating the same thanks she had cried the night her child had been born, while the words of Connal himself had thickened in his throat, his gratitude obvious for the healing of his injured leg.

They had talked far into the wee hours, Caitlin brewing pot after pot of tea, but in all of their conversation the name of Liam Riordan had not been spoken. They had nursed a stranger, a man whose senses were shrouded in a mist that had not cleared. He had walked from the house at the breaking of dawn, leaving behind the one thing he had, a small wooden box.

'*It held letters all tied together with a velvet band,*' Bridie had told her. ''*Twas Connal O'Malley himself had the reading of the name penned on the top one. Maura Deverell, so it was. It was to you . . . yourself had the belonging . . . no more was read in this house.*'

They had not read the words poured from Liam's heart, had Aiden Shanley too read only the name? She knew there was no foundation for the question, he would have respected both her own privacy and that of the writer.

The turf soft beneath her feet, morning sun warm on her face, she trudged on. The stranger had not returned to their cottage, Connal had told her, they had heard no more of him. Was he well, had Liam's senses returned enough to take him home to Eyrecourt? She would not call at that house but enquire in the village of Clonfert, people there would tell her of the sons of Seamus Riordan.

Parting so soon with her friends had brought the tears to Caitlin's eyes and Bridie's too had filled with moisture; but like Bella, Bridie had understood that deep inside was a need that drove, that would give no peace until it was satisfied: and that need was to kneel beside those simple graves, to whisper to her parents one more time the love that she felt for them. So she had held Maura tight in her arms while her soft voice had murmured a blessing and the surety they would meet again in God's good time.

To whisper her love for her parents. Halting in her stride she let her glance travel far ahead. That was only part of the need that was in her heart, the part she had confided to Bridie; but the look in those bird-bright eyes had seen beyond her brief confiding, glimpsing a truth that lay beneath it, a truth Maura admitted only in the deepest recesses of her being but one which would never be realised . . . to whisper her love to Liam Riordan.

The pain of the thought resting like a stone in her heart she walked on, her gaze searching the heath for the small heap of stones that covered her mother's last resting place. Had she missed the way? She glanced at a sky beginning to lose the brightness of the sun. She had walked in a straight line the morning she had left that grave . . . and she had retraced her steps; but had she? Her heart sinking she stared ahead, how did you judge a straight line on an empty heath . . . how could she be sure she had not been walking in the wrong direction!

She must not give in. Maura tried to talk herself into rising from the ground where she had slumped in despair. She had come too far to give up now, another dozen steps and that tiny cairn she had raised over her mother's body might appear on the horizon. And if it did not? Pushing the thought away she rose to her feet.

These were the stones . . . they had to be the stones! The sun had touched the horizon when she first spotted them, a smear of white against the green of the heath. Now, with the rim of the sky bathed in the brilliance of a scarlet sunset, she stared at the scattered rocks on the shallow depression in the earth that had once held that beloved form but now held no more than a smear of newly growing heather.

Who could have moved them, thrown them aside like petals plucked from a daisy and tossed carelessly away? And why do such a thing . . . had some homeless traveller been so desperate as to rob a grave? Staring at the small hollow she pressed both hands to her mouth, stemming the scream her next thought brought to her lips.

Dogs! Dogs left to run wild over the moor or belonging to gypsies who sometimes set up their camps near to the river . . . other creatures that roamed the heath at night?

'No!' The scream reached between her fingers as she fell to her knees. 'Holy Mother, not that . . . please not that!'

The sharp staccato bark of a dog fox echoing in her brain,

Maura moaned as she pushed to her knees. The glory of red-gold had gone and in its place were great sweeps of purple-grey tipped with pink. Dawn! She glanced at the shadowed indentation over which she had thrown herself, sobbing at the terrible pictures in her mind, pictures of her mother's body being ravaged by animals. She had been unable to stop the pictures or the sobs that had wracked her; but nature must have taken a hand, drawing her eventually into sleep for it was now the brink of a new day. Why had she come back to Ireland, she should have known . . . she had known . . . there would be only heart-ache for her here . . . but this! Feeling an unhappiness so bitter she could scarcely breathe she knelt again, her limbs stiff and sore as she touched her fingers to the heather-covered hollow that had held her mother.

'Forgive me,' she whispered, 'I did not think of such a thing happening . . . forgive me, Mother.' With tears running un-controlled down her cheeks she lowered her head, her lips touching where that cherished figure had lain. 'I love you,' she whispered again, 'I love you so much.'

Sinead O'Toole shaded her eyes against the brightness of the day. She had watched the speck moving in the distance for several minutes. It was no illusion, no trick of light or shadow, the speck was definitely moving. Curiosity ever her master she waited, her stare keening against the sunlight.

A woman? And what else could it be after being? She answered her own question derisively. No animal was after wearing skirts and no man either, not in Ireland anyway!

Watching the figure draw closer she lifted the willow basket from her arm, resting it beside her on the ground. The rishawn of herbs and plants she had gathered from first light seemed to grow heavier as her bones grew older.

She had known this day would come. She smiled to herself

as the figure became a person, one she had known from the hour of its birth. The child of Mairead Deverell was home.

'Good day to ye, Maura Deverell.'

The greeting was lost on Maura, making no impression on tiredness that screamed in every limb.

The child of Mairead Deverell was home. Sinead thought again as she saw the pallid drawn face, watched the footsteps, each of which threatened to be the girl's last . . . she was here but where was her heart?

'Is it no word ye have for Sinead O'Toole?' She spoke louder and this time the figure halted, red-rimmed eyes looking vacantly in Sinead's direction, then, her breath scarcely a sigh, Maura crumpled to the ground.

She must leave her bed and help her mother with the breakfast. Warm and comfortable, Maura glanced about the small room she knew so well. Everything was as her mother liked it, a fire glowing in the freshly swept hearth, dishes each in its place on the shelves her father had set to one wall, the table he had made with his own hands set as always with a bright clean cloth. There would be oats with warm milk and honey . . . throwing back the covers she moaned softly, the room spinning around her as she sat up. Why did something inside her feel that all was not right and why when she moved did her body ache so? The cottage was as it always was, as it had been the day . . . as memories flooded in she covered her face with her hands, hiding the misery reflected there.

She had left Bridie's house, walked a full day across the heath, found her mother's grave, a grave that had been . . . Crying against the pain of remembering she stood up, holding a hand to the bedpost to steady herself. She had left that place, that shallow hole in the earth that was slowly covering itself with grass and heather and she had walked again . . . but she had not walked into this house; so who had brought her here and who had taken her clothes before laying her in that bed?

Reaching them from a chair over which they had been draped she dressed, then rinsed hands and face in water taken from a tall tin jug. Mother O'Toole! The sharp bite of cold water washed the last of the cobwebs from her mind. Was it truly Mother O'Toole had spoken to her or had that been simply a dream? But this cottage was not a dream, the hearth, the table, the bed, it was all real yet somehow unreal, for how could it be so cared for? It was as if she and her mother had never been away. She must go to Mother O'Toole's cottage across the brook, the explanation would surely be there. Tidying her hair she took the water she had washed in, carrying it to be emptied behind the house.

'Mother!' It was a whisper lost among the clatter of the bowl falling from nerveless hands. The dish unheeded at her feet, her whole body numb with shock, she stared at the simple oval block of grey-flecked stone, at the name carved upon it, Mairead Deverell!

Pausing beside a clump of gorse the man stepped behind it, the better to shield himself from view. It was a woman . . . a young woman knelt there before that stone. Watching the glint of light play on rich chestnut-coloured hair he felt his insides kick. Was she alone or had she some man with her, perhaps sitting in that cottage? He must make no move . . . remain unseen.

Across from him, Maura's head turned, her cry winging over the quiet space as she moved to another stone, identical in form and shape to the first, dropping to her knees as she touched it. There was no sound from that cottage, no movement, no figure emerging in response to a cry that was part agony, part delight; so she was alone! Seeing her head lift he caught a long glimpse of a profile and again his stomach kicked. The girl was beautiful.

Unaware of being watched, Maura touched her lips to the

stone, tears flooding her eyes. 'Father,' she sobbed, 'oh Father you are together . . .' It did not matter how, her fingers rested on the black earth adorned now with summer flowers, her parents lay as they would have wanted, one beside the other for all eternity.

The flood of emotion spent she pushed to her feet at last, allowing her mind to fill with unspoken questions. She had seen her mother's grave, the place she herself had buried her on that lonely heath; it had been opened, the cairn of piled-up stones strewn across the ground, but the hollow beneath them had held no trace of her body. Now in this patch where her father had lain with the tiny brother she could hardly remember, where when she and her mother had left this house only two rough-hewn wooden crosses marked their graves, there were now three headstones each carved with the names of her family. Who had raised them, who had paid her parents so much respect? But most important of all her questions was the one stabbing her like the blade of a knife; did the body of her mother truly lie beneath that stone . . . or was it merely a pretence?

But no one knew where she had lain her mother. She had told of that awful night only to Bella and one more person beside . . . she had told Aiden Shanley and he had returned to Ireland! Had he prolonged his stay in this country, made his way to that cairn, taking his sister's remains and bringing them here to Clonmacnoise?

'Holy Mother –' hands crossed on her breast, Maura prayed softly ' – you have listened to my prayers since childhood, heard the joys of my heart and comforted its sorrows; I pray you now, let it be that the body of Mairead Deverell lies in the ground beside the husband and child she loved so much.'

Her head bent on her breast, eyes closed in prayer, Maura did not see the tall figure step from the cover of the bush.

       ★   ★   ★

'Is it the whole day entirely ye mean to stand beside that bush?'

His eyes still on the girl, Aiden did not answer directly.

'The business ye came here to do will not have the doing of itself . . . or have ye no longer the courage?'

Turning his gaze as he was spoken to again he seemed poised to walk away.

'Ye cannot run and rest with a quiet heart, one has no place with the other; ye must face what it is cries to ye, only then can you find peace.'

A world of torment in his eyes, Aiden glanced at the girl who, hearing their voices, had turned in their direction. 'Peace!' he said bitterly. 'Did they who lie in that patch know peace . . . or the girl whose tears fall for them?'

'Life has a divergence of which Sinead O'Toole has not the explaining, for some 'tis a rosebed while for others 'tis a bed o' thorns; it smiles on one man with the sweetness o' honey but looks on another with the sourness o' bitter aloes. But ye can rest yer mind for the one ye came to say goodbye to, yer sister's body lies alongside her man and her soul be safe in the Lord's hands.'

He had been so careful not to tell his name to anyone, to speak of himself only as the tinker, yet the old woman's stare said she knew him. Surprise edged a little of the torment from Aiden's eyes.

' 'Tis how do I know who it is the tinker be is the question ye be asking ye'self.' Sinead's bird-bright glance flicked over the dark hair touched with grey, the face handsome despite the lines that told of the hardness of its years. 'Who but the brother of her childhood would leave tears on the stone o' Mairead Deverell? Oh it was herself told me of ye, wept in these very arms for ye and the son heaven saw fit to take from her . . . and it can be no lie I tells when I says it be the same man I saw near this clochan but a few weeks from the finding o' Seamus Riordan at the bottom of that hill.'

'It was not meself was after sending him over that cliff, though given the chance I would not have turned from it.'

'That I understands,' Sinead nodded, 'for Seamus Riordan had dubh heart.'

'He was black-hearted in every way . . . 'tis only a wonder some man of the valley was not after killing him long ago . . . and his son the same, that one had not the worth of dying peaceful in his bed!'

Let not all yer ears have the listening of a truth to be held in yer heart! The words living only in her mind, Sinead looked again at the slight figure stood at the graveside. Died of the pneumonia. That had been the word spoken in Eyrecourt, but it had not been the only lie ever to come from that house. Sinead O'Toole had been given the truth of it and it was not what Liam Riordan would have believed; his protection of the name of the filthy jackeen who had raped that girl and taken the flower of many a colleen had not the fooling of one who carried in her the powers of the old ones; given to her was the hearing of words which came not from mortal tongue, and pictures borne on the shadows of night were not seen by the eyes of others, and it was herself had seen the death of Padraig Riordan. It was no peaceful passing in his bed had seen the man from this world, that the powers had shown her; just as they had told how the man facing her now had once before come to take the life of the second son of Seamus Riordan.

38

He had held her hands, had called her 'girl dear', but he had not owned her the daughter of his sister. Watching him now taking a pipe beside the fire, Maura felt a weight of sadness rest in her. Was it true what Bella had told her, that this man had claimed to be the brother of Mairead Deverell? But Bella would not lie, nor, surely, could he gain anything by not speaking the truth; the soul in her longed to know but she could not ask what it seemed he had no wish to speak of. Aiden Shanley must be afforded the secrecy he desired.

'The business which saw me come back to Ireland is finished, it is over and done.' Aiden Shanley spoke quietly.

'All o' it?' Sinead's jet-bead eyes glittered as they rested on him. 'Be sure o' that afore ye takes yer leave this next time, for fate does not deal a second kindness lightly.'

A second kindness! What was the meaning behind those words? Silent in her unhappiness Maura waited.

'It is over and done.' Staring into the fire, Aiden repeated the words.

'And what o' the daughter of Mairead Deverell?' The glittering eyes swung to Maura. 'Will it be leaving the shores of Ireland ye'll be after doing now that ye've knelt beside the graves of the two that gave ye life?'

'I promised my mother I would.'

'Yet ye be back.'

Maura felt the sharp eyes on her but did not look up to meet them. Her hand resting against the letters in her petticoat pocket, she replied, 'It was to return some property I came. A box was left in Birmingham, the contents had my name written on them but when I opened them I realised that though they had been addressed to me it was not intended I should see them, therefore I will take them to the person to whom they rightfully belong.'

Lowering his pipe Aiden Shanley looked at the girl his heart longed to own; yet he was feared to speak lest she turn from him for ever. She had travelled all the way from England's very centre to give back a pile of old letters. Why? She could so easily have fed Bella's fire with them and so been sure no other eyes would ever see what had been set to paper; but the look on that sweet face, a face so like the one he remembered, held the shadow of pain. Maura Deverell had returned to Ireland for more than the returning of letters.

''Tis no beag way to come when ye could have sent what it be by the carrier!'

Mother O'Toole was right in that, it was no small distance to travel, but it was a journey she had known she had to make. Meeting those dart-like eyes, she said quietly, 'A field is never ploughed by turning it over in the mind. I spoke bitterly to Liam Riordan before leaving this land, I held him responsible for the sin of his brother and the ambition of his father . . . I would speak my apology as I now give Aiden Shanley my thanks for raising those stones over my family.'

His pipe laid swiftly aside, Aiden twisted in his chair. 'I? It was not meself had the raising of the stones.'

'But I thought—'

'Ye were wrong in yer thinking, child, as ye were in placing blame,' Sinead said quietly. 'It was Liam Riordan himself had the carving and the raising as it was himself had the bringing of Mairead Deverell's body to where it rests beside her man.'

'Riordan!' Aiden was on his feet, disbelief darkening his features. 'I have not the believing any Riordan would raise a stone, all they have ever lifted was a hand . . . and that to strike a man down!'

'*T'cha!*' Sinead slapped a hand against her dark skirts. 'Is it the dingle o' a fool ye carry, the mark o' stupidity! Sure, and if we fought temptation the way we sometimes fight common sense 'tis a nation o' saints we'd be after being! 'Twas Liam Riordan had the doing for did I not see it with me own eyes, and it be himself and no other has had the caring o' this clochan, his the coin that pays for it to be scrubbed and cleaned as Mairead Deverell would have it.'

'Liam brought my mother home!'

'He did so, child.' Moving to the side of the girl she had seen enter the world, Sinead O'Toole laid a gentle hand to the trembling shoulder. 'Not many days after ye left was she brought home and laid out there in the spot her heart longed to be.'

'Then it is thanks I must give as well as apology.'

'Apologise!' Resentment and anger laced Aiden's words. 'To a Riordan!'

Touching a hand to the one resting on her shoulder, Maura felt the strength of the older woman flow into her. Meeting the anger full on she smiled. 'To a man, Mr Shanley,' she said quietly, 'I shall apologise to a man.'

There was something deeper in her words. Aiden saw the shadow of pain disappear, leaving her face with a look – he caught his breath – it was a look of regard, of tenderness . . . the girl thought to speak words of apology to the son of Seamus Riordan, but it was words of love were in her heart . . . she was in love with Liam Riordan . . . the man he sought to kill! The man whose father had placed the act of murder on the shoulders of a young boy and looked on while his life was snatched away. The daughter of his sister could not love the son of a murderer and the brother of a rapist . . . she couldn't!

'Liam Riordan!' The words spilled of their own accord.

'You would apologise to the very man whose life I came back to Ireland to claim . . .'

'You . . . you have killed Liam?'

The depth of misery so deep in those wide brown eyes that Aiden felt he would smother in it, he shook his head. 'I went to Eyrecourt but he was not there.'

'But why would you want to kill him? Mr Shanley, please . . . you must tell me.'

That look was more than he could bear. Aiden sank back into the chair, his hands covering his face. Pain . . . God knows he had suffered all of that, but the look on that sweet face, to know the grief and anguish his act would cause her, even the angels in heaven could not wipe the memory of that from his soul.

'Don't be visiting the past too often, Aiden Shanley, nor stay in its presence too long,' Sinead said, a deep pity in her voice as she looked at the man her heart told her was suffering his own torment. 'Neither put the name o' experience to what drives ye, for that be the word a man too often sets upon his mistakes. Follow now where the soul o' ye tells ye to tread for that be the path o' yer own happiness.'

Lifting his head as Maura came to kneel beside him, Aiden touched his fingers to the shining chestnut hair.

'Girl dear,' he began softly, 'I was nobbut a child, a lad of no more than ten years . . .'

The tick of the tin clock the only accompaniment to his voice, Aiden Shanley told the story of his life, of the bitterness that had ridden him all of those years and of the promise made to himself.

'But Liam was not the one who robbed you of your life, he did not rape my mother nor was it him forced himself upon me.' Maura lifted a face stained with tears. 'Liam Riordan tried to give back this house . . . to put right the wrongs his family had done.'

'He could not give back the life of your mother . . . of her who was my own sister.'

He had said it! Maura's heart leaped. He had acknowledged their relationship.

'He could not,' she whispered, 'but the one we both loved would not have your hands commit the very crime Seamus Riordan committed. Don't let bitterness take you from me again.'

Fate had led him to this girl, to the daughter of his beloved sister, could he risk losing one as he had lost the other? Lifting his glance to Sinead O'Toole he heard the words she had spoken echo in his heart . . . *'fate does not deal a second kindness lightly'*.

'When it was a sickbed you lay on in the house of Bella James, I heard the words of your rambling. "Refuse the inheritance", was what Maura Deverell said, 'a legacy of hate is the gift of despair, it can only destroy.' It was a man ye spoke to, one only you in your sickness could see standing beside ye, one ye said had ever been kind and polite to Mairead; how those words speak again in your eyes. I will refuse, girl dear, refuse the inheritance and the legacy.'

He no longer wished the death of Liam. Leaving the two of them inside the cottage, Maura had gone to stand beside the rippling waters that were a finger of the Shannon. Tomorrow she would go to Clonfert, to the house of Liam Riordan, to give him her thanks and return the letters held beneath her shawl, but first she would go to the Abbey grounds of Clonmacnoise and offer a prayer of gratitude in the tiny chapel of Saint Ciaran, a prayer of thanks that Aiden Shanley no longer had a wish to kill Liam and to ask the health of Seamus Riordan's son be returned to him. Then she would return with Aiden to England.

It would pain her to leave her home, but it would pain her more to stay, to know Liam was no more than a few miles distant, to see him one day marry . . . Touching the letters she had read once more she fought the tears. She would have the memory of them for ever, no one could take that from her.

'Maura . . .'

Quietly spoken it was the murmur of grief, an utterance of the anguish that was tearing her soul apart.

'Maura.'

Staring at the gleaming waters, hearing her name ripple on its surface she gathered it to her, locking it inside, storing it against the coming years, a memory that must help her live.

'Will you not speak to me?'

It was the voice of her heart, but she could not listen, the pain was too great. Turning quickly she almost cried out as she caught sight of the figure watching her, his hair catching the light and gleaming as it framed a fine-boned face whose dark brown eyes seemed to hold her to the spot.

'I had not the knowing you had returned to Clonmacnoise.'

As if by some unseen miracle a great weight was lifted, the figure stood tall, the shoulders straight, one almost even with the other.

'Liam.' It broke from her like a sob.

'I had given up hope—' He broke off abruptly as she stepped away from his outstretched hand. 'I saw you as I was passing, I wished to ask if you are well.' Liam Riordan turned his glance to the stream. The hope he had nurtured, the dream he had kept alive in his heart had turned into a nightmare. The girl he loved, who stood not a yard from him, had shuddered at the prospect of his touch. But then what had he truly expected? A man could dream but that is all it would ever be for him, for what woman could love Seamus Riordan's misfit, his cripple of a son!

The emotion too strong he turned away across the heath, his words coming over his shoulder. 'God give you long life, Maura Deverell.'

He was the soul inside her, the one her heart yearned for, the one it called to in the long hours of the night.

'Liam,' she called brokenly, 'Liam, wait, I—'

He was beside her but the words would not come, caught by the sobs in her throat they remained imprisoned.

'Maura,' it was soft, tender as a breath on the breeze, 'I prayed that one day I would see you again, hear your voice other than in dreams, I thank heaven for this blessing.'

'My thanks go with yours.'

Forced from her the words sounded stiff and stilted; it was the rejection every fibre of him knew had to happen. Resting his gaze one minute more on that lovely face, her downcast eyes laying a sweep of dark lashes along pale cheeks, he lifted a hand then let it fall. He could not stand that again; the pain of her drawing back a moment ago was enough for one lifetime. 'God keep you, Maura Deverell,' was all he said as he turned away.

'I have something I must return to you.' It was not what her heart wanted to say, the words that cried deep within her. 'These were given to me but I feel you would want them returned.' Her fingers trembling she held out the letters she had read for the last time beside that quiet brook.

'How—' He broke off as he took them, pushing them deep into the pocket of his coat. What did it matter how she had come by them, it was obvious she did not want them.

'Did you read them?'

There was an anger in his question, a demand that she say she had not but Maura would not lie. Lifting her glance to his she nodded.

'Then I'm sorry. I would not have embarrassed you with such words, they were the ramblings of a fool.'

'No,' she whispered, 'they are beautiful words.'

There was a smile on that beloved mouth, a gentle smile holding no derision . . . and no rejection?

Despite the hurt of moments ago, the pain of her drawing back from him, he held out a hand and his very heart was in the one word, 'Maura.'

Reaching towards it she felt a flood of happiness, golden and warm, spread through her.

'They were words I could not say,' his fingers closed on hers, 'words that must stay in my heart, for after what my father and my brother did you could only hate a Riordan.'

'I did not hate you, Liam,' she answered softly. 'I told you the day we parted on the heath I would always value your friendship.'

Was that all she wanted from him . . . friendship? The thought like a knife blade in his heart he looked deep into velvet eyes. If so, he must give it and never let the truth show. He had begged of God that a moment such as this would be given him, had minutes before thanked heaven it had, now he wished his prayers had gone unanswered for how could he suffer to part from her again, how could he bear the emptiness?

His hand closing more tightly on hers he looked down on the small elfin face, painting the image of it deep inside.

'You will always be in my heart, Liam.'

She had said it quietly, a touch of colour rising to her pale cheeks, the blaze of truth flaring in the look that lifted to him.

'You *are* my heart, Maura Deverell,' he muttered, drawing her into his arms, holding her tight against his body. 'You are the soul within me, the air I breathe; the words of my letters are the words of my being. I love you . . . I have always loved you.'

'And I love you.' Shy at the words spilling instantly from her lips she moved against his hold but it tightened fiercely.

'Don't step away,' he breathed, 'never step away from me again.'

Lifting her head to answer, Maura heard the whole universe sing as he pressed his mouth to hers.

★　　★　　★

He loved her but they could not marry. Sat with Sinead and Aiden she listened to Liam tell what had passed between himself and his father, how he had learned during one of Padraig's wild rages of her mother's visit, and the words his father had told to his brother.

'To no Riordan would child be born, the house and all it stood for would be wiped from the valley, the Riordan line would die, cursed out of existence.' Glancing at Maura he went on, 'I could not be the man to bring you unhappiness, to watch your heart pine for the child that could not be born of my body.'

Crossing quickly to him, Maura dropped to her knees. 'It would not matter . . .'

'No, my love –' his finger touching her lips he smiled, a sad desperate smile which echoed deep in his eyes '– it would matter to me. The thought of my being the cause of a heart-ache you could not prevent is more than I can endure.'

Sitting silent until this moment, Aiden Shanley rose from his chair, drawing Maura to her feet. ' 'Tis wise words the man speaks,' he said quietly, 'the pain of an empty womb cannot be known to ye now but the years will bring it, fight it as ye may.'

'They too be wise words, Aiden Shanley, and spoken from the love yer heart holds for the daughter o' your sister, but they are not after being the wisest of words.'

'Then if you have the knowing of others that will soothe, say them, for the heart of the child be near breaking.'

'Mrs O'Toole.' Liam put in gently, 'I love Maura Deverell with all my heart, I would not see her suffer but my house was cursed . . .'

'By a Deverell woman!' Sinead's eyes glittered like black diamonds. 'And it can be lifted by a Deverell woman.'

'Lifted?'

'I had the saying of it,' the old woman answered the

tremulous query. 'What be done can be undone, but only ye' self has the way.'

Her brows pulling together Maura stared at the lined face. 'The way?' she said. 'I know no way.'

'But have ye the faith, the trust to follow what I say?'

The slight frown of perplexity keeping its place between her brows, Maura answered simply, 'Have I not always had faith in the woman who has been a second mother to me, did I not always trust the word of Mother O'Toole?'

'Thank you, child,' Sinead smiled, 'now with the help of the ancient powers yer mother called upon we will do what herself would have had the doing of . . . the giving to ye of yer heart's love.' Turning to where her willow basket had sat in a corner during the nursing of an exhausted Maura she set it on her arm. 'Come with me, girl, but both ye men stay here. What I do is not for yer eyes to have the seeing of; but rest yer hearts easy for Sinead O'Toole will let no harm come to the daughter of her friend.'

Across the stream the moon was rising silver-gold above the rim of the horizon when Sinead at last declared that all was ready. Taken from her basket and laid on the soft earth were seven tiny slivers of wood and beside them a shallow indented stone held clear water taken from the stream. Slivers of the same trees would, she knew, have been used in Mairead's curse, for had herself not given the teaching of the old ways.

Maura had gathered dry sticks while she herself had searched for a stone of just the right sort. Sinead looked at the rising moon; soon it would be time. Setting a match to the dried grass set beneath the sticks she looked at Maura.

'Ye have no fears, child?' she asked, watching the face for any sign of hesitation, smiling when none came. 'Then listen carefully. Ye will speak no word other than that which came from my tongue, make no action other than we have discussed; make no mistake for there will be no second chance.

Ye remembers what it is I've had the speaking of?' Waiting for
Maura's nod she went on, 'Then is it ready ye are?'

She would remember; whatever Mother O'Toole asked of her
she would do if it meant the chance of happiness with Liam.
Maura watched the gnarled hand take each twig from the basket
then hand it to her. Lifting it, as she had been instructed, towards
the rising moon, her breath trembling, she whispered.

> 'Spirits of air and water,
> Spirits of sky and earth,
> You who are of old,
> I do you honour.
> Bring to the hand the power it seeks,
> Let this night the ancients speak.'

It seemed the twig twitched in her hand, a ray from the silver
orb tipping its end and endowing it with radiance.

'Now, child,' Sinead murmured, 'quickly, as I told ye and
no more.'

Her throat tight, Maura felt the hot rise of panic. The words
Sinead had had such a short time to teach, she could not
remember them! Help me, Mother . . . The cry rose inside her
. . . Help me, please.

Think, child . . .

Gentle as always the answer whispered back and with it her
fears faded. In the light of the climbing moon she looked at the
twigs laid on the ground and suddenly the words came.

> 'Elder, Ash, Beech and Oak,
> Over each these words are spoke,
> Elm and Chestnut then with Yew,
> I call the powers which flow in you,
> Each to the other held in thrall,
> Let twig of Bay free them all.'

Touching each twig first with the sprig of bay leaves she scooped them into her hands, holding them towards the full moon.

> 'Three lives did thy power enchain,
> Two are taken, the third I claim,
> A woman's love did vengeance make,
> A daughter's love may that curse break.'

The incantation finished, Maura's lips stilled but in her heart a different plea spoke brokenly. Take back your words, Mother . . . lift the curse you laid, he . . . he did no harm, I love him, Mother, I love him!

With the last thought it seemed to Maura the world was held in a vast silence. No rustle of night creatures among the heather, no ripple of water tumbling over stones, no sound of earth penetrated its barrier. She was alone with the moon, caught in a net of shimmering silver radiance. Hands uplifted, the twigs dark in her fingers, she knelt like some lovely marble carving, every line bathed with incandescent beauty.

Beyond the rim of light, lost among the blackness it closed out, Sinead O'Toole watched, every nerve in her old body tense. The girl had called upon the ancient ways, called upon powers whose might she could never define; she stood now in mortal danger. Should the choice have been given her . . . should Sinead O'Toole have put her in the peril that now hovered close? The answer in her head was no, but the answer in her heart said otherwise. What had taken place here beside the stream was the one chance the child had to know her soul's desire, to live a life of happiness with the man of her heart, how could that chance have been denied? Save yer daughter. She prayed silently. Save yer child, Mairead Deverell.

Within the gleaming circle Maura felt a touch against her brow; soft as the brush of lips, gentle as a mother's kiss, it rested a few brief seconds then with its going the silver light that surrounded her intensified, its brilliance drawing together, gathering itself into one great luminous column, the tip almost touching the upraised hand. Then from its centre came the quietest of sounds, the whisper of breeze on a summer meadow, and the twigs held in Maura's hand vibrated.

Closed away in darkness, Sinead O'Toole caught her breath. The ancient powers were close, now was the moment. As the thought solidified in her mind the sound grew in volume, the shining silver beam began to spin and suddenly the twigs were snatched from Maura's fingers, twisting upwards through the centre of light, caught in a vortex which shattered, the remnants swallowed in its glistening spiral. Then it was gone; benign and golden, the moon spilled its yellow glow across stream and heath. Releasing her pent-up breath Sinead murmured her thanks for the protection that had been placed about the daughter of her dead friend. The curse was broken, the house and son of Seamus Riordan were released of its hold, but what of the daughter of Mairead Deverell? She had made a vow, much as her mother before her, but hers was the vow to leave for ever the shores of Ireland, and a vow given a dying mother was sacred! Pushing to her feet she glanced at the girl who a moment before had knelt in an aura of light. Maura Deverell had freed the man she loved but she could not free herself.

39

It had been a week of heartbreak but also of joy. Liam had
come to the cottage every day, and on each of those days had
held her close, whispering his love. But she must not accept
that love for she could not ask him to leave his homeland and
she could not stay in it. She had made a promise to her mother,
one she would not break.

Aiden had said his sister would never hold her child to such
a word, that she should wed with Liam, but Maura knew her
heart would always tell her she had betrayed her mother.

Entering the grounds of the great Abbey of Clonmacnoise
she stood a few seconds before each of the tall Celtic crosses
that rose like beacons from the soft green turf, then before the
smaller less significant headstones that marked the resting
places of several *Ard Ri*, the high kings of Ireland, whispering a
blessing on their names.

They had talked long, herself and Aiden Shanley. She
turned from the lichen-covered stones, walking slowly towards
the tiny chapel stood a little apart from the Abbey church. He
would return to England he had said, but she had seen the
longing in the eyes that had roved the land embracing his
sister's home, touching the glistening stream, lifting to the
smoky hills, and she had known his heart too would ache for
the wanting of Ireland.

'*You have feelings for Aisleen McCullough?*' she had asked.

'*I have so, it be a rope that pulls me from this land.*'

Maura smiled, remembering the simplicity of his answer

and the nod that replied to the question of would he wed with her and if so would he bring her to Clonmacnoise, take the house that was his sister's, live there and care for the land she and her husband had loved?

So it had been agreed. If Aisleen was consenting, the pair would return to live in the tiny clochan Brendan Deverell had built himself; and Bridget . . . Aiden had smiled at her asking, that colleen would wed her English goldsmith or Aiden Shanley was no Irishman!

But what of herself? The words of her mother had been lifted, Liam no longer lay beneath that curse, but her own promise must stand. Tomorrow she would leave her mother's house for the last time.

How could she live! A sob breaking from her lips she entered the minute chamber, falling to her knees before the spot long believed to hold the body of the blessed Saint Ciaran, her hand lifting to mark the holy sign on her brow and breast. How could she go on without Liam! But she must be strong, strong for them both.

'I love him, Holy Father,' she whispered, 'give me the strength I need, the courage to leave him.'

Leaving the chapel she gazed out over the gentle emerald pastures that rolled away on either side of the glistening river. There was a peace to this place, a tranquillity that reached deep into the soul, a harmony that called to the heart.

She must drink deep of it, carry it with her; it would be the memory she would cling to in the long nights when she could not hold back the tears. Breathing hard to stay the longing, she let her gaze follow the gleaming waters to the bend that carried them from her sight.

In a week she would be with Bella and in the place of green fields would be the smoking stacks of factories and the wide black mouths of coal mines; but there she would find the friendship that had welcomed a tired frightened girl and the woman she knew would do so again; no matter what the future held for Maura Deverell one thing was certain: she would always love and respect Bella James.

On the opposite side of the river a bird swooped low, skimming the water, the sun glinting on its plumage. Watching a moment longer she turned away. Her goodbye had been said to Clonmacnoise, it was time to go. Her eyes lowered, unable to bear the pain of leaving this peaceful place she retraced the steps she had known from childhood. Almost to the gateway the shadow of the soaring O'Rourke's Tower fell across her path and she thought she heard her name called softly.

Glancing at the great round structure she saw that no one stood there. Was her longing to stay so strong it was playing tricks with her brain?

Maura . . .

It was stronger this time yet still a whisper in her mind. Turning her glance towards the gateway she caught her breath. Liam stood framed in its entrance, but it was the figure beside him had her whole body trembling.

Clothed as she had last seen her yet with a happiness in her eyes Maura had not seen for so many years, the image of her mother smiled at her.

Resting one hand on Liam's arm the figure seemed to lift it, holding it towards her.

Stay child . . . take your heart.

The whisper sounded again and the beloved face smiled.

Too choked to cry out, Maura stood as the figure faded. Stay, it had told her, she had been released of her promise.

Tears sparkling in her eyes she looked at the man whose eyes seemed to say his heart was breaking.

'I love you, Maura,' Liam said quietly, 'stay with me, my love.'

Her mother's smile and the words that had whispered in her mind, they had told her she was absolved of her promise, she could go to Liam; but what of Bella and the others . . . the herb shop?

Unaware her words were spoken aloud she saw only the love in those dark eyes.

'You have my word, we will speak with Bella, we will leave nothing which could give you grief; only be my wife, my love . . . never leave me.'

His arms opening she stepped into them and in the cloistered shelter of the gateway she lifted her mouth to his.

'*Never leave me.*'

With the words singing in her soul, Maura knew she never would.

If you enjoyed THE DEVERELL WOMAN,

here's a foretaste of Meg Hutchinson's new novel,

SIXPENNY GIRL.

I

'Shut yer mouth, you mewlin' bitch!'

Enoch Jacobs snatched the broad leather belt from around his waist, cracking it several times and savouring the sound.

'You don't ask no question o' Enoch Jacobs.' The belt whistled on the air before slicing across the shoulders of the slight figure crouched on the ground. 'You don't ask no question . . .' the belt rose and fell, 'no question . . . no . . .'

Breathless with the effort, Enoch Jacobs's heavy-set figure slumped back against a tree, sliding downward as his legs folded.

Curling her body tightly against the savage fury of the man, her arms thrown protectively about her head, Saran Chandler waited for the next slash of the belt, the next of the stinging blows that followed through her every day.

Where had the money come from? How had he paid for the ale that had him roaring drunk? She had not dared ask those questions . . . not this time!

Folded in on herself she held back the tears, her teeth clenched against the smarting pain burning across her back and shoulders, breath held against the next onslaught. But the whine of leather slicing the air had stopped . . . the next blow had not come. As the realisation seeped into her brain, she waited a moment, then slowly raised her head. Sagged against the tree, his heavy-jowled face flushed, the belt fallen from thick fingers, Enoch Jacobs snored loudly.

If only she could run away now, leave and never have to

look upon his face again; but while Enoch Jacobs took care always to find a tavern to satisfy his thirst, he was just as careful to make sure that what he saw as his property remained that way.

Easing her cramped legs, Saran felt the rope bite against her neck. Yoked like an animal, the slightest movement had the knot slip a little tighter against her throat.

Where had the money come from? Leaning her head against the trunk of the tree Saran thought of that day a week ago when she had dared ask that question. He had been an hour in the alehouse, an hour drinking away the last farthing they had, a farthing that could have paid for a loaf of week-old bread, bread that would have fed her mother and her sister. Then he had come outside. The ale already telling on him he had hit against the doorpost before staggering across to where he had tethered them like beasts, his heavy face flushed, his eyes bloodshot.

She had thrown an arm about her mother and sister, holding them as close as the rope about their necks would allow, her own body tense as it waited for the blows that followed them through the days like a constant companion. A beating was what they had come to expect almost from the day her mother had remarried. '*Let me take care of you all,*' Enoch Jacobs had said, smiling, the day of his marriage; but the only care he had taken was of himself, selling every stick and stone, every item they possessed to satisfy his own needs, quieting any objection with blows. That had become the pattern of their lives. When sober, Enoch Jacobs delivered those blows with an air of regret, as if the pain of driving evil from them was a more bitter pain for himself, but she had known the true force behind them was self-gratification, every punch, every slash of his belt an outlet for a wickedness that consumed him; and when drunk that gratification glowed with an intense pleasure.

'*On yer feet you mewlin' bitch!*'

Her stomach churning at the remembered words Saran stared at a sky strewn with a million stars. Such a beautiful world, yet so full of misery . . . knuckles pressed against her lips she tried to stem the pictures in her mind but, relentless, they flooded on.

He had cut away the length of rope holding her mother and sister, kicking away the hands that tried to hold on to them, then yanked the thin figures to their feet dragging them behind him into the beerhouse. He had ignored the sound of her mother's choking – the cord digging so savagely into raw flesh she could not breathe – and the cries of an eight-year-old.

It seemed a lifetime later her mother and sister had emerged, their yoke held by another hand, a hand that tugged hard on the rope as her mother had turned to look at her. She had tried to call . . . to speak . . . but only her eyes had said the words.

Pressing her fingers so hard against her lips her teeth cut into them, Saran could not stop the sobs trembling in her chest.

The afternoon sun had sparkled on the tears filling those gentle eyes, eyes that had said goodbye. That same day she had asked the questions, where is my mother and my sister . . . what have you done with them.

He had been even heavier in drink, his words mumbling from a saliva-drooling mouth, his small eyes bleary as he had looked at her. Then had come the blows. Like savage rain they had fallen on her head and body as Enoch Jacobs had sought to relieve his own guilt by beating her senseless.

It had been during that same night she had learned the truth. Closing her eyes against the agony of it, Saran remembered the drunken mumblings.

''Alf a crown . . .' Enoch Jacobs had twitched and moaned as he lay sprawled on the ground, *''alf a crown for the woman . . . bloody daylight robbery, should 'ave bin twice that, got years of work in 'er . . .'*

With every bone screaming its own pain she had scrambled as close as her tethering rope allowed, straining to catch each muttered word.

'. . . *but it weren't work 'e 'ad in mind fer the little 'un, 'e wanted 'er for 'is own pleasures; I seen that when I set 'er on the table . . . Zadok Minch's eyes glowed when they lit on 'er, likes 'em young, do Zadok Minch . . .*'

He wanted her for his own pleasures? Her blood had run cold as she had listened. What had this brute of a man done with her family?

'. . . *come close to that table, then, 'e did . . .*' the mutterings had gone on, '. . . *couldn't resist runnin' 'is 'ands over that body, feelin' the buds just beginnin' to pop, strokin' up them legs to the very top, knowin' by the way the kid squirmed and cried out that he was first man to play his fingers in that tight little 'ole . . .*'

She had wanted to kill him then, wanted with every fibre of her being to grab a stone and dash it hard against that heavy-jowled face, to keep on smashing it down until no trace of life was left in the man she hated; but the rope had held her too tightly and all she could do was listen.

'. . . *'elp in the 'ouse was what 'e were buyin' 'em for . . .*' Enoch Jacobs's laugh had snuffled in his throat, '. . . *that might 'ave fooled the others who were bidding for the goods on offer but it d'ain't fool me, I knowed what the wench were wanted for an' I med Zadok Minch pay; I let 'im feel 'er all over, then when 'is mouth were waterin' I med 'im pay . . . 'alf a sovereign was what I asked, 'alf a sovereign for a babby to play with in 'is bed . . .*'

As if guessing that she already knew what had transpired the afternoon before, Enoch Jacobs had smirked when dragging her to her feet next morning, had taken a cold sadistic pleasure in retailing the account in full. He had led her mother and sister into the beerhouse, shoving first her mother on to a table shouting loudly she was for sale to any with money to buy. They had bid in pennies and halfpennies, gloating as her skirts were lifted to show her legs were capable of 'carrying a load during the day an' spreadin' wide enough at night to take the load of any man 'ere'.

He had enjoyed seeing the blush of colour that had brought to her cheeks, but Saran had known his real enjoyment had lain in seeing the pain she could not keep from showing on her face.

'*Then come the wench's turn . . .*' The words sounded again in her ears as though they were still being spoken. '*Lifted 'er on to the table, I did, pulled 'er frock up to 'er face . . . let the fox see the rabbit. Them little tits just startin' to sprout set the bids comin' thick an' fast but Zadok Minch were the only man could spend 'alf a sovereign. That be what I done wi' yer mother an' sister, I sold 'em, sold 'em as any husband and father 'as the right to do.*'

Sold them! Hard as stone the words settled on her heart, stilling the sobs in her chest, banning the tears from her eyes. Only hate remained, cold impervious hate coupled with a burning desire for vengeance.

The thick cord biting into the soft flesh of her neck, Saran stumbled as it jerked, almost pulling her off her feet. Enoch Jacobs had slept fitfully, crying out at intervals as some unseen dread plagued him, a dread the constant spending from the money got from the sale of her family did nothing to abate.

'Pick yer bloody feet up, you clumsy bitch!'

Jacobs snatched again on the rope he never removed from her throat, mumbling to himself as he walked. He had not been properly sober from the day he had sold her mother and sister, auctioning them like cattle to the highest bidder; nor, since that day, had he once settled to sleep until he had tied her hands together then secured her to a tree. And she knew the reason for this; the reason, despite the ale he consumed, was fear, fear of her. Enoch Jacobs had seen what gleamed every day in her eyes, heard what laced each word that left her mouth, knew what rested in her heart, the prayer that rose nightly from her soul, the yearning to see him dead!

Six steps in front of her, he paused. Saran turned her head away as, making no attempt at privacy, he relieved himself. The man was an animal! Keeping her eyes tight shut she swallowed hard. What lies had he told her mother when persuading her to wed him?

'I needs a bite o' summat to eat.'

The rope jerked again and Saran caught the sneering look as she opened her eyes, the look that said she belonged to Enoch Jacobs to do with as he pleased; and what did he intend to do with her? Trailing her around the country would bring him neither peace nor profit so what was to be her fate . . . auctioned off in some beerhouse as her loved ones had been?

'There be a tavern up ahead, I'll get meself a meal and a bit o' decent company, an' a bit o' decent company will mek a fine change from looking at your surly face the day long. I'll find somebody as knows 'ow to smile at a man.'

How could he call himself a man! Three people tethered like beasts for market, two of them sold into God only knew what sort of existence, herself dragged from tavern to tavern then staked to the ground or tied to a tree while he drank himself into a stupor. But at least the hours spent waiting were hours when she did not have to look up on that hated face, when her ears were free of a voice that scarred her soul.

'Sit you 'ere.'

Tugging viciously on the rope, Enoch Jacobs hauled her to where a group of tall bushes stood a little way off from a low-slung building, small-paned windows glinting in the late spring sunshine. Checking her hands and assuring himself they were still firmly tied, he smirked.

'Mebbe I'll bring you a bite o' summat out . . . mebbe!'

Laughing loudly he swaggered away, the first of his remaining coins already in his hand. Watching him bend to enter the low doorway Saran felt her stomach rumble. He had not brought her more than a crust in days and there was little doubt but he would not bring her anything today, his own needs were all that occupied the mind of her stepfather. But hunger she could cope with and she thanked heaven for these precious moments when she was alone.

Drawing up her knees she rested her forehead on her tied hands. What had happened to her life? One minute they had all been so safe and secure, so happy in their small house in Willenhall, her father's locksmith workshop attached to its rear. Then had come that accident. Her father had gone to the steelworks as usual to order a fresh supply of metal for his business, and it was whilst he stood talking to the overseer in the yard that a loaded cart overbalanced, tipping its load of metal bars. There had been no warning, her mother had been told by men carrying her father's broken body home on a door used for a stretcher, no time for her father to escape the rush of heavy steel, he had been killed almost instantly. Two weeks on from the burying of the father she loved, Enoch Jacobs had come upon the scene. What money they had could not last many weeks . . . eyes tight shut, Saran remembered her mother's words.

'*Mr Jacobs is a locksmith, he has served his years of apprenticeship and he will work for us.*'

But Enoch Jacobs had worked for himself, duped her mother with his quiet concern for the welfare of her family and the business that supported them, inveigled himself so deeply in her trust that she turned more and more to him, asking his advice, following it to the letter even though in her heart she must have known it was not always sound. But her mother had in turn been taught by her mother always to believe that a man was superior to a woman, in mind as well as in body, so she had refused to listen when Saran had tried to point out that Enoch Jacobs was not conducting the business as her father had done, nor would he any longer have herself keep the account books; in fact, he had gradually drawn more and more into his own hands until finally, with marriage to her mother, he had it all.

Life for her family had gone downhill from that point. Less and less of the money from the business had been given to the housekeeping and more and more to the tavern-keepers and brothels, with any complaint bringing a blow to the mouth.

It had been one such blow had brought on her mother's miscarriage. Now clenching her fingers tightly where they rested on her knees, Saran tried unsuccessfully to wipe the pictures from her mind. There had been no fire in the grate the night Enoch Jacobs had staggered home from the tavern, the small house was cold with the frosts of January. He had ranted and raved, demanding a fire be lit and a hot supper produced. Her mother, seven months gone with his child had trembled as she answered that there was neither food nor coal in the house. He had stopped shouting then. Beer-dulled eyes had rested on her mother then he had swung a doubled-up fist, hitting her full in the face and sending her crashing backward into the fireplace. Minutes later her mother was gasping with the pain of childbirth.

She had not known what to do. Saran flinched, seeming to feel again her mother's hands clawing at her arm as she writhed. Jacobs had left the house as her mother had fallen; only Miriam was there. But Miriam was no more than eight years old. Her mental vision switching, Saran saw a small white-faced girl, her dark eyes wide with terror as they looked at the woman groaning with pain.

'*Fanny Simkin . . .*' her mother had gasped between spasms that left her breathless, '*send for Fanny Simkin!*'

Should she go? Leave her mother like this with only a terrified child to care for her? What could Miriam do should anything happen? Saran remembered the thoughts that had been a whirlpool swivelling her brain . . . That was when she had made her decision. Miriam must go fetch the woman who acted as midwife for half of the town. Tying her own shawl over her sister's head she had told her to run, to find Fanny Simkin and bring her to the house. She had looked at the prettily enamelled clock stood on the mantelpiece as the child had fled from the house. It had showed a little after ten. Somehow she had got her mother to bed; holding the worn figure, taking the weight against her own, they had paused on almost every step for waves of pain to subside. And the time had rolled slowly by, each minute seeing her mother's agony grow. But Fanny Simkin did not come.

'Help me, Saran . . . help me, child!'

Tears hot against her closed lids, Saran heard the cry again in her head. She had never seen a child birthed, how could she help? But without assistance her mother might die. That one thought had quieted the doubts, stilled the chaos in her brain. She had run to the room she shared with her sister and snatched a clean cotton nightgown from a drawer of the dresser, laying it across the foot of her mother's bed; then she fetched the threadbare sheet they had washed and set aside for the purpose, and spread it beneath the panting figure. If only her mother had explained the process of childbirth as she had spoken of the need for the sheet . . . but she had not. Saran remembered the desperation that had swamped her. But somehow she had kept it a controlled desperation. Outwardly calm she had talked quietly to the heaving figure, soothing . . . quiet . . . holding an air of reassurance she herself had been far from feeling. Praying for guidance, asking heaven for the help she needed, she had placed her mother's legs so the knees pointed to the ceiling, then, speaking with a new-found authority, had told her to breathe long and slowly, doing it with her while the pain-filled eyes had clung to her face. Then the child had come. Exhausted, her mother had sunk into the pillows and she, Saran, had washed the tiny dead body of her half-brother.

It had been all over when, at one o'clock in the morning, Miriam and the midwife had returned, the older woman saying she had been at a birth on the far side of Shepwell Green.

'*There were naught you could 'ave done that you didn't do.*'

Fanny Simkin had looked at the marble-cold body of the newborn baby.

'*At seven months they don't stand a lot o' chance o' bein' born alive. You need set no blame agen yourself for 'twas a deal o' sense you showed and 'tis like enough you 'ave your mother's life to show for it.*'

She had looked once more at the poor little body, marking the sign of the cross on forehead and chest before wrapping it again in the cotton nightdress.

'*Where be Enoch Jacobs?*'

Stunned as she had been by all that had happened, Saran had not failed to notice the woman did not afford him the usual courtesy of calling him 'the man of the house'. Hearing he had not returned as yet she had simply looked at the tired figure in the bed then back to Saran.

'*When you hears the whistle along of Priestfield pit calling the miners to their shift you get yourself to Lizzie Beckett's grocer shop along of Froysell Street; tell 'er Fanny Simkin sent you, 'er'll gie you a soapbox to lay the child in, and for sixpence Joby Crump will see it laid in 'oly ground.*'

She had thanked the woman, moving with her to the bedroom door. There Fanny Simkin had paused, her voice lowering as she glanced back over her shoulder at the bed. '*Your mother be worn out . . . 'er don't be well enough for the kind o' attention Enoch Jacobs be interested in, you understands me, wench? Your mother be too weak to carry more babbies, the next one be like to see the end of 'er.*'

The woman's words had been more than kindly advice, they had been a warning, one Saran had done her utmost to heed. Beginning that same morning she had begun to sell everything which belonged to her personally; the locket her father had given her to mark her thirteenth birthday, saying proudly his little wench were now a young lady, the ivory bracelet that had been a gift on her Confirmation. One by one they had gone and after them had gone Miriam's little treasures, the doll she cherished going last of all.

Lifting her head Sarah gazed at the sky, the last of the sun's scarlet setting spilling like blood on the horizon.

Selling the doll had been the hardest task of all. Miriam had tried not to cry but tears had trembled in her soft eyes. It had all but broken her own heart and their mother had pleaded with her to give the toy back, yet Fanny Simkin's warning had been stronger. While there was one item in the house, one thing that would bring money to pay for Enoch Jacobs's beer and women, then it must be sold; only that way could she keep him from taking his pleasure from her mother, only that way could she keep her safe.